A HASTILY CONVENED MEETING IN THE MIDDLE OF THE NIGHT . . .

The chairman of the Joint Chiefs of Staff was the first to speak.

"We're not going off to fight World War III, are we, Donald?"

The CIA director, Donald Shupe, didn't respond to this attempt at humor. "Gentlemen," he began, "I received word under an hour ago that the drop at the restaurant was intercepted."

No one spoke. The initial shock was such that questions hadn't yet formed in their minds. They had worked for over two years to develop a desperate plan to save the country. In just a few hours it had been threatened.

Shupe continued.

"The Russians are thinking about encircling the United States with missiles that'll put Washington and New York in a crossfire just minutes away. SRVs under the Arctic already give them military superiority, but together with land-based ones in Cuba, they'll have a delivery system of under two minutes anywhere along the eastern seaboard."

"There's only one defense," Shupe added, "and this hatcheck girl, Cheryl Branigan, has it. . . ."

Also by Robert Neidhardt

ROOT OF ALL EVIL

THE FINAL DECEPTION

ROBERT NEIDHARDT

JOVE BOOKS, NEW YORK

THE FINAL DECEPTION

A Jove Book / published by arrangement with
Robert Neidhardt

PRINTING HISTORY
Jove edition / May 1990

ISBN: 0-515-10324-1

Jove Books are published by The Berkley Publishing Group,
200 Madison Avenue, New York, New York 10016.
The name "JOVE" and the "J" logo
are trademarks belonging to Jove Publications, Inc.

PRINTED IN THE UNITED STATES OF AMERICA

10 9 8 7 6 5 4 3 2 1

"Neither the United States of America nor the world community of nations can tolerate deliberate deception and offensive threats on the part of any nation, large or small. We no longer live in a world where only the actual firing of weapons represents a sufficient challenge to a nation's security to constitute maximum peril."

—President John F. Kennedy,
  in reference to the Cuban missile crisis,
  October 22, 1962

1.

October 6, 1994
Korseakov Air Base
Sakhalin, USSR

IT WAS NOT a good night for surveillance.

The temperature had dropped to three below and the wind was swirling clouds of snow over the huge Siberian air base. Two inches of fresh powder had fallen in the past hour, covering the SU-15 fighters lined along the tarmac with a veil of white lacework. It was just the beginning of a storm, moving east over the Kamchatka Peninsula, that was expected to last the night, with temperatures falling yet another ten degrees.

At the far end of the base a chain-link fence separated the runway from a service road that ringed the entire complex. A row of army trucks were parked along it, their windshields covered with snow, except for one that had its wipers running. Inside, two agents from the GRU section of the KGB sat staring at the fence and the howling mass of twisting white shapes beyond it. All that could be seen of the base now were the security lights above the control tower, which looked like two red spots suspended in space.

The agent behind the wheel, a short, overweight man named Leonid, wiped the windshield with a cloth to clear it. It was freezing up so quickly the defroster in the ten-year-old vehicle couldn't keep up with it. He cursed it. He cursed the cold. He cursed the assignment. As his partner poured some hot cocoa from a thermos, he checked his watch: two A.M. Six more hours to go before they would be replaced and could return to the warmth of their compound, just four kilometers away. He wondered if they had enough cocoa to make it. Mikhail read his mind and held up the thermos, pointing to the half-full mark. He shrugged, gulped down the steaming drink and settled back in his seat. Mikhail would keep watch for the next three hours while Leonid slept.

Leonid turned in the seat to sleep on his side and noticed a dark shape moving toward them. Using his hand, he wiped an opening in the window to see through. There was a light coming closer. It was a small van. Its lights were off but the driver was using a flashlight to search along the fence. Without looking away, Leonid tapped Mikhail on the shoulder and quickly turned off the truck's motor.

The van passed in front of them. Leonid saw it was one of the new Polstoys, imported from Czechoslovakia. He looked for a name on the door or the side panel but there wasn't any. Slowly it continued on until it began to disappear into the snowy darkness. Mikhail was already talking to the command post. They had agreed earlier that if anyone came, Leonid would follow while Mikhail stayed on the radio. Leonid grabbed the walkie-talkie lying beside him, zipped up his parka, and slid from the truck into the icy darkness.

The wind was swirling around him but he could still hear the sound of the van's motor up ahead. It was moving more slowly now. As he walked between the tire tracks he felt inside his jacket for the security of a .45-caliber revolver holstered over his right hip and two phosphorus grenades clipped beside it. He noticed that the road was curving and that the chain-link fence was getting closer. A gust of wind blew straight at him, and when it passed, he realized the truck had stopped.

He ran through the snow and left the road, moving between two warehouse buildings. His plan was to get slightly past the van and put it between himself and Mikhail. A long row of storage barrels enabled him to move into position without being seen. By the time he emerged from behind them, he could see that a man had gotten out of the van and was playing the beam of his flashlight along the edge of the fence. Leonid got behind a large oil drum about twenty meters away. Through the falling snow he saw the man return to the van, where he opened the rear door and took out some digging tools, along with a small square box.

For the next fifteen minutes he watched as the dark figure dug a hole deep enough to contain the box. The man worked slowly, oblivious to the danger that might be around him. When the hole was dug, he carefully lowered the box into it, then filled it in with dirt and snow. Satisfied that it was well hidden, he reached down and pulled up a small antenna. It was thin and stood about six inches over the box. Reaching into his pocket for a tool to make a final adjustment, he heard something behind him. He turned and found himself staring into the beam of Leonid's flashlight. Behind it was a .45 automatic.

"GRU. Don't move!" Leonid shouted.

The man raised his hands to cover his eyes from the blinding light, and his own flashlight fell into the snow. For a moment he seemed about to run but decided against it. As Leonid came closer, he dropped his hands to his side, resigned to his fate. Leonid turned him around, handcuffed him, and called Mikhail on the walkie-talkie. Within minutes he could see the truck's lights moving toward them through the falling snow.

The ride back to the command station took over thirty minutes. Visibility was near zero, and they had to stop several times to clear the wipers of snow and ice. The man was handcuffed to the backseat and sat there in obvious fear. Both agents had identified themselves as GRU and charged him with trespassing on a military installation, and, more importantly, endangerment of national security. They had recovered the box, which was now lying at the man's feet. Leonid turned to look at it. It was the third one they had found in two weeks. Maybe now they wouldn't have to spend any more nights in the freezing cold. Now they had the box and the man to go with it.

Inside the command station, the prisoner was ushered into a small interrogation room while the box was taken to another area to be studied. He was given some coffee and then observed through a two-way mirror by a GRU captain named Berkhin, who would soon interrogate him. For twenty minutes Berkhin watched as the man fidgeted with the coffee cup and smoked three cigarettes while he paced the room nervously. He was small, slightly built, with jet-black hair and a neatly trimmed beard. His round, wire-rimmed glasses occasionally slid down his nose, and he seemed annoyed with adjusting them. He probably never had been in a police station before and seemed very frightened with his situation.

Satisfied that he had evaluated his character sufficiently, Berkhin and a stenographer entered the small gray room. Leonid and Mikhail followed them in and sat in the rear with the stenographer. Berkhin, a powerfully built man resplendent in his neatly pressed uniform, began the questioning.

"Who are you?" he asked, taking the man's cigarettes from the table. It was a sign that he was his prisoner and no longer owned anything.

"Vladislav Shaktyor," he answered slowly, pushing back his glasses. Berkhin already knew who he was. Leonid and Mikhail had found a driver's license and an identification card in the glove compartment of the van. It was the first thing that had puzzled him. A mistake like that was the mark of an amateur. But why was an amateur burying a sophisticated device at an air base at two in the morning? Alone. In a blinding snowstorm. Berkhin organized his opening questions and then fired them in quick succession at the frightened suspect.

"What were you burying at the air base?"

"A box," he answered nervously, running his finger along the rim of the empty coffee cup.

"What kind of box?"

"I don't know."

"Have you buried any others?"

"Yes."

"How many?"

"Three."

"All here at the base?"

"Yes."

"Where did you get them?"

"From a man who paid me to bury them."

"What man?"

"A man I met at a trade show in Khabarovsk. An electrical trade show. I'm an electrician, you know."

"We know. Who was the man? Did he give you a business card?"

"No, but he was an American."

Berkhin stopped. He walked over behind Shaktyor and looked at Leonid and Mikhail. All of the boxes they had recovered were marked in English. That concerned him. If they were some sort of destructive devices, the fact that they were made in America was alarming. He lit one of Shaktyor's cigarettes and continued.

"What did the American say the boxes were?"

Shaktyor stared at his hands, which were beginning to shake.

"He said they were microwave radio receivers that would pick up signals from a satellite. His company wanted to test them under severe weather conditions."

"So he told you to bury three of them as close to the air base as you could," Leonid said from across the room. "Are you totally stupid? Those boxes could be something that could blow up the whole base." He got up from his chair and went over to Shaktyor. The captain had told him to play the heavy, and he was going to enjoy the role. For three weeks he had spent long, cold nights waiting to catch this guy. Leaning against the table, he put one hand in his pocket, revealing his holstered pistol.

"Do you know what you're charged with?" he asked in what was almost a whisper.

"Yes," Shaktyor answered, barely able to say the word. "With trespassing and—"

"And with endangering military security," Leonid said, interrupting. "Do you know what we could do to you? We could take you back out to where we found you and shoot you. It would save us a lot of trouble and paperwork. And believe me, nobody would be the wiser."

"But," Berkhin continued, "we hesitate to do that because you certainly know more about the box and the American than you're telling us."

Shaktyor looked at the two men. Like all Russians, he had grown up fearing the GRU but doubted they would summarily march him off and shoot him. However, he had heard of people being beaten and tortured. One thing was certain. They would never stop investigating him until they knew as much about the boxes as he did. The short, stocky man frightened him. He addressed himself to the captain, who seemed more reasonable.

"Of course I wondered what was in the box and why he wanted me to bury it," he said, staring at the table. "But he offered me a lot of money to do it. It was more money than—"

"How much?" Berkhin asked quietly.

"Eight thousand rubles," he answered. "That's more than I make in a whole year."

"So for rubles you forgot that this box could maybe kill hundreds of comrades and destroy the entire base." Leonid practically spat the words out at him.

"I didn't know that for sure," he answered with a shrug.

Berkhin offered him one of his cigarettes, and he accepted it. He fumbled for his matches and tried to light it, but his hands were trembling. After two attempts Berkhin reached over and lit it with his lighter.

"How were you paid?" he asked as Shaktyor deeply inhaled the cigarette.

"He paid me in cash right at the show. The boxes were delivered to my shop a week later by a delivery company."

"What delivery company?"

"I don't know," he answered nervously. "The truck was parked outside. I never saw it."

"Did you have to sign anything, a receipt or a voucher?"

"Yes, a receipt, but the driver didn't leave it behind."

"And there was no return address on the packages?"

"No, nothing."

Berkhin crossed the room and leaned against the wall. During an interrogation he always looked for a pattern to develop in the suspect's answers. One was emerging now. Everything Shaktyor had said or done was amateurish. Leonid and Mikhail had reported that he simply drove onto the base, picked a spot and began digging. He wasn't in communication with anybody and apparently hadn't reconnoitered the area. Although the truck was unmarked, he was carrying identification inside. A new registration indicated that it had just been purchased a month ago. He probably hadn't gotten around to having a name painted on it yet.

But unlike Shaktyor, the American who'd hired him was a professional. He left no identification, and, more importantly, had covered up any means of tracing him. Berkhin needed to find out more about this man.

As he walked back over to Shaktyor he gave Leonid a quick look that told him to remain silent while he pursued a point in the questioning. Taking a chair, he turned it backward and sat down next to the suspect.

"Tell me," he began, "how was this American to know whether or not you buried the boxes at the base? You could have just taken his money and done nothing. Isn't that so?"

Shaktyor smiled for the first time, relieved that Berkhin was shifting the emphasis of his questioning to the American.

"He must have thought of that," he answered. "When he gave me the money, he said that if I didn't bury the boxes, he would know about it."

"How?" Berkhin asked.

"There are two connections that have to be activated when the boxes are put in the ground. Then the receiver sends a signal to a satellite, which tells where they're located. He would know whether I buried them near the base or not."

"And if you didn't?" Berkhin left the question open.

"Then he said he would come back to my shop."

The captain turned to Mikhail and Leonid.

"Did you apprehend him before he activated the box?"

Leonid shrugged.

"Once he had it buried and pulled up the antenna, I came up on him. I didn't see him activate anything."

"Did you?" Berkhin asked Shaktyor.

"No, I was just about to when he flashed the light in my face," he answered.

"So we have a box here that the American will know hasn't been activated, don't we?" Berkhin replied with some amusement in his voice. "That may bring him back to your shop. And when he comes, we'll be waiting for him."

The questioning went on for another two hours. Shaktyor described the American in detail and retraced his meeting with him minute by minute. But Berkhin knew it was unlikely he would return to the shop or would, in fact, ever be found.

What continued to bother him was why this professional had selected a complete novice to plant what was most likely a sophisticated destructive device. In fact, they had selected a man who would most certainly bungle the job. Hiring Shaktyor was like delivering the devices to the KGB personally.

But that wouldn't be in his report to KGB headquarters in Moscow. It wasn't every day that his unit was involved in an operation this important, so why should their success be lessened? If the Americans had bungled this one and put the weapon right in their laps, they would take the credit. They would show those *Kegebeshnikis*, those elitist agents in Moscow, that even though they were stationed on the fringe of civilization, they too were professionals.

2.

CHERYL BRANIGAN STOOD in front of a mirror in Bloomingdale's trying on a one-piece blue lamé bathing suit. She turned slowly in front of the angled glass, which gave the effect of looking into a prism. There she was, twice, four times, a dozen times, her body receding off into infinity.

With one smooth motion she moved into another pose to see the strapless back of the suit. She liked what she saw. Her back arched gracefully down to the low-cut bottom that hugged her firm buttocks. Slowly she turned on her toes, putting one arm up into her long blond hair and the other on her hip. From the side, her full breasts pressed against the bodice and the long, curved line of her hips arched gracefully into the high cut of the suit. Terrific. She could see herself in this number on the beach at Malibu, making a few heads turn. Tomorrow she would be there, away from the cold of a late New York winter. Southern California in September . . . it would be great to be back there.

She went into the dressing room and slipped behind the curtain, where she'd left her clothes. Lying on the bench were the other items she had purchased during her two hours in the store: two tank tops; three pairs of shorts; a white peasant skirt; three pairs of slacks; and, most important of all, a man's raincoat.

The raincoat was the main reason she had come to Bloomingdale's. It was the only place in town that had the exact one she was looking for. She held it up and examined it one more time. The color was perfect, a light tan. It was single-breasted with four front buttons. The epaulets tapered out from the collar and there was no belt. It couldn't be better.

She had gotten it in the men's department and carried it with her to try on in the ladies' dressing room. It would be too big for her, she knew that, but the length had to be just right. Slipping it on over the bathing suit, she went back out and stood in front of the mirror. The shoulders were big, as expected, but she would wear a heavy sweater underneath. Turning around, she saw that the length was about four inches too long. That was all right. She would need that much for the hem.

Through the mirror she saw an elderly man staring at her. He looked like he was waiting for his wife to come out of the dressing room. The old guy was looking her over from top to bottom. She smiled. From the back she could imagine what she looked like with her bare legs under the coat. As she caught his eye he turned away, embarrassed, but then she saw him looking right back at her again. Cute. He probably had never seem a female flasher, but he was about to. With one quick movement she spun around and opened the coat, revealing the low-cut bathing suit.

"Flash!" she said in a high, playful voice.

The old man turned a bright red and practically ran from the department just as his wife came out of the dressing room. Cheryl pulled the coat back around her and went on studying it in the mirror. The woman gave her a quick look, then ran after her husband.

Satisfied with the coat, she changed into her street clothes and paid for the purchases. It was three o'clock. There was just enough time to get back to her apartment and make final preparations for the evening. There was a lot to do. Work had to be done on the coat and she had to gather up some last-minute things. The next few hours were important. They were leading to an evening that could change her whole life.

Outside the store, she found a cab immediately. She was about to give the driver her address on Ninety-sixth Street when she changed her mind. There was something she had to see just one more time. Instead she told him to head down Lexington Avenue and then cross over to the West Side at Forty-fifth Street. It had started to rain, a cold, damp drizzle that spattered against the taxi windows as it traveled down Lexington. From inside, the buildings took on an eerie, distorted look. The cab went across to the West Side and then crossed Broadway. Lights from the marquees danced on the beaded panes in a spray of reds and yellows. Broadway. This was where she had walked the streets for the past six years, going from audition to audition. There had been some successes but mostly disappointments. Now it would be over with.

She had come east from California with high hopes. New York was where she would become an actress. Her career had started in Los Angeles with bit parts in B movies, but then she got a part in a stage production that led her to an agent. At first he was successful in getting her small TV parts; in fact, there was one meaty role in a series, but it was canceled after three months. For the next three years she worked sporadically, with just one or two parts that made any real money. Finally she decided to come to New York. It meant leaving a small group of friends and a man she had lived with for three years. But that relationship really wasn't going anywhere, either. She needed a fresh start, a whole new circle of friends, a new challenge.

She asked the driver to pass by the Winter Garden Theater. As they drove by the marquee lit up the inside of the car. This was the first theater she had played in New York. She thought back to the audition. It was for the part of a maid. Three lines were all she had: "Would madam like some tea?"; "I'm sorry, she's not in right now"; and "Can I get you something else?"

For five days she studied those lines, practicing every inflection possible. From morning to night she would repeat them over and over in front of a mirror, into a tape recorder, anyplace where she was alone. On the next audition she got the part, and the show ran for three years. There were six performances a week plus two matinees. During the day she took more acting lessons and auditioned for TV commercials. She was a tooth fairy in a toothpaste commercial, a young mother for floor wax and a mermaid for a dishwasher detergent. Her residuals that year amounted to over sixty thousand dollars. But then it all went downhill. The show ended and the commercials ran less often. The constant rejection became impossible. "You're too young, too old, too tall, too short, too attractive, too everything." Finally, to make ends meet, she took a part-time job in a restaurant as a hatcheck girl.

It was a small Italian restaurant in the Village called Armando's. Armando Lucci, the owner, was a fat, vulgar man who somehow had put together an elegant restaurant with an excellent menu. The clientele was mainly yuppies who lived uptown but were willing to make the trip for some good Italian food. After three months she discovered they were coming for more than food.

Every now and then she would catch Armando with a small packet of what looked like cocaine, which he said was for a certain customer. She never saw him make an actual transaction but assumed he was selling it regularly when he came to her with an offer. He said the demand for cocaine had increased at the same time the police were cracking down. What he needed was a method of getting quantities of it into the restaurant that could be distributed to several of his large customers. When the son of a bitch explained how he was going to do it, she was surprised at his ingenuity. He was going to pass it through the hatcheck room.

The plan was very clever. On a prearranged evening a drop would be set up. A man would come into the restaurant wearing a raincoat. Two packets containing up to fifty grams each would be sewn into the lining. The customer receiving the delivery already would be seated in the restaurant, having checked the same type of raincoat. All she had to do was switch them. The man who made the delivery would walk out with the other man's coat, and he would leave with the cocaine. For each drop she made five hundred dollars, in addition to her regular salary. She hated the fact that she was involved in something as sleazy as cocaine, but the money was decent. Now she thought it was far too little for the risk she was taking, and she told Armando so. He refused to give her more.

Three or four times during the year there would be what Armando called "a delivery *grande*," an especially large order for a foreign customer. One was scheduled for this evening.

Tomorrow she would be on a plane for California and, within a week, would have more money than she would ever need again.

The cab drove out of the theater district and headed up the West Side.

Turning onto Ninety-sixth Street, the cab pulled up in front of an old four-story brownstone. Cheryl got out, paid the driver and went into the building. She checked the mailbox in the hallway. There was just a bunch of bills she wouldn't have to pay now. Tucking them under her arm, she climbed the four flights to her apartment.

As she came through the doorway a sudden weakness came over her whole body. Was she going to be able to pull this off? It meant leaving the apartment, her friends and a whole way of living that had developed over the past five years. She had always been a creature of habit, and routine was important to her. Why did she feel she had to leave it all behind? She leaned against the door and took a deep breath. The answer to her own question was that she was going nowhere. Let's face it, all those rejections were because she wasn't really that talented. At auditions she often saw people who were much better, but she refused to admit it. Well, it was time to face up to it, kid. In three months she would be thirty years old. If she really was going to make it, her career would be showing signs of it by now. She wasn't going anywhere in life unless she did something dramatic. And that's what she was about to do, something dramatic.

She looked at the small studio she had decorated over the years until it was just the way she wanted it. Now there was practically nothing left. She had sold the last of the furniture the day before, along with the television and the stereo. Clothes that she couldn't take with her had been donated to the Salvation Army. All that remained was her convertible sofa, some books stacked next to the telephone, a radio and a cabinet full of odds and ends. Piled next to the closet were some cardboard boxes, full of old cassettes, records, a broken hair dryer and junk she just didn't care about. Hanging on the closet door was the outfit she would wear to work that night: a bulky white sweater and dark brown slacks.

She took the raincoat from the shopping bag and put it on. Standing in front of a mirror mounted on the closet door, she checked the length again. The coat was about four inches too long. That was all she needed. With some straight pins she marked the turned-up hem, took off the coat and laid it out across the sofa. From the kitchen she got a box of sugar and two plastic bags.

Carefully she poured the sugar into them until they were almost full. Then she pinched them shut and taped them with thick strapping tape. Within a few minutes she had both bags sewn into the lining, and the hem sewn to the proper length. Back in front of the mirror, she checked her work. The coat sagged a little at the sides but was hardly noticeable. Turning to the side, she winked at herself and said softly, "Cheryl, you kid you, you're a genius."

She hung the coat up on the closet door and returned to the sofa. Taking off her shoes, she fell back on it and pulled the answering machine onto her lap. She pressed the play button and a woman's voice crackled over the speaker.

"Cheryl, Diane. If you're not working tonight, call me. There's a Woody Allen movie playing. Let's go."

She pressed the rewind button and Diane's message played again. It probably would be the last time she'd ever hear her voice. She'd miss Diane and their weekly Friday night movies with coffee afterward. They had a good mixture of fun and crying on each other's shoulders over the years. Now she would have to leave without saying good-bye.

"Miss Branigan, this is Globe Cleaners. The suit you left won't be ready until tomorrow. Sorry."

Goddammit. Her good blue suit. It wouldn't be going to L.A. with her. Maybe it was just as well. She had to travel as light as possible if she was going to get through the check-in at LaGuardia quickly.

The tape squealed forward to the next message. A young man's voice came over the speaker. He didn't identify himself and his message was very short.

"I'll be waiting for your call tomorrow," he said hurriedly. "See you then."

A cold chill ran through her as the voice suddenly brought about the reality of what she was going to do. Tomorrow she would deliver cocaine to this man in exchange for more money than she had ever seen in her life. His name was Barry Rossiter, and she thought she had left him in her past forever. But as it turned out, he needed to enter her life one more time. Then she would be free to do anything she wanted . . . forever.

The tape ran forward and there was another message.

"Cheryl, baby. We've got a big one tonight. Get your sweet

little ass over here. I'm gonna squeeze it like a beega fatta watermelon. Ciao."

She laughed. The tape had backed up to a message from that morning. It was the message that had alerted her to tonight's special drop. She could hear the excitement in Armando's voice as he thought about how much money he would make from this delivery. Big fat Armando, who expected her to pass coke for peanuts. She laughed and answered back the faceless machine.

"Fuck you, Armando. Tonight we'll see who squeezes who."

Cheryl usually took the subway to Armando's from her Upper West Side apartment, but tonight she took a cab. The A train to Times Square and the switch to the downtown local would be too much with the two carry-ons she had. Besides, she should get used to the good life. From now on she'd have enough money to afford it.

At six o'clock sharp she arrived at the restaurant and went inside. The place was empty, except for two waiters who were making last-minute adjustments to the table settings. Armando was standing behind the maître d's desk, checking the evening's reservations. A glass of anisette was in his hand.

"Ah, Cheryl," he said, looking over his wire-framed bifocals at the bags she was carrying. "Where are you taking that luscious body off to? You gonna go to Tahiti; Rio, maybe—"

She cut him off. He would go on and on if she let him.

"I'm going to see my mother in Florida."

"Ha, you told me your mother was in California," he said, moving out from behind the desk to block her way.

"That's my other mother, Armando. I have two. That's why I have everything doubly good."

"I know . . . I know . . ." he said. His stubby hands left the glass and started toward her. She pushed one of the bags against him and edged her way past the desk. However, he got hold of the bag and held it firmly.

"You gonna be here for my two special customers," he said in what was more a statement than a question.

"Yeah, what do you think? You pay me big money for this," she answered sarcastically. She looked down at his hand. It had moved on to the handle of the bag in which she was carrying the raincoat. "I'll be here. But like I told you on the phone, I've got to catch a ten o'clock flight."

"This is a big delivery tonight," he whispered, as if there were people that could hear him. "It's very important to me." A smile curled under his pencil-thin mustache. "Maybe I give you a little extra tonight. Then you can visit your *two* mothers."

His hand moved across the bag to get closer to her body. She didn't want to draw any more attention to the coat. With a quick motion she raised her left hand to check her watch and knocked the drink from his hand at the same time.

"Sei stupida, ignorante!" he shouted. A few drops had gotten on his black tuxedo. *"Hai rovinato la mia giacca!"*

"It's after six and I have to get ready for your special customer," she said calmly, slipping by him. He was still cursing when she got behind the checkout counter to set up for the evening.

She waited. Finally he went to the back of the restaurant to clean his tuxedo. As he went through the kitchen door she took her raincoat from her bag, tagged it as number one and hung it up. Within a few minutes Armando was back out, to check a party of four's reservation. The women both wore furs, one man a topcoat, the other a raincoat. Good. There were two on the rack now. Armando would not be suspicious.

At six forty-five the man who would make the pickup came into the restaurant.

It was the same one who had been there the last few times. He was heavyset and very stern-looking. Armando greeted him at the door.

"Good evening, Mr. Volpe. How nice to see you again. I have a very nice table for you tonight." He took the man's arm, walked him over to Cheryl and helped him out of his coat.

"Cheryl will take your coat. Here you are, dear," he said, handing it to her. She hung it in the number nine slot and gave him the ticket. He gave it to the man and escorted him to his table.

Her heart started beating faster when the second man entered the restaurant ten minutes later. By now the place was half full, and he had to wait behind a couple that Armando was checking in. He glanced over at her. She smiled in recognition but he turned away quickly. She thought he looked unusually nervous.

Finally Armando got to him. Apparently he was a little late and some juggling had to be done to get him seated. In the meantime he came over and handed his coat to her. Immediately she felt the weight in the lining on the right side.

"Hello, Cheryl," he said as she hung it up in the number twenty-seven slot. "Looks like they're keeping you pretty busy tonight."

"Yeah," she answered. "The place is really jumping. You're a little late, aren't you?"

She handed him his ticket. His hand was trembling and he fumbled with it as he put it into his breast pocket. Without answering, he looked past her into the restaurant. He seemed to be looking for the other man who had come in earlier. When he finally saw him, he looked back at her.

"Yes, yes," he said, taking deep breaths between the words. "It took me a while to check out of the hotel, and I ran into a lot of traffic on the way over. Friday night, you know."

"I know," she said, looking over at Armando. If he didn't hurry to seat the man soon, the other one would leave with the cocaine before she could make the switch. She had to get rid of this guy. This was no time for one of his casual conversations. Another couple came up to Armando's desk. She thought he would take care of them first, but he asked them to wait and came over to the man. He whispered something in his ear, then took him to his table.

Cheryl looked at the rack behind her. All three coats were on it now, along with two others that were quite similar. She ran the numbers through her mind again. Number one was hers, nine had the check in it and twenty-seven the cocaine. All she had to do now was switch hers with twenty-seven. She physically would have to move the coats, not just the tickets; the slots had fixed numbers. People were still coming in and Armando was nearby. She waited.

For the next hour, making the switch was impossible, but then it became quiet. Armando looked over at her a number of times, waiting for her to do it. Finally she appeared to adjust the rack but quickly switched the two coats. A slight nod to her acknowledged the fact that he knew they were in place. Then he turned and looked at the first man, who had finished dinner and was paying his check. Seeing Armando's signal, he got up from the table. Now she was desperate to make the final switch. If he got to her before she could do it, he would end up with the cocaine and she would lose everything. Armando was watching.

The man started across the restaurant. She could see his reflection in a glass door that led to the street. Another few seconds and he would be too close to make the switch. Armando was coming out from behind his desk to meet him. It had to be now. Armando's phone rang.

As he turned to answer it she reached for the coats and switched them. Now she was committed. If anything went wrong now, she would be in terrible danger.

The man came up to the counter and handed her his coat-check ticket. He glanced over at Armando, who was hurrying to end his conversation. Cheryl turned and took the raincoat from the rack. She felt the weight of the sugar in the lining as she held it out for him to put on. He turned around and extended his arms. Her hands began to tremble. Was the coat going to fit him properly? Would he notice any difference in the fit from the one she had switched? Slowly it went up over his arms, and she felt it fit snugly around his shoulders.

He took a few steps from the counter with his back to her. With a few quick movements he adjusted the coat higher on his shoulders. Then he put both hands in the pockets and pulled up on it a little. He turned around and stood facing her. There was a slight curl to his mouth that seemed to be the beginning of a smile.

"Thank you," he said, holding out a five-dollar bill.

"Oh . . . ah . . . yes," she said. The words came tumbling out of her mouth. Her eyes were still fixed on the coat. "Have a nice evening."

"Yes, I will," he answered.

That was the most he had ever said to her. For the first time she thought she detected a slight accent but dismissed it because of her nervousness.

Armando had hung up the phone and was escorting the man to the door. He seemed very subdued as he spoke to him. Cheryl's eyes never left them. Was everything all right? The man was nodding to Armando. Would he suddenly discover he had the wrong coat? He shook hands with Armando and left.

Slowly she exhaled the long breath she was holding in her lungs. As Armando went to greet two more customers she looked at her watch. It was getting close to seven-thirty. This was the part of the plan she dreaded the most. She couldn't leave until the other man picked up his coat. Armando insisted that she always complete the final switch of the coats. However, the longer she stayed, the more she was in danger. If the man who'd just left found out what he was carrying and came back to the restaurant, it would be all over. She had to get out of there within the next twenty minutes—no matter what.

Through the mirror she could see that the man who had brought in the cocaine was paying his check. Thank God. He got up from his table and was coming to the counter. Armando came out from behind his desk to give his usual good-bye spiel. He took the coat-check ticket from the man and handed it to her.

"Cheryl, dear, Mr. McFarland's coat, please."

That was the first time she had ever heard his name mentioned. She took the coat from the number twenty-seven hook and was about to help McFarland into it when Armando took it from her. He slipped the coat over McFarland's shoulders and they walked to the door. It was over. All she had to do now was get out of there. Quickly she took her coat down from the rack and laid it over her bags. She was about to get up when she felt Armando behind her. He had come right into the coatroom.

"Leaving so soon?" he said, pressing against her. She could smell the anisette on his breath.

"I told you I had to leave early to catch a plane. I have to go, Armando," she answered, her back to him. She couldn't turn around. He had put both arms around her and was pulling her away from the window and into the rack of coats.

"I have something for you," he said, breathing heavily. "You're going away, and I said I was going to give you something extra."

"You're crazy," she answered, trying to keep her voice down. "Let go of me. I have to leave."

He held her with one arm as his other hand went into his pocket. She continued to struggle but was surprised at how strong he was.

"See what Armando has," he replied as his hand came in front of her with two fifty-dollar bills. It continued down into the opening of her sweater until it found her bra. She felt the bills slipping under it and his fingers spreading over her breast. His fat body pressed against her, and she felt him hardening.

Her mind was racing but she fought to maintain control. The

man with her coat could be coming back to the restaurant any minute. Everything had been planned so carefully. Why was this happening to her now? Something told her to remain calm, maybe even lead him on. She took slow deep breaths. He relaxed his grip and she was able to turn toward him.

"I've been waiting for you to do that for so long," she whispered. To his surprise she brought her arms up around his neck. Then he felt her lips against his, along with a sudden surge of pain in his groin as her knee came crashing into his testicles.

He fell backward into the rack of coats as she picked up her raincoat and bags. There were two people waiting at the window and she practically ran over them. The door was only a few feet away, but there was a crowd of people in front of it waiting to be seated.

"Excuse me, excuse me," she said frantically as she used the bags to push them out of the way. The line parted in front of her and she burst through the revolving door and onto the street.

It was raining more heavily now, and her first thought was that it would be impossible to get a cab. With the rain pouring down on her, she looked up and down the block. There wasn't a cab in sight. Then she looked directly across the street. There were two men in a parked black Buick staring at her. The man on the driver's side had rolled down the window to get a better look. She ran.

At the corner, a taxi was coming down Broadway with its directional light on. She dropped the bags and raised both arms over her head to signal it. If she was lucky, maybe it was pulling over to let someone out.

It passed, splashing through a puddle near her, then stopped at the end of the next block. A man got out.

"Taxi!" she screamed at the top of her voice. She ran as fast as she could but it was starting to pull away from the curb. Again she yelled. This time the man who had gotten out heard her and stopped the driver. He held the door for her as she ran up and threw her bags into the backseat. She was soaking wet, and she got inside.

"Thanks," she said, turning to the man who was still holding the door. She was out of breath.

"You really should wear that raincoat instead of carrying it," he said, smiling at her.

She looked down at the coat, which was draped over her lap.

"Yeah, I guess I should," she said quickly. He closed the door and she turned to the driver. "La Guardia airport, please, and I'm in a hurry."

"What's new?" he said without turning around. "Everybody is."

He started uptown, later turning east toward the Midtown Tunnel.

Cheryl settled back in the seat and realized that a chill had come over her whole body. She took the raincoat and pulled it around her shoulders. The last few minutes had been so frantic. She was still shaking. But so far she had pulled it off. Son of a bitch, she had pulled it off.

The driver was looking at her in the mirror but now had turned away. She reached down and felt the hem of the coat. There were two bulky packets sewn into the lining. She smiled. There was probably enough here to supply half of Los Angeles.

But then fear returned. She really hadn't pulled off anything yet. The black Buick across the street from Armando's—who had been in it and were they following her? Quickly she turned and looked out the back window. All she could see through the rain was a truck and a small van. What about the man who was carrying the sugar? Had he discovered it yet? Had he contacted Armando? He knew she was going to the airport. Oh, Jesus, she had to get there quick. She looked at her watch. It was eight-thirty.

"Can't you hurry," she said to the driver, who was now pulling in behind a line of traffic at the entrance to the Midtown Tunnel.

"Lady, ya gotta go through this hole to get to the other side of the river. The only other way I know is on top. But you're pretty wet already. What time's your flight?"

"Ten o'clock. American."

He looked at a wristwatch that was hanging on the dash.

"You'll make it. Once we get through this mess, it's only fifteen minutes."

She opened up one of the carry-ons and pulled out her ticket. She already had her boarding pass. She had to check her bags, go through security and get to the gate before ten o'clock.

Security. She had planned for that. Anything metallic was in her purse which they were welcome to open. All the bags would go through the X-ray machine, where they would find nothing. She would be wearing the raincoat going through what was only a metal detector. Unless she raised some suspicion, the pouches in the lining would never be found.

Traffic finally started to move, and they made it through the tunnel in a few minutes. The rain had kept people off the Grand Central Parkway and the cab moved along, making good time. At nine-twenty they pulled into the American terminal.

Cheryl could feel her heart pounding again. They could be waiting inside for her. She wouldn't even know who they were. The cabbie got out and opened her door. Reaching into her purse, she took out a twenty-dollar bill and gave it to him. Forget about the change. She put on the raincoat, picked up her bags and went into the terminal.

To her surprise it wasn't crowded inside. She wished it was. Now it would be easier to spot her. She hurried across the large ticketing area dragging her bags behind her. An agent took her ticket and assigned her the last available aisle seat. As she stepped away from the counter she saw a TV monitor with the departing flights listed on it. There it was: LOS ANGELES, FLIGHT 3, 10:00 P.M., GATE 3.

She looked to her right. There was a line of people waiting to go through security. It was moving slowly. Two bored armed guards stared at the endless parade of anonymous faces moving through. One of them was playing with a rubber band between his fingers in an attempt to keep some part of his body moving while his mind stood still. Good. Maybe it was the end of the shift and they wouldn't be alert. She took her place in line.

Her eyes darted from person to person as she scanned the line and the people waiting around the area. Who looked suspicious? Who was waiting for her? Would she have time to run? She looked in back of her. There was a large clock on the far wall and two men were standing under it. One of them was staring at her. She turned away.

They must be looking for her. Armando had gotten them here on time. They knew what she looked like, and if they weren't sure, the raincoat was a dead giveaway. Maybe she should take it off and carry it through the gate. No, that would raise too much suspicion now.

"Next, please."

The words startled her. The security guard was motioning her to put her carry-on bags on the moving belt to be X-rayed. She placed them on it and a green light went on over the metal-detector doorway.

"Step through, please."

The guard spoke in a monotone born of sheer monotony.

She hesitated for a moment, then took the three steps that were necessary to walk through.

"Thank you. Next, please."

She stood there. That was it? No alarms? No questions? She had made it.

Her carry-on bags were coming out of the X-ray machine. As she picked them up, she turned to look back at the men under the clock. Two women had joined them and they were laughing together. "Paranoid. You're paranoid," she told herself. "Stop worrying, you've made it. You've probably got over three hundred thousand dollars worth of coke in your pocket. You pulled it off, baby, now relax. You're just a passenger going to L.A., like a hundred others. Just get to the gate and get on board. You're home free."

She hurried down the corridor to Gate 3. They had nearly completed boarding the airplane and she went right on. A stewardess helped her put her carry-ons in the overhead compartment and she slid into an aisle seat, next to an elderly lady.

Settling back into the comfort of the seat, she let out a long, deep breath.

"Just made it, I see," the woman next to her said, looking up from her paperback romance novel.

"Yes," she answered, hearing the irony in her voice. "I just made it."

The woman noticed her raincoat, which was still wet.

"You're going to catch your death of cold in that wet raincoat, dear. Why don't you take it off and put it in the overhead?"

Cheryl reacted instinctively and pulled the coat tightly around her.

"No . . . uh, thank you. I'd rather wear it."

"You're sure?" the woman persisted.

"I'm fine . . . really," she said, raising her voice slightly. Nobody was going to touch the coat. She had come too far to risk blowing it all now. The woman shrugged her shoulders and went back to her novel.

Cheryl turned and looked out the window. A man in a bright yellow slicker was directing the plane out of the gate. His hands came together and it stopped. The taxi tractor was unhooked from the nose wheel and he turned around to signal the pilot. With one hand he pointed to the runway and with the other he saluted. The plane moved forward and taxied out of the terminal area to the main runway, where it was immediately cleared for takeoff. Cheryl felt the thrust of the engines push her back against the seat as the 767 roared down the runway. She watched the ground fall away and then saw the lights of Manhattan shimmering in the rain. Through the window they looked like the theater marquees she had seen from the cab just a few hours ago. The plane continued to gain altitude, and then they were gone.

Without turning from the window, she reached down and felt the packets inside her raincoat.

"Good-bye, New York. Hello, L.A.," she whispered.

At precisely one minute after ten o'clock, the phone on Armando Lucci's reservation desk rang. It rang several times before he picked it up. Something inside told him it wasn't for a reservation.

"Armando's Restaurant. May I help you?" he asked tentatively.

"Is this Armando?"

"Yes. Is this Mr. Vogel?" Armando recognized the accent immediately. His heart began to race. There had been a problem with the drop. Vogel wouldn't call for any other reason. It was too dangerous.

"We seem to have a problem with what was delivered this evening, Armando. It is not what we contracted for."

The voice was cynical yet deadly serious.

"What was delivered?" he asked. Beads of sweat were forming on his forehead.

Even though there was a danger of the phone being tapped, Vogel's answer was simple and direct.

"Sugar."

Armando was silent. The air seemed to rush out of his lungs. He looked over at the hatcheck counter. One of the waitresses was behind it now. There were only a few coats remaining on the rack, none of them tan raincoats. That fucking bitch Cheryl had done it. She was the only one who could have made a switch. He had believed her story. She was going away and had to leave early. Of course she had to leave early—before they found out. He could still feel the soreness in his crotch where she'd kicked him. If it was the last thing he ever did, he would get her for this. But what about Vogel? He had to protect himself from him right now.

"I had nothing to do with it. You must believe me," he heard himself whispering into the phone.

"We believe you," Vogel answered, dismissing the thought. "You wouldn't be that stupid. However, you realize the importance of this particular delivery to us."

"Yes, yes of course," he said quickly. He was beginning to feel the phone shaking in his hands.

"We must act quickly if we're to recover it," Vogel continued in what was now a restrained monotone. "We've contacted McFarland and we're reasonably sure he delivered what was ordered to your restaurant."

"Yes, of course . . . it wasn't him . . . it was . . ."

Vogel interrupted. "We know who it was. What is the hatcheck girl's name, and where is she now?"

Armando took a deep breath. They knew Cheryl had done it. They were professionals and were way ahead of him. He blurted out the information.

"Her name is Cheryl Branigan . . . she left the restaurant about an hour ago."

"For where?" he asked quickly.

"For the airport . . . La Guardia . . . she said she had to make a flight. . . . She—"

"Where was she going?" Vogel's questions were coming in rapid succession as he began to realize that the switch may have been carefully planned.

"I don't know. To visit her mother, she said. I think it was Florida," Armando answered weakly.

"In what city?"

"I don't know."

Vogel was breathing heavily as he tried to get control of himself. Finally he spoke in a calm voice that was almost apologetic for having lost his professionalism.

"Apparently it's too late to stop the Branigan girl now. She's probably already in the air, headed for any one of a hundred places. What we need to know now is her apartment address. Do you have it?"

"Yes, of course," Armando replied, not really knowing where it was in his cluttered desk drawer. He held the receiver against his shoulder as he searched through piles of paper. Where was it? He was literally throwing things on the floor in an effort to find it.

"Well?" Vogel asked impatiently.

"I have it here," he answered excitedly. Luck was with him. He held a crumpled piece of notepaper in his hand, with her address scrawled across the top of it.

"One seventy-eight West Ninety-sixth Street," he said, enunciating each word for clarity. "Apartment 4A."

"When did she give you this address?"

"About three months ago."

"You're sure she still lives there?"

"Yes."

"Good," Vogel said, relieved that he was coming away with something. "You're to do nothing further this evening. However, tomorrow we'll want to meet with you to talk in more detail."

"Of course." Armando felt a sense of fear building inside him. What were they going to do with him? "The usual place?" he asked.

Vogel hesitated.

"I don't know yet. Someone will be in touch with you."

"I see," he said softly. The conversation was ending too abruptly. He needed more assurance that he wouldn't be blamed for what had happened. Cheryl was the one. She had gotten greedy and intercepted the most important drop they had made in two years.

He started to babble something more that was an attempt to put all of the blame on her, but then he heard a click. The line went dead.

Slowly he put the receiver down and thought about what could happen to him now. That fucking Cheryl. There were other drops she could have taken off with; why did it have to be this one?

Why did it have to be the one that the KGB had been waiting for?

3.

CHERYL'S CAB PULLED up in front of the Belmont Hotel in the Westwood section of Los Angeles. She had always wanted to stay at the elegant hotel just off the UCLA campus but had never had the money to do it. She felt along the lining of her raincoat for the pouches inside. Now she could afford it.

The doorman took her bags and escorted her into the spacious lobby. She stopped in the center of it and looked up at the high glass ceiling. Hanging from it was the largest crystal chandelier she had ever seen. It sparkled like a thousand diamonds as the crystals reflected in the glass above them. She looked within the crystals and saw her own image. How fitting, she thought. Yes, this was her new life. Diamonds, crystals, sparkle and glitter. *Cheryl, they would be all yours.*

She stepped up to the front desk and found an attractive young clerk ready to assist her.

"May I help you?" she asked pleasantly.

"Yes, I'm checking in," Cheryl answered a little nervously. This was the first time she would be using a new identity. From now on she would be establishing a new name and a new life. She had to be careful. Armando and whoever he was working for wouldn't waste any time trying to find her. Every step of the way had to be covered. Armando was loud and vulgar but underneath the facade was a clever, cunning man.

"Your name, please?" the clerk asked.

"Carolyn Mulcahey." She loved the name Mulcahey. It had been her mother's maiden name.

The young girl turned to a computer next to her and typed in the name.

"Oh, yes, Miss Mulcahey, we have your reservation. This is for a two-week stay?"

"Yes, it is," Cheryl said. She had reserved two weeks, anticipating it would take that long to find a permanent place, establish credit and get a new driver's license. It had taken most of her savings to do it, but she felt it was absolutely necessary.

"I see you've paid in advance for your stay with us," the girl continued.

"That's correct," Cheryl answered. "I sent you a money order two weeks ago for the full amount, and you sent me back a receipt."

The girl referred to a file next to her.

"Yes, I have a photocopy of the money order right here.

Cheryl looked at her new name on the back of the photocopy. It even looked good on paper. She had swung the y in Mulcahey off into a half circle at the end of the signature. It felt good to do it again.

The girl rang for a bellman and Cheryl was taken to an elevator and whisked off to the nineteenth floor. Her room was at the end of a long carpeted corridor. The bellman opened the door and ushered her into a large luxurious room. It had a queen-size bed, large modern overstuffed chairs, a Chippendale desk and a beautiful walnut wall unit that contained the TV and opened up into a fully stocked bar. On each side of the bed were two lamps that had huge globe bulbs resting on white-lacquered pedestals. The room was almost as big as her entire New York apartment.

She examined the bathroom and the closets while the bellman brought in her bags and adjusted the heating unit. He explained all of the hotel's amenities, and then she tipped him. He was about to leave when he turned and walked over to a large drapery covering one entire wall.

"There's one thing I forgot to tell you about his room," he said as he opened it. "It's got the best view in the hotel."

Cheryl walked over to the window. Los Angeles was a beaded mosaic of sparkling lights spread out in front of her. The window framed it as if it were a work of art done by an Impressionist painter.

Behind her, she heard the bellman say, "Enjoy it," and he left the room.

She pulled up the hem of her coat and felt the packets in her hands. Then she turned around and ran to the other side of the room. In one bounding motion she leapt onto the queen-size bed and rolled onto her back. Tearing at the hem, she began to laugh hysterically. One packet fell out of the lining, then the other. She threw them both in the air and caught them. Holding them against her, she rolled across the entire length of the queen-size bed and onto the carpeted floor. It felt so good to be free of everything, worries, debts, all her troubles.

Gradually her laughter subsided and she lay there a moment, catching her breath. This was the way life was going to be from now on. It was going to be a ball.

She raised the two packets over her head and felt the weight of them. They seemed heavier than when they were in the coat. It looked like the plastic at the seams was ready to burst. Then she noticed something odd. The one in her left hand had a corner of something sticking out of the white powder. It looked like the edge of a small white box. She shook the packet to shift the powder away from whatever it was. Now she saw more of it. Yes, it was a box about a half-inch thick.

Suddenly a chill ran through her. She got up from the floor and went over to the closet where the bellman had put her bags. There was a utility kit in the outside pocket of the smaller one. She took a scissors from it and went into the bathroom. On the sink was a glass, from which she quickly tore the plastic wrap and poured some of the powder into it. Wetting her finger, she dabbed it into the powder and tasted the white granules.

Sugar.

Her first thought was that she had the wrong coat. No, it was the right one. These packets were sealed differently and had something inside them. Quickly she emptied the rest of the sugar into a wastebasket, leaving the small box inside, which she now saw was about three inches square.

Her hands trembled as she held the packet, in front of her. Through the plastic she could see that the top of the box was held down with a piece of Scotch tape.

She looked up and saw herself in the mirror. Perspiration was forming on her forehead and the corner of her lip was trembling. Reaching down to the sink, she took the scissors and cut away more of the packet in order to remove the box. Then she slowly slid it out and opened the lid. There was film inside.

It was on a red-plastic spool with a notched hole in the center to fit onto a projector. The film was much smaller than the eight-millimeter size they used at some of her auditions.

Her fingers were shaking and she had difficulty pulling off the tape stuck to the end. Finally it came off. She stretched out a section of film and saw dark images between the tiny sprocket holes at the top and bottom. What was on it? The images were too dark. She had to see what they were.

There was a round magnifying makeup mirror over the sink. It had a light in the center of it and would make a perfect light box. Pushing herself onto the vanity, she got into a kneeling position. Then she took the film and held it against the bright light. Each frame was less than a quarter of an inch high. It was microfilm. The word sent immediate terror through her body. This was the type of film that the KGB, CIA and other government agencies used to pass secret information. She had read all the espionage thrillers. It was tiny film that could fit inside a pen, a cigarette holder, a watchband, anything small.

She moved closer, straining to see the tiny images. By moving the film a little to the right, she was able to get it over the brightest part of the magnifying glass. What she saw terrified her. There were six panels on the film, each containing some sort of mechanical drawing. There were technical drawings and the objects appeared to be in space. They were plans for something. For what, she didn't know. The images were much too small. It would take much more magnification to make anything of the tiny, almost microscopic, lines, but God, they were definitely plans for something.

She rewound it back on the reel and opened the second packet. A quick taste of the powder revealed it was also sugar. Again there was a box inside that contained microfilm. Holding a strip of it to the light, she saw that this wasn't a series of still drawings but a continuous movie sequence. There were tiny flecks of white light and then a brightness that filled the entire frame. She stared at the length of film in her hand. What was it? It looked like an explosion, a nuclear explosion. Whatever it was, it would be more valuable than any cocaine she could have stolen. Lucci had meant to pass it on to somebody. Oh, God, he would be looking for her. He wouldn't stop until he found her.

A feeling of weakness came over her entire body. She put the film down and slid off the vanity. Her legs were numb and could barely support her weight. The room seemed askew and was spinning around until it started to whirl. She gave in to a feeling of vertigo and let herself slide down the vanity to the floor. There she was able to put her head between her legs and allow blood to get to her brain. Gradually the faintness subsided.

Her fingers felt something coarse. Some sugar had fallen on the floor. She picked up the crystals and felt the hard texture between her fingers. Sugar. What a fool she had been. Lucci was very clever. That son of a bitch knew she might pass coke for money but would draw the line at military secrets. He knew her better than she thought.

"It's a chance for you to make some real money," he had told her. "All you have to do is mix up a few raincoats. You do that often enough, anyway. Now you'll get paid for it. And if you fuck it up," he had warned, "somebody is going to come after your little ass and kick it good."

They would do a lot more than that now. But who was he working for? The Mafia? The Russians?

The man who picked up the drop had a slight accent. She could never quite place it because he never said very much, but yes, he could have been Russian. Leaning her head against the vanity, she took a few deep breaths.

Her whole body was shaking and she couldn't stop it. Using the vanity, she pulled herself up and made her way slowly to the bar in the bedroom. Some Scotch on ice might help. She poured the drink and then sat on the edge of the bed with it. Maybe it would calm her nerves. There were two things she could do at this point; she could become hysterical, which she was on the verge of, or she could try to think things out.

The first thought that ran through her mind frightened her. She needed to call Barry. He wasn't expecting her call until morning, but she needed to call him right now. But that could be dangerous. Lucci's people were probably professionals. Just picking up the phone could be the end.

The ice cubes clinked against the side of her glass as she held it. Alcohol worked slowly on her and it would be a while before she stopped shaking. However, her mind was beginning to organize thoughts in a more rational manner.

Maybe she should simply call the FBI. They would know how to deal with getting her safely to them. Yeah, sure. She could imagine the telephone conversation now.

"Hello. My name is Cheryl Branigan and I just found a box of microfilm in a plastic packet that I thought was cocaine. I was passing it in a restaurant in New York when I just happened to stumble on it. What's on the film? Well, I'm not sure. It looks like plans for some kind of weapon but I can't really see them very clearly. Oh, you want me to make an appointment in the morning? Well, I can't do that because people are after me and are trying to kill me. How do I know that? You're right. I don't really know that."

The whole thing sounded ridiculous.

And what about the fact that she had taken part in passing secret film? Would they believe that she didn't know what was on it? Would they believe she thought she was only passing cocaine? Yeah, just cocaine. They'd find her guilty of that too.

She fell back on the bed and stared up at the ceiling. Before anything could be done, she had to find out more about what was on the film. Then she would have a better idea of who was after her and where she could bring it. Also, she had to find a safer place to stay. What if Lucci's men had followed her. What about the apartment in New York? Did she leave anything behind that showed she'd made a reservation at the hotel? Oh, God, she needed someone to help her. As much as she hated to, she had to call Barry now.

Barry had been meant simply as a means of getting rid of the coke. "Here it is. Give me my two hundred thousand and good-bye." She didn't want to get involved any more than that. Their relationship had ended over five years ago because he was using coke, and she had sworn never to see him again. But once she thought of stealing from Lucci, he was the only one she knew who could deal it. And now he was the only person who could help her. Getting anyone else involved would be too dangerous. Besides, there wasn't anybody else.

They had lived together for three years when she first came to Los Angeles. He was already established as an up-and-coming film editor, assisting on features while she was just starting out. He had connections who could help her and she used them. Within just a few months she had a small part in a new television series. There she was, Cheryl Branigan, on television every Thursday night. Barry asked her to move in with him and she did. Life was wonderful. They both were making money and having a ball at the same time.

It didn't last very long.

Suddenly the series was canceled and she was out of a job. Although Barry tried to help as much as he could, she couldn't get anything else except for small bit parts and a few television commercials. Meanwhile his career began to move. He won a technical award for an independently produced documentary and it had led to a job with KNBC, the largest television station in L.A. He was overjoyed. She was miserable.

The constant rejection began to gnaw at the relationship. At first they both tried to cope with it by talking things over. But then the talking wore out. She couldn't hide the failure that happened every day by pretending to be cheerful. If she could have worn a smile on the outside while being miserable on the inside, things might have worked out. But she wasn't that kind of person. Her feelings were what drove her life, for better or for worse.

Barry began to see other women and got into the drug scene. It was mild stuff at first, but gradually it got to coke. He would come home in the middle of the night stoned, and they would have violent arguments that lasted into the early morning. Coke turned him into a different person. He became a kind of Jekyll and Hyde. One moment he was warm and tender, the next violent and totally unpredictable. After two months of it they both knew the relationship had to end.

Finally one night they decided to have dinner in a fancy Beverly Hills restaurant. Although neither of them said anything, they both knew it would be their last night together. As soon as they sat down at the table Barry ordered drinks. When they came, he raised his glass and offered a short toast. She still remembered every word of it.

"Here's to us, not for what might have been, but to what was.

"Here's to the fork in the road where we choose our separate ways. Maybe not because we want to, but because it has to be.

"Here's to where the roads will lead us. May it be to places where we find happiness, but, more importantly, where we find ourselves.

"Here's to us."

He must have written it earlier and memorized the whole thing. She was so moved that her eyes filled with tears. Why was having a career so important to her? Why couldn't she be happy just being with him? Why couldn't he lay off the coke? She needed a handkerchief. Barry handed his across the table.

They promised to stay in touch with each other. She told him she was going to New York to get a fresh start. Most of her work had been in TV commercials, and more and more of them were being shot there. He said he would write and he did. But they hadn't seen each other until last year, when they met for lunch in New York to arrange the coke deal.

At that time she had told him she didn't want to get involved again. She was going to start a new life in L.A. She was even going to change her name. Cheryl Branigan would cease to exist.

But now she had gotten involved in something far more dangerous than stealing coke. God knows who was looking for her right now. She needed help desperately.

Unfortunately there was only Barry.

Prague, Czechoslovakia

Inside a large hunting cabin thirty-five kilometers from Prague, a CIA agent pressed a series of buttons that rotated a large satellite disc outside the cabin. The disc was not uncommon in this mountainous area, as it was very difficult to get good television reception. But this was no ordinary disc. It was a transmitter linked directly to a communications satellite monitored by the Pentagon.

Minutes ago he had received a message from an informer working on the docks at the Russian port city of Tallinn. Land-based Russian SRV missiles were being loaded there. They were being carefully crated to appear on deck as gas turbines.

The message had not been totally unexpected. For the past three years Russian SRVs had been operational inside typhoon-class submarines stationed deep beneath the polar ice. The submarines had operated from a base at Gremikha and sailed through the Barents Sea to the Arctic, where they ran undetected by radar under the ice. Over two hundred missiles were now said to be positioned for possible strikes against the United States.

SRV development had started secretly in the fall of 1988. *Glasnost* and *perestroika* were the formal policies of the Soviet Union, but the United States had insisted on following through on its Star Wars program. As a result, there was a position of friendliness on the surface but a mistrust underneath. While both countries leaders met to discuss a new openness, Russian scientists secretly worked to develop a new means of missile delivery to counteract Star Wars. Their efforts resulted in the SRV.

The missile was only eighteen feet long, but its eight warheads each packed an explosive power of 150 kilotons of TNT. Its solid-fuel, two-stage design enabled it to fly at Mach 2 over 8,000 kilometers in just three minutes. It was the first submarine-launched missile with the power to destroy a major city.

Meanwhile the United States Star Wars program had failed to produce anything that could provide a defensive shield capable of repelling attack. Ground-based lasers, high endo-atmospheric interceptors and missile decoys had either proven too costly or were not technically feasible. By January of 1992, the program had been officially abandoned. The following month, the Russians test-fired the first SRV. With it they now had military superiority over the United States.

It was only a matter of time before a land-based version was developed. That, apparently, was now at Tallinn.

The agent took a small pad and wrote the message he would send Washington while the transmitter's computer homed in on the communications satellite.

TOP SECRET
10335Z4 REDSTAR

RADCOM OPS

CONTACT BLUESTAR MESSAGE 60 SECONDS. XX REPORT SRV
LAND MISSILES ARRIVE TALLINN FOR SHIPMENT XX SRVS
DISGUISED AS TURBINES XX SHIPS ARRIVE 16 OCTOBER XX
POLTAVA LEAD SHIP.

The name *Poltava* triggered something in his brain. Where had he
heard the name before? Poltava was a city in Russia, but he had
seen it in another context somewhere else. Where was it?
Suddenly it came to him, and he added two more lines to the
message.

Now he knew where the missiles were going.

Langley, Virginia

A chauffeured limousine turned off the George Washington
Parkway and went down the exit marked CENTRAL INTELLIGENCE
AGENCY/INTELLIGENCE COMMUNITY STAFF. It went through the stop
sign at the end of the ramp and made its way toward a seven-story
building silhouetted in the moonlight. As the car got closer, the
man in the back could see lights going on in a corner office on the
top floor. Good. They were there already.

He looked at his watch. It was two A.M. A helluva time for a
meeting, but they now had a helluva big problem on their hands.

Two security guards waved the car into a huge underground
parking garage, which was empty except for four other limousines
parked at the far end. The license plates indicated that two
belonged to senators, one to the chairman of the Joint Chiefs of
Staff and the others to high-ranking intelligence officials. The car
pulled in between them and the chauffeur opened the door for his
passenger. A tall man in his early sixties, dressed in a tan blazer
and corduroy slacks, stepped out. He had been awakened just
thirty-five minutes ago and decided that a meeting this early did
not call for formality.

"Shall I come up with you, Mr. Shupe?" the chauffeur asked as they headed for a private elevator.

"Yes, why don't you," he answered. "You'll be more comfortable waiting upstairs. This is going to take a while."

They stepped into the elevator. There was only one button on the panel inside. It was marked with the number seven. The chauffeur pressed it and a panel lit up over the closing doors. It read CENTRAL INTELLIGENCE AGENCY. OFFICE OF THE DIRECTOR, DONALD A. SHUPE.

Neither man spoke as they traveled up the seven floors, directly to Shupe's office. As they came out into the reception area voices could be heard coming from the private conference room. Shupe walked into the room while the chauffeur remained outside. The conversation stopped as he sat down at the head of the table and took some papers from a worn leather briefcase.

"I'm sorry to have to call you all here in the middle of the night, but I'm afraid we've got a serious situation on our hands. What we've been working on for the past two years may have been lost tonight in New York."

Everyone in the room knew what he was referring to. They had all gone home hours earlier, hoping that everything would go as planned. Apparently something serious had happened in the past few hours.

General Cabot, chairman of the Joint Chiefs of Staff, was the first to speak.

"We're not going off to fight World War III, are we, Donald? What on earth could be so terrible?"

Shupe didn't respond to Cabot's attempt at humor. Instead he stared at the papers in front of him. Finally he looked up and addressed the group.

"Gentlemen," he began, "I received word under an hour ago that the drop at the restaurant was intercepted. Special Agent McFarland notified me as soon as he could get to a safe telephone."

No one spoke.

He looked to each man for a response but saw that none was coming. Their initial shock was such that questions hadn't as yet formed in their minds. They had all worked long and hard for over two years to develop a desperate plan to save the country from losing military superiority to a new Russian regime. In just a few hours it had been threatened, if not lost.

He continued. "McFarland is certain that the hatcheck girl at Armando's intercepted the drop. She's the only one who could have done it. Two things have to be accomplished immediately. One, she has to be found at all cost. Two, the film has to be placed back in the hands of the Russians immediately. It's our only defense against the Russian SRVs."

Senator Park, chairman of the National Security Committee, asked the question that everyone else was afraid to ask.

"Do we know who this girl is?"

"Her name is Branigan . . . Cheryl Branigan. That's about all we know. New York is trying to get more information on her right now," Shupe answered quickly.

"Goddammit," Park said, slamming his fist down on the table. "Just when we were making progress toward the Russians finding our receivers at Sakhalin and the other military installations, this has to happen. What about replacement film? Can McFarland get another copy in time?"

"I don't know if that's possible," Shupe answered, lighting his pipe for the third time in less than an hour. "However, it was my first thought, and I've already contacted California. The lab there will start on a duplicate immediately."

He paused for a moment and then went on. "Two hours ago I would have thought it possible to get another one to the KGB, but a second phone call from Colonel Weinstein at the Pentagon makes me think it's unlikely. Weinstein received a coded SAT-COM message during the night from our intelligence station in Prague. The agent's contact in Tallinn reports that land-based SRVs arrived there last night, to be loaded on ships. The timing is incredibly bad. With the loss of the film, it leaves us defenseless against missiles that are going to be aimed right down our throats."

General Cabot took off his glasses and looked hard at Shupe.

"We've been expecting to see land-based ones any day now. But why at Tallinn? We thought they'd haul them by rail into Kishinev or Melitopol, where they could reach Germany in minutes."

"That's the whole point, General. They're not thinking about Germany—or Europe, for that matter. They're thinking about encircling the United States with missiles that'll put Washington and New York in a crossfire just minutes away. The agent in Prague gave us the name of one of the freighters that'll arrive at Tallinn to take on the missiles. It's the *Poltava,* the same freighter that led the Russian convoy to Cuba in 1962. They're going to give us another Cuban missile crisis, only this time it'll be 1994 style."

There was silence in the room. The impact of what he had said was too incredible to believe. The timing of this information, combined with the loss of the film, stunned everyone. Shupe's deputy director, Joseph Matava, was the first to speak.

"SRVs under the Arctic already give them military superiority, but together with land-based ones in Cuba, they'll have a delivery capability of under two minutes anywhere along the eastern seaboard."

"One minute and fifty seconds to be exact," Cabot said quietly. "There's no defense against that."

"There's only one defense," Shupe said, watching the smoke from his pipe curl up toward the ceiling, "and this hatcheck girl, Cheryl Branigan, has it. Only now we're running out of time to get it back into their hands. You asked why Tallinn, General. I think it's because the *Poltava* left from there over thirty years ago, and I'd bet my last dollar they're going to go even one step farther to repeat history. They're going to leave on the anniversary of the day they sailed for Cuba against Kennedy—October twenty-second. That's just two weeks away. We've got to get that film back into the KGB's hands before then. Once those ships leave, they won't turn back.

He turned to General Cabot.

"If we don't have Branigan and the film before then, we may very well be going off to fight World War III."

The Upper West Side
New York City

Two dark, silhouetted figures climbed the fire escape of a brownstone building on West Ninety-sixth Street. Both men wore tight-fitting leather jackets and jeans, which enabled them to move quickly. One of them carried a small black case and a short length of pipe. The other had rope and a grappling hook slung over his arm. At the fourth floor they stopped in front of a wooden casement window and knelt beside it. They checked the window for an electrical alarm and found none. The hardest part of the break-in was over. Catching the fire escape from the ground in the darkness and pulling it down without being heard was difficult. Entering the apartment would be relatively easy.

The man with the case opened it and took out what looked like a modified car jack. He placed it on the windowsill and adjusted the telescopic length of pipe over it to fit the height of the window. He then took a small handle and inserted it into the jack. As he pumped it, the pipe exerted upward pressure on the window. Inside, the sleeve lock on the top frame began to bend, until it finally snapped. The window was raised and both men slid through it into the dark apartment.

One of them remained crouched near the window while his partner checked the rest of the apartment. No one was there. For once their KGB superiors had been right.

They began a systematic search of what was left in the small apartment. However, they found what they were looking for almost immediately. There was a Manhattan Yellow Pages directory in the bottom of a cardboard box next to the wall. When they looked under the heading "Airlines," they found that the page had been torn out. For the next ten minutes they went through wastebaskets and boxes looking for it. Finally one of them opened a plastic bag of garbage and found it crumpled in the bottom. Using a penlight, they looked down the page and saw two departure times penciled in the margin next to American Airlines. The first was too early—six-thirty P.M. But the other was a nine-o'clock flight.

One of them put the paper in his pocket, then they searched the rest of the apartment. Nothing else significant was found. Within twenty minutes they had left through the window and were back on the fire escape.

Two men watched from the building super's apartment on the first floor as the KGB agents dropped the fire-escape ladder to the ground. One took careful note of the time they were leaving and entered it in a notebook. Then both watched as the Russians ran down the darkened alley along the building to report back to their office. The two CIA agents never thought they would be part of helping the enemy, but this time they needed all the help they could get. The film had to get back into KGB hands and they would do everything they could to help them find it.

So far they had been lucky. Jim McFarland knew the hatcheck

girl's name and they had been able to get to the apartment quickly. With the help of the super, they got in and searched the place. The Branigan girl had been very careful. Nothing was left behind. The missing page from the directory was already in a trash can that would have been picked up the following morning. Also with the super's help, they had found it and placed it back in the apartment, where the KGB would find it. Now, with one phone call to American Airlines, they would know what the CIA already knew.

Cheryl Branigan was in L.A.

The Bolshoi Ballet
Moscow

The Bolshoi Theater was bathed in light, highlighting the majestic columns rising to support the building's ornate triangular facade. Melting snow glistened along the top of the peaked roofline, disturbing the smooth line of Gothic architecture. It was a cold October night, perfect for the women to show off their sables as they walked into the theater with men dressed in black tuxedos. Tonight's performance was one of the most popular of the season, the opening of Asafyev's *Flames of Paris*. Muscovites, like most Russians, loved history. Tonight they would get their fill of it.

Inside, the theater glowed from the warm light of huge crystal chandeliers hanging from the vaulted ceiling. The soft light radiated over the audience, reflecting pinpoints of light from diamonds and rubies that seemed to be everywhere. The classless society of Lenin was not in evidence that evening. Wealth and power were.

In a box directly over the stage, a group of people were carrying on a lively conversation as they waited for the ballet to begin. One of the women was recognized by many in the audience as being one of Russia's former great prima ballerinas. Ivana Parkofsky was not only beautiful but had been a great dancer. She danced with the best male performers Russian ballet had to offer. Vasiliev, Nureyev, Gudonov, all of them had been partners to her magnificent talent and had become better dancers as a result of it. Now a teacher at the Bolshoi, she was married to a man also recognized by many in the audience: Viktor Karpolov, the newly appointed head of the KGB and member of the Politburo.

Karpolov stood and shook hands with an elderly man who had just entered the box. The new KGB chief was an imposing man who stood over six-foot-three and had the trim figure of a man much younger than his forty-four years. He did not have classic good looks; instead there was a sense that his features had been chiseled out of the land, out of oak or ash. Everything was angular, the nose, the mouth, the shape of the cheekbones, even the forehead that tapered back to meet a full head of wavy, dark hair. His hands suggested that at one time they had been used to cope with nature but now enjoyed the luxuries of hand cream and weekly manicures.

The old man patted him on the back and then turned to Ivana who kissed him lightly on the cheek. The other six people in the velvet seats greeted General Alexei Parkofsky warmly with handshakes and the traditional embrace. Standing in front of Karpolov and his daughter, he took both their hands and held them in his.

"How wonderful it is for this old man to be here tonight, celebrating with you," he said. "I honor you, Viktor, for your great achievement, but more importantly, I honor you for the happiness you have brought to my daughter. That is most important to me."

Karpolov felt the old general's grip. The man was almost twice his age and still had strong hands.

"Thank you, General," he answered. "Without the two of you, this evening never could have happened. Your support and Ivana's encouragement are what got me this honor. I am grateful."

He put his arm around Ivana and added, "Now, if I could only beat him at chess, I would be encouraged to be premier."

The general laughed loudly and pointed a finger at him.

"Never," he said. "It's the only thing left I can beat you at. I find that at my age you relinquish the body's agility but treasure the agility left in the mind."

"You still look pretty agile to me, Father," Ivana said, putting both her hands on her father's square shoulders. "I've seen you come running up the steps to our apartment when you're late for dinner."

"How did you see me?" he asked in mock puzzlement.

"She was spying from the window," Karpolov interrupted.

"We KGB men teach our women a few tricks, don't we?" he said, looking at Ivana.

"Well, I must admit that when it comes to Ivana's food, this old body finds a way to run to it," Parkofsky answered.

Karpolov turned and noticed that the American ambassador, George Hodges, and his wife had come into the box. Hodges stuck out his pudgy hand and spoke in a high voice that had irritated Karpolov from the first time he met him. Another Ivy Leaguer. Another product of a capitalist system that produced spineless intellects who never got their fingers dirty.

"Congratulations, Viktor," he said, shaking his hand while his wife smiled at Ivana. "We were very happy to hear last week of your promotion at Two Dzerzhinsky Square."

Karpolov laughed to himself. Hodges couldn't bring himself to say KGB. First of all, he was embarrassed about using the acronym rather than the full name, Komitet Gosudarstvennoy Bezopasnosti, which he couldn't pronounce. But more importantly, the acronym represented a threat to his government that he preferred to avoid. Instead he referred to the location of the agency rather than by its name.

"Thank you. It's very nice of you to stop by," he answered politely, trying to hide his dislike for the man. He had never trusted him. Like most U.S. diplomats, he was tied to big American military contractors. As a result, he had appeared to be open to *glasnost* policies of friendliness and cooperation but at the same time had supported Star Wars to fill the pockets of those corporations.

"I know everyone from the president on down is delighted that we'll be working with you in your new position on the Politburo," Hodges continued. "It's particularly pleasing to me because we've known each other for a while. Ballet buffs, you know."

"Oh, yes," Karpolov said in a voice loud enough so the others could hear. "It's rumored that Grigorovich's *Golden Age* is one of your favorites, but I really don't believe it."

Golden Age was a thirties revival that dealt with a decadent capitalist society. The ballet's main character was a voluptuous siren, danced by Tatiana Golikova, one of the Bolshoi's newest stars.

"No, I believe *Golden Age* is more of a parody than a

representation of any reality. I prefer something with more substance myself. Don't you?" he replied.

Karpolov was about to answer, but the orchestra started playing and the houselights were dimming.

Hodges shook his hand again and turned to leave. "Congratulations again. We'll be seeing you soon."

You certainly will, Karpolov thought to himself. And it will be a lot sooner than you think.

The curtain opened and the ballet began. Ivana took his hand and put it in hers, as she always did. How soft and warm it felt. Then she put her head on his shoulder and kissed him lightly on the cheek.

"I love you and I'm so proud of you," she whispered.

He kissed her on the forehead.

Karpolov had seen *Flames of Paris* a number of times, but tonight it would have a special meaning.

The setting was Paris during the French Revolution, and it depicted the struggle of the masses against a tyrannical monarchy. It was a struggle that all Russians related to. The 1917 February Revolution and the overthrow of Czar Nicholas II was the Russian equivalent of the story line. The audience loved it.

The tempo of the music became slower and his mind drifted off to a meeting of the Supreme Soviet, held over a week ago. At that meeting his promotion to head the KGB and his appointment to the Politburo were announced. But more importantly, his plan for Russia to gain complete military superiority over the United States was approved. It was a daring plan but one that would succeed where Khrushchev had failed thirty-two years ago. It would send missiles to Cuba.

Khrushchev had made the mistake of trying to establish a presence in the Caribbean without having the military muscle to back it up. But now, after three years of intensive submarine-pen construction at Gremikha in the Barents Sea, and the development of new submarine-fired missiles capable of being launched from beneath the polar ice, they had military superiority. The United States Star Wars program had failed. American scientists had not been able to develop a protective shield of laser satellites that were impervious to Soviet missiles. And now they had even better missiles—SRVs. Missiles that were impossible to defend against because of their tremendous speed and accuracy.

His plan would place medium-range missiles in Cuba within a month, which would give the Soviets unquestionable military superiority. It would in effect surround the U.S. and shorten travel time to the target to under a minute. There would be no defense against this capability. With their current technology the Americans would be helpless.

There was a second aspect to the plan that was more psychological than practical. It would turn the moral defeat they suffered under President Kennedy into a moral victory. This time they would not be stopped. Their missile-carrying ships would sail undeterred to Cuba, and they would establish themselves before the world as the unchallenged military power. And he, Viktor Karpolov, would be in a position to be the next premier.

His attention returned to the stage as Asafyev's music swelled. Dancers, playing the role of French revolutionaries, were leaping across the stage. Behind them, Paris was burning. The city was aflame in a brilliant display of red, orange, and hot yellows. Smoke poured from buildings that were silhouetted against the roaring flames behind them. There was total chaos as people ran for safety into the streets. The lavish production gave such a sense of reality that the audience broke into applause.

"Isn't it wonderful, dear?" Ivana whispered softly to him.

"Yes, very realistic," he said.

But he wasn't seeing Paris in front of him. It was New York, Los Angeles, Washington, Chicago. All of them would be in flames unless the United States acceded to the new Soviet military superiority and the demands that would stem from it. By the end of the century, Russia would dominate all of Europe, and the United States wouldn't be able to stop them. His plan would have missiles pointed at them from all sides. They would be caught in a cross fire that could destroy them in seconds.

He remembered Premier Chebrikov's words when he'd first proposed the plan to him.

"I like it for two reasons," he had said. It was one of the few times Karpolov had ever seen him smile. "I have always believed that we would have to threaten American soil directly in order to accomplish our goals in Europe. This plan will achieve that. But more importantly, we will avenge the humiliation of 1962. Even if we gain nothing beyond getting those missiles to Cuba, it will have been worth it."

But they would achieve more. When the American people found their country directly threatened, interest in protecting Europe would wane. Already they were amassing Russian land troops around the Czechoslovakian border. With the Americans held in check, they would move quickly through Germany and France, to threaten England within sixty days.

He settled back in his seat and squeezed Ivana's hand. She was staring intently at the stage, studying the dancers' technique and style. They were so unlike in so many ways. Her life revolved around beauty, form, and grace. His was a life of espionage, collusion, secrecy, and sometimes death. Often they spoke of how they remained so compatible over the years. Her answer was that she provided a respite of calm and peace to his fast-paced life. On the other hand, he represented to her a chaotic, threatening world that needed the influence of culture and serenity. She was right.

He noticed a sliver of light to his left and saw the door of the box opening. His aide, a man named Anton, signaled that there was a telephone call for him. Anton knew he was not to be disturbed unless there was an emergency. The emergencies always seemed to happen at the wrong time. It was inconvenient, but his position required he be in contact with the communications center at all times, even if it meant carrying a portable decoding radio with him.

He excused himself and left the box with Anton.

"What is it?" he asked. The fact that he had been disturbed showed in his voice.

"It's Com Check Central. They've got a Code 1 ready and another standing by. They say both are hot."

"I understand," he answered. Two Code 1s at once were unusual, but to come at this hour even more so.

They walked down the carpeted staircase to the lobby and into a small private office where the communications decoder was set up. Karpolov sat next to the operator, who handed him a headset with a microphone attached. What he would hear was a digitized voice from the computer. Com Check, located on the other side of the city, was sending a coded signal. The computer decoded it and converted it into a voice. When he spoke into the microphone, it reversed the process. An elaborate device to make a telephone call, he thought, but necessary. These days the Americans were listening everywhere.

"This is Com Check 2-A01."

The code surprised him. It was from the GRU. A Code 1 from the internal security force was unusual. He gave his own code number and waited for a response.

"We have a communication from the Institute of High Energy Physics at Serpukhov."

"Go ahead with the communication," he answered.

The mechanical voice from Com Check droned on.

"The laboratory has issued a report on a receiver device found last night near the air base at Sakhalin. Although a quick examination of it is inconclusive, the device appears to be a receiver for a laser satellite transmitter."

Laser satellite receiver. The words rang in his ears. For the past six months, information on American attempts to develop a laser weapon had been passed to them through a drop in New York. Laser-reflected satellite technology had been the only development in Star Wars with any promise at all. He never believed, however, that the weapon would be a success. Both American and Russian scientists had tried for over four years to develop lasers with military capabilities and had failed.

He looked over at the operator for a reaction to the transmission and realized only he was hearing it. The operator was simply monitoring some dials that showed the signal was coming through clearly.

"How many receivers were found?" he asked.

There was a two-second delay while the computer decoded both the response and the reply, but then it came.

"A total of eight. Three at Sakhalin, three at Magadan, and two at Kamchatka."

All three were important bases on the Siberian mainland. They were important both offensively and defensively to operations taking place in the Sea of Japan or, for that matter, the entire Pacific.

"How were the receivers found?" was his next question.

"Through surveillance at the bases." The computer voice sounded matter-of-fact and mechanical. "The latest one was found by Sector 14, commanded by Captain Berkhin. His report accompanied the lab's."

"Give me a summation of the report."

"It is quite long" came the reply.

"A paragraph is all I want. Give it to me now!" he said, raising his voice.

There was a pause. Finally the automated voice responded with what appeared to be selected lines from the total report.

"A man was apprehended three nights ago at Sakhalin, after burying the receiver boxes near the base. He was interrogated. During questioning he claimed he was paid to bury the boxes by someone he met at a trade show, an American. He said that . . ."

"He was paid by whom?" Karpolov asked.

It took a moment for the computer to stop, translate his question, and repeat the statement.

". . . at an electrical trade show. By an American."

"Who was the American?" he asked, not expecting to get back a definitive answer.

"They don't know, and it doesn't appear he can be traced" came the reply.

"What else is in Berkhin's report that's significant?" he asked.

The voice droned on, reciting a checklist of facts.

"The markings on the device were in English. When activated, it verifies that it's operating and signals its location to a satellite. In the case of the last box, it was discovered before it was activated. It's hoped the American will make contact again because of that, but Berkhin doubts it."

Karpolov agreed.

Maybe the box was some sort of receiver, but he doubted the Americans could have developed a laser weapon that quickly. Clouds, pollutants, and atmospheric distortions were just a few of the factors that made lasers ineffective as weapons. Relay mirrors, used to reflect the beam down to a target, were not sufficiently accurate to insure destruction. After expenditures of over five billion dollars, the idea was essentially shelved by the Hayden administration.

He needed time to think. Why did this have to happen now? His plan had been enthusiastically approved and he'd been rewarded with a promotion and a seat on the Politburo. Not only that, but in two weeks he would commit an armada of Russian ships to Cuba, with the assurance to his superiors that the Americans were defenseless. Could he be sure of that? Once those ships were sent, there could be no turning back.

"How long will it take Serpukhov to have definitive information on the capabilities of these receivers?" he asked quickly.

"They say anywhere from two to three months. It will require testing various degrees of laser strength directed at the receiver from different altitudes."

That was the answer he wanted to hear. Time was what he needed, time for his plan to be executed before any doubts about the weapon could develop. In the morning he would order further testing on the devices and the stepping-up of intelligence operations inside the U.S. military. That might lead to some answers, but it would take months. By then his plan would be in effect and he couldn't be held to blame. Yes, that was the answer. Sometimes delay was the key element to success in a bureaucratic system. If delaying didn't solve the problem itself, it got so entangled in the system that it automatically became less critical. Working in a bureaucracy was not for the impulsive. It was the procrastinators who thrived.

His thoughts turned to the second call and he put the headset back on. The operator turned to another channel and he heard him give the call sign and frequency. He recognized them as the KGB Communications Center in Dzerzhinsky Square. The officer on duty was Colonel Zarov.

Zarov was a workhorse and a stickler for detail and procedure. What he lacked in creativity, he more than made up for in getting things done. Over the years he had become Karpolov's right-hand man in the GRU and had been given more and more responsibility. His latest assignment was the monitoring of the drop being maintained in New York.

"Is this 1A-100?" The numbers were his new designation as KGB head.

"Yes it is, go ahead," he answered.

Zarov hesitated for a moment, waiting for verification of the call number, then spoke in an uncharacteristically slow voice. Karpolov sensed immediately that something was wrong.

"At 0500 hours this morning, Moscow time, the New York drop was intercepted. I wasn't notified until an hour ago."

The decoded words were calm and mechanical, but their impact on Karpolov was explosive. He couldn't believe this could be happening, along with what he had just heard from Sakhalin.

"That was over twelve hours ago," he shouted into the phone. "You were just told now?"

"Agents in New York were reluctant to report it until they had a chance to recover the film. They thought it could be done within hours."

Karpolov slammed his fist on the table, sending an ashtray crashing to the floor. This New York drop was supposed to provide them with the latest information on laser development. What had been just an updating of the technology had suddenly become critical. It was one of the covert operations that could have provided him with answers as to whether the Americans had a laser weapon or not. The timing of all this was incredible.

"How did it happen?" he snapped at the microphone, knowing that his voice would lose all its emotion in the decoding.

"They had a hatcheck girl making the switch. Thought she was dealing with narcotics and got greedy. She probably doesn't even know what she walked off with."

"She's got what we need now more than ever," he answered, shouting into the microphone. "We need the information from that drop and we need it immediately. She is to be found! I want her found within forty-eight hours! Tell New York that."

There was a pause. He knew he had overreacted, and Dimitri was considering a more realistic time frame.

"I've already taken action and issued orders to them," he replied. "A search of her apartment showed that she's left for Los Angeles. Agents there will be alerted, along with Station 20 in San Francisco. I will stay here until their first reports come in. By morning, New York will have checked her friends, neighbors, the usual. We'll find her."

"I want her found quickly," he shouted, wishing the computer would translate the emotion in his voice.

"I'll do my best," Dimitri answered.

Karpolov looked down at his hands. They were folded in front of him and were trembling. That hadn't happened in a long time, not even when he'd found himself in life-threatening situations in dark alleyways years ago. In those situations the key words to survival were *hide, cover up,* and *conceal.* That's what he needed to do with this situation now.

Again, the bureaucracy could work for him. The GRU and the KGB sections lacked coordinated communication. The military always felt that intelligence operations within the Soviet Union were nobody's business but their own. He could prevent the finding of the laser receivers in Sakhalin and the loss of the weapons information in New York from ever being linked.

Together they could put his plan in jeopardy with the more conservative members of the Politburo. But if he could conceal information, his plan would remain intact. He was lucky it was Dimitri who was on the other end of the line.

"I want you to tell those bungling idiots in New York that I find it difficult to believe that a hatcheck girl stole important information right out from under their noses. Their stupidity reflects on me personally, at a time when I've been given greater responsibility by our leaders. Tell them that."

"I will transmit that to them."

"Good," he continued. "This is such an embarrassment to both of us that I don't even want it on the record, do you understand?"

"Yes, I do . . . but I don't know if we can—"

He answered before Dimitri could finish. Even though it broke the rules to name an agent during a decoded transmission, he needed to appeal to him on a personal level.

"We need to keep this between us, Dimitri. We can't afford a mistake like this right now. At least not until I've established myself in this new position with the Politburo. The operation in New York is to be reduced to Code 3, and the communication excluded from POL-1 review. The computer tape is to be stricken from the log. I want you to repeat those instructions back to me so there is no mistake in the decoding."

There was a pause. Karpolov nervously drummed his fingers on the wooden desk.

Zarov's reply was short and clipped.

"Code 3, exclude from POL-1 review, communication stricken from log." Then he added, "I hope you know what you're doing."

Karpolov motioned for the operator to end the transmission, and he placed his headset on the table. Everything inside him was in motion. He felt his stomach churning and he was breathing deeply. The operator and Anton turned to him and he struggled to maintain his composure.

"I'll go back and join the others now," he said slowly.

Anton opened the door and they walked back to the private box.

There was no conversation. He quietly slid into his seat beside Ivana. The first act of the ballet was almost ending. There was celebration in the streets. The monarchy was being overthrown. Asafyev's music soared as the dancers leapt high in the air. Ivana took his hand and noticed that it was trembling.

New York City

Armando Lucci hadn't slept most of the night. It was after two A.M. by the time he had closed up the restaurant and returned to his apartment. He had immediately taken two sleeping pills and gone to bed. But they hadn't helped. The phone call from Vogel had left him so terrified, he couldn't stop himself from shaking. No matter how many blankets he piled on top of his large body, he couldn't stop the trembling. It had gotten so bad that several times during the night he had run to the bathroom and thought he was going to vomit.

He stared at the ceiling and asked himself why he had gotten involved with the KGB in the first place. As usual, money was the answer. His drug operation was about to be closed down by the police when he was approached by Vogel. The KGB needed a safe place to use as a drop. They would pay enough money for him to buy protection from inside the police department. In fact, they even knew who to buy. It would be good business for everybody. His operation would run without interference from the police, and the KGB would have a safe drop.

But that fucking Cheryl had ruined the whole thing. Vogel had warned him that this was the most important drop they had yet made. It had to go smoothly. He had called Cheryl early in the day to make sure she would be there. Yeah, sure. That had been his biggest mistake.

He looked at the clock radio beside his bed. Six-thirty A.M. He had been lying awake for over four hours. Maybe if he took another sleeping pill he would still be able to get some sleep. He started to get out of bed when he heard a loud knock on the door. Who the hell could it be this early in the morning? He put a robe over his pajamas and went to answer it.

"Who's there?" he asked hesitantly from behind the door.

"Vogel" came the reply. "Open the door."

He felt his heart begin to race. Vogel said Armando would hear from him. A meeting place would be arranged. But he had come directly to the apartment. Instinctively he unlocked the latch and was about to turn the knob when the door burst open. Two men stormed into the room, the first pushing him backward until he fell into the sofa. Vogel came in behind them.

"Where did you say Cheryl Branigan was going last night?" he shouted, towering over him.

"Florida. She told me she was going there to see her mother." He could hear the fear in his own voice. His chest was pounding.

"That's what she told you?"

"Yes."

"Well, she's in Los Angeles. She left on a nine-o'clock flight last night from La Guardia."

"I didn't know. She told me—"

"She told you lies," Vogel said, taking off his raincoat and throwing it over a chair. "And if you weren't stupid enough to listen to them, we wouldn't have lost what belongs to us. We pay over two hundred thousand a year to protect your drug dealing, and this is what we get for it!"

"I didn't know it was going to happen. Believe me. I thought everything would go all right. I never thought she would run off with it."

Lucci could feel himself beginning to perspire. He didn't even know exactly what Cheryl had taken. All he knew was that he had been warned that it was important to the KGB and that it was lost.

"But now you're going to help us find it, aren't you? My superiors in Moscow want it found immediately." Vogel continued to raise his voice. "Do you hear me?"

"Yes. Yes. I'll do whatever I can."

"How much do you know about her?" the KGB agent asked, sitting down in a straight-backed chair next to the sofa.

"Not much," he answered meekly.

Lucci's mind was racing to gather whatever information he knew about Cheryl that would help them. L.A. That's where they said she had gone. He thought back to the first time she had applied for the hatcheck job.

"Cheryl . . . used to live in Los Angeles," he said, stammering. "She lived there before she came to New York five years ago."

"Where in Los Angeles?"

"Westwood, I think. She liked that part of the city. She always used to talk about how many movie theaters there were."

"Where in Westwood? Give me a street, an area."

"I don't know. All she said was Westwood. She liked it there."

"Did she live alone?"

"I don't know."

"What about friends?"

"I don't think she had many."

"She's an attractive girl. Did she have a boyfriend?"

Lucci shrugged his shoulders.

"Did she have a boyfriend? Think! What did she tell you?" One of Vogel's men grabbed him around the lapels of his robe and jerked him to his feet.

"She didn't tell me anything else about herself," he said, gasping for air as the man pulled the robe tightly around his neck. "She was always just kidding around, saying a lot of nothing."

"What kinds of things?" There was a desperate tone to Vogel's voice Armando had never heard before. Whatever Cheryl had, Moscow must be frantic to get it.

"Silly things. She would pretend to be a big movie star, staying in all the best hotels and having people wait on her." He was beginning to perspire, and his words came out, one on top of the other, as he struggled to remember. "She loved fancy hotels. She said once that she walked through the lobby of the Waldorf every day for a week, pretending she was a big Hollywood movie star. She dreamed. She was a dreamer. Then she would come to me and say she didn't make enough money. She always wanted more money. The bitch never had enough. Maybe that's why she stole from me—so she would be able to stay in her fancy hotels."

"Yes, maybe so," Vogel said. He nodded to the man holding Lucci. He released his grip on him and Armando sank back down into the sofa. "She probably thought she was stealing enough cocaine from you to do anything she wanted for a very long time, including staying in the best hotels," Vogel said. His voice was calmer now. He looked at his watch and said nothing for a few moments. Finally he took a small notebook from his breast pocket and wrote something in it. Then he got up from his chair.

Lucci watched as he walked across the room and picked up the phone. He dialed an eleven-digit number and spoke calmly into the receiver.

"This is Vogel in New York. Who am I speaking to? . . . Yes, very good. I have a question for you. What is the best hotel in Los Angeles? Westwood in particular. . . . I see. . . ." His eyes narrowed slightly as he looked back at Lucci. "Check both of them," he continued, "immediately." There were a few more words of conversation and then he hung up.

Lucci was questioned for over an hour until Vogel was sure he had gotten every bit of information he could out of him. In the meantime the KGB in Los Angeles was rushing to check two luxury hotels in Westwood.

One of them was the Belmont.

4.

Los Angeles

WHEN CHERYL AWOKE, she was lying fully dressed on the bed, the empty glass of Scotch beside her. As her mind began to focus, the chill returned to her body. The events of the last twelve hours played through her mind like instant replays. Only this wasn't make-believe. This was real. She was in big trouble and she needed help. She needed Barry.

God, he had to help her. She hadn't told him how she was getting the coke, just that she would call him on the tenth when she got to L.A. He was just expecting a simple transaction; she'd give him what she had and he'd pay her. Now when he found out what she was involved in, he might just forget the whole thing.

The numbers on her digital watch were blurry but she managed to read them; 4:27 A.M. Sleep had spared her from three and a half hours of terrible fear. Her body ached and her clothes had a dank smell from the rain in New York. She had to get out of them, and then she would call Barry. Slowly she got up and went into the bathroom. The packets of sugar and the two boxes were on the sink. That nauseous feeling started in her stomach again as she stepped out of her clothes and went into the shower.

The warm water felt good as it cascaded down over her body,

but inside she was trembling. Would Barry help her? It was almost a year since she had seen him last. Why hadn't she stayed in closer contact with him? If he wouldn't help her now, nobody would.

If only the soapy water could wash away the whole thing. Why did she get greedy? Why didn't she just go on getting what acting jobs she could in New York and been happy? No. She had to get involved in something so far over her head, it probably would get her killed. The thought made her shudder and the water didn't feel warm anymore.

She dried herself quickly, wrapped the towel around her body, and went into the bedroom. Barry's phone number was in her bag. She dug through the airline stubs, combs, pens, and makeup items and finally found a blue notebook near the bottom. Quickly she fumbled through the pages and found the number.

After four rings a tired voice answered.

"Whoever you are, do you know what time it is?"

The words were slurred and barely understandable but it was him. She tried to speak but nothing would come out. She managed what was just a whisper.

"It's Cheryl."

There was a pause, and then his voice sounded stronger.

"Yeah, uh, Cheryl. You're supposed to call me in the morning, aren't you? This is the middle of the night. Where are you?"

"At the hotel." She swallowed hard and then added, "Barry, I need your help . . . I'm in trouble."

"What kind of trouble?" His voice was cautious, noncommittal. "Do you have what you said you'd bring with you?"

"No, I was supposed to but—" Her voice was cracking and she had to stop to take a deep breath. "I can't really get into it on the phone. I've got to see you. I stole something by mistake and now I think I might be in terrible danger. There are people who are after me . . . they—" She couldn't finish the sentence without breaking down, and she wouldn't let herself do that.

"Calm down," he said. There was confusion in his voice as he tried to understand what she was saying. "Who's after you?"

She took a deep breath and continued.

"I thought I had stolen coke from the restaurant where I was working in New York. I thought it was cocaine. It turned out to be more than that. It's film, Barry."

"It's what?"

"Film. Microfilm for some kind of plans."

"What kind of plans?"

"I don't know, but I need your help. I'm in way over my head."

There was a long pause that seemed like an eternity, then finally he spoke.

"Listen, we had a deal to unload some coke. If you don't have it, I don't really want to get involved in—"

"Please, Barry, you've got to help me!" She was losing control of her voice as tears ran down her face. "I can't call the police. You've got to help me. I don't have anybody else."

There was another pause. God, if he didn't help her, who could she turn to? It seemed forever before he spoke again.

"What hotel are you in?" he asked. His words sounded tentative.

"The Belmont, in Westwood," she answered quickly. "Can you come now? I'm so frightened."

She could feel his hesitation on the other end of the line. It was over five years since they had severed their relationship, and in just a few minutes she wanted help that even the closest friend would give reluctantly. She waited for his answer.

"All right," he said hesitantly. "Give me about an hour. But listen, our deal was coke. I don't know if I want to get involved beyond that."

"I know," she replied quickly. She had to get him there as soon as possible. "I'm in Room 1937, checked in under Carolyn Mulcahey."

"Mulcahey?" he asked. She could tell he was writing it down.

"Yes . . . and, Barry?"

"Yeah?"

"Thanks."

She hung up the phone. Then she put her head down on top of it and cried.

The next thirty minutes were spent just keeping busy. She dried her hair and put on a simple white sweater over a pair of designer jeans. If she could get Barry to take her from the hotel, it would be better to be as inconspicuous as possible. She took the packets and the microfilm from the bathroom and moved them to the desk in the bedroom. She had to keep her hands and mind busy. The TV. She turned it on, saw a commercial, and turned it off. Finally, running out of things to do, she sat on the bed and faced the apartment door, waiting.

Staring at it reminded her of when she first had dated Barry. He was always late and she would sit and wait in front of her apartment door. This was like old times. Yeah, sure.

The telephone startled her.

Instinctively she picked up the receiver but then was terrified at who could be on the other end.

"Miss Mulcahey? This is the front desk."

"Yes?" she answered hesitantly.

"There is a Mr. Ross to see you. Shall I send him up?"

A Mr. Ross—that would be Barry. Barry Rossiter. "Yes, send him up."

She practically ran to the door and looked through the peephole. It seemed an eternity before the elevator door halfway down the corridor finally opened and a man stepped out. It was Barry, his image distorted by the peephole's wide-angle lens, but yes, it was Barry. She fumbled with the latches and opened the door.

They stood for a moment facing each other, not knowing what to say. Finally she held out her hands and he took them in his.

"Thanks for coming," she said, trying to catch her breath.

"Yeah, I got here as soon as I could," he answered. "There's traffic even at five in the morning."

She stepped aside to let him into the room.

He was dressed in jeans and a pullover with a sailing emblem. California casual was still his style. His hair wasn't combed and he hadn't bothered to put on socks under his docksiders. A year hadn't changed him much. His dark hair was still thick and wavy. The pullover fit snugly around his broad shoulders and the jeans hugged his narrow waist and thighs. When he turned toward her, she saw that his thirty-two years weren't showing. He still had that handsome, boyish look that had attracted her from the very beginning.

"Now, what happened?" he asked, looking around the room.

She went over to the dresser and picked up the boxes of microfilm and the packets of sugar.

"This happened," she said, trying to control the emotion in her voice. The tears were starting to well up in her eyes. "I stole these bags from the restaurant where I work. I thought they were full of coke. Instead I found these boxes inside. They had microfilm in them."

Barry wet his finger and tasted a few of the granules from the packet.

"This is sugar," he said.

"Yes," she answered quickly. "I thought they were just passing cocaine through the coats I was checking there. So I said to myself, why should they make all the money while I take all the risk? It would be easy to walk off with a couple hundred thousand dollars worth of coke. All I'd have to do is simply put it into a coat just like the ones they were using. So I switched coats. They ended up with mine and I ended up with this."

"What was in yours?" he asked.

"Sugar, to make it look like the coke I was passing."

"But they weren't just passing coke. They were also passing microfilm," he said, holding up one of the boxes and taking the film from it.

"Yes. I looked at it over the makeup mirror in the bathroom. It magnified it enough to see lines forming some kind of shape. I think they're plans for something."

He took the film into the bathroom and laid it over the makeup mirror. Slowly he passed the first strip of film over the light, examining it carefully. By holding it slightly farther away from the glass, he was able to magnify even more than she had. The images were very small, but appeared to be technical in nature.

She handed him the shorter strip. "This is microfilm, isn't it?" Her hands trembled at the very mention of the word. "It's got some secret plans on it. Oh, Barry, I'm so frightened."

Barry took more time with this strip. Carefully he passed it between his thumb and index finger, enabling him to get the maximum magnification.

"It's plans for something," he said without looking up. "Maybe they're military secrets. Or they could be for some new machine design or jet engine, practically anything. You'd have to magnify it much more than this to really see," he said calmly. "You can't tell much here."

He thought for a moment and then asked, "Do you know who's passing this stuff?"

"This fat pig, Armando Lucci, owns the restaurant. I figured he was tied in with the Mafia and passing coke. But the guys making the drop don't look it. The one who brings in the stuff is, you know, a typical businessman type. The other one has—and I never thought about it till I saw the microfilm—a slight accent."

"What kind of accent?"

"I'm not sure . . . but it could be Russian."

She could feel the tears forming in her eyes now.

"Armando, and whoever else he's involved with, will be looking for me. He knows I'm the only one who could have taken the stuff. Suppose he's working with the Russians? I stole film from them. They're not going to stop until they find me. And they will. Who knows, they could be downstairs right now. I don't know what I'm going to do. I—" She had to stop. Her voice was starting to break, and she couldn't get the words out. She sat on the edge of the bed and buried her face in her hands. Barry stood over her.

"Listen," he said, "when you first planned to steal the coke, you knew they'd find out who did it, didn't you?"

"Yes," she said without looking up.

"So you must have made sure no one knew where you were going."

"Yes."

"Did you leave anything in your apartment that could tell anybody where you are?"

"No."

"You didn't tell anyone, your friends, your neighbors, nobody?"

"No."

"And you checked into the hotel under a different name, right?"

"Yes."

"Well, then," he said, "how could anyone know where you are? I doubt if there's a KGB agent hiding behind a plant in the lobby. At least I didn't see one on the way in."

She tried to manage a smile as she wiped the tears from her eyes.

Barry walked over to the window with the film in his hands. He stood facing the city below, the light behind him casting his reflection on the window. She knew he was making his decision either to help her or to leave right then and there. And why shouldn't he leave? He didn't owe her anything. They'd had an arrangement to deal some coke and she didn't have it. Instead she was caught up in a dangerous situation that he didn't have to become a part of. Her heart was pounding in her chest. He had to help her. Oh, God, he just had to.

He turned and held the film out to her.

"The first thing you need to find out is exactly what's on this film. I can do that for you. Once that's done, we'll take it from there."

She let out a deep breath. He was going to help her.

"Right now," he said, walking toward her, "we have to get you out of here. We'll go to my apartment and you can stay there for a few days. Tomorrow I'll take this film over to the station and see what we're dealing with here."

"Thank you," she said. It didn't seem like enough.

He simply nodded, then looked at his watch.

"Get your bags together and we'll go downstairs and check you out. Be careful not to leave anything behind. When we get to the lobby, I'll put the bags down and go over to the desk. You stay with them. I'll explain that you're not feeling well, that I'm your brother and I came for you. Is the bill charged or something?"

"I prepaid it by check," she said anxiously. "It was almost two thousand dollars for two weeks. It's nearly all I have."

"I'll see if they'll refund anything. If not, forget it. Your life is worth far more. It's Carolyn Mulcahey, right?"

"Yes," she said softly.

She looked at him. He was the same old Barry. "Come on, let's do it. Take charge." It was the same as when she had met him. "You're new in L.A. You need a job. Let's find one. I'll call an agent I know this afternoon. By next week you'll be working twelve hours a day and you'll hate me for it. Life moves on, keep up with it." All he saw in front of him was the problem. If it needed fixing, he would simply fix it.

"Listen," she said, wiping her eyes. "God knows I need your help, but do you realize what you could be getting yourself into? If somebody's following me, they could be dangerous. You could get killed. I want you to think about this before you plunge into it."

"I thought about it before I left the apartment. You didn't have the coke, so why the hell was I getting involved in this? I still don't know. I even thought about calling you back. But I didn't. So get your stuff together and let's get the hell out of here."

She looked up at him and said, "I don't know how I'm ever going to repay you for this."

"That's not important now," he said. "Let's go."

She repacked her things, along with the film, and they left the room. The elevator came almost immediately and took them down to the first floor without stopping. As they stepped into the lobby, they saw it was empty, except for a man vacuuming the carpet and two clerks behind the desk. Barry put down the bags and walked over to them.

Cheryl sat in a wing chair next to the bags and waited. One of the clerks glanced at her as Barry handed her the key. She took it and typed some information into the computer. After conferring with the other girl, she gave him a piece of paper and he walked back over to her with it.

"She'll refund the rest of your money," he said quickly. "Just sign this."

Without even looking, she wrote her new name on it and he returned to the desk.

A man came into the lobby. He was dressed in a dark business suit and was carrying a black shoulder bag. For a brief moment he looked at her, then turned toward the desk. Slowly he came up in back of Barry and reached into his breast pocket. What was he reaching for? She wanted to scream but couldn't. His hand came out of the pocket and there was a billfold in it that he held up for the clerk to see. He said something to her, which Barry overheard. Whatever it was, it caused him to hurry away from the desk. He rushed over and quickly picked up her bags.

"Everything okay?" she asked.

"Yeah, let's go," he said, glancing back toward the man, who was now looking over the hotel register with the clerk.

They hurried through the automatic glass doors out to the parking lot. She practically had to run to keep up with him. He threw the bags in the trunk of a red Porsche and got in beside her. Quickly he started the engine and threw the car in reverse. With a squeal of the tires, they turned onto Wilshire Boulevard and headed for the freeway.

"What's the matter?" she asked excitedly. "Is someone following us?"

"I don't know," he answered, checking the rearview mirror,

"but that guy who came up to the desk was looking for Cheryl Branigan."

Her hand automatically came up to her mouth. She thought she would scream, but instead there was just a muffled gasp.

"Who was he?" She could barely get the words out.

"He said he was FBI, and he flashed his identification at the clerk," Barry answered without taking his eyes off the road.

"Oh, my God, how did they find the hotel so fast?" Her fingers were clutching her purse and were digging into the leather.

"I don't know, but whoever your friend Lucci was passing the film to, the FBI was on to it."

Twenty minutes later they exited the Ventura and came into one of the better sections of Burbank. They drove through the downtown area, then turned onto a tree-lined street with modern, two-story garden apartments. About halfway down the block, Barry drove the Porsche into an underground garage. He opened the trunk and took the bags over to the elevator. They went up three floors and the doors opened on a thickly carpeted hallway. Barry led her down the corridor to a door at the end. He unlocked it and she went inside.

The apartment was sensational.

A large foyer led to a modern, sunken living room. One entire wall was glass and looked out on a golf course. Golden rays of light filled the room with a warmth as the sun came up from behind trees on the horizon. All the furniture was leather, with brushed-metal arms and legs. A wall unit containing an oversize TV and stereo was covered with dark suede. It all contrasted with white carpeting that came up three steps to meet the hand-painted tiles in the foyer.

"What do you think?" she heard him say behind her.

"Terrific," she said slowly. "You must be doing great."

"Well, KNBC doesn't pay me what I'm worth, but I manage. Let me get you a drink? To tell you the truth, I think we both need one."

She accepted a vodka and orange juice. Barry made two of them from a bar that pulled out from a sidewall and then sat down beside her. As he placed the drink in her hand it shook so that she could barely grasp it.

"They're going to find me," she said, without looking up at

him. "Already the FBI knows I'm in L.A. If they don't find me, Lucci's men will. And when they do, they'll kill me."

She felt Barry's hand on her shoulder.

"Nobody is going to kill you. You're safe here. That FBI agent at the hotel found a dead end. There wasn't a Cheryl Branigan registered, remember? You're Carolyn Mulcahey. That's what was in the register. Listen, nobody knows you're here. As long as we don't make any mistakes, there's no way they can find you."

"But they're professionals," she said, taking a sip of the drink, "both the FBI and Lucci's men. They have ways of tracking people down that we don't even know about."

"Maybe so," he said. "But they can't find you if they don't have any leads. You got to the hotel safely and were there for over six hours. You used a phony name checking in, and you got out safely. The hotel doesn't know where you went; neither does anybody else. Cheryl Branigan has disappeared, right, Carolyn?"

"Maybe," she said, turning to him, "but I'm frightened to death. I thought about calling the police before I called you. Maybe I should still do that. It's too dangerous doing nothing."

"I don't think we should call anybody just yet. First of all, you don't know what's on that film. You have to find that out before we do anything else."

She noticed the change from *you* to *we* in the middle of his sentence. It was comforting. Inadvertently he had stated his intention to help her.

"The first thing you have to realize is that you're safe here. And you can stay for a while. Okay?"

"Okay, thank you," she answered with a faint smile. Between the drink and his reassurance, her body was starting to relax again.

"Tomorrow," he said, holding up the reel of film, "I'll take this over to the station. It's Sunday and most of the editing rooms will be empty. Once I get it transferred to videotape, we can look at it on my VCR right here in the apartment. Then you can decide whether or not to call the police, the FBI, or anybody else."

"Should I go with you?" she asked tentatively.

"I don't think so," he said. "You might be seen. I just don't think it's worth the risk."

"But what if somebody sees me in the apartment?"

"You won't look any more suspicious than the thousands of women that have stayed here since you left."

He was kidding, of course, but she was surprised to feel a hint of jealousy.

"Yeah, they weren't carrying stolen military secrets with the FBI on their tails, either."

He put his hand on her shoulder. It was the first time he had touched her in five years.

"That's true," he said. Suddenly his somewhat hard features seemed vulnerable. His boyish look still had an effect on her. "Most of them just had old boyfriends and husbands on their tails. That can be even more dangerous."

"For who?" she teased.

"For me, of course. One of them could come in the bedroom and blow my brains out."

"Which is the same thing the girls were doing to you, anyway," she answered.

"Aha, touché," he said, stepping back from the bar. "My God, Carolyn, you're as quick as this girl Cheryl I know."

She smiled. Somehow in the middle of all this terror he still could make her smile.

"Now that's more like it," he said. "Smile number one. I've got to frame that and put it over the bar with my first dollar bill."

"I don't think you've got it anymore. It must have taken every cent you own to afford this place." She was, of course, thinking that coke money paid for it all.

"Want something to eat? How about some breakfast?"

She wondered if her stomach could keep anything down, but yes, maybe she would feel better if she ate.

"Yes, I'd like some," she said, standing behind him.

He started to open the refrigerator. She removed his hand from the door and led him to the table.

"I think you should sit down and let me take care of this. Since you're providing the room, the least I can do is provide the board."

"Okay, if you insist."

"I do. If I remember, Saturday is two fried eggs, sunny-side up; bacon crisp but not burned; rye toast; decaffeinated coffee with milk and two sugars. Also orange juice, fresh squeezed. Right?"

"Right. I'm surprised you still remember."

"Yeah," she said, "because after I left you I continued to eat the same thing in New York every Saturday."

"You're kidding. Why?"

"I don't know. I guess I was so busy trying to change everything in my life that I decided to keep one thing the same."

"Well, I'm glad you remembered," he said. For the first time she noticed a softness to his voice.

They sat and ate breakfast, talking about her life in New York and his in L.A. While she was struggling, he had moved up steadily at KNBC to senior editor. Now he was responsible for two top shows originating from the station, along with an hour news program airing on Thursday nights. Although happy with his success, he was still frustrated that he wasn't editing feature movies. That's where the real money and prestige were. But he was still tinkering with his inventions on the side. Last year he had gotten two new patents on a technique that would enable editing to be done electronically. If he could raise the necessary capital, there was a manufacturer ready to start producing the equipment. "Electronic editing is where the future lies," he had said, "and whoever gets there first will make a bundle. Unfortunately it won't be me, unless I inherit a million dollars."

She got him to talk about his involvement with coke. He had stayed on it for almost a year after they had split, but now he supposedly was off it for good. There were a few big dealers in town for whom he sold it, but only if people he knew were involved. Her deal would have been the first one that year.

She talked about her loneliness in the most exciting city in the world. At first her early success had made her feel like a part of the Manhattan scene. But later, when things had gone bad, it was a terrible place to be. Everything had just seemed to move around her while she stood still. Her friends were all in the business and most were working. Eventually the frustration, the constant ups and downs, had all been too much. She had to do something to catapult her into another life-style, even if it meant taking a risk. For months she had thought about stealing the coke, until one day, after yet another rejection by an agent, she had decided to do it. Unfortunately she had ended up with more than she bargained for.

After breakfast she unpacked her things. Barry insisted on her having the bedroom. He would sleep on the living-room sofa, which pulled out into a double bed. Again she resisted, saying she was just happy to be there and didn't want to take over the whole place. His reply was that it was impossible for a woman to move into an apartment without taking it over.

With the unpacking finished and nothing else to do, her fear returned. She stared at her reflection in a full-length mirror on the back of the bedroom door. It was the reflection of a woman who had microfilm she felt men would kill for. She had changed her name, but that wasn't enough. Her looks had to be changed too.

Barry got up from the kitchen table and stood behind her.

"I've got to change the way I look," she said without turning from the mirror.

"But you'll be here. Who's going to recognize you?"

"I don't know," she said, grasping for reasons. "Suppose we have to leave for somewhere else quickly, even if it's to get to the police."

He shrugged his shoulders but answered her in a concerned manner.

"Okay," he said. "If it'll make you feel better, I'll go out and pick up whatever you want. I've got some other things to get, like food. We bachelors don't cook much at home, you know."

He took a small pad from a drawer next to the refrigerator and made a list of the things he would need to buy.

"You'll need some dark glasses. A hat. Hair color. What color would you like to be?"

"Brunette. I always wanted to be a brunette."

"Okay, brunette it is. You'll need some new clothes to hide that figure of yours. Maybe a loose-fitting dress. What size do you wear?"

"Six."

"Okay, I'm on my way. If I think of anything else you might need, I'll buy it."

He got up from the table and went to the door. "I'll be back in a few hours," he said. "The place is yours. There's some good albums and tapes by the stereo. Help yourself to them and anything else you want. And don't worry. Everything is going to be all right. See you later."

As the door closed behind him a sudden chill went through her. Suddenly she realized how tenuous was her ability to handle this alone. In just a few hours she had gone from being a strong-willed individualist to a person totally dependent on someone else. It frightened her as much as the situation itself.

She took his suggestion and opened the walnut cabinet next to the stereo. There were rows of albums stacked neatly on three shelves. When they lived together, his taste in music was limited to pop and country western. Now it had expanded to classical. It included Brahms, Stravinsky, Mozart, and Beethoven. She scanned the bottom row and selected a Barbra Streisand album.

Music filled the apartment as she explored the rest of it. There was other evidence of Barry's newly found good taste. The bedroom closet was full of custom-made clothes, Gucci shoes, and Ralph Lauren sportswear. On the dresser was a picture of a sailboat. He had owned a small eighteen-footer six years ago, but this was much bigger. She could see the name painted on the transom, *The Escape*. It was appropriate. If ever there was a workaholic, he was it. Work dominated his life. There was little time for anything else.

A wine cabinet in the hall contained French Chardonnays. He talked of not having money to get his inventions manufactured. No wonder. He was spending it all on himself.

She went into the spacious living room and looked at the bookcase. His collection of technical manuals had nearly doubled. There were books on electronic frequency modulation, video and audio synchronization, and new laser-scanning cameras and recorders. He thrived on technical knowledge. It was his forte, but at the same time, creativity was his weakness. She would never tell him that was the reason he couldn't get into feature films, but she felt he knew it, anyway.

However, he continually studied any kind of film he could get his hands on. Cinematography, sound, lighting, editing, even the actors' performances came under scrutiny. From the filmic simplicity of Chaplin to the technically sophisticated *Star Wars*, he dissected films into areas to be studied. She had seen him spend hours at it. But he confessed to her once that he never could find the creative inspiration that enabled an editor to turn a piece of film into heart-stopping action or an emotional high. He realized that technical expertise had little to do with it. Some editors just sensed when two pieces of film put together felt right. It was almost something magical when it happened. The feeling constantly eluded him, and it was frustrating.

She looked along the row of videocassettes, which he had neatly marked, and selected *The Maltese Falcon*. It was one she had never seen. She put it into his VCR and settled back to watch it. Halfway through the film, she heard a key in the door. Barry was back.

He came in carrying some newspapers and some shopping bags, which he put on the coffee table.

"I got back as soon as I could," he said. "Are you okay?"

"Yes." She really wasn't. The time he had been gone had seemed an eternity.

"I got everything we need and more," he said.

"I see," she answered, turning off the VCR.

"Were there any calls?" he asked.

She hadn't thought about the telephone.

"No, there weren't. I wouldn't have answered it, anyway."

"Good," he said. "I was thinking about it in the car and figured I could explain it away once, but it would be better if you didn't answer." He looked at the tape lying on the VCR. "What were you watching?"

"The Maltese Falcon."

"Great movie. Love Sydney Greenstreet. And Bogart? One of his best. Did you notice? Almost all of the movie is shot in one room. Like a play, only on film; it's great. It's the way it's shot. Lots of close-ups edited together so there's still enough interest. I must have watched it twenty times."

He took a smaller bag out from inside one of the larger ones and emptied four pair of glasses onto the table.

"Let's see what these look like on you."

She tried them on and they decided on a black pair for outside and horn-rimmed for inside. The hats he'd bought were wide-brimmed and ran from silly to ridiculous. One was a tan safari hat large enough to get all her hair inside.

"You look like you're going to hunt tigers, but it works," Barry said.

"No," she answered, "they're hunting me."

After trying on three dresses she selected a khaki-colored, shapeless cotton that just hung on her. If she ever gained ten pounds, it would fit her snugly. She hated it, but it did hide her figure.

Turning in front of the mirror she studied the whole disguise and was surprised at how much her appearance had changed. Unless you knew her well, you'd probably walk right by her.

"Well, what do you think?" she said, turning to Barry.

"You don't look like anybody I know," he said confidently. "With your hair darkened, it'll be even better."

She went into the bathroom and applied hair color. She couldn't get it as dark as she wanted with one application, but there was a noticeable difference. When she came out, Barry was on the living-room floor, the newspapers spread out around him. He looked up at her.

"Looks good," he said. "It's a whole new you."

She agreed. With glasses and the appropriate clothes, she could feel confident outside the apartment. It would be very difficult for anyone to spot her.

"Is there anything in there about me?" she said, sitting down beside him.

"Yeah, on the front page—Woman steals military secrets and wants over three hundred thousand dollars for them. Call 555-3000."

She took the paper from his hands and threw it across the floor. "It's not funny. If that film has military secrets on it, the CIA could even be looking for it."

"Not really," he said calmly. "The guy making the drop was probably a private individual selling information. It happens all the time. You read about people who work in research companies developing weapons for the government. The Russians approach them to buy information about what they're working on. Before you know it, they're in the laboratory taking pictures with microfilm cameras to sell to the KGB. They pay millions if it's something they want to find out about. You said the guy picking up the film had a Russian accent. I think he probably was Russian. What you have is something they definitely would want to know about."

"Why?"

"Because it sounds like they set up an elaborate drop in that restaurant. It was very well planned, with you switching coke for payment to the guy making the drop. How many times did you say one of Lucci's special switches were made?"

"I don't know, about eight or nine."

"That's what I thought," he said, getting up from the floor. He began to pace around the room, organizing his thoughts. "This guy who made the drop was building up whoever it was being passed to. It probably was the KGB if you recognized a Russian accent. If that's so, after eight or nine drops this film has to be the grand finale on something big."

"Like what?" she asked. "We don't have any idea what's on the film yet."

"It could be anything. You read in the newspaper that they pay huge sums of money for high-tech computer data, secret codes, intelligence locations, all that kind of information. You thought the coke would bring a lot of money; that's nothing compared to what this might be worth."

She looked up and could see his mind working. His eyes darted around the room as he processed the possibilities and their consequences. He reminded her of the first time she'd thought of stealing the cocaine. It sent adrenaline rushing through her veins, and the challenge sent a wave of excitement through her body. Danger became an emotional high, to the point that it overcame the fear of being caught. Barry was right. This time the stakes were much higher than the two hundred thousand she expected for the cocaine. It could be worth millions.

"Do you think it's really worth a lot of money?" she asked.

"I've got a feeling it's worth plenty, but we'll know tomorrow when I examine it closely at the station."

He came over and put his hand on her shoulder.

"How would you like to be a millionaire, kid?"

That evening he barbecued steaks on the terrace. They sat and watched the long shadows of the trees on the golf course gradually darken until they became one large shape silhouetted against the moon. The light played across his face as they sat across from each other. She wondered how he managed to stay so sane and rational through this whole thing. His taking charge of the situation had calmed her. There hadn't been anybody to do that in a long time, and it felt good.

"Why are you doing all this for me?" she asked. His eyes lowered upon hearing the question, and he didn't answer immediately.

"I don't know," he replied. "Maybe it was the tone of your voice. You sounded so helpless. And then again, maybe it was just hearing your voice again. I can't say I haven't missed you."

She didn't say anything, so he went on.

"Now I'm caught up in the problem. You know me, it's broken, so fix it. That's what I want to do now, help you. Who knows where that may lead us."

"Who knows," she said, taking his hand. "But wherever it leads, I want to thank you for what you've done for me. I really don't know what I would have done otherwise."

He reached over and took her hand. Then he kissed her lightly on the lips. Something inside her wanted to respond but she couldn't. Before she could feel what was there before, it would have to be out of love, not out of gratitude or fear.

She didn't feel that yet.

Washington, D.C.

President Alan Hayden sat behind his desk in the Oval Office, facing General Cabot, Secretary of Defense Walter Commack, and CIA Director Shupe. The early-morning sunlight was streaming through the large windows to his right, highlighting their faces. Hayden could see that the three men were exhausted, having come directly to the White House from their two A.M. meeting in Langley, Virginia. When Shupe called at six A.M. and told him what had happened during the night, Hayden had immediately set up an eight-thirty meeting. It had meant canceling a briefing on environmental controls, but from what Shupe had told him on the phone, clean water was totally unimportant by contrast. This meeting was about preventing World War III.

"It looks to me like we've got two critical issues to deal with, gentlemen, and they've both come together at the same time," Hayden said, sipping the last of his coffee. "The first is the loss of film we desperately needed to get to the Russians, and the second is an intelligence report that SRVs are being loaded at Tallinn. If that's true, and I assume it is, we don't have much time to get that film back into Russian hands. You think we have as little time as the twenty-second, is that right, Donald?"

"Yes, Mr. President," Shupe answered, pouring himself another cup of coffee. If the lead ship is the *Poltava*, my hunch is that the Russians aren't just flexing their military superiority muscles, they're out to score a psychological coup as well. The *Poltava* was the ship President Kennedy turned around thirty-two years ago. It left Tallinn for Cuba on October 22, 1962, and the anniversary of that date is just two weeks away. I think they're going to leave on that same date, knowing we can't do anything this time to stop them."

Hayden lit a cigarette and leaned forward in his chair. Every time he heard the words *military superiority*, it angered him so much that he had to light one up. For over a year he had tried to quit smoking, but since the Russians had developed SRVs, he was back to a pack a day.

The last administration had put them in the situation they were in now. His predecessors' insistence that Star Wars be pursued to the fullest had resulted in complete failure. None of the weapons had been tested satisfactorily, and billions had been spent. On top of that, it had hurt friendly relations with the Russians and now *glasnost* had turned to wariness, mistrust, and finally hostility. Now they were back to square one; who had the best military hardware and who posed the greatest threat to the other? Well, now the answer was clear. The Russians held the upper hand and were about to use it. And they couldn't be stopped unless that film got back into their hands.

"Have you heard anything from the Russians about this, Walter?" he asked, looking over his cup at the Secretary of Defense.

"Nothing," Commack answered. "I just met with Marshal Borskeyev in Oslo two weeks ago and didn't get any indication they were about to make a major move. It was the usual rattling of swords but nothing out of the ordinary. Sometimes he'll let something slip if we're alone and I get a few drinks into him, but not this time."

"And you, General?"

"Nothing, except we do suspect they're moving reserve divisions into Czechoslovakia. Nothing concrete yet, but intelligence supports it. Donald's people have also gotten some indication of it."

"That's right," Shupe answered. "The Czechs have just completed a major airstrip south of Prague, and that's usually the first sign. If they move armor in there, they'll have a very short run to the German border."

"So Chebrikov is about to send missiles to Cuba to surround us with them, and at the same time they're building up their forces in Europe." Hayden thought for a moment and then added, "And with SRVs in Cuba, they'll have a missile down our smokestack in less time than it takes you to tie your shoes."

He flicked an ash into the silver ashtray to his left. The ashes drew an image in his mind of what Washington would look like after an attack. He closed his eyes for a moment and then said, "We've got to convince them we've got a weapon that can retaliate swiftly and destroy major targets inside Russia once an SRV is launched. They've got to believe that even though we may not be able to defend against it, we'll still be able to destroy their cities simultaneously. We've got to convince them we've got a laser weapon operational that can turn their cities to ashes. They know we've been working on it and they know we've got receivers inside Russia. The film will prove we've tested it. We've got to get it back into their hands . . . immediately."

He took another sip of his coffee and then directed his questions to Shupe. They came one after another, reminiscent of the style he had used as a special prosecutor before he was elected to the Senate.

"Can we get another film to the Russians that will be credible?"

"If it means before the twenty-second, I don't think so. But we're trying."

"Any leads on the girl who stole it?"

"She's in L.A. We know it and the KGB knows it. We made sure of it."

"Who's going to L.A.?"

"We've assembled the emergency task force. They're on the way."

"Who heads it?"

"Frank LaSala. Who else."

"Good. What about more receivers?"

"We've planted more at five locations. A total of twenty in all. Six were discovered."

"Good, that helps our credibility."

He turned to General Cabot.

"How quickly can NATO exercises be planned in West Germany?"

"A month, maybe six weeks, no sooner than that."

"What about putting two divisions of our own troops in Germany? Put it under the cover of military maneuvers."

"That's possible," Cabot answered, looking at a small plastic calendar stuck in a flap of his notebook. "The 180th Airborne out of Fort Bragg can be there in ten days."

"Do it. We'll worry about the doves in Congress later. And leak it to the press. I want the Russians to know about it as soon as possible."

He reached over and snuffed out his cigarette in the ashtray. Suddenly everything that had started over two years ago was coming to a head. What had begun as a desperate attempt to counter the Soviet SRV threat was now facing the reality of whether the Russians believed the United States had a laser weapon or not. They had painstakingly fed the KGB information about the weapon through the New York drop. They had planted receivers inside Russia so they would be discovered and had developed film that proved the weapon had been tested. Now he would have to make additional moves, moves that placed troops in Europe, head to head against the Russians. And within two weeks he would have to stop Chebrikov's ships from reaching Cuba with the American people clamoring for him to do so. He would do his best to stop them. But what the American people and most of the Congress didn't know was that unless the film got back to the Russians, he was fighting with both hands tied behind his back. All he could do was bluff Chebrikov. The Russians now had unquestionable military superiority. There wasn't any laser weapon.

It didn't exist.

5.

THE IMAGE WAS blurred, like an out-of-focus snapshot, but it still held the same terror for CIA agent Frank LaSala that it had over twenty years ago. Even while he slept in the comfort of a Lockheed Gulfstar headed for Los Angeles, his body trembled as the scene was replayed in his mind. He thought that time had enabled him to live with the memory, but a meeting with Director Shupe just hours ago had rekindled the fear and anger he felt on that night so long ago. The whole thing was happening all over again, this time right down to the smallest detail.

He remembered the stairway. It was carpeted with an intricate floral pattern that contrasted against gold velour wallpaper. A brass chandelier hung from an arched ceiling that had a mural painted on it. Two white doves were sitting in the center of a billowy cloud ringed by a circle of gold stars. It was elegance atypical of Berlin apartment houses, even those in the wealthy Tiergarten district. It was elegance that would be tarnished with the color of blood.

Voices. He could still hear them plainly behind the closed door at the top of the stairs. Anxious, nervous men were speaking hurriedly in Russian. LaSala and his young partner, Mark Ellis, began to retreat down the stairs. They were too late. The KGB had beaten them to the apartment, which a wealthy German financier named Helmut Ecker had just entered. Two days ago it had been proven that Ecker was a Russian agent. He was not the trusted informer for the CIA in Berlin that everyone thought but was a double agent, a major in the KGB. In intelligence parlance, a mole.

Over twenty agents were assigned to apprehend him. He and Mark had followed a hunch, and it had paid off. Ecker had been known to be seeing high-priced prostitutes along fashionable Kurfurstendamm, prostitutes with apartments in the area. It was possible that he was hiding out in one of them until he could leave Berlin. They canvassed the area, talking to over thirty of the higher-priced girls. Finally they found one who knew where Ecker was and was willing to talk. A prostitute who had stolen away two of her best customers was hiding him. Now she would pay her back.

The apartment was just around the corner on Lietzenburger Strasse. They could be there within minutes. Their orders were to report any lead to their superiors in a small house on Bergstrasse, over six kilometers away. Youth and inexperience overruled the order. The result was fatal.

The voices grew louder. They were coming toward the door. Mark was behind him as they moved back down the stairs with their guns drawn. If they could get to the bottom without being seen, they could find cover in the vestibule. But suddenly the door opened, and they were spotted immediately. Before they could fire, he heard two shots ring out behind him, one of them tearing through his chest next to the left armpit. Mark screamed and his body fell backward down the stairs, landing at the feet of a KGB agent who had been left outside to cover the building.

LaSala lay against the wall with blood pouring from his chest. Mark was still alive, even though part of his stomach was splattered on the floor in front of him. Both his arms were raised up to the agent standing over him with a Magnum pointed at his head. LaSala managed to raise himself up enough to plead for his partner's life.

"No, please . . . please don't kill him," he said in what was little more than a whisper.

A smile came over the agent's face as he pulled the trigger.

Three men and a woman rushed down the stairs past him and raced for the door. The last man, who seemed to be the leader, grabbed the young agent by the arm to get him out of the building. But the agent stood firm, and LaSala saw him point the Magnum directly at him. Just one squeeze of the trigger and he would be dead too. Seconds became an eternity as the agent resisted the orders of his superior. LaSala stared at the barrel of the gun and the face of the man behind it. The face was hard, with features chiseled in sharp, angular planes. Closely cropped jet-black hair fell low over the forehead just inches above thick, black eyebrows. The eyes were very small and at first seemed to be brown, but when light reflected from them, they were a fiery red. He would never forget them.

Finally the Russian lowered the gun and followed the older man out of the building. LaSala's head slumped down on his chest and he fell unconscious, the memory of his friend's killer etched forever in his brain. For six months he searched through every file of known KGB operatives in Europe that he could get his hands on but found nothing. It wasn't until two years later that he came across a folder containing pictures of three agents who were returning to Moscow. Those small, fiery eyes stared out at him. Underneath was a typewritten name: Viktor Karpolov.

Through the years he followed Karpolov's career. As he rose through the ranks he became more visible in the news media. Pictures of him constantly renewed LaSala's hatred and frustration. Now Karpolov was totally removed from the field. There wasn't even the remotest chance they would ever cross each other's paths again—until last night.

LaSala felt a hand gently shake his shoulder. His young assistant, Steve Jankowski, was standing over him holding a cup of coffee.

"You all right, Frank?" he asked. "You really were tossing and turning in your sleep."

"Yeah, I'm okay," he answered quickly, trying to regain his composure. "Never could sleep on planes, anyway."

Jankowski put the coffee down on the tray in front of him, took two sugar packets and a stirrer from his pocket, and dropped them on the saucer.

"Who's Mark?" he asked.

The question caught him by surprise. He had always prided

himself on his ability to guard against divulging anything about his professional life. When something came up, his mind went on double alert to edit out pertinent information. But now he was blurting things out in his sleep.

"He was just a guy I knew a long time ago," he answered matter-of-factly.

"I see," Jankowski said. He knew his boss well enough not to pursue the question any further. "The men are about ready to be briefed when you're ready," he continued. "They're anxious to hear what this is all about."

LaSala took a sip of his coffee and studied his assistant over the rim of the cup. In a way Steve reminded him of Mark Ellis. Physically they resembled each other. Both had blond wavy hair, round ruddy faces, and were slightly overweight. Steve was older, probably about thirty, and had the same kind of unassuming manner. It masked a hard-driving, tenacious personality that would stop at nothing to reach a goal. The unassuming part he liked; the overzealous part needed to be watched. Ellis had died from it.

He got up from his seat and took the coffee with him. Somewhere he had read that coming into a meeting with a cup of coffee was supposed to communicate to people that you were calm and in control of the situation. "Bullshit," he said to himself. "If you watch their hands around the cup, more often than not you'll find them trembling." He looked at his own hands and decided to finish the coffee and leave the cup behind.

"Have you told them anything yet?" he asked as Steve was about to open the door to the rear section of the plane.

"No," he answered, picking up a manila folder from the seat he had occupied earlier, "they don't know anything except that they've been ordered to L.A. for an undetermined amount of time."

"Great," he said, brushing back his gray hair. "They're going to love looking for a needle in a haystack."

As Frank came through the door twelve men looked up from what they were doing. Some were playing cards, others were reading, but all of them directed their attention to the man who was to lead them on an unknown assignment.

Most of them either had worked with Frank or knew of him. He was known as a real "field man," an agent who hadn't moved up through the ranks to a supervisory desk job but one who preferred to work in the trenches. His experience encompassed the entire globe. It included Laos, where he had gathered intelligence on the Pathet Lao forces; Berlin, where he was involved with arrangements to swap captured agents with the Russians; Iran, where he infiltrated Shiite forces; and most recently Japan, where he aided the Japanese in identifying Soviet intelligence operatives inside their country. He had earned the respect of three CIA directors, and when Donald Shupe took over, in 1988, he offered him the New York area command. Frank refused. The field was his place, not some stuffy office with piles of paper waiting to be pushed from the in box to the out box. Shupe did convince him, however, to be his troubleshooter. He was given a Priority-One Clearance and now reported directly to Shupe's office.

What the men liked best about him was his easygoing, direct manner. He didn't pull any punches. If he had something to say, he said it in the clearest way possible. You never heard a four-syllable word come out of his mouth when a two-syllable one would do the same job. As a result, those who didn't know him well underestimated his intelligence. They soon learned, however, that he was extremely bright, with a capacity to absorb a tremendous amount of information and draw upon it in critical situations. Under fire there was nobody better.

His looks were also deceiving. Although he had just turned forty-six, he looked older. He blamed it on his hair. It was thick and full but a snowy white. (He always said it wasn't from the pressure of the job but from watching extra-inning Mets games.) It contrasted against the dark skin of his full, round face, which sat on a body overweight by about twenty pounds.

Clothes were made strictly to cover his body, and Frank wore them as such. It didn't matter if a brown sportcoat ended up over a blue pair of trousers as long as they were clean. Pressing was optional. Today he was exercising his option. A five-hour flight, followed immediately by a three-hour meeting with Shupe, left him no choice. He took off his rumpled jacket and hung it over the edge of an empty seat. Then he sat down and swung his legs over the armrest to face the group, some of whom were now standing in the narrow aisle to hear better. Jankowski handed him his manila folder.

"So," he began, "we got ourselves a big one here. I know you

all volunteered for this . . ." He waited for the expected response and got it—a loud groan.

"At three o'clock in the morning I don't volunteer for
anything," one of the men said from the back.

"I know," he answered, taking the top sheet from the folder.
"You all were called on short notice because this one is hot. I'll
tell you right up front, we've got no time, one lead, and the top
brass is breathing down our necks."

He put on a pair of bifocals and continued on without waiting
for questions.

"I think I've worked with everybody here except two of you.
Jim Sweeney and Jesse Moscowicz, where are you?"

Two men on his left raised their hands.

"You both come highly recommended as communications men
fluent in Russian. You're going to be very important to us.
Welcome."

He read down the rest of the list and greeted each man
individually. The last man was Gene Zeller, an expert on the KGB
and its operating procedures. He had a deck of cards in his hand
and a pile of money in front of him.

"As always," Frank concluded, "I like to operate without an
elaborate chain of command. Everyone is equal, and Gene is here
to assure that. Because of him you'll all start out the
same . . . poor."

Zeller nodded in agreement and stuffed the money into his pants
pocket.

Frank put the personnel list back into the folder and handed it
to Jankowski. There was nothing else in it that he hadn't already
committed to memory. He then paused for a moment, waiting for
the group to settle down until he had their complete attention.

"I wasn't kidding when I said we have a 'hot one' ", he began.
"It's hot enough for Washington to bypass the usual 'fragmented
information' method of working a case. In the past many of you
only knew what was necessary to perform your job. It protected
against the whole house of cards crumbling if you were caught and
questioned, but this time we're going to have to run that risk and
tell you everything. There just isn't time to do it any other way.
We need every man to have all the information if we're going to
succeed."

He took off his glasses and cleaned them with a handkerchief as he went on talking.

"What I'm going to tell you now is top secret. Only some members of Congress, Cabinet members, and other key people needed to develop the project know about it. It began over two years ago when it became evident that we would lose military superiority to the Russians. The project involved the creation of a powerful new laser weapon to serve as a deterrent to Russian SRVs. I use the word *creation*, gentlemen, because the weapon doesn't really exist. The entire project was designed to dupe the Russians into thinking we have a laser weapon that we don't really have."

The men stared at him, not quite grasping the magnitude of what he had said. He waited a moment until he felt they had absorbed it fully and then went on.

"Two nights ago a young physicist at Space Technologies named Jim McFarland was to make his ninth drop at a restaurant called Armando's in New York. The drop was intercepted.

"McFarland had been working for the SR section for two years, passing information to the Russians on this new weapon. The weapon is still two more years away from being fully developed, but the film he was carrying would have convinced the Russians that it was operational right now. Losing that film couldn't have happened at a worse time. It was our only defense against a major military move Intelligence says the Russians will make in two weeks.

"As some of you may know, they've constructed new submarine pens at Gremikha, two hundred miles from their main base on the Kola Peninsula. The pens will house new typhoon-class subs capable of launching missiles from under the Arctic ice. The missiles are also new; SRV-60s with travel time to Washington and New York at under two minutes. Since their intelligence knows that our whole Star Wars project has failed, they find themselves sitting with military superiority. And guess what— they're going to use it.

"Cuba, gentlemen. The sons of bitches are going to rub our faces in it. Thirty-two years ago they didn't make it, but in two weeks they'll have short-range missiles there. Combined with the SRVs, time to major targets will be under forty seconds. And there's not a damn thing we can do to stop them."

He paused for emphasis and then added, "Unless we convince them we have a high-vibration weapon ready to go right now. That's what the film McFarland was delivering to them was supposed to do, and that's why we have to get it back."

The men remained silent. Even the veterans were stunned at the importance of the mission. Zeller was the first one to jump in with a question.

"What exactly is on the film McFarland was carrying?"

"A demonstration of the power of the weapon. We created it inside a studio in California using models and a new film technique. It showed a vibration laser destroying a missile silo in Colorado. You would never know it wasn't the real thing."

"Who intercepted the film at the restaurant?"

"The hatcheck girl," he answered.

"You're kidding."

"No, she probably thought they were passing coke, because McFarland was putting film inside packets of sugar. She got greedy and ended up with the film."

"Where's she now?"

"L.A."

"How do you know that?"

"Because of quick action by the guys in New York. When the Russians found they had a packet of sugar instead of film, they called McFarland and told him a switch had been made. He notified Washington immediately of the hatcheck girl's name, and they set up a break into her apartment. Her name is Cheryl Branigan, lived on the Upper West Side. A sift through her garbage turned up that she's in L.A. Our guys left the information out in the open for the KGB, when they broke in an hour later."

"So we're helping the Russkies to find her. That's a switch," added Sloan, an agent LaSala had worked with in Iran.

"Exactly. But it's got to be done very carefully. They can't know we're doing it or we blow McFarland's credibility. As far as they know, he's an unhappy, underpaid physicist making a lot of money for his information."

"Why don't you just get new film to McFarland?" Sloan asked.

"We're trying, Jim, but it doesn't look like the film can be replaced in time. Two weeks is all we've got, gentlemen . . . three at the most. We've got to find Cheryl Branigan."

The men were silent as they absorbed the information. They were professionals who had all been on tough assignments, but LaSala could see an intensity on their faces he hadn't noticed before.

Finally one of the new men, Moscowicz, continued the questioning.

"What do we know about the girl?" he asked.

"Not much," LaSala replied. "At least not yet. New York is checking every angle, and we'll know more in a day or so. In the meantime we do know she headed for L.A., and the office there is starting with the airport. There wasn't a Cheryl Branigan on the nine-o'clock flight two days ago, but that doesn't mean she didn't travel under another name. They're talking to cabdrivers who met the flight. Unfortunately all they have is a verbal description from two agents who saw her leave the restaurant. It's not much, but it's something."

Another agent was about to ask a question, but LaSala cut him short.

"I'm sure you've got a lot more questions about the girl, the details of the drop, and the weapon itself. Steve can fill you in on that later. What I'd like to do now is impress upon you the importance of what we have to do."

He got up so he could see everyone in the back, but more importantly so that he could use his hands. Maybe it was his Italian heritage, but he always found a need to express himself with the movement of his hands. Somehow a gesture, however small, seemed to underline verbal points for him better than if he raised his voice or changed an inflection. It sometimes resulted in some playful abuse from his audience, but it was worth it if he was making a point effectively.

As he started to speak, he found his hands already in motion. They moved with the tempo of his voice, which was beginning slow, each word carefully selected.

"First of all, each of you must look upon this operation as one of the most important you'll ever be assigned to. The KGB will have their best men out to find the girl and recover the film. We've learned that Karpolov himself is personally running their whole operation. The plan to send the missiles to Cuba was his, so you can bet they want a thorough check of what's on that film. He'll stop at nothing to get it back. And we'll stop at nothing to make sure he does."

He felt like a coach pumping up his players before a game. In a sense, that's exactly what he was doing. Motivation. He had always believed that not only was it the key to winning, but also, in this business, the key to survival.

His hands returned to his side and he asked the men if there were any more questions. There were none. He turned the briefing over to Jankowski, who began it by taking them back to 1984, when lasers were first being tested. Once Steve started to field some initial questions, LaSala left the group and returned to the front cabin. A member of the Air Force flight crew was waiting for him.

"This just arrived for you," he said, handing him a piece of notepaper with a jumble of letters on it. This was the first tangible evidence of the mission's importance. Normally the message would have been transmitted in a standard Air Force code, but this was in a priority code specially developed for the group's use.

"Thank you, Sergeant," he said, and sat down. Taking a small plastic disc from his briefcase, he matched the transmitted letters with those on the disc and in minutes had the decoded message in front of him. Unscrambled, the message read: "Branigan traced to Belmont Hotel, 174 Wilshire Blvd, Westwood. Come in through Casita Place. Meet you there—Bud."

He folded the paper and stuck it into his shirt pocket. Maybe Bud Kovacs and the L.A. crew had gotten lucky. Apparently a cabdriver had remembered taking Branigan to the hotel. Over twenty years of experience had taught him not to get his hopes up, but maybe they would find this girl quickly and could concentrate on getting the film back into Russian hands. If that happened, it would be the first time that anything this important had gone this easily.

Twenty minutes later the group came off the plane in Los Angeles. Each man came through the departure area separately or paired up with another agent. Luggage was sent to the baggage area and mixed in with another American flight from Chicago. LaSala picked up his bags from the carousel and joined Jankowski at the Avis counter. Within ten minutes they had picked up a car and were on the San Diego Freeway, headed for the hotel.

The traffic thinned out as they came into the Westwood section of the city. It was getting dark and the street signs became difficult to read. Frank followed Steve's directions through the winding back streets until they came to a long driveway that was marked as the service entrance for the hotel. At the end of the driveway was a small parking lot next to some loading docks. They parked the car. As Steve opened his door to get out, a light went on in the doorway next to one of the docks.

As they crossed the lot a silhouetted shape appeared behind the door and then it opened. A man was standing in the light and he motioned with his hand for them to come forward. Frank and Steve stayed along the left side of the lot, keeping a car between them and the door. They didn't emerge from behind it until they were close enough for Frank to recognize Bud Kovacs's six-foot frame, topped off by a military crew cut.

"Welcome to L.A.," Kovacs said as they stepped through the door into a small loading area. "Sorry you had to come through the servants' entrance, but I guess we can't be too careful on this one."

"Staying in the shadows is what this one's all about," Frank replied. "The name of the game is going to be giving Ivan all the help we can without him knowing it. But you fellows seem to have gotten the jump on him already."

"Well, maybe," Kovacs said as they started down a corridor past the hotel kitchen. "We were lucky enough to find an airport cabbie who said he had taken a woman answering Branigan's description to this hotel. When we got here, we found the same girl had been seen by someone else. So she was in the hotel, all right, but only for a short time. Where she went from here is anybody's guess."

"Who saw her?" Steve asked.

"A young female clerk checked her in and later checked her out. We'll talk to her and the night manager. They're waiting for us now in his office."

They came through a side door off the main lobby and entered a small, neatly furnished office behind the service desk. One of Bud's agents was questioning the desk clerk but stopped when he saw the others come into the room.

Kovacs made the introductions.

"Janice Linder, I'd like you to meet Special Agent Frank LaSala and Agent Steve Jankowski. Mr. Alan Midler here is the night manager. . . . Agents LaSala and Jankowski"—he turned to the man who had been questioning the pair—"Agent Kevin Tomlinson from our office."

Everyone shook hands and Tomlinson moved from behind a walnut desk, allowing Frank and Steve to sit facing the two hotel employees. Kovacs sat on the edge of the desk flipping through a pad already full of notes. He directed his attention to the young clerk, who was wearing her hotel uniform, a blue suit with a gold emblem over the breast pocket. She fidgeted with one of the pleats in her skirt.

"Ms. Linder," Kovacs began, "I know you've already answered a lot of questions for us, but Mr. LaSala here may have some areas that we haven't touched on. Do you mind?"

"No, certainly not," she answered. Her voice was soft and pleasant.

LaSala leaned across the desk. "Tell me, Jan, what was it about this girl that made you remember her?"

"It's unusual for someone to check in and then out again during my shift. She had paid in advance for a two-week reservation and didn't stay seven hours. Besides, it's unusual to check out at such an ungodly hour of the morning."

"What name did she register under?"

"Carolyn Mulcahey." She reached for a computer printout on the desk and handed it to LaSala. "See, she checked in at 11:07 P.M. and left at 5:27 A.M. With a pretty nice-looking guy too. He said he was her brother and that she had gotten sick, so he was taking her home. In fact, she waited across the lobby while he checked her out."

"What did he look like?"

"He had dark wavy hair, a cute face, and a nice build. I'd say he was about twenty-eight. Had on a, let's see, jeans and a T-shirt with some kind of emblem on it. Said his name was Mr. Ross. No first name."

"Did you believe him?"

"I didn't think he was her brother, but she did look kind of down. But then I thought, even if she wasn't sick, he was cute. I'd leave with him too." She paused for a moment and looked around at the men in the room.

"Tell Frank about the other visitor you had this morning," Kovacs said, reminding her of what she had told him earlier.

She looked at LaSala and continued tentatively. "Well, while this Ross was standing there, another man came up to the desk and identified himself as an FBI man. He was looking for Cheryl Branigan."

Frank looked at Kovacs.

"How did he identify himself?"

"He showed me identification inside his wallet." She looked away for a moment. "I didn't get a really good look at it, but it seemed very official-looking."

"What did he say?"

"He asked if there was a Cheryl Branigan registered in the hotel, and I said no there wasn't. Then he gave me a very detailed description of a girl I realized would look very much like Miss Mulcahey."

"Where were Mr. Ross and the girl then?"

"They had just gone out the door no more than a minute or two earlier."

"Did you tell this man that Carolyn Mulcahey matched the girl's description?"

"Yes."

"And that she had just left?"

"Yes."

"Did you tell him she left with a man?"

"Yes."

"And did you describe him?"

"Yes, in detail."

"What did he do then?"

"He hurried outside but then came back a few minutes later to use the phone in the lobby. After that he left and never came back."

LaSala stared at the woman but said nothing. The man wasn't an FBI agent, he was a KGB agent. They had gotten there ahead of them. Good. He was impressed. Information left out in the open for them in New York had been used well. Now both he and Karpolov knew Branigan was in L.A. and had a good description of the man she had left with. He hoped Karpolov would find them quickly and recover the film. Then he would have the only weapon in the U.S. arsenal that could prevent him from sending missiles to Cuba.

6.

IT WAS THE gunshots that woke Cheryl.

They seemed to be exploding all around her as she bolted up in the leather recliner she had been sleeping in. Her first instinct was to run to the window, but then she realized where the shots were coming from. Barry's expensive quadriphonic speakers had taken the sounds from the movie *High Noon* and turned them into reality. She stared at Gary Cooper on the screen. His six-shooter was smoking and three men lay dead at his feet.

Slowly she exhaled the air that tension had built up in her lungs and reached for the VCR remote control. She aimed it at Gary and pressed the off button. Immediately he was reduced to the size of a dot and swallowed up by a black screen.

She went into the kitchen and checked the wall clock over the refrigerator. Four o'clock. What was keeping Barry? He had left for KNBC over five hours ago to examine the film. Had something gone wrong?

She took a Pepsi from the refrigerator and went into the bathroom. Leaning over the sink, she splashed cold water over her face. Whenever she needed to wake up quickly, cold water did it every time. It was a lot quicker than making coffee.

As she dried her face, she looked over the towel at her image in the mirror. It startled her, just as it had yesterday. Who was this dark-haired woman she was looking at? Who was she and what was to become of her?

The thought of the possibilities was terrifying. Armando's men already had had two days to look for her. What if the clerk at the checkout desk had identified her to the FBI?

She couldn't go on living like this. She was a woman on the run, a woman terrified to go outside, a woman who had to fear her every move. It had to end soon. Where was Barry? Why hadn't he come back?

The telephone rang. Instinctively she picked it up.

"Hello," she said automatically.

"Oh, uh, hi," a woman's voice answered. "Is Barry there? It's Judy."

She slammed the receiver down. Barry had told her not to pick up the phone. Who was Judy? Why was she calling? Why had she picked up the phone? Now someone knew she was there. She sank into the sofa and began to cry.

Tears continued to run down her cheeks. God only knew what was on that film, but it couldn't be worth all this. It had to end.

Finally she thought she heard the electric overhead door going up in the basement. It was Barry. In an instant she ran from the den to the kitchen and opened the door to the basement. The Porsche was pulling in. Barry was back.

The car door slammed and she heard his footsteps on the concrete floor of the garage. He came into the basement and started up the stairs, carrying a small plastic bag labeled, KNBC TELEVISION, CHANNEL 4. Halfway up the steps, he noticed her. She was wiping tears from her eyes with a handkerchief, and her whole body was shaking.

He rushed up and put his arm around her.

"Calm down," he said, stroking her hair with his free hand. "I'm here now. Everything is all right."

"It's not all right," she said, sobbing. "Everything is all wrong. I'm so afraid."

"Afraid of what?" he asked gently.

"Of everything. I forgot what you said and answered the phone. It was a woman named Judy. Now she knows I'm here."

"So what. It's no big deal. Judy knows I date other women."

"Every time you walk out that door, I'm scared out of my mind."

"You're a little paranoid, that's all. You think the whole world is looking for Cheryl Branigan. And besides," he said, holding up the plastic bag, "wait'll you see what's in here. Your fat friend Armando was passing some pretty heavy stuff, and it's going to be worth a lot."

He waited for a response from her but she didn't say anything.

"C'mon," he said, taking her hand. "Let's take a look at what's going to make us millionaires."

She followed him into the den where he took a videocassette from the bag and put it into the machine.

"What took you so long at the station?" she asked as he made adjustments to the TV.

"I had trouble getting an editing room," he said with his back to her. "I needed some special equipment to enlarge the microfilm and had to wait until one was free. It turned out to be almost an hour and a half."

"Oh, I was afraid something had happened," she said, settling into the recliner directly in front of the set. Her attitude had turned totally passive now. The anticipation of seeing what might be on the film had been overwhelmed by fear. She sat staring at the blank screen.

He turned around and faced her. "Just watch this."

He hit the play button of the VCR and the screen lit up.

There were some numbers that clicked down every second: four . . . three . . . two . . . one. An image appeared. It was a large control room with men seated in front of computers. Above them was a screen that was half the width of the room. It showed a stretch of desert with low mountains off in the distance. A full moon cast eerie shadows off a concrete structure in the foreground that looked like the top of a giant coffee can.

"That's a missile silo," Barry said in response to the questioning look on her face. "Those covers open hydraulically if a missile is launched."

The camera pulled back across the room to show a group of dignitaries standing along the sidewall. There were some high-ranking military officers and two or three civilians watching intently.

Although the film was silent, Cheryl could sense the intensity in the room. The technicians were busy at their computers. Screens flashed as information scanned across them. Words were spoken into headsets and pieces of paper were handed from one desk to another. Finally their attention was drawn to a large digital readout under the screen that read, THREE, TWO, ONE and then ZERO.

"Watch this closely," Barry said, anticipating what was about to happen.

A narrow strip of brilliant light came out of the night sky. It was blazing with color, its center white with heat, the edges flaming yellow and orange. Within seconds it hit the missile silo with an impact that shook the earth. Concrete crumbled and flew into the air while the beam bored deeper and deeper into the earth. Large masses of concrete and steel crumbled and flew into the air. Huge sections of earth caved in to replace the debris now spread over the entire area. Finally the light stopped. A cloud of dust began to settle, revealing the destruction below. In seconds a silo that was the size of a football field had been totally destroyed.

Barry pressed the pause button. Cheryl's eyes were now riveted to the screen. She was unable to speak.

"What is it?" she asked. Her tone reflected the incredible scene she had just witnessed. "What is it that can destroy something so massive in just a few seconds?"

"Fourteen seconds, to be exact," Barry replied. "I timed it at the station." He paused for a moment to look at the screen. The scene was frozen in time. Dust and fragments of concrete still hung in the air, suspended over a hole in the ground over a hundred yards long.

"It's got to be a laser weapon," he said, turning to her. "But I don't think it's a conventional laser like what was attempted for the Star Wars program. This seems to be using some sort of vibration frequency. When the beam hit the silo, there wasn't an explosion. It was more like the laser bored into the concrete, shaking it until it crumbled. Let me run it again and you'll see what I mean."

Cheryl watched as the tape ran in reverse. Fragments of concrete fell back into place, the silo was intact, and the laser beam flew back into space. Then Barry ran it forward again. The beam hit the silo and bored its way into the concrete, like a giant jackhammer shaking the earth. The power of the beam was awesome. But Barry was right. There wasn't an explosion. Vibration seemed to be the cause of the destruction.

This time he let the film run. As the dust cleared, the camera pulled back to show a wide shot of the control room. The technicians were cheering, slapping each other on the back, and throwing papers into the air. The dignitaries were shaking hands and congratulating one another. As the camera moved closer to them, Cheryl suddenly pointed to the screen.

"Stop," she said excitedly. "Stop the tape right there."

Barry again used the remote control to pause the tape.

"That man between the two generals. He looks familiar. He's . . . wait a minute. Who's the secretary of defense?"

"Walter Commack," Barry said, hesitating momentarily.

Cheryl sank back into the recliner.

"Then it must be some important new weapon, isn't it?" Fear had come back into her voice again.

"You better believe it," Barry replied emphatically. "If Commack is there, it's very important. I also recognized two other people. One of the generals is Dwight Cabot, chairman of the Joint Chiefs of Staff, and one of the civilians is Senator George Park, chairman of the National Security Committee. It's important, all right."

"That's what I was afraid of," she said quietly. "Now there's no question about it. This is important enough for whoever wants it back to do anything to get it . . . even kill us."

"Not if we get to the KGB first."

"The KGB? Why not the FBI, Barry?"

"Because it's the KGB that will pay. This guy at the restaurant must have been getting a fortune for his information. Can't you see? This fell right into our laps. We have information on a new laser weapon that can bring millions. Let me show you what was on the rest of the microfilm."

The last few seconds of the film showed more celebrating, then the screen went black. It flickered a few times and then the first image from the microfilm appeared.

It showed a satellite high over the earth. A dotted line representing a beam came up from below, bounced off it, and returned to earth. There were tiny lines at the point of impact, indicating an explosion. The second was a cutaway of the satellite itself. Some of the headings around it were readable. TARGET

MIRROR, LASER BEAM, LASER RODS, TRACKING TELESCOPE, POST-
BOOST ROCKETS and MEGAHERTZ ACCELERATOR were just a few of
them. The last three frames were some kind of receiving device.
They showed various angles of a box buried below ground level.
The cutaways were complicated mazes of wiring and electromag-
netic cells. Insets detailed the circuitry and electrical diagrams. It
looked very complete.

"I don't understand any of it," she said, turning away from the
screen.

Again Barry reversed the tape to show the first frame of the
microfilm.

"I've done some reading about lasers. They're being used now
for video and sound recordings, so I know something about them.
The laser on that diagram can be directed up from the ground to
an orbiting satellite with reflecting mirrors on it. They reflect the
laser back to a target on the ground. Some technical magazines ran
articles on it when Star Wars was being developed."

"But Star Wars failed by the end of 1991, didn't it?" she
replied.

"That's right, and supposedly this type of weapon was part of
the failure. The problem was that the reflecting satellite had to be
in a low orbit for the laser to reflect enough power to destroy a
target. That meant the Russians simply could use missiles to shoot
them down. It was unfortunate, because the laser had the strength
of a seventy five thousand ton blast. The bomb that devastated
Hiroshima was thirteen thousand tons. They also had problems
with atmospheric disturbances."

"So maybe the film is showing an obsolete weapon," she said
hopefully.

"I don't think so," he said, walking away from the set. He
began to pace around the room, organizing his thoughts. "This
looks like something different from a conventional laser. The
diagram shows the satellite orbit to be over forty miles up. That's
probably beyond Soviet missile capability."

"But then the laser wouldn't be strong enough. You just said
that."

"Unless it was something different. The diagram mentions a
'megahertz accelerator.' Hertz is a measure of cycles of frequency. I think the satellite is reflecting high-frequency waves,
high enough to cause vibration that's destructive. Like I said

before, the explosion wasn't really a blast. The ground just seemed to shake apart. That had to be caused by a beam vibrating at millions of cycles per second."

"But what about the atmosphere disturbing the sound waves coming down to earth?" she asked.

"That's probably been solved by a receiver buried below ground level. Remember? It's in the next diagram. The beam is drawn to it with tremendous force, enough to cause the destruction we saw in the film. If they buried receivers near military targets, the beam would be drawn to it, just like it was to this missile silo."

He paused, then walked to the end of the room and looked out on the golf course. With his back to her he said, "I think the Russians would be very interested in this and would pay a lot of money to get their hands on it."

He paused, waiting for a response, but instead she got up and switched off the set. Then she turned around and faced him, her hands spread out behind her, blocking the screen.

"I'm going to contact the FBI and turn in everything . . . tonight."

"You what?" he asked, walking back toward her. "I'm telling you, we've got something here that the KGB will pay millions for."

"I don't care," she said calmly. The hysteria and fear were gone from her voice. "I'm not going to spend the rest of my life being afraid to go out the door. No amount of money is worth getting up every morning and wondering if it's going to be my last."

"That's being a little overly dramatic, isn't it?"

"No, it's not. I saw today what it's like and it was terrible."

"But don't you understand, once we sell the film, we'll have the money to go anywhere we want. We can go to South America, Europe, anywhere."

He came toward her, but she moved back closer to the set.

"Somebody will always be following us," she insisted. "They'll—"

"And if we contact the FBI like you want to, then what?"

"They'll protect us."

"Bullshit. They'll question you, and when they're through, they'll throw you back on the street for Lucci's men to come and put you six feet under. Think about that before you call them." He paused for a minute and then said, "And on top of that, they'll get me as an accomplice. At any rate, we certainly won't be lying on a beach somewhere with a million dollars in our pockets."

"I don't care."

"Maybe I do," he said, turning away from her.

She took her hands off the screen and put them at her side. It was the first time he had asked for any consideration at all.

"They don't have anything on you," she said softly. "You can simply walk away. I can turn it in myself."

"I think that's a little naïve," he said, sitting down in the recliner she had just gotten up from. "I was seen at the hotel, they know I'm involved."

"So what," she answered quickly. "That doesn't mean you had anything to do with the film."

"C'mon. I'm a film editor. I had to be involved. They'll be after me too. Let's face it, I'm in this as deep as you. Just because I didn't steal the film doesn't make me any less vulnerable."

"Suppose I just return it. I don't have to say I know what's on it. It's microfilm. It has to be something valuable to the military, so I'm returning it."

"Nice try," he answered, "but again they know you were with me. People saw me at KNBC today and they could probably connect me to the film. I'm involved no matter how you slice it."

Neither of them spoke for a moment. Each avoided the other's glance as they considered their positions. Finally they began to speak together. Barry allowed her to go ahead.

"All I know is I can't play this terrible charade any longer. I can't have all this fear hanging over me. No amount of money is worth it. But I also know I'm the reason you're mixed up in all this. I don't want to hurt you, Barry. You've done so much for me already. I never would've gotten this far without you. But I can't play Carolyn Mulcahey anymore. Can you understand that?"

Barry stared at the blank TV.

"I never should have called you from the hotel," she continued. "Once I saw what was sewn in the lining, I should've called the FBI myself. Then you wouldn't be involved at all."

"But you did call," he said, looking up at her. "I'm involved, and I say we're throwing away an awful lot of money. More than we'll ever see again in our lifetimes."

"I'll never be able to enjoy it," she said. "Every time I turn around, I'll be expecting to see a gun pointed at me. I can't live that way. I just can't."

She watched Barry carefully. He was going to press her to the limit, but she wasn't going to back down. She had made a terrible mistake in New York stealing the packet. Then she didn't know what living in fear would really be like. Now she knew. Running from Armando would have been bad enough, but this was impossible. She had to stand her ground. What she did now would affect the rest of her life. But then Barry surprised her.

"Well, then I guess we don't have much choice," he said softly. Suddenly his voice was steadier, more in control. "If we're going to stay together, it sounds like one of us has to give in, doesn't it?" He paused for a moment that seemed like an eternity. His hands were folded together under his chin and he leaned forward a little in the chair. Finally he said, "It's going to have to be me. Our staying together has become too important."

His eyes went to the television set behind her.

"That film could bring us a lot of money, but if you're not going to be happy, it won't mean a thing. So-o-o . . ." He dragged out the word, as if it gave him one last chance to change his mind, but then he went on to finish the sentence. "I guess instead of ending up with a million dollars, I'll have to settle for being able to stay with you instead. Think you're worth it?"

She stood looking at him. It was amazing what he had done for her. He came out in the middle of the night like a knight in shining armor to save her. He welcomed her into his home and calmed her fears. Now he was passing up a chance to be wealthy for the rest of his life so she could live hers in peace. This wasn't the Barry she had known six years ago. This was a kind, considerate man who cared about what she felt. Already she could feel the terrible burden of fear being lifted from her shoulders. It was replaced by a warm, loving feeling that moved through her entire body.

"Yes," she whispered. "I think I'm going to be worth it to you."

She moved to the recliner and leaned over it. Her hands on the armrests, she slowly lowered her body onto his. Then, moving her arms forward, she pushed the back of the recliner and it fell into a horizontal position.

Her mouth found his and she brushed her lips against it. "Thank you," she whispered. "Thank you for caring." Before he could say anything, her tongue had found its partner and the two darted in and out like two flaming swords slashing at each other. They moved faster and faster, in a frenzy of wild circles. Her fingers undid the buttons on his shirt, starting at the top and working their way down. She felt his hands over her breasts and her nipples hardening under his touch. It had been so long since she had felt like this. Her whole body was crying out for him as she unbuckled his belt and tugged at his jeans. She moved down his body, pulling clothes with her until they were a bundle at the end of the recliner. Then she tore off her clothes and started back up over his body. The recliner had moved to a vertical position and Barry's hands were outstretched to her. Just as she reached his erect penis he lifted her until her knees could get astride him. The recliner fell back again and she was over him.

Slowly she lowered herself onto his penis. It felt like a burning fire as it moved inside her. She threw her head back and moaned with pleasure as she felt his lips on her nipples. His tongue darted back and forth from one to the other while his hands held her breasts against his mouth. Her weight shifted from his thrusts, causing the recliner to move forward and then backward. It was as if she were on top of a wild steed, his strong, muscular body moving beneath her.

The fire within her reached a fever pitch. Every nerve ending in her body was ready to explode into a shower of ecstasy. Then she climaxed once, and then again. She heard herself cry out, making some shrill animal sound she had never heard before. Her lungs were bursting. Barry pulled her down to him and she felt his hot breath against her breasts. His body was thrusting wildly and she moved into the rhythm of it. She was soaring higher and higher, up through the clouds to a point she had never reached before. Then she felt Barry climax and her whole body released the fire inside with a final orgasm that left her falling back toward earth with a feeling of exquisite peace and serenity.

Neither of them spoke as they returned to a world of harsh realities. Her head was resting on his chest and she could hear his heart slowing down to a normal beat. His hand moved up the small of her back and into her hair. He began stroking it in long, gentle movements that relaxed her whole body. Days of constant torment had finally been broken by a few moments of calm, peaceful bliss.

"I think you're right," he said softly. "You *are* worth it. It was never like that before."

"I know," she answered. "I guess it's because I never owed you so much."

"You don't owe me anything. What's important now is we're together. If this whole mess gives us that, it'll be payment enough."

She kissed the side of his neck, then snuggled in close to his shoulder.

"Tell me," she said softly, "why did you come to the hotel? It was the middle of the night. You could've just hung up and forgotten about me."

"You sounded so frightened and vulnerable. It wasn't the Cheryl I'd known six years ago, or even the girl I saw in New York last year. That girl never needed me at all. She knew exactly what she was doing and how she was going to get there."

"And this girl?"

He turned on his side and looked into her eyes. "This girl's name is Carolyn and she needs me. She's everything Cheryl was, but she needs me. That's the difference, and it's why we'll return the film and maybe start all over again."

She leaned back and held his face in her hands.

"Here's to where the road will lead us. May it be to places where we find happiness but, more importantly, find ourselves. Remember when you said that?"

"Yes," he answered. "The night we left each other. It took me half the afternoon to compose it."

"Well, maybe the road has led us right back to each other and this is where we'll both find the happiness we're looking for."

He put her hands in his and drew her close.

"I think we will," he replied. "In fact, I know we will."

They lay in each other's arms for another half hour. Most of the time was spent in silence, holding each other close. When they spoke, it was in whispers of assurance that now they had each other and everything would be all right. She tried to avoid the practical questions of how they would return the film, but finally she felt compelled to ask them. Barry's response was to bring the recliner to an upright position and pull her out of the chair. He put his arms around her and pointed toward the kitchen.

"Know what's in there?" he asked.

"No."

"Chinese."

"How many?" she asked playfully.

"Food, you silly person. I got it on the way back. Why don't you jump in the shower and I'll put together a dinner, complete with wine and everything. Then we'll talk about how we're going to get rid of the film, okay?"

"Okay." She gave him one final kiss on the forehead and went into the bathroom.

Later she heard the stereo playing over the hiss of the shower. Barry had put on the Barbra Streisand album she had played the day before. He must have seen the tape lying on top of the record player and known she had played it. How thoughtful.

She stepped from the shower, dried herself off, and slipped into his white terry-cloth robe. It felt warm and snug around her. Maybe she was going to come out of this all right, after all. She turned and saw her dark hair in the mirror again. This time it didn't frighten her. Soon she would be free of this other woman she had become.

Barry was pouring wine from a crystal decanter as she came into the dining room. The table was set with china and silverware on a white embroidered tablecloth. Two white candles in porcelain holders glowed in the soft, subdued lighting. She came around the table and put her arms around him.

"The lady has already been seduced," she said playfully. "I expected paper plates and plastic forks."

He put the wine down and kissed her lightly on the cheek.

"This is not some ordinary meal we have here. This, my dear lady, is a celebration."

"What are we celebrating?" she asked, teasing.

"Each other," he answered, brushing his index finger across her lips. "And besides . . ."

"Yes?"

"This nuked Chinese food needs all the help it can get."

He turned her around slowly and held the chair out as she sat down.

"But first a toast."

He moved to the other side of the table and sat down across from her.

"This one is a lot less eloquent than the last one I made but, I hope, even more meaningful."

He raised his glass.

"To us."

"To us," she replied.

They sipped the wine and then Barry put his glass down.

"Now," he said, "I'm serving all of column A followed by B, C, D, to Z. There's enough food here for an army. Let me get it before it turns into a disaster."

They shared wonton soup, egg rolls, shrimp with lobster sauce, spareribs, and chicken with honey sauce. At the end of the meal Barry took away the dishes and they opened fortune cookies.

His read: "Follow your instincts, they are truer than you think."

Hers read: "Look to your past for the future."

"How appropriate," she said, and leaned across the table to kiss him.

They spent the rest of the evening just as they had the afternoon, enjoying each other's closeness. Cheryl agreed with Barry to postpone the task that lay before them until the morning. The evening had been too perfect; no sense in shattering its serenity.

After more wine and more conversation, Cheryl was exhausted. It was only nine o'clock, but she couldn't keep her head up.

"I'm so tired," she told Barry. "I think I'll go to bed if you don't mind."

"Of course," he said, kissing her lightly on the cheek.

He picked her up in his arms and carried her to the bedroom. When he got there, she was already asleep. Gently he put her on the bed and pulled the covers over her. Then he walked over to the door and turned out the light. He looked back at her one more time. She would sleep soundly for the next ten to twelve hours.

The three ccs of Valium he had put in her wine would assure that.

Moscow

Viktor Karpolov sat with his hands folded as a waiter poured French wine into his glass. He raised it to his lips and tasted the 1980 Château de Beaucastel, his favorite. The bouquet was perfect, the dryness exquisite. Why couldn't his country produce wine like this instead of the coarse, overly fruited liquid that even common peasants refused to drink. Well, that would soon change. If they couldn't make French wine, they would simply take it from them. Soon his plan would hold the United States in check while the Russian Army took all of Europe, including France's vineyards.

He nodded his approval to the waiter, who filled the other glass at the table. A hand lined with age but steady in its grip lifted the elegant crystal goblet until it touched Karpolov's over the center of the table.

"*Na zdorovie*, Viktor. To your health and to your good taste in fine wine." General Ivan Parkovsky brought the glass to his lips and savored the sparkling wine. "I must say, Viktor, that I look forward to these luncheons—not only for your company but also to see what new wine you come up with. This is very pleasant. What is it?"

"Château de Beaucastel, 1980. I suggested that it be added to the wine list over two months ago, but it just arrived last week."

"What was the cause of the delay?" the general asked, looking over his wire-framed bifocals.

"The usual, bad weather."

Parkovsky looked out the draped window of the Politburo private dining room. Two feet of snow covered the Kremlin from the last storm they had gotten three days ago. The white, onion-shaped spires of the Spassky and Nikolskaya Towers contrasted against a bleak gray sky.

"Ah, a pity that nature hasn't blessed us with a better climate. In the old days our harsh weather had a certain romantic charm, but now it has become a nuisance. Not only can we not produce the necessities of modern life, we can't even import them quickly into the country. Roads are blocked, transportation snarled, and"—he pointed to the wine—"decent grapes can't even be grown. I've always believed Mother Nature has doomed our people to suffer the inconveniences of life."

"But we're trying to change all that," Karpolov interjected. Premier Chebrikov's new policy of raising the standard of living should alleviate much of this."

"Yes, things are changing," Parkovsky said, gesturing to the modern, elegant surroundings of the new twelve-story Politburo building, "but sometimes change is brought on too fast. When this wing was added last year, I criticized it as a break in the traditional architecture of the Kremlin. Where is the continuity with the past, I asked? The answer from many, including Chebrikov, was that we needed to break from the past if we were to make dramatic strides forward. 'We need to think modern, dress modern, and live in modern surroundings. We need to keep pace with the rest of the world militarily and economically,' he said. That may be so, but it all moves too fast for this old soldier."

"It moves too fast for most of us, General," Karpolov said sympathetically. He addressed Parkovsky as General, as he had done since he had met him. He was his father-in-law but was also a highly decorated hero and deserved his respect. Calling him Ivan just seemed out of place. "But nevertheless," he continued, "we must keep up with the fast-paced, fast-talking businessmen that run the capitalist countries of the world. They operate from modern glass towers equipped with desktop computers and the latest communications equipment. They deal in business around the world at the drop of a hat while our people wait in line to buy a new pair of shoes." He picked up the glass. "They drink wine like this when it strikes their fancy, while only people in our position can even think about it in this country.

"And what's most disturbing is that despite our attempts to adapt to capitalism, we're still not accepted. The Americans have still continued to develop militarily despite our attempts at glasnost, and they do so because basically they're a militaristic society intent on fueling the coffers of their so-called 'defense' industries."

"You paint a gloomy picture, my dear Viktor."

"Not at all," he answered, finishing the rest of his wine. "Because despite the hardships we face, we've managed to achieve superiority over these so-called sophisticated capitalists. We may not have outdone them in the world of business and finance, but we have surpassed them in the most important area of all: military superiority. With that advantage we can use our strength ultimately to bring the better things in life to our people."

The general picked up the menu and glanced at the selections as he spoke.

"I would hope that military superiority could bring that about, because it would be a major achievement. The temptation has always been to use an advantage to go on the offensive. That has meant war. And war has never raised anybody's standard of living."

"I agree," Viktor replied, "but taking the offensive doesn't necessarily mean armed conflict. Ultimately it can mean preventing one. When you have the upper hand, there's the opportunity to weaken your enemy. You can move aggressively against him and he can't retaliate because he fears your advantage. That's the position we're in now."

"And that brings us to your plan, does it not?"

"Yes. Placing missiles in Cuba is the first step toward weakening the Americans."

"Then how will you move aggressively against them?"

"By taking Germany," he answered without hesitating. "Then we'll move across Europe. Also we'll expand farther into South America."

"That's a tall order," the general answered, looking over the top of his menu. "And you think the Americans will sit still for that?"

"They'll have to. With our submarine-launched missiles aimed at them from under the polar ice caps, and land-based missiles in Cuba, they'll be in a nuclear cross fire that can destroy them before they're able to retaliate. Our new supersonic SRV-60s can be launched from under the Arctic Ocean and travel the six thousand kilometers to Chicago in less than two minutes. Missiles from Cuba can hit Washington in less than sixty seconds. Even if the Americans decided to fire retaliatory missiles immediately after detecting ours, it would take longer than that to launch them."

He paused and noticed that the general had lowered his menu and was paying strict attention to him.

"In effect, the United States will be militarily immobilized. They will no longer be a factor in preventing us from reaching our goals in Europe. Once we have included Germany, France, Italy, the Scandinavian countries, and others into the Eastern bloc, we will have access to world banking, computer technology, the arts, high-tech manufacturing, outlets to the sea, and yes . . . fine wine readily available to our people."

The general laid the menu on the table and took a cigarette from inside his shirt pocket. Viktor had noticed that lately he carried four Turkish cigarettes there to limit what he smoked daily.

Although Viktor didn't smoke, he carried a gold lighter, which he used to light the general's cigarette.

He inhaled it deeply, then tilted his head back to blow the smoke into the air.

"I assume you've consulted the proper military and civilian advisers to assess the feasibility of this plan," he said, looking up at the smoke rising toward the ceiling.

"I have," Viktor answered, "on numerous occasions."

"The key question, though, is if the Russian army can move through Europe even if the Americans aren't involved. There could still be considerable resistance without them."

"Resistance, yes," Karpolov replied, "but not enough to stop us. Essentially it's the American nuclear capability that protects Europe. But in a conventional encounter we're vastly superior, even more superior than American intelligence believes. For the past year we've concealed three divisions in Czechoslovakia that they aren't even aware of."

A waiter appeared behind them to take their order. Viktor allowed the general to order first. He ordered borscht to start, then beef Stroganoff and *morozhenoye* (ice cream). Viktor began with *akroshka* (a cold soup with a beer base), *kotlyety po Pozharsky* (chicken cutlets cooked in a cream sauce), *krasnaya ikra* (red caviar), and *prostakvasha* (yogurt). The waiter left and Viktor continued to speak.

"But there's more to be gained from the plan than a military advantage," he continued. "There's also a psychological one. In 1962, when the Americans turned our ships around, they prevented us from establishing a presence in Cuba. Kennedy was able to do that because he had military superiority. This time we have it, and there's no stopping us. We will reach Cuba and place missiles there that will not only be a terrible military defeat for the Americans but a moral one as well. When NATO and the rest of Europe see that America can no longer defend herself, all hope for any assistance will die. Then Europe's defenses will crumble."

The general flicked the ash off his cigarette and then pointed it at Viktor.

"I support your plan and have told the premier personally. However, I support it for different reasons than you've mentioned. At my age, one tends to think only of the immediate future, so I cannot get much beyond the ramifications of putting missiles into

Cuba. But I believe they're considerable and in our favor. The first is the psychological one you cite. I was a high-ranking military officer in 1962, involved in the planning of that abortive mission. I was personally humiliated, as were many of my comrades who today serve on the Politburo. And I can tell you that this triumph will not only be a moral blow to the Americans but also a tremendous boost to the morale of the Russian people. It will uplift them and at the same time remove a terrible burden. And that burden is fear. Fear of a nuclear attack that could ultimately destroy them. Once they're assured we hold a definitive military edge, that pressure will be removed.

"Which brings me to the other reason I support it. I believe the arms race between us and the United States will never end. *Glasnost* and *perestroika* were at best superficial attempts to disguise a basic mistrust that will always exist between our two countries. It has gone on for over forty years now, with one side trying to outdo the other in an effort to maintain a so-called posture: They will never attack us if we're stronger. It is costly and our people suffer because of it. The forty-two billion rubles that went to the military last year could have been spent on raising our people's standard of living. It could have bought cars, appliances, better clothing and housing. Instead it went to increase this huge stockpile of weaponry that will kill us all if it's ever used.

"But now, for the first time, we have a distinct advantage. With the failure of America's Star Wars and our success with the SRVs, we can move to assure that the Americans will never be able to attack us in the near future. I think you're right. Now is the time to position ourselves so that we completely dominate the United States."

He flicked the ash from his cigarette as if it were the Americans he was discarding.

"I don't know if you'll ever bring all of Europe into the Eastern bloc, but you may be able to move into South America. You may be able to move into the Persian Gulf and take over the oil, and into Spain and Portugal, where our party is already strong. Sweden, the Netherlands, and Norway are also vulnerable. There is innovative technology in those countries that can be of great use to us. At any rate, your objective, I believe, is correct: use our present military advantage to hold the Americans in check, removing both a psychological and economic pressure from our people."

Viktor leaned back in his chair and studied the general. He hadn't seen him this animated in a long time. For an eighty-three-year-old man, his body movements were suddenly quick and expressive. There was optimism in his voice and a smile on his face when he spoke of avenging October 1962. He tried to consider the reason for this attitude change and decided it stemmed from the general's background. The man had fought in two world wars, both of which were strictly defensive. Now, for the first time, Russia would be on the offensive, and initially it would be without firing a shot. This was something he probably never thought he'd see in his lifetime.

The general's support had been extremely important throughout his career. Since his marriage to Ivana, he had been influential in his moving through the ranks of the KGB. He saw that they went to the right parties, met the right people, and constantly commended him publicly to higher officials. At first he thought it was mainly for Ivana. The higher he rose, the better it would be for her. But eventually he saw that the general truly believed in his ideas and proposals. They were essentially on the same wavelength, although sometimes his ambition for power irked the older man. However, he considered him a friend and ally who had gotten him to where he was today. Hopefully he could continue to count on his support in the future.

"I don't know how far we can go to capitalize on our military advantage," he said, responding to the general's conclusion, "but we have prepared an option to move into Europe once our missiles are secured in Cuba. Whatever is decided must be done quickly, though, if we're to keep up the momentum."

"I understand, and I'm sure the Politburo will choose the proper options," the general replied, "but I would offer you a word of caution about the first part of the plan: the placement of missiles into Cuba."

Some of the animation had left his voice. The normally dour, serious character was surfacing, and Viktor could see he was about to stress a point of deep concern.

"As I've said," he began, "there will be a great psychological lift to many of our people when the missiles are brought to Cuba. However, there will be terrible humiliation if 1962 repeats itself.

You must be certain that the United States has no recourse militarily that can stop us. There must be absolute certainty that President Hayden cannot stop the ships once they leave for Cuba."

He paused for a moment, looked directly into Karpolov's eyes for the slightest doubt in his conviction. Finding none, he continued.

"I understand that our intelligence people have made a comprehensive check on U.S. Star Wars weapons-testing at your request. Is that true?"

"Yes, it is," Karpolov answered firmly.

"And your conclusion is that nothing came from the program that can threaten our military advantage?"

"That is correct," Viktor answered immediately. He felt his heart quicken slightly. The general knew many people, both in scientific research and his own KGB. In fact, he knew his friend Colonel Zarov, who was helping him withhold information on both New York and Sakhalin. Was the general leading him on to admit there was some doubt about U.S. military capabilities? Had word leaked out? He fought to keep his voice steady as he continued with his answer.

"The U.S. tested five of what they termed 'defensive shields' to prevent missiles from reaching them. They ranged from particle-beam accelerators and interceptor rockets to X-ray lasers and kinetic-particle weapons. None of these were successful. The only device that remains viable is a form of laser that can destroy ground targets. The Americans call it Radio Frequency Quadrupole, or RFQ. It accelerates subatomic particles for use in lightweight space-based beam weapons. Our scientists at the Institute of High Energy Physics at Serpukhov worked on the concept for three years and saw no merit in it. They still doubt that the United States can ever develop it to where it will be a military threat. And if they could, it would be several years before it would become operational."

"You're sure," the general said. It was more a statement than a question.

"Yes," Viktor answered, hoping the general could not see the beads of sweat he felt forming on his brow.

He began to tremble inside and tried desperately to control it. How much did the old man know?

Suddenly two waiters appeared with the food. They served it

quickly and refilled the empty wineglasses. As the general picked up his knife and fork he looked directly at Viktor.

"Well, if you're absolutely sure," he said, smiling, "let's eat."

An hour later Karpolov sat in his office, staring at the white telephone on his desk. It had just been installed the previous month and was a mass of buttons and flashing lights. Suddenly it was very important which buttons he pushed. The decisions he made in the next few days would not only be important to his career but to the country itself. The general had raised doubts that were still in the back of his mind. Was it possible that the Americans could have developed a laser weapon so quickly? Sources inside the Federation of American Scientists assured him they had not. Government scientists at Sary Shagan, the largest Soviet antimissile research center, had said it was impossible. There was no way American scientists could have solved the problem of a laser losing its destructive force when placed at an altitude safe from Soviet ground-launched missiles. At best they were two or three years away.

But he needed to be certain. The general had pointed out what he feared most: the ships having to turn back. If that happened, the morale of the Russian people would be devastated . . . and so would he. He had to know if a weapon existed or not. And he had to know soon.

7.

CHERYL BRANIGAN AWOKE to find a dry, slightly salty taste in her mouth. Her eyes had a pasty layer of film over them and the lids stuck together when she opened them. The first thing she noticed was that every muscle in her body ached and that she was still fully dressed. She tried to remember the night before, but it was a blur in her mind. All she remembered was the wine. It had made her feel very good.

Slowly she rolled onto her side to check the clock radio beside the bed. The digital numbers were fuzzy and she rubbed her eyes to bring them into focus: 1:37 P.M. It couldn't be. It had to be A.M. She couldn't have slept that long. But light was streaming through the sides of the closed venetian blinds; the clock was right.

She turned and stared up at the ceiling. Oh, how wonderful yesterday had been.

Barry's pillow was beside her. She pulled it over and snuggled against it. It felt cold. He must have gotten up hours ago. She listened for sounds in the apartment. There weren't any.

Slowly she pushed her body up into a sitting position. For a moment the room turned slightly askew and then straightened up again. She had been groggy after a drunk before, but never like this. What the hell kind of wine was that, anyway?

She pulled the covers off her legs and swung them over the side of the bed. Feeling around the floor with her toes, she found her slippers and stepped into them. Then, using the wall for support, she walked to the bedroom door and opened it. Barry was nowhere in sight.

Maybe he had gone out for a while and left a note in the kitchen. A quick search revealed nothing. Standing over the table, she found it an effort just to keep her balance. She needed to hold on to a chair for support.

Slowly she made her way from room to room. There wasn't any note to be found, nor a clue as to where he had gone. Something was wrong.

Back in the kitchen, she made some coffee. Her mouth was so dry. The coffee would feel good and wake her up. As it perked, she looked for signs of Barry. There weren't any coffee cups around, the cover was on the toaster, and the dishwasher was full of dirty dishes. He was a maniac about running the dishwasher every night, yet he hadn't done it. Maybe he'd just forgotten.

She looked at the clock. The coffee had about five more minutes to brew. It was now five minutes to two. Where the hell was he?

Holding on to the kitchen counter for support, she watched the coffee drip down from the filter into the pot. It had a hypnotic effect that added to her grogginess. She began to wonder if it was something more than wine that had caused it. Was it something she had eaten, or was it simply because she had slept so long?

The coffee felt good against her dry lips. As she sipped it her mind started to focus on the previous night with more clarity. The film. It had been on top of the TV set when they were making love. Later, during dinner, she had noticed it was still there. Suddenly her body was turning cold. The coffee cup felt hotter in her hand. Was the film still there?

She sprang out of the chair, forgetting that she needed support. But now she didn't. Adrenaline had replaced whatever was in her system, and now she was practically running into the living room. As she came into it she noticed immediately that the tapes were gone. A *TV Guide* and the remote control were all that remained on top of the set.

She tore open the cabinet where he kept his tapes and albums. The film wasn't in any of the drawers. Maybe they fell down behind the set. Nothing. She checked the closet shelf. They weren't there, either, but she noticed that his leather jacket and two windbreakers were gone.

In the dining room she looked on top of the hutch, in the drawers, on shelves lined with books, and under some newspapers. In the bedroom closet she found three empty pants hangers and two empty drawers in the dresser where he usually kept his shirts. His shaving kit was missing from the bathroom. She had used a razor from it yesterday. Every room was searched carefully, but she found nothing. Then she practically ran into the living room and stood in front of the recliner where they had made love.

Her fingers tightened into a fist and her shoulders began to shake uncontrollably. Tears formed in her eyes and ran down her cheeks. She brought her hands up to her breasts and held them, as Barry did just hours ago. A sound came out of her mouth that was either a whimper or a scream. She didn't know which. All she knew was that she wanted to shout at the top of her voice, but instead the words came out in barely a whisper. They were not meant for Barry. They were meant for her.

"You idiot," she said, sobbing. "You stupid fucking idiot." She said it over and over again until the words were drowned out by her crying. Slowly she felt her body weakening again and she sank to her knees in the middle of the room.

How could she have been so gullible to believe he wanted to spend the rest of his life with her? How could she have given him her body, believing that his caring for her was real and sincere?

The whole thing about deciding to go along with her had been bullshit. The son of a bitch knew when he got back to the apartment what he was going to do. He must have spent half the afternoon making preparations. It hadn't taken five hours to examine that film.

Then came more lies: "If nothing else, this served to bring us back together again." Those words were just an excuse to get his cock into her, which was the final degradation.

She saw her reflection on the darkened TV screen. She looked pathetic. Her body had been violated and used. She felt filthy.

Well, now she would take her life back into her own hands. It's what she had been doing for the past five years until she called

Barry. That call put her back to being the dependent little wimp
she had been when they first met. "Barry, what shall I do now?
Barry, is this all right? Is that all right?" She couldn't make a
move without him.

But now she would do what she should have done before. She
would contact the FBI. Even though she no longer had the film,
she had to stop running. For once and for all, this whole thing
would come to an end. Besides, now she had another reason to
call them: Barry. She would tell them everything she knew about
him. She would get the bastard if it was the last thing she did.

Her body felt steadier as she got up from the floor. The phone
book was in a drawer next to the wall phone in the kitchen. She
went and got it. Quickly she flipped through the pages . . .
F . . . FBI. No listing. F . . . Fe . . . yes, here it was,
Federal Bureau of Investigation, 555-7000. She dialed the number.

"Federal Bureau of Investigation. Agent Massey speaking."
The man's voice sounded terse and professional.

"My name is Cheryl Branigan and I'd like to—"

"Excuse me, can you repeat the last name, please."

"Branigan." She spelled it out for him. "First name is Cheryl."
She started to speak again, but he interrupted immediately.

"Miss Branigan, I need the address where you are right now."
Suddenly his voice sounded unsteady, a little hurried.

She didn't know the address. What the hell was it? She looked
on top of the phone. An electric bill was wedged in behind it.
There was an address on it.

"1679 Cayuga Drive, Burbank."

"And the phone number?"

"It's 555-7790. Listen, I stole some . . . co . . .
some . . . *thing* in New York that turned out to be—"

"We know, Miss Branigan. Please stay where you are and
someone will call you back within fifteen minutes. Will you be
there?"

"Yes, I uh—"

The agent hung up.

She put the receiver back on the hook. They had been waiting
for her call. As soon as the agent heard her name, all he wanted
to know was where she was. He knew what she wanted and didn't
need any explanation.

They would want the film back, and she didn't have it. But she knew who had it now. And she would tell them everything she knew . . . with great pleasure. The wall clock over the refrigerator ticked off the seconds. Three minutes passed, four, five, and then the phone rang. It was too soon. Oh, my God, she thought. Maybe it was Barry.

"Hello?" she said anxiously.

"Is this Cheryl Branigan?" It wasn't Barry. The voice was older and had a rough edge to it.

"Yes, it is," she answered nervously.

"My name is Frank LaSala. I'm with the CIA, working with federal agents here in Los Angeles. Are you alone?"

"Yes, I'm ah . . . I'm alone in somebody else's apartment. He took the film and is gone. That's why I'm calling you. I . . . "

"Miss Branigan, I want you to listen very carefully. It's now 2:20. In exactly thirty minutes, at ten minutes to three, a black radio cab will pull up outside the apartment. The driver will honk his horn twice. Only after you've heard the horn are you to leave the apartment. Pack only what you can carry with you. He will not get out of the car. Can you do that?"

"Yes," she answered. "I'll be ready."

"Good," he said, and the line went dead.

She stood for a moment, holding the phone. The importance of what she had stolen now was apparent. It wasn't just the FBI that was looking for it, it was the CIA.

She ran into the bedroom, pulled a suitcase out from the closet along with a small carry-on, and tossed them on the bed. Then she opened all the dresser drawers and threw everything into the bags. There were two dresses in the closet that she would leave. Grabbing the carry-on, she went into the bathroom and put all her toilet articles into it, along with a bathrobe.

On her way back to the bedroom she heard a garage door opening. She froze. Was Barry back, after all? She walked to the front window. A car was pulling into a garage two apartments away. She let out a sigh of relief and sat down on the sofa. Thank God it wasn't Barry.

Leaning her head back, she closed her eyes and thought about what she had just done. Without any kind of negotiation she had told the FBI where she was. Just like that. Why? she thought. The answer to her own question was that she was incensed. Incensed with Barry and wanting revenge for what he had done. Maybe it was irrational not to have been assured of her own situation first, but she was glad she had done it. They wouldn't prosecute her, anyway. Without her help they would never find Barry. And unless they gave her immunity, she wouldn't tell them anything.

The strength had returned to her arms and legs. Her body was almost back to normal now, and she was steadier on her feet. She must have been drugged. Barry must have put something in her wine. The son of a bitch. She had mentioned the poem he had written, and now she remembered two of the lines: "Here's to the fork in the road where we choose our separate ways. Maybe not because we want to, but because it has to be." This time he had chosen the fork in the road and decided to travel it alone. But she would find the road, and when she did, he would pay.

The sound of a horn outside startled her.

She waited for the second one. When it sounded again, she ran to the window. There was a black radio cab parked at the curb. The driver was leaning across the seat, checking the number on the front door. He was a middle-aged man, maybe in his early forties. She grabbed her bags and went to the door. Fumbling with the lock, she opened it and stepped outside. The man motioned for her to hurry from inside the car. She ran down the sidewalk and opened the rear door, threw her bags on the seat, and jumped in.

"Cheryl Branigan?" he asked.

"Yes."

"I'm Gene Zeller, a special agent working with Frank LaSala, who spoke to you on the phone before." He flashed an identification card, which bore his photograph and some sort of seal in the upper left-hand corner. "I'm going to take you to a house in Van Nuys, where you'll be questioned."

"I understand," she answered hesitantly.

He looked at her in the rearview mirror while at the same time checking to see what was behind them.

"This is going to be a kind of roundabout route to Van Nuys, so don't be concerned." He smiled for the first time.

"How long will it take?" she asked.

"About thirty minutes."

She sat back and watched him carefully. As he pulled away from the curb he checked both the side- and rearview mirrors. At the end of the block he did the same thing. His eyes constantly darted from one mirror to the other as he came into heavier traffic. As he approached each intersection he slowed down to check the streets coming into it. If a car was in back of him for more than five or six blocks, he turned onto a side street to lose it. After four or five minutes he picked up a microphone and radioed another car. The message was a jumble of numbers and code names which she couldn't understand. They passed a supermarket, and another radio cab came out of the parking lot and slid in behind them. Over the next few miles she noticed that it would leave occasionally and then come in back of them again. The radio communication continued back and forth. She sat quietly, nervously fumbling with the handle of her suitcase, which was beside her.

Finally they turned onto a tree-lined street, which was in one of the better sections of Van Nuys. There were elegant private houses on large properties with walls in front. Zeller drove past them until he came to a cul-de-sac at the end of the street. In front of them was a high brick wall with a black wrought-iron gate. He reached up and flipped over the sun visor. There was a remote control unit clipped to the back. He pressed it and the large gate opened.

They drove up a long paved road with elms on either side. It led to a spacious Victorian fieldstone mansion. As they pulled up to it two men emerged from inside. One of them opened the door for her.

She got out of the car, and the man introduced himself as Special Agent Frank LaSala, CIA, the man she had spoken to on the phone. She had imagined someone much younger. His voice was a little high-pitched and had a youthful quality to it. LaSala then introduced Steve Jankowski, who she thought had a rather butterball physique that wasn't her image of a CIA agent. Both men seemed friendly and glad to see her. Jankowski led the way and they went inside.

The foyer was circular, with a slate floor and high stucco walls. French doors led to rooms on either side. A plush carpeted staircase was directly ahead. LaSala opened the first door on the right and they entered a large, dark-paneled study.

"Won't you sit down," he said, pulling a Colonial ladder-back chair out from an elegant rosewood table. She sat down, facing a microphone and a tape recorder already set up in front of her.

"Would you like some coffee?" Jankowski asked.

"Yes, thank you," she answered. Actually she was starved, not having eaten since the night before. However, she wanted to get the questioning over with before she asked for anything more.

Jankowski left the room and LaSala turned to her. His hands were folded under his chin as he leaned forward on the table. She noticed he was wearing an inexpensive Timex watch and that his white shirt was wrinkled.

"You're very pretty," he said.

She lowered her eyes. "Right now I look a wreck. I slept until just before I called you. I think I was drugged."

"By whom?"

"By my . . ." She hesitated to use the word. "By my friend, I should say my ex-friend, Barry Rossiter."

"You were staying at his apartment?"

"Yes."

"He's the one you mentioned on the phone that has the film now."

"Yes."

"I see." His voice was sympathetic and he seemed genuinely concerned.

"Miss Branigan, may I call you Cheryl?"

"That's fine," she answered.

"Good," he said without really considering her reply. "Cheryl, you look like a bright girl who I'm sure by now realizes she's stumbled into something that's extremely dangerous. We wouldn't be sitting here if you simply had stolen a bag of coke from a restaurant in New York. Right?"

She nodded. So far he seemed pleasant and nonthreatening. She relaxed a little.

"But obviously you stole more than that. You stole film. Film I'll tell you we're very interested in."

She saw a sudden coldness in his eyes and his smile disappeared.

"Did you know you had stolen microfilm in New York?"

"No. I thought I had coke." She was frightened.

"So it was just by chance that you ended up with film instead?"

"Yes."

He put both hands under his chin and seemed to be waiting for more of an answer. When none came, he continued.

"All right, so you thought you had coke. What were you going to do with it?"

"I had an arrangement with Barry. Barry Rossiter. He's a guy I knew here in L.A. six years ago. We lived together for a while. He was going to pay me cash on the spot for what I had. From the weight of the packets I described, he thought it would be worth about three hundred thousand, depending on the quality."

"And when did you discover you had more than coke?"

"At the Belmont Hotel. Then I called Barry."

Jankowski came back into the room carrying a tray of coffee cups. He put it down on the table and they each took one. LaSala took a sip, then put it aside.

"So at the Belmont Hotel you saw what you had, and called Barry." LaSala repeated her statement for Jankowski's benefit.

"We saw it was microfilm," she continued. "Right away I wanted to bring it to the FBI, but Barry said we should examine it more closely to see what it really was."

"Examine it . . . how?" LaSala asked, taking a small pad next to him and passing it to Jankowski.

"Barry is a film editor," she answered, looking at both of them alternately. "He works for KNBC here in Los Angeles. Yesterday he took it there and examined it on some special equipment."

"What kind of equipment?"

"Something called an ADO. It blows up the film so it can be put on a videocassette. Then you can play it on a VCR."

"And what did he find?" LaSala asked. He looked at Jankowski, who was no longer taking notes. There seemed to be an unspoken communication between them.

"When he came back to the apartment with the videocassettes, we played them on the VCR. It showed a weapons demonstration. The secretary of defense was watching it along with some other people. There was a powerful explosion that destroyed a missile site in seconds. The people watching all cheered. It was very successful."

"What else did you see?" Jankowski asked. LaSala was watching her very carefully now, studying her every move.

"Some schematic drawings. Barry said they identified the weapon as a laser device."

"How did he know that?"

"He knows a lot about lasers. He's involved in laser technology, to develop a new electronic editing system. He says lasers are the thing of the future in editing and he wants to know everything about them he can."

LaSala seemed disturbed by her answer. His next few questions came in rapid succession.

"You looked at the tape on the VCR. Then what happened?"

"Barry said he wanted to sell the tape and the film to the Russians. He said it would be worth millions to them."

"Why?"

"Because it was a weapon they probably didn't know about."

"And did you agree?"

"No," she said emphatically. "I wanted to turn it over to the FBI. I wanted the whole thing to end because I was terrified. Then Barry . . . he . . ." She was starting to lose her voice to the anger that was coming back.

"Barry what? Go on." LaSala was tapping the table with the tips of his fingers.

"He said we'd turn it in if I was so frightened. But when I woke up this afternoon, he was gone, and so was the film. The son of a bitch had no intention of turning it in. He knew from the minute he came back to the apartment that he was going to run off with it."

"And do you know where he went with it?"

"Well, I can make a pretty good guess," she said angrily. "He probably went straight to the KGB to sell it to them."

LaSala looked at her for a moment. He seemed to be summarizing in his mind everything she had said. Jankowski was scribbling notes on his pad. But suddenly LaSala got up and motioned for him to do the same.

"If you'll excuse us, Cheryl, Steve and I are going to leave you for a few minutes. I'll be back shortly. If you need anything, there's someone right outside the door."

He turned and left the room with Jankowski right behind him.

She leaned back and took a deep breath. The questioning had ended abruptly and she hadn't said everything she'd wanted to. What about a guarantee of protection? She had forgotten about that. Like always, she had gone ahead and blabbed everything without thinking first. When they came back, she promised herself she'd find out where she stood before saying anything more.

Across the hall, LaSala and Jankowski listened to a replay of the questioning with the rest of the CIA team. When the tape ended, Jankowski was the first to speak. There was excitement in his voice as he switched off the tape recorder.

"Well, our job's a lot easier now," he said, flipping his empty Styrofoam cup into a wicker wastebasket. "Now we've got somebody else doing it. A few hours ago we were worrying about finding Cheryl, and then she calls up to tell us where she is. We had no idea how we were going to get the film back to the Russians, and now we have Barry delivering it for us. Talk about luck, we've had it in spades so far. All we have to do now is monitor the Soviet missions and diplomatic agencies to make sure Barry contacts them."

"That can be done pretty quickly," Moscowicz said. "I've already alerted our guys to reactivate the taps we have in them."

Jim Sweeney was punching the keys of a computer with a modem on direct line to Washington. "I'm getting that going right now, along with an identification check on this Rossiter," he said over his shoulder.

LaSala was sitting in a chair, staring at the now silent tape recorder. His hands were folded, the thumbs nervously circling over each other. Jankowski sat down next to him.

"I think we should get back in there, Frank, and find out more about Rossiter," he said.

LaSala turned to Ross Ward, the film expert who had helped create the "explosion effect" on the film.

"What's an ADO, Ross?" he asked.

"It's a video recorder that can blow up film frame by frame once it's been transferred to tape," Ward answered.

"So the microfilm was transferred onto another machine."

"Yeah, a tape deck that transfers from a film negative, but in this case from the film positive."

"That means he didn't need the ADO to make the cassette. So why would he use it?"

"He didn't have to . . . unless he wanted to examine every frame blown up."

"I see," LaSala said, looking again at the tape recorder. "And if he did, could he detect anything?"

"No, it's next to impossible. We used an Ulta Matte process to create the film. Two synchronized cameras controlled by a computer shot the model of the missile silo and the control room

simultaneously. The images matched perfectly when they were
put together electronically. Even under severe magnification the
match was perfect. Don't forget, it had to be. The Russians sure
as hell will scrutinize it very carefully when they get their hands
on it."

"What are you thinking, Frank?" Jankowski asked. It was
unlike him not to have acted immediately to instruct the group on
their next moves.

"I'm thinking we better make sure Barry doesn't know any
more than he should about the film he's carrying."

"But the film's perfect. Those Ulta Matte scenes are put
together so no one can tell the difference. What are you worried
about?"

"I don't like the series of events she describes in there," he said,
gesturing to the room next door. "This Barry comes to help her.
He's a film editor. Not only that, he knows about laser technology.
He takes the film to KNBC and transfers microfilm to videotape.
But he uses this ADO, which really isn't necessary. Why? The
next day he takes off after drugging Cheryl. Now something's
wrong with this picture. And I want to find out what that is before
I let this guy walk up to the Russians and deliver that film. We're
talking about preventing a possible third World War here. We
better not leave any stones unturned."

The group sat silent for a moment, evaluating what he had said.
Most of them had been caught up with finding Cheryl so quickly,
but now they were beginning to realize that Frank's points were
valid.

LaSala turned to them. They were awaiting their assignments.

"First of all . . ." he said, "we're going to check out KNBC.
I want to talk to everybody Rossiter saw when he was there with
the film. I mean everybody. Petersen, get in touch with them and
have those people assembled as soon as possible."

Petersen replied, "They may not be able to—"

"I don't care if they have to go off the air to do it," LaSala said,
raising his voice. "I want it done."

Petersen left the room to get to a private phone.

"The next thing we need to do is stay on Barry's trail just in
case we have to stop him or just to verify that he's contacted the
Russians. Pagano, Tracey, Fuller—get to his apartment and shake
it out from top to bottom. Jim, get that computer busy finding out

everything you can about him—motor-vehicle records, bank accounts, withdrawals, the works. Moscowicz, we need those Russian diplomatic houses and missions covered that Sweeney was talking about. That means Washington, San Francisco, New York, Glen Cove, Riverdale, everywhere. We need all the taps going and our informers talking. If Rossiter even comes close to talking to the KGB, I want to know about it.

"The rest of you will go to KNBC as soon as we've made arrangements to get their people together. Ross, you'll be in charge of the initial questioning. Steve and I will get there as soon as you've got somebody for us to talk to. In the meantime we're going to ask our Miss Branigan a few more questions."

LaSala got up and motioned for Jankowski to follow him out into the hallway. Steve quietly closed the door behind him, and they stood next to the staircase speaking in low voices.

"What do you think?" LaSala asked his young assistant. Jankowski knew the question wasn't meant to elicit some new thought or insight.

"Well," Jankowski said, "if Rossiter used specific equipment, we ought to know why. Plus, if the guy is as technically oriented as she says he is—who knows? He could have stumbled onto something."

"Yeah, but it's not going to be easy finding him," LaSala replied. "We can't put out an all-points bulletin on him without raising suspicion with the KGB. We're going to be operating with one hand tied behind our backs." He checked his watch. "It's almost five o'clock, eight in Washington. I'm going to call Shupe and tell him what's happened. He'll probably contact the president before the evening is out."

Jankowski watched as he straightened his tie. He swore LaSala was the only man who constantly wore a white shirt in Los Angeles. Even the most fastidious businessmen let their hair down a little when they came here, dressing more casually. But on the other hand, Frank had his own way of looking casual. The shirts were never pressed.

LaSala gestured toward the door behind him. "I want you to question her some more. Find out all you can about Barry. She said they lived together. Find out where. Also, where did he hang out? Who are his friends? What are his hobbies? You know, the usual stuff. And see if she has a photograph of him. Then get her settled. When they're ready for us at the station, I'll call you."

Two hours later Frank and Steve walked into KNBC, having compared notes in the car. Cheryl had given Steve a list of clubs and bars where they had gone together, but that was six years ago. Some of them didn't exist anymore. Nevertheless, he had passed the list on to another agent, along with a seven-year-old snapshot of Barry. Steve reported that Cheryl was reluctant to get involved any further. She wanted assurance that she wouldn't be prosecuted, assurance Steve couldn't give her.

LaSala reported that Shupe had panicked when he heard Cheryl didn't have the film. He agreed that a complete investigation should be made at KNBC immediately and promised assistance from his office should it be necessary to obtain their cooperation.

As Frank and Steve entered KNBC's main office, they were met by Agent Ross Ward and the station manager, who assured them that the entire facility and staff were at their disposal. Ward told them that Barry had come in contact with six people the previous day but had only worked with two: Tom Faxon, an ADO film editor; and Elise Farrell, the videotape librarian. Both of them were standing by for further questioning. Ward said he had already questioned the editor and suggested that he and LaSala follow up with him. Steve would talk to the librarian.

Ward took LaSala to the third floor, where they stepped out of the elevator into a small reception area. Beyond it was a door marked VIDEOTAPE EDITING. Ward opened it and they entered a large room full of whirring computer discs and tape machines. There was the screeching sound of audiotape as it ran in reverse, and the clatter of film as it flew off the ends of takeup reels. It was a maze of sophisticated electronic equipment, with men shouting to be heard above the din.

They passed through the room into a corridor with dark rooms on either side. LaSala could see the silhouetted shapes of men facing rows of blinking lights and illuminated video screens. The sound of a Coke commercial came from one room and blended in with crowd noise from a football game in the other. At the end of the corridor was a door marked ADO EDIT.

They opened the sliding glass doors and entered a small, darkened room crammed with equipment. A man was seated at a large console, which was a maze of dials and switches. Rows of red, yellow, and green flashing lights reflected into his glasses in a kaleidoscope of color. Above him were four TV screens, all with images frozen on them, waiting for electronic commands to send them back into motion. The man turned in his swivel chair and stood to introduce himself.

"Hi, Tom Faxon," he said with a smile. "Pleased to meet ya." He was tall, dressed in a light vee-neck sweater (the air-conditioning was set for the computers, not for him), light chino slacks, and sneakers. From his voice and demeanor he appeared to be a Midwesterner.

"Frank LaSala, Special Investigator." Frank shook Faxon's hand and turned to the massive control panel in front of him. "This is a very impressive piece of equipment. How long did it take you to learn to play it?"

Faxon smiled. "Haven't learned yet. I find a new button and light every day. Someday I'm gonna learn what they all mean. In the meantime I just kind of muddle along."

"That's not what we hear from the tape editors," Ward interjected. "They say you've saved a lot of asses around here with this ADO."

"Well, maybe a few," he said, wiping his glasses with a handkerchief.

"Like maybe Barry Rossiter's?" LaSala asked.

"Well, not very often. Barry's a technically sound editor. Comes in here sometimes to experiment, though. He's always been interested in finding out just what all this stuff can do."

"And just what *can* it do?" LaSala sat down in a high swivel chair at the end of the console.

"Essentially blow up images," Faxon replied. "We measure screen size in terms of 'fields.' The ADO can blow something up as much as fifteen fields without losing quality. That's about fifteen times the size it appears on your TV set. And it can do it in a smooth move with varying speeds. If you have a scene of a man looking at his watch, this machine can move in close enough so you can tell the time."

"Was that what Barry was using it for yesterday?"

"Yeah, for the most part." Faxon hesitated for a moment and then added, "Ross, here, tells me that it was classified film. Could've fooled me. Barry said it was a demonstration for an upcoming documentary on weapons testing. He came in here with

some videotape he had transferred and said he had to blow up
some scenes so that they'd have more impact."

"Who made the film transfers?" Ward asked.

"He did. On a film-to-tape recorder down the hall. I worked
with him on it for about two hours. I can show you the tape."

LaSala was surprised and turned to Ward, who was pulling
another chair up to the console.

"We're lucky, Frank," Ward said. "Barry didn't know it, but
Tom made a master of the tape as he was working on it. He also
recorded all of the computer commands from the ADO into the
station's mainframe. As a result, the master can be replayed with
all of the moves that Barry asked for."

Faxon was seated at the console, pressing a series of buttons
that had removed the images from the screens in front of him.

"Yeah. I copy everything onto a master now and hold it for a
week or two," he said with a cynical smile. "These editors
constantly want changes, and if I haven't recorded what I've done,
I'd spend most of my time recreating it. Now watch this." He
jabbed at a row of red buttons, and the countdown numbers from
Barry's tape appeared on one of the screens. "That's all there is to
it."

Suddenly LaSala was staring at an image he hadn't seen in over
two months. There was the control room filled with technicians in
front of a large screen. The screen showed the missile silo
silhouetted against a night sky, just the way he had remembered it.
Only in his mind, the missile silo was a model, no more than four
feet long and made of cardboard and clay. The control room was
an elaborate set with actors playing the parts of technicians. He
remembered the two stage sets. They were in a studio in the
Burbank section of Los Angeles and had been photographed
secretly at two in the morning.

The countdown appeared on a digital clock over the screen—3,
2, 1—and suddenly there was a flash in the sky. The laser beam
blazed through the darkness and hit the silo, sending huge chunks
of concrete flying into the air. As the beam continued to bore
through the silo cover, the camera pulled back to include technicians in the first two rows at their computers. This was the first
point in the film that the Ulta Matte process had been used. One
camera had shot the men and the control room, including the

screen. The other had shot the laser and the model exploding. The two images had been put together later, using the Ulta Matte.

The film stopped. Bits of concrete were suspended in midair, and the laser was a stationary line of brilliant white with soft yellow edges.

"Here's where Barry made the first blowup," Faxon said, referring to a column of numbers on the computer screen in front of him. "This went up about ten fields, keying on the back of the technicians' heads against the explosion. Why he wanted this I'll never know. It's a pretty dull shot."

The blown-up image appeared on the screen. With ADO resolution, it was sharp and clear. LaSala looked at the edges of the technicians' heads, superimposed against flying bits of concrete and dust. Here he had been told edges can get jagged, even out of focus, but they were clean and in perfect focus. He looked over at Ward, who nodded approvingly.

The image jumped back to normal size and the tape went forward. Concrete continued to explode in the air until the screen was obliterated with flying debris. Then the laser stopped. Clouds of smoke and dust gradually dispersed, revealing a smoldering hole the size of a football field. Chunks of twisted, tangled steel lay inside it. The technicians jumped to their feet, cheering along with a group of dignitaries standing against the sidewall. They were wearing military uniforms, and most were high-ranking officers. LaSala knew them all, including Secretary of Defense Walter Commack, who was partially hidden by two other civilians.

Again the film stopped, the image frozen on the screen.

"See the guy in the middle, hidden by the two generals?" Faxon asked. "Turns out he's the secretary of defense. Barry wanted a close-up of him to show the importance of the demonstration. Here it comes."

He ran the film forward, and Commack's face filled the entire frame. His hands were raised over his head as he celebrated the success of the demonstration. LaSala looked at the image and tried to link it to the other scene Barry had selected. That one had appeared to be a close examination of the film, but this was strictly for identification. Barry wanted to make sure it was really Commack. Why?

"There's one more blowup," Faxon said as he advanced the

film. "This one's fourteen fields, just about the maximum the machine can handle."

The tape flickered as he ran it forward frame by frame. It was the opening scene of the film. The technicians were seated at their computers and the countdown was about to begin. The camera was moving along a row of computers. Information flashed on the screens. There were rows of numbers, digital displays, and graphics. Suddenly the film froze on one of the screens. There was text on it, along with columns of numbers. At the top was a heading that wasn't legible.

"Barry thought the information here could be used as a close-up in the documentary, so he blew it up as far as it would go," Faxon said.

Gradually the image grew larger, until it was large enough to read. It snapped into focus.

LA 4623 DEMO, USAF DEPT. 0620, CHEYENNE, WYOMING, 6 MARCH, 1994, 2230 HRS. LaSala saw the words and again wondered why. Why was the date of the demonstration important?

"After this blowup Barry left the room for about twenty minutes," Faxon said impassively.

"Why?" LaSala asked.

"Don't know. He said he had to go back to his editing room and check something out. It was supposed to take only a few minutes, but it turned out to be nearly twenty."

"Do you know what time that was?"

"Yeah." He checked the computer readout in front of him. "At 1:32 P.M. I didn't start the tape again until 1:50."

"What happened when he came back?"

"He was very excited. He wanted me to run through the microfilm. I did, but he didn't want any blowups. Then he asked to see everything one more time. After that I made him two cassettes of the entire film—one with blowups and one without. It only took a few minutes, and then he was out of here."

Again LaSala reviewed the blown-up scenes in his mind but still couldn't make any connections. But Barry must have. Something had made him leave the room in a hurry. Something had triggered an idea that made him leave and later return to have the date of the demonstration blown up. What was it?

There was a knock on the door.

Faxon reached over and opened it. Steve was standing in the doorway with a videocassette in his hand.

"How'd you make out?" LaSala asked without turning away from the screen.

"I've got something you should take a look at," Jankowski said, closing the door behind him.

"Well, we've got something here too," he answered, pointing to the image in front of him. "Rossiter had Tom blow up three scenes from the microfilm, but we can't make any logical connection between them."

Steve moved closer, to read the information on the screen. The image showing the time and date of the explosion was frozen in front of him.

"Is this one of them?" he asked. LaSala noticed his eyes. They were wide open, staring at the image. His hand had gone up under his chin, and he leaned closer to get a better look. Something on the screen had triggered an excitement that was very apparent in his voice.

"Yes," LaSala replied.

"Can I see the others?" he asked. He hadn't taken his eyes off the screen.

Faxon ran the tape backward again. LaSala watched his assistant carefully. His mouth had opened, and it looked as if he were about to say something but nothing came out. His eyes darted across each image, studying it in minute detail. As the last frame flashed off, he spun around and picked up the cassette he had brought into the room with him. He handed it to Ward.

"Can you run this cassette and the blowups on Tom's machine?" he asked excitedly.

"I guess so . . . sure," Ward replied.

"If you'd excuse us," Steve said to Faxon, "but we've got something we have to look at in private." The editor nodded, got up, and left the room. Ward took the cassette and inserted it into the machine.

Steve turned to LaSala.

"The link you're looking for is on this tape," he said. "Elise Farrell, the film librarian, showed it to me about twenty minutes ago. Barry came to her and asked for it right after he left Faxon." He hit the play button.

A KNBC logo appeared, followed by a second scene that

showed a large white rectangle with a single line of computer type. LaSala stared at the letters. "Washington Report, Secretary of Defense Walter Commack, March 6, 1994, 9 P.M., Tape #683, 4 min. 38 sec. For airing 10 March, 1994."

Steve pressed the stop button and pointed to the date.

"That's the same date we just saw on the computer screen in the control room. When Barry saw it, he must have made the connection between the date of the explosion and this interview. The date was one that stuck in his mind. He told the librarian he remembered being called in that day to edit an interview with the secretary of defense that had been taped earlier. It was a Sunday and he was pissed off, because he was going sailing and had to come in instead. Now they wanted him to do more work on it, so would she please make him a copy? She did, and he left with it."

LaSala's mind was racing ahead, putting this new information together with what he had seen on the blown-up tape. The conclusions were horrifying. Ward ran Jankowski's tape.

The interview opened with Commack seated in front of a graphic representation of the Pentagon. The host, Charles Browning, of NBC's Washington bureau, turned to the camera.

"Good morning, ladies and gentlemen, and welcome to *The Washington Report*. Our guest is Secretary of Defense Walter Commack, who has taken time out from a busy schedule to be with us today. Welcome, Mr. Secretary."

"Thank you, it's a pleasure to be here," Commack replied with a pleasant smile.

"The media released a leaked report yesterday . . ." The interview went on, but LaSala didn't hear a word. He stood, staring at Walter Commack's image on the screen. He couldn't believe what he was seeing. And what Barry had also seen.

"So our friend Barry knows that Commack couldn't have been at a demonstration in Wyoming on March sixth because he was doing an interview right here at KNBC." His own words shocked him.

"Right," Steve said. "And if he knows that, he can draw some very logical conclusions."

"Exactly. The first being that Commack couldn't be in two places at once, and the second being that Ulta Matte was used and the demonstration must have been simulated."

Now his hands were out of his pockets, and he moved about the room like a fighter shadowboxing with an unseen opponent.

"Then he says to himself, 'Wouldn't the Russians just love to get their hands on this?' They thought they were buying film on a weapon that could threaten their military superiority, but now he has proof that the weapon isn't real. That was worth millions. He goes back to the apartment, and Cheryl is insistent on turning the film in immediately. He pretends to go along but slips her something that will buy him time until morning. Then he's off to the Russians and it's screw you, Cheryl."

He stopped in the center of the darkened room and stood with his back to the screen, which was the only source of light.

"What this all means," he said, looking at some point off in the darkness, "is that now we have the reverse situation of what we had hours ago. Instead of doing everything we can to get the film to the Russians, we have to do everything we can to prevent it. If Barry manages to show them the tape, along with the Commack tape, we've blown the whole thing. He's got to be stopped, and he's got to be stopped fast."

He paused for a moment and then added, "Even if we have to kill him to do it."

Cheryl lowered her head into a sinkful of warm water and began to massage the rinse out of her hair. For the last hour she had been alternately applying and rinsing the color remover, trying to rid herself of the dark brown that had made her Carolyn. Her fingers dug into the scalp as if they could rip the color out so she could throw it away forever. Now this nightmare was ending. She was safe in a house surrounded by CIA men that would protect her. Good. Safe is what she needed to be.

She raised her head out of the water and reached for a towel. The lush terry-cloth felt good against her face as she dried it. Now maybe all the color would be gone. But when she opened her eyes, it wasn't. Carolyn was resisting. She wouldn't go away that easily. There was a knock on the door.

Quickly she pulled the opening of her robe together and tightened the sash at her waist. Then she walked through the small Colonial-style bedroom to answer the door.

"Who is it?" she asked, looking at the clock on the dresser. It was almost midnight.

"Frank LaSala" came the muffled reply. "I saw your light on and wondered if I could talk to you for a few minutes."

She had wanted to talk to him too. When she spoke to Jankowski earlier about immunity from prosecution, he hadn't given her any real assurances. Maybe LaSala could. She opened the door. "Come in," she said, partially hiding herself behind it.

LaSala walked slowly across the room and sat down in a small, soft chair in the corner. He looked tired. She sat in a white wicker rocker next to him.

"I hope you're comfortable here," he said, looking around the pink-and-white bedroom. "If there's anything you need, don't hesitate to ask."

"Not really," she answered. "Everyone has been helpful."

"Good," he said, leaning forward in the chair. His hands were under his chin, holding it up. She could see he was struggling to keep his eyes open, and there was something important on his mind. He looked up at her as if to assess her mood, then spoke in a surprisingly loud voice.

"We need your help," he said. The words came out as more of an order than a plea.

"That's a switch," she said, trying to hide the sarcasm in her voice. "I thought I was the one who needed all the help."

"We ran into a dead end at the station. We have no leads on Barry and we need to find him quickly."

"Look," she said, getting up from the chair, "I want some assurances before I start remembering everything, and nobody around here is giving me any."

"What kind of assurances?"

"Like I won't be prosecuted for what I've done. I didn't know I was passing military secrets, but I did know I was passing coke. I could be charged with that. And even if you didn't decide to press it, how long are you going to protect me? When you're finished with your questions, I could end up back on the street, with Lucci's men waiting for me."

"Whoa, hold it, stop," LaSala said, waving his hands in front of his face. "Calm down. There're answers to all of those questions, but let me take them one at a time. First of all, we're not going to prosecute you. We need your help too much for that. As far as protection is concerned, that depends on how much you cooperate with us."

"How do I know that for sure?"

"You'll have to take my word for now. I'll get you more assurances later."

She looked at him closely for a moment, studying his eyes carefully. Finally she decided he was telling the truth and she relaxed a little. LaSala took a quick look at his watch.

"In the meantime Barry has to be found, and we need your help to find him."

"Well, I told your friend Steve everything I know about him, which isn't very much."

"We know that, but we still need your help. You're all we've got right now."

She got up from her chair and walked across the room. When she got to the bed, she turned and faced LaSala.

"You know, I'm tired," she said. "I'm tired of running, tired of looking over my shoulder, tired of the whole goddamn thing."

LaSala wrote something on his pad and then said, "Well, I'm afraid the 'whole goddamn thing' is far from over. And you can't just walk away from it, because you're already being hunted by the KGB. You see, Lucci was working for them. They were using his drug operation to obtain military secrets. So when you called, both of us were looking for you. They still are. And quite frankly, if you don't help us, we could put you right back out on the street for them. They'd find you pretty fast because they're very close. That man you saw when you checked out of the hotel wasn't FBI. He was KGB."

"Oh, my God," she said softly. Suddenly the fear was coming back. It was the KGB that was after her. They had almost caught her.

LaSala went on, holding the end of his pen against his chin. "Unless you help us find Barry, I really don't know why we should protect you from them."

"You've got to protect me," she said. Her voice was rising. "They'd kill me!"

"Probably," he said calmly.

LaSala saw the fear in both her face and body movements. Her hands were trembling and her eyes darted back and forth, as if looking to escape the mental terror her mind was conjuring up. He had succeeded with the first part of his plan: to instill fear and a reliance on him for her survival. The second part was to instill yet a second emotion: anger. It meant revealing what Barry had discovered at KNBC, that the weapon didn't exist. Even though she would be one more person who knew, the secret would be safe. Cheryl Branigan wasn't going anywhere for a long time.

He shifted his position in the chair by crossing one leg over the other.

"There are some other things you should know," he said. "Then maybe you'll understand what stealing that film really meant."

She stood behind the bed with her hands at her side. Suddenly she felt the need for a large object between herself and LaSala.

"You see." he continued, "the informer that was passing the film to Lucci was actually working for us. His name is James McFarland, and he's a physicist working for the company that's supposedly developing the weapon. McFarland was passing information on it through Lucci to the KGB—information that we wanted to fall into their hands. We *wanted* the Russians to know about the laser weapon that was on the film. So when you ran off with it, you negated a top secret two-year plan designed to demonstrate to the Russians that this weapon wasn't only fully developed but operational as well."

He paused for a moment, making sure she fully understood what he had said.

"Our immediate objective was to get that film back into KGB hands, and that meant finding you. And as soon as we found out you were in L.A., we did everything we could to help the KGB find you."

He could see her mind working now, drawing conclusions about what he had said. She started back around the bed, coming closer to him.

"So when I finally called you, why didn't you just tip off the KGB and let them know where I was?"

"We almost did, until you told us you didn't have the film."

"But now your problem is solved. Barry has the film and is on the way to the Russians with it. He's going to personally deliver it for you."

"That's true, but he's delivering more than just the film."

"What does that mean?"

"We found out tonight at KNBC that he's got proof the weapon on the film doesn't really exist."

"He what?" She couldn't have heard the words right and needed them repeated.

"Barry discovered through careful examination of the film that the explosion came from a weapon that doesn't exist. The film was made with the use of models and sophisticated film techniques. Barry saw through them once he discovered another tape that proved the secretary of defense couldn't have been at the demonstration."

She couldn't control the smile she knew was on her face. The fucking son of a bitch. All that technical knowledge had finally been put to creative use. He always said that someday he would work on a film that would make him millions; this was it.

"So we need your help," she heard LaSala say.

Her fingers closed into a tight fist and her body began to shake. LaSala saw the anger in her eyes as she thought about what Barry had done to her. But when she finally spoke, it wasn't about Barry.

"Do you see my hair?" she asked, pulling at the dark strands with both hands. "I'm trying to wash away this whole thing and you want me to get in deeper. The reason I called you was because I wanted to be free of this whole thing. I gave you all the information I know. So let's call it even. I can't take any more."

LaSala glared at her. Instinctively she moved back a step, expecting a loud reply, but his voice was soft and controlled.

"You listen to me, lady, and you listen good. This isn't a child's game we're playing here; this game is called the survival of the United States. You blew our only chance for military survival when you walked out of Armando's with that film. Now your boyfriend's found out the truth about it and is off to spill his guts to the Russians. If he succeeds in getting there before we can stop him, the whole country is going to pay the price. And it's going to be a steep one. It's going to be living with missiles aimed right down our throats. So don't tell me you're tired and you don't want to get in deeper or any other bullshit. Whether you like it or not, you're in this about as deep as you can get."

She stood with her hands hanging limp at her side. The whole thing was hitting her like an avalanche crashing down all at once. LaSala was on his feet, his hands moving to underline each sentence. "I know you're frightened and I know you want this all to end. But it's not going to unless we stop Barry. And I don't think we can do it without your help."

She saw her reflection in the mirror behind him. But it wasn't her. It was Carolyn Mulcahey, the girl that was her dream of a life full of fun and freedom. Now the promise of all that had ended quickly, in just a few days. Now she would have all she could do just to survive. And it wasn't just her survival that was involved; it was the survival of the country.

Her eyes returned to LaSala and a sudden realization sent a chill running through her. Now that he had told her the film wasn't real, she was as dangerous to them as Barry. The thought was terrifying.

"Will you help us?" he asked. The sentence was posed as a simple question, but the tone held an underlying threat.

"Yes," she answered. "I don't think I have any other choice."

"That's right," he said calmly. "You don't."

He turned away and walked over to the door. For a moment he stood with his back to her, but then he turned around. "I want you to know you're safe here," he said softly. "We'll protect you as long as you're helping us—and beyond that. I promise you—."

Without waiting for a reply, he opened the door and left.

LaSala walked down the hallway and went into his room. Jankowski was waiting for him.

"Well, how did it go?" he asked, snuffing out a cigarette into the ashtray beside his chair.

"She knows everything we do now, and she'll help us find Barry," he said, slumping down on the edge of the bed. "But there's one thing I didn't tell her."

"What?"

"That after we find him we'll need her to return the film to the KGB."

Washington, D.C.

President Alan Hayden took off his white terry-cloth robe and handed it to Secret Service Agent John Miklos. Miklos draped it over a chair near a staircase that led up to the first floor of the White House. He then sat down on a white bench near the pool as the president prepared to do his daily laps.

Hayden stepped onto the low diving board. Head erect, arms high, stomach in, feet together, push off . . . go. His body sprang forward and cut into the water at a perfect thirty-degree angle. He opened his eyes and saw the illuminated bottom of the pool coming up at him. With a quick kick of his feet his body turned and sped up to the surface. He broke the water with a loud splash and took in a breath of air.

The sixty-degree water felt good. At six o'clock every morning it was a quick wake-me-up. Doing the laps was exhilarating and served to get his mind started. This was the time when he ran the day through his mind. What meetings did he have to attend? What were the issues to be discussed? How would he handle them? The answers came easily. His mind was fresh and alert.

But this morning had been different. The phone next to his bed had rung at four A.M. The call was from CIA Director Donald Shupe. Word had come from Los Angeles that Cheryl Branigan had been found. At first he had been elated. But then Shupe told him what else had transpired in Los Angeles, and he was furious.

The goddamn Pentagon had blown it again. Nobody had bothered to check the date on the phony test film against those of Commack's public appearances. What a blunder! And what was the chance that the film would fall into the hands of someone who could recognize that blunder? One in a million?

He pushed off the edge of the pool and began the first lap. Breaststroke . . . back straight, keep feet kicking in rhythm with arms, head out, breathe, head in. Stroke, breathe, stroke, breathe.

Shupe also told the president he had received a report from S-1 intelligence agents inside the Soviet Union. Six freighters docked at the port of Tallinn, loaded with SRV-60 missiles, would sail for Cuba in four days. They would be led by the *Poltava*, the same ship that had led the convoy in 1962.

Thirty-two years ago, the decision to confront that convoy had been made in this very pool. On the day of his address to the American people, President Kennedy had swum here in the morning, preparing for the speech. Hayden imagined him moving through the water, organizing his thoughts and gathering the courage to make his stand. He had been eloquent and forceful, with the final result being one of the finest hours in American history.

But this time the Russians were confident there would be no turning back. Kennedy had stopped them, but he had operated from a position of strength. Now the United States was weak. They had spent twenty-five billion dollars on a Star Wars defense program to counter Russian submarine-launched missiles and had failed. This time the *Poltava* would have clear sailing all the way to Cuba.

He looked up at the white-tiled ceiling. Steam from the heated water was rising up to it, forming a small billowy cloud. It looked like a face. The face was President Kennedy's, and he was standing in front of a podium ready to speak to the nation. Hayden had studied the speech many times and now heard Kennedy's voice echoing through the cavernous pool area.

"This secret, swift, extraordinary buildup of communist missiles is in violation of Soviet assurances and in defiance of American and hemispheric policy—this sudden, clandestine decision to station strategic weapons for the first time outside of Soviet soil—is a deliberately provocative and unjustified change in the status quo which cannot be accepted by this country if our courage and our commitments are ever to be trusted again, by either friend or foe. The cost of freedom is always high, but Americans have always been willing to pay it. One path we shall never choose, and that is the path of surrender or submission."

They were strong words and they were backed up by strength. Kennedy had complete military superiority over the Soviet Union in 1962. America had a larger nuclear arsenal, advanced space technology, and superior conventional land and sea forces. It was easy to stand up to the Russians and wave a club when you had a bigger club. But he didn't even have one. His was just make-believe.

At this point the best he could hope for was to prevent the truth from reaching Karpolov and the Politburo. If they failed at that, there wouldn't be any point in even trying to stop the convoy. They would be defenseless and he would have to accept the wrath of the media and the American people for allowing what Kennedy had so courageously defended against years ago.

He turned in the water and began a sidestroke. His heart rate was climbing, and he wasn't certain whether it was from exertion or because of the anxiety of a hopeless situation.

Shupe's final words were being replayed inside his brain: "Our only hope is to find this Rossiter before he gets to the Russians. He must not reach them with the film."

The president agreed with Shupe that Rossiter should be

officially declared a threat to national security. That gave Shupe the authority to eliminate Rossiter, if necessary, to prevent what now seemed to be inevitable.

The next week would be crucial. Shupe told the President it would take six or seven days for the Russian convoy to reach Cuba. But he warned that once the missiles were in place, it would be nearly impossible to get them back out. The Russians would have achieved a tremendous moral victory in the eyes of the world, along with an irreversible military advantage.

At the end of his tenth lap the president took a deep breath and dived under the surface. He opened his eyes and saw a large underwater light at the end of the pool. As he swam toward it, it looked like a giant spotlight shining directly at him. Yes, that's where he would be for the next week, and maybe long afterward; in the spotlight. World attention would be focused on him as he tried to beat back the Russians with a weapon made of celluloid. But he was determined to handle it one step at a time, and the first was preventing Barry Rossiter from reaching the Russians.

The next was adding whatever credibility they had to the nonexistent weapon. Cabot had informed him that orders had been issued to the 181st Airborne and word leaked. By tomorrow the Russians would be aware of a new aggressiveness in Europe. Hopefully it would signal them that the U.S. was getting tough and had the weapon to back it up.

He had also instructed Ambassador George Hodges to confront the Kremlin directly with the intelligence report from Tallinn. So far the Russians had denied any existence of missiles at the docks, saying only that turbines were being readied there for shipment abroad.

Before any steps could be taken, the film would have to be in Premier Chebrikov's hands, along with other support that the weapon existed. He would have to delay any direct threats to him until then. But time was running out. If the October 22 date was accurate, there were only four days left.

With one quick motion his body recoiled off the wall as he turned to begin another lap. His head came above the surface as he took in a deep breath. At the same time he heard the phone ring. Miklos answered it and after a few moments motioned him over to the side of the pool. As he swam toward the ladder the agent hung up the phone and met him with his robe and towel.

"That was General Cabot," he said. "The group is en route now and will be here in half an hour."

"Good," Hayden replied. "I'm ready for them now."

He put the robe on and walked along the wet tile to the opposite end of the pool. As he turned around he saw Miklos standing against the far wall, shrouded behind a thick vapor rising off the water. His body was a gray silhouette framed in a veil of smoky white. Again he heard Kennedy's voice echoing off the tiled walls.

"Our goal is not the victory of might but the vindication of right; not peace at the expense of freedom but both peace and freedom here in this hemisphere, and we hope around the world. God willing, that hope will be achieved."

He looked at the silhouetted figure and said in a voice that was just a whisper, "Let's hope God is willing, because we haven't the power to do it any other way."

Moscow

Viktor Karpolov leaned back in his whirlpool as 110-degree water swirled around his naked body. He reached for a glass of cognac on a silver tray beside him and took a sip. The liquid warmed his throat and he felt its relaxing effect spread out into his arms and legs. A jet of water pressed against his back as he shifted slightly, and its gentle massaging action moved up and down his spine. His legs relaxed and began to float effortlessly toward the surface of the bubbling water. Slowly all the tensions of the past few days started to leave him. For over a week now the pressure had been unbearable. Every minute now brought him closer to where a decision would be made that not only would decide his future but also the future of the country.

The whirlpool had been a gift from Ivana. When he was promoted to director of operations for the KGB, he had felt real pressure for the first time. Overnight he had a staff of several hundred reporting on assignments around the world. His workday suddenly jumped to fourteen hours. There were meetings to attend, planning sessions with key managers, and social functions in the evening. He needed to relax. Ivana had come up with the perfect solution.

He remembered the first time he saw the whirlpool. While he was away on a three-week trip a new den was to be built in the basement. But the trip was cut short unexpectedly and he got home a week early. When he walked in the door, Ivana tried to keep him from seeing what progress had been made, saying it was a mess. Finally, when he insisted, she stepped aside and opened the door. Instead of a den nearly completed, he saw a concrete hole in the floor with unfinished tile on the walls.

"They got a little carried away digging out the floor," she had said with a sheepish grin on her face.

"And the tile?" he asked innocently.

"Oh, I thought it was very practical. It's washable, you know."

"I see," he had said, trying to keep from bursting out laughing. "And where will I do my work now?"

"I left a small space over in the corner," she answered. "I think it's in proper proportion to the room; ninety percent relaxation, ten percent work."

He had taken her in his arms and thanked her for knowing what he needed better than himself. And then she had said, "I wanted it for you, but also for us. There's room for two, you know."

And they had used it many times together. Making love in the warm swirling water had been ecstasy, and he felt himself growing erect just thinking about it.

But his mind quickly returned to his plan, which was about to receive final approval in four days from the Politburo. Once they signed off on it, orders would be given immediately for the ships to sail for Cuba. Then he and the country would be totally committed.

He reached for a two-hundred-page report from the Institute of High Energy Physics at Serpukhov that was lying beside him. After his lunch with General Parkovsky, he had ordered it immediately. The Institute's position remained the same; the Americans could not possibly have a laser-charged weapon operational at this time. There was also a report from the Army Satellite Reconnaissance Unit at Kharkov. As of one month ago there had been no sightings of an aboveground weapons test over North America. They were absolutely certain.

But other things were not as certain; things he was hiding from the Politburo. The receivers found by Captain Berkhin at Sakhalin had since been identified as capable of generating a blast in the 100,000 to 150,000 ton range from a laser-reflected beam. Also, he found it hard to believe the Americans hadn't taken better precautions in hiding them.

And what about the drop in New York? For over two years now, this McFarland had been passing them information from the supposed laser weapon's prime contractor, Space Technologies. But again, Russian scientists had rejected all the information, calling it "beyond state-of-the-art" or just "technically not feasible." At some point he had even considered that maybe they were biased. Maybe there was jealousy on their part. Had the Americans achieved something they couldn't and they were loath to admit it? He concluded that it was unlikely but ordered the drop continued in the hope that it would offer something definitive one way or the other.

That definitive answer would have come with McFarland's final drop, had it not been intercepted by this Branigan girl. By now he would have known if the Americans could prove they had the weapon or not. He took a sip of the cognac and considered what he would do if they really did have it. He would have to advise the Politburo, and his plan would be scrapped immediately. His saving the country from a terrible embarrassment might be rewarded.

But once the plan was approved and the ships sailed, General Parkovsky was right, there was no turning back. Once those ships left Tallinn, he would have to conceal any information that could prove the Americans had the weapon operational.

They would leave four days from now, on October 22. Kennedy's victory on the same date, thirty-two years ago, would be avenged. Premier Chebrikov had been adamant. "If we are to go at all," he had said, "it will be on that day." The entire Politburo had stood up and applauded.

The warm water relaxed his muscles, but his mind still felt the pressure of the decision he would have to make. If only he knew for sure. Did they have the weapon or not?

He thought about President Hayden. They had met only once and had gone through the motions of politeness, but personally he didn't like the man. He was too much the Wall Street business type: perfect clothes, perfect hair, perfect nails, perfect everything. His biography was even perfect: Choate School, Harvard Law School, special investigator, congressman from New York, and then five years in the Senate before becoming president.

He tried to picture him playing poker, because that's what they were doing now. What kind of player was he? Underneath those perfect clothes, did he have the balls to try to bluff him? He and the Politburo held all the high cards, submarine-launched missiles far more sophisticated than anything the U.S. had, and now land-based ones that soon would be in Cuba. Hayden, according to his own KGB, had nothing. But was he bluffing? Like a good poker player, was he doing the best he could with a weak hand? He had to find out, and there was very little time left to do so.

The cognac began to take effect. He closed his eyes and leaned back on an inflatable pillow. For a moment he thought he heard the sound of a door opening behind him but discounted it as just the whirlpool's jets blowing water to the surface. Beads of perspiration were beginning to form on his forehead, and his hand fumbled for the towel lying beside him. Just as he touched it he felt warm, slender fingers move down his forehead, along his nose, and on to his lips. He kissed them.

"Hello," Ivana whispered. "I hope I'm disturbing you."

"You are and I love it," he replied, holding her face in his hands.

Her lips pressed against his and he felt her naked body lowering into the water. The steam rising off the surface gave her face a soft glow as she moved her body gently over his. She was weightless, and her nipples brushed against his chest with a delicate sensation that was exquisite.

"Cognac," she murmured as her mouth found his and tasted his breath. "The perfect aphrodisiac."

Slowly her tongue moved over his lips until it found his. In a dance as delicate as a ballet, they circled and touched, withdrew, then touched. As the dance progressed, it reached a crescendo until delicateness and control gave way to sheer passion.

His hands moved over her body, feeling, touching, caressing. She moved back down over him and lowered herself onto her knees. Resting on his elbows with his body floating, she moved between his outstretched legs. Then he was inside her, floating effortlessly on the surface of the water. Swirling masses of bubbles enveloped them and they moved in an ever-quickening rhythm. The sound of the gushing jets was a roar in his ears. Ivana's mouth was open, but he didn't hear her cry out as she climaxed once and then again. Then he followed her with an orgasm that erupted as violently as the water rushing out of the jets around him.

Every part of his body luxuriated in a feeling of serene pleasure. Ivana moved alongside him and they lay together in the warm water, locked in an embrace.

"That was wonderful," she whispered. "I love making love in here."

"So do I," he replied. "There's something about warm water and sex that go hand in hand."

"I know," she said, turning to him. "I don't know why, but it's awfully good."

At moments like this he marveled at the body's capacity to experience pleasure. In just a few seconds it could be excited with great intensity. The heart raced, sending blood to each corpuscle to heighten the senses while at the same time the mind dulled, fading into a sensual daze. It all worked together to produce a symphony of ecstasy. He stretched his legs out into the warm water to feel the bubbles against his thighs. And then it came to him.

Yes, the way to find out what cards Hayden was holding didn't necessarily lie in the stack of reports beside him. And it didn't lie in sophisticated maneuvering and deception on both sides. It was in something much more basic; it was in pain. The body had a great capacity to feel pleasure, but it had an even greater capacity to feel pain. A man suffering unbearable pain was what would give him the answers he needed. He wished he had thought of it earlier, but there was still time.

He would call Colonel Zarov later in the evening and would find out the truth about this weapon. There was one man who knew what was on the film: James McFarland.

Yes, Mr. McFarland would tell him what he wanted to know.

Stamford, Connecticut

Chuck Atkins tried to hold his binoculars steady while he scanned the rolling waves in front of him. Somewhere ahead was red buoy number five, marking the entrance to Stamford Harbor.

The rain beat down heavily as his friend, Bob Lehman, steered the boat into four-foot waves. They were right in the middle of one of those unexpected squalls that hit Long Island Sound in the late fall. They should have stayed in the marina and readied the boat for the winter like they had originally planned, but the day had started out warm, and they decided to take one last sail across the Sound.

Now the sky had turned black, a large anvil-shaped cloud forming over the Connecticut coastline, a sure sign of a squall. As it came closer, the winds increased, forcing them to drop their sails and turn on the nine-horsepower outboard. The little Evinrude did its best against a rolling sea and thirty-mile-an-hour winds, but it was slow going all the way. Now it had turned dark and they were heading into a wall of darkness.

"Are you still on a 340 degree heading?" Chuck shouted back to Bob, who was leaning against the tiller, trying to hold the boat on course.

"Yeah, between waves I am. See anything yet?"

"No."

"Well, we better pretty soon or we're gonna find ourselves on the rocks."

"Tell me about it," Chuck answered as a wave came over the bow, heeling the boat onto its starboard side. It pushed him against the cabin bulkhead, knocking the glasses from his hands. Regaining his balance, he picked them up and stared out again into the darkness. Through the rain-spotted lens he saw a small red light flash and then disappear.

"That's it," he shouted. "Over there. To port. About eleven o'clock."

He kept the glasses on the position, afraid of losing it. Bob turned to the new heading and increased the speed. The light flashed again in Chuck's binoculars, this time revealing a stone breakwater behind it.

"See it now?" he called back to Bob.

"I got it. It's number five, all right. We just need to find the ramp now, and it's Miller time."

Bob guided the boat in behind the breakwater while Chuck went below to get the portable searchlight. The water was much calmer in the protected channel, and he was able to move about the cabin with ease. He took the red searchlight from beneath the chart table and went back on deck.

"Shine it along the port side," Bob said. "The launch ramp should be coming up any minute."

Chuck moved the light along the shoreline, and the number-three marker appeared through the rain. Beyond it was the ramp, which was illuminated by a streetlight on either side of it. As the boat came around the marker, he went up to the bow and readied the anchor. They had done this many times before. When the boat got in four feet of water, he would drop the anchor. Then he would wade ashore and back the trailer down the ramp. All Bob had to do was pull the anchor back up and motor on to the trailer. He dreaded going into the cold water, but there wasn't any other way.

"Okay, drop it," Bob shouted from the stern. Chuck let the anchor go and the boat backed off it, pulling the line taut. Sitting on the edge of the bow, he took off his sneakers and jumped into the forty-five-degree water. The rain was still coming down heavily as he waded through the muddy bottom. He could see it was low tide and that it would be difficult to get the boat in close to the ramp. As the water got shallower, he started to move faster. Dry clothes and a couple of beers were starting to look awfully good. Then suddenly he tripped and fell flat on his face into the mud.

Slowly he pushed himself back onto his knees. There was something in the water behind him, a black shape with white at the end of it. He crawled over and felt the black. It was cloth. He pulled at it and a man's head came up to the surface. Large white eyes stared at him. The mouth was open, frozen in what might have been a final scream.

Instinctively he let go of the jacket and the head fell back into the water. "Bob," he shouted as loud as he could. His stomach was retching and he felt like he was going to vomit. He yelled again and again but there wasn't any reply. The wind was howling even more now. Bob couldn't hear him.

He stood there for a moment, not knowing what to do. Finally he closed his eyes, took a deep breath, and grabbed the lapels on the man's jacket. Digging his heels into the sand, he tried to pull the body forward. It wouldn't move. Something was holding it in place. He felt underneath and found the man's hands tied behind him. Then, to his right, he saw the top of an old wood piling sticking out of the water. The other end of the rope was tied to it. Someone had taken great pains to insure that the body wouldn't wash out to sea. He untied the rope from the man's hands and slowly dragged him up onto the muddy beach.

In the light from the street he saw that he was about thirty and dressed in a dark blue suit. He reached into his jacket pocket and found a leather billfold. Inside was a plastic identification card. It had a picture on it, and the name of a firm located about two miles away in downtown Stamford. The firm was Space Technologies, Inc. The man was James McFarland.

8.

"DID YOU OVERHEAR him make any calls?"

"No."

"Were there any calls made at all?"

"Not that I remember."

"You mean to say that the three days you were in the apartment he didn't make any goddamn calls at all?"

"I don't know . . . I can't be sure."

"Well, think. Think hard. This all didn't happen six months ago, you know. You're supposed to be an actress. Where's your memory?"

"Well, maybe I fuckin' lost it, okay? Maybe your big fuckin' star witness here lost her memory. How d'ya like that? The whole country is going to go down the tubes now because I can't remember every goddamn detail you want me to."

Cheryl glared at the group sitting around the dining-room table. The table was filled with coffee cups, the air was filled with cigarette smoke, and her eyes hurt. Eight men had been alternately firing questions at her for over three hours now.

At first they had seemed reasonable, asking questions and accepting whatever she could remember. But as the morning went on, there were phone calls, and individual members of the group were called out of the room. When they returned, the pressure on them seemed to have been increased. Apparently it was coming from above, and then was passed on to her.

Frank LaSala got up from the table and walked over to a bay window that looked out on the backyard. The early-morning sun was streaming through some tall palm trees, sending long shafts of smoke-filled light into the room. His hands were on his hips and he stretched backward to loosen muscles that were aching from hours of sitting. His clothes looked like he had slept in them, and his hair was sticking up in five different directions. He straightened an indoor plant hanging in a pot and then turned to the group.

"Listen, I think we've reached a point here where it's getting a little nonproductive. Going on like this isn't serving any purpose except to get us all pissed off at each other. And if that happens, we're never going to find this guy at all."

He came around the table and looked for a place to sit closer to Cheryl. Finding nothing more comfortable than a corner of the hutch, he leaned against the edge of it.

"What's happening is that time is running out and we're getting desperate. Washington is climbing all over us, from the president on down. So we're looking for anything that will help us find Barry. Anything at all; even things you might think are insignificant might be important."

"But I told you, it's been five years since I lived with him. His whole life has changed."

"We realize that, and we're questioning other people who know him now. But you're the one he discussed the film with, and you were the last to see him. You're the one he talked to about returning the film. He didn't talk to anyone else but you.

"The other problem is that we can't launch an all-out effort to find him like we normally would. The most we can risk is to have the local authorities help us find the car and to quietly put Rossiter on a missing persons list. If the KGB finds out we're looking for him, then we become associated with the film. It has to continue to look like McFarland was passing that film on his own, that you intercepted it and still have it. And we have to stop Barry before they think otherwise."

"Look," she said, "I hope you guys aren't missing something

real simple, like just giving McFarland new film and having him go back to Armando's before Barry gets to them."

"Yeah, that would certainly be a simple solution," LaSala said, glancing quickly at the group. "A lab is working to get us another film, but we won't be able to use McFarland to get it to the Russians." He paused for a moment and then added, "McFarland is dead. We found out during the night."

Cheryl felt a chill run through her entire body. She saw McFarland standing in front of her that last night in Armando's, looking frightened. He had such a young, innocent face and she had wondered how he'd gotten involved with passing what she thought was cocaine. Now he was dead. She would be, too, if they had found her. They wouldn't stop at anything to get that film, and now she wondered about the men in this room. They were desperate too. She had the feeling that if she needed to be eliminated in order for them to succeed, then maybe she was expendable. She looked around the table. Every man was staring at her.

"What happened?" she asked. She was trembling in anticipation of what the answer would be.

"The KGB got to him," LaSala said in a soft voice. "Let's just say we know because it was evident that he was interrogated very heavily."

"Oh, my God," she said, putting both hands up in front of her face. She wanted to shut out this whole thing. She wanted to be back in her New York apartment, where she didn't have to worry whether she'd be dead or alive tomorrow.

But then she thought about what McFarland's death really meant. They'd said, ". . . interrogated very heavily." That sounded like a polite way of saying "tortured."

"How do you know he didn't tell them everything before he died?" she asked.

"We don't," LaSala said, accepting a cup of coffee from Jankowski, who had just come into the room. "But we have to assume that he didn't, or else we might as well pack it in right now."

He stopped for a moment, and Cheryl saw a quick look in his eyes that betrayed doubt about what he had just said. He went on, however.

"These next few days may just be an exercise in futility if

McFarland talked. But Washington's decision is to go on. The problem is, we don't have anything yet on Rossiter. So far he's vanished into thin air."

He stared at a pad filled with notes for a few moments, then turned again to Jankowski.

"Is somebody checking the airlines?"

"Yeah, Moscowicz just finished. Nothing."

"Did he go through the routine?"

"Males traveling alone, booked during the last twenty-four hours, destinations to cities with Soviet embassies or diplomatic agencies, he did the whole bit. The computer narrowed it down to just under eight hundred."

"That's about what I figured," LaSala said, tapping a pencil against the side of his cup. "I think all we can do now is wait for Rossiter to approach an embassy. With the limited facilities we have and the short amount of time, there's no way we'll get to him before that." He turned to Jim Sweeney. "Are all the taps operating?"

"Just three of them," Sweeney answered. "One in San Francisco, one in Chicago, and one in Riverdale, New York. The last one's an embassy residence, but we pick up good information there. It's a good source."

"So that leaves Dallas and Washington uncovered with taps."

"Right. We'll just have to watch those closely. In Washington we've got an informer working as a chef's assistant, and in Dallas we've got one internal bug inside a chandelier. It gets changed at the beginning of every month when it's dusted. But that's over two weeks away yet."

"We'll just have to watch them closely. Get them operating around the clock now. We'll have to take a chance that our Russian friends don't find the taps on."

He turned his attention back to Cheryl, who was fidgeting with a spoon. She was getting tired.

"Maybe we should focus on a different area," Jankowski offered. "Like the money. Did the two of you ever talk about what you'd do with any money you got from the Russians?"

"No, not really . . ." she answered, trying to remain alert. She'd never realized how tiring an interrogation could be. Trying to remember things that happened in the past was taxing her mind and draining her whole body. After a moment of thought she finished the sentence. "We didn't get into it because I kept insisting we turn the film over to the FBI."

"So he didn't suggest anyplace at all, like maybe Switzerland, the Bahamas, Monaco, or any of the more commonly known places to hide money."

"Not that I remember. We just never got that far. Our immediate concern was to find out what was on the film, and then we'd decide what to do with it."

"You never really talked about it, then."

"No," she answered. But then her eyes went up to the ceiling and darted around the room. LaSala could see she was processing many thoughts in her mind at once.

"There was something," she said, slowly trying to get the memory fixed in her mind. "Barry once mentioned—not this time, but when we were together five years ago—some bank in the Bahamas that was laundering money for the Mafia in Florida."

"What bank?"

"I don't know, some big bank—in Nassau, I think."

"The National Bahamian Bank?"

"Yeah, that could be it. Barry was really pissed off that a bank would actually help someone like the Mafia."

"Do you think he would remember that bank and try to use it now?"

"I wouldn't be surprised," she said with anger in her voice. "The son of a bitch remembers anything that could make him a buck. He'd file that away in the back of his brain for future use."

LaSala turned to Steve.

"Check out National Bahamian."

By late afternoon a feeling of helplessness came over the group. The dialogue around the table became strictly hypothetical. "He'll probably do this, but what if he does that? The odds are he'll go here, not there." Finally they all came to the simple conclusion that the best thing to do was nothing at all. They would just have to wait. If they were fortunate enough to intercept a call from Barry to the KGB, then they would have to act fast. But nothing could really be done in advance to prepare for it. Nobody knew how he would contact them, in what city or at what time.

Wait. It was all they could do. At five P.M. she was allowed to go up to her room. Her body was drained and her mind numb.

She lay on the bed, staring up at the ceiling. Nothing had really come out of the questioning that would lead them directly to Barry. The Bahamian bank had also been a dead end. They hadn't heard from anybody sounding like Barry but would contact LaSala if they did. It was decided, though, that by the time Barry called the Bahamas, he would be only hours away from turning over the film. It would be too late, anyway.

She watched a pattern of light move slowly back and forth across the ceiling. She had left the window shade open, and the setting sun was shining through a palm tree, its branches moving in the wind. Her eyes became heavy as she watched the gentle motion move from side to side. Then finally sleep came, a welcome escape from a day filled with the pressure of a thousand questions and no real answers.

Hours later Frank LaSala stood outside the safe house, looking at the full moon shining in the clear night sky. The gables of the French Victorian mansion jutted up into the perfect circle, making it look like a pie with triangular pieces missing from it. That's what he had: missing pieces; missing film, missing information, and a man on the loose who could put the country at a military disadvantage from which it would never recover.

He drew the collar of his windbreaker up around his neck and closed the top snap. The cool Los Angeles night was typical of this time of year, seventy-eight during the day and forty-five at night. Good weather for sleeping, if you could.

As he came around the back of the house he saw Moscowicz and Sweeney leaning against the wrought-iron gate at the end of the driveway. Their cigarettes glowed and illuminated their faces in the darkness.

There was a tall hedge to his left, casting long shadows out over the back lawn. He walked along it, staying in the darkness so he wouldn't be seen. He needed to be alone with his thoughts now. He needed a break from the others. Washington had been firing information and questions at him all afternoon. From the president on down, the urgent message had been the same: Find Rossiter, and destroy both him and the film.

That would take not only some good intelligence work but, more importantly, a lot of luck. And right now luck was heading toward Viktor Karpolov. In fact, Karpolov might have already learned everything he wanted to know. McFarland had been tortured with an electric fire starter. Twenty burn marks had been found on his body by the Stamford medical examiner.

LaSala reached into his jacket pocket and took out an old imitation leather wallet. Tucked in back of his credit cards was a small black-and-white photograph. He took it out and held it up to the light from the full moon. The edges were worn and the image was stained from age, but the two men standing arm in arm were clearly recognizable. He and Mark Ellis were in front of a beer hall in Berlin. They each held a stein and were raising it up in a toast. LaSala remembered that the picture was taken the day Mark died. The day Karpolov killed him.

Taped to the back of the picture was another one. It was from a newspaper and had faded to a yellowish brown. But the image was still clear enough for him to see those eyes that had haunted him for years.

He thought of them staring behind the .350 Magnum, and of the thin smile as he pulled the trigger. Those same fiery eyes had since ordered a red-hot fire starter pressed against the skin of another man just days ago. He thought of a film interview he had seen with Karpolov recently. How smug, how impeccably dressed, how well spoken and mannerly he had been. But underneath it all, those eyes were there, the eyes of a man obsessed with gaining power and stopping at nothing to get it.

He probably would never meet him face-to-face again. But he swore that he would do everything possible to prevent him from getting those missiles to Cuba—for the country and for Mark.

San Francisco

Jack Reynolds took the last mentholated cough drop from a bright yellow box and popped it into his mouth. One drop an hour for the last twelve hours had fought off the exhaust fumes from an Avis garage above him. As he started to suck on the drop, a piercing screech came through his earphones as another car tore down the ramp to be delivered to a customer.

This was the worst duty he could remember in fifteen years of working for the FBI. He had run phone taps in filthy holes in the wall all over the world, but this one took the cake. Twelve hours a day he sat at a broken-down wooden table in a space no bigger than four feet square. It was cold, a water pipe leaked down on him, and the exhaust fumes . . . they were unbearable. He looked at the digital clock on the recorder in front of him: 8:52. Just another eight minutes and his shift would be over.

The garage had an exhaust system that sucked fumes from the upstairs down into a filtering system that exited out the back of the building. But the vents leaked and fumes swirled around the basement. By late afternoon his eyes burned so much from the carbon monoxide, he had to go up into the street. If it weren't for those fifteen-minute breaks he took every two hours, he wouldn't have made it through the shift.

In the old days he wouldn't have been able to leave the room at all. The tapped line was kept closed until a call came in. Then it was manually activated before the receiver was picked up and the call recorded. The system prevented the suspect from checking for a tapped line when the phone wasn't being used. With the advent of fiber optics, the technology became much more sophisticated. Now the taps were done electronically. There were no wire connections at all, and everything was recorded on quarter-inch tape automatically. He really didn't have to be there, except in this case Washington wanted to know immediately if a particular call came in. Taps had been placed in every city with a Russian embassy or diplomatic agency. They were looking for a Barry Rossiter to make contact to sell top secret film. It was another CIA 01 Priority. Big deal. Lately they were all priority.

He was tired of listening. Over a hundred calls had come in during the twelve hours, most of them unimportant drivel. The bulk had been travel arrangements for diplomats leaving L.A. for a meeting in Washington. He never heard so many requirements for a hotel reservation. Did the hotel have a heated pool? Was there twenty-four-hour room service, valet service, and same-day dry cleaning? He loved these low-level Russian diplomats. Some of them had never been out of Russia, and when they got here, they went wild.

A few conversations were in Russian. Out of habit they sometimes reverted to their native tongue when they thought they were saying something important. But for the most part, the calls were a steady drone of political gossip. Who was being promoted or demoted in Moscow, and who was getting choice assignments?

At least it was a chance to use his Russian language skills, which, by the way, needed brushing up.

Reynolds heard a door close behind him and footsteps coming down the metal stairs. He didn't bother to look up. It would be his relief, Tony Parisi. For once he had gotten there on time. His earphones buzzed. A call was coming in on the line.

"Good evening, 555-7090," the slightly accented voice answered. Reynolds smiled. The Russian was tired. His shift ended at nine o'clock also.

"Is this the Russian consulate?" a voice asked. It was American, young and friendly.

"Yes, it is. To whom do you wish to speak?"

The line was always the same. "To whom do you wish to speak?" It was proper use of the word *whom* by this Russian automaton. Reynolds loved it. He turned and nodded to Parisi, who was taking off his rain-spattered coat. Christ, he had forgotten his umbrella.

"Well, I don't know," the voice continued. "I'm here in L.A. on business and have a client who loves Russian food. I thought someone there could recommend a good Russian restaurant."

Parisi leaned against the damp wall and opened up the *L.A. Times*. The space was so tight, he had the paper folded vertically. Reynolds saw half a headline: RUSSIANS MASS TROOPS INSIDE CZECHOSLOVAKIA.

There was an audible sigh from the Russian operator. Reynolds was already putting the call into a mind classification called "routine and unimportant." The operator's voice was a monotone as he gave his stock answer.

"I'm sorry, but we don't give out that information. I suggest you consult the telephone directory. You'll find many good restaurants listed there."

Parisi was unwrapping a hot pastrami sandwich. The aroma from it cut through the carbon monoxide, and Reynolds thought about the Italian restaurant he would stop in on his way back to the hotel. He barely heard the caller's next words.

"Well, a friend of mine, Armando Lucci in New York, suggested that you'd be able to recommend something really good for my client."

Reynolds watched Parisi bite into the sandwich and expertly flip the page of the paper with his other hand.

"Just one moment," the operator said. "I'm going to switch you over to someone who may be able to help you."

There was a long pause. Reynolds checked the digital readout on the recorder next to him to see if it was working. The frequency modulator moved back and forth, showing that the electronic impulses were being recorded. Reynolds decided he could use a good restaurant himself. He unplugged his headphones and laid them on the table. Turning to the last page of the logbook, he wrote in the time of the call and a brief description: "American looking for a good Russian restaurant."

"Anything interesting?" Parisi asked, munching on his sandwich.

"Twelve hours of listening to Russian soap operas, that's what. Same bullshit as yesterday," Reynolds answered, getting up from his backbreaking wooden chair.

"No Rossiter, huh?"

"Everything but. This last guy's asking them to recommend a good Russian restaurant and they're doing it. It'll be the Volga Boatman again. It's the only one they know."

"Yeah," Parisi replied. "Haven't been there myself. The prices scare me."

"Right now I'll settle for Pietro's down the street," Reynolds replied. "Some good wine and a veal saltimbocca will do just fine."

"I'm staying with sandwiches. I need to lose all the weight I can to fit into this place," Parisi said, surveying the cramped area.

Reynolds moved aside so his relief could sit down in the chair.

"Well, at least you won't have the fumes to deal with tonight. It'll be slow upstairs until morning."

"The log up-to-date?" Parisi asked, putting his sandwich on the top page.

"Yeah, just put down the time that this last call stops recording."

"When do we submit what we have so far?"

"It can wait till morning, unless you get something hot during the night." Reynolds looked at Parisi's wet jacket.

"By the way, can I borrow your umbrella?"

"No."

"Why not?"

"See that pipe there?"

"Yeah, it leaks."

"That's why you can't borrow my umbrella."

Reynolds laughed and patted his partner on the shoulder. As he started up the metal staircase Barry Rossiter finished his call.

San Francisco

The man in the back of the crowded elevator adjusted his wire-framed glasses farther up on his nose, then glanced at the woman beside him. She smiled pleasantly, then resumed her study of the floor indicator arrow, which was flashing toward the letter *L*. A bell sounded and the elevator gently came to rest on the ground floor of the Mark Hopkins Hotel. The door opened and Barry Rossiter stepped into the elegant lobby.

There was a long line of people checking in that stretched across the entire room. He excused himself to cut through it and hurried for the front door, which was already being opened for him. The doorman was a tall black man dressed in a burgundy-colored tuxedo with gold trim. Barry stopped outside the door and turned to him.

"Can you tell me how to get to Ghirardelli Square?"

"Yes, sir. Go to your right to the next block. That's Powell. Make a left down the hill. The square is about a ten-minute walk. Or if you prefer, take the Powell Street cable car. It's right there on the corner."

"Thank you."

The street was crowded. Good. That's where he wanted to be, in a crowd. There would be less chance of his being spotted. But the hardest part was over. He had made it through two airports without being recognized. That's where the FBI would most likely have been, but apparently the glasses and dyed hair had worked. Either that, or Cheryl was very late in contacting them.

There wasn't any doubt in his mind that she had called the FBI. It was the only choice she had without the film. Besides, after what he had done, she'd help them in any way she could to hang him by his balls. He smiled to himself. Tough little Cheryl. She thought she was so street-smart. Miss Independent. Knew her way around the world. Well, she had always been a naïve, frightened child inside. And she still was.

Sometimes it touched him and he felt sorry for her, like when she had called. And for a while he thought maybe they had something going between them. They could have lived the rest of their lives as millionaires, but she never would have had the guts to do it. And besides, why should he split millions with her? He didn't need her anymore, just like she suddenly hadn't needed him six years ago. Fuck her. He smiled to himself. That's just what he had done.

At the corner of Powell he looked to his right and saw a cable car coming down the hill, its lights reflecting off the tracks ahead of it. He looked at his watch. His instructions were to make contact with the restaurant before eleven o'clock. It was almost ten-forty. The cable car stopped and he jumped on. There were some seats in the rear and he rushed to get the last one. "Stay close to people," he said to himself. "Blend in."

The car started down Powell Street, its bells ringing. At the end of the block it braked suddenly and a woman bumped against him. She excused herself, and he felt in his pocket for the piece of hotel stationery that had a number he was to call on it. He took it and moved it to his breast pocket, which had a zipper. It would be secure there.

Ahead, he could see Ghirardelli Square. The lights from the buildings reflected off the bay like fireflies dancing on the water. Thousands of people looked like dots of color from an Impressionist painting. He had seen in the paper that the stores in the square would be open until eleven o'clock that evening. Good. Crowds. He needed them.

As soon as he got off the cable car, he saw a telephone booth. It was an enclosed one with graffiti smeared over the Plexiglas doors. He went inside and took the crumpled paper from his pocket. The name and number had been written quickly, and he was barely able to read his own writing. Holding the paper directly under the overhead light, he finally was able to make it out: The Volga Boatman, 555-3860.

He dialed the number. It rang three times, and finally he heard an accented voice.

"Volga Boatman. May I help you?"

"Yes, I'm a friend of Mr. Armando Lucci. I was told by the Russian Diplomatic Office to make a reservation tomorrow evening for two."

"Ah, yes," the voice answered quickly. "One moment please."

He waited. A group of teenagers walked by. One was carrying a portable stereo that was blaring out a heavy-metal number. The sound blocked out everything for a moment, and he hoped they would keep moving. They did.

"Mr. Hines?" a voice asked as he picked up the phone at the restaurant.

"Yes," Barry replied, suddenly remembering that he had used that name when he'd called the consulate.

"This is Andreas Dukoff. We spoke earlier in the evening at the embassy. Are you calling from a phone booth?" Again Barry was surprised at the agent's English. There was hardly the trace of an accent.

"Yes."

"Very good. I've relayed what you told me to my superiors and we're interested in talking further with you."

"Good," Barry replied. He heard his own breathing in the telephone receiver. It was hurried, and he felt the receiver shaking against his ear.

"You said you have the information we were to have received in New York. Is that true?"

"That's correct," he said too quickly. He was aware that his nervousness was beginning to show through. "I have the film." He had already anticipated what the next questions would be and had rehearsed his answers.

"How did you obtain the film?"

"From Cheryl Branigan."

He could see what Dukoff was thinking. Cheryl's name was further verification that he wasn't some crank caller.

"I see," the agent said slowly. "And where is Miss Branigan now?"

"With me."

"What is on the film?" The question was blunt, and it was asked with a tone of desperation that caused Barry to relax a little. He was the one in command, not them. This guy had his bosses breathing down his neck, and they needed to know what was on that film.

"You'll find out tomorrow evening," he said with a confidence that surprised him.

"We need to know now" came the reply. "My superiors need some indication of what you have."

"They'll just have to wait until tomorrow."

There was silence on the other end of the line. Finally Dukoff replied, "Very well. We'll meet at the Volga Boatman at the predetermined time, eight o'clock. You will bring the film." There was a curious mixture of resignation and determination in his words.

"I'll be there," Barry answered, and hung up the phone.

There was a click on the other end of the line. Barry opened the door of the booth and the din of the crowded square rushed in. He let out a long breath and stepped outside. The conversation had lasted only a few minutes, but he felt it had been much more. Nevertheless, he decided he had handled it well.

Tomorrow he would give the Russians more information than they could ever hope for. They expected no more than the film they had lost to be returned. But he was going to sell them much more than that. He was going to prove that the United States didn't have the means to stop them from doing whatever they wanted to militarily. Their one deterrent was nothing more than a piece of film created with sophisticated trick photography.

And he could prove it.

Moscow

Colonel Dimitri Zarov stood at the living-room window of his small apartment, watching the street ten stories below. It was five A.M. and the apartment buildings along Sadovaya Boulevard were tall, dark, rectangular shapes rising up to a black sky. The only light was from the streetlights that stretched like a string of pearls to the Hotel Peking in Mayakovsky Square. That was always lit up. Foreign correspondents staying there kept the bar open until dawn.

Zarov's small apartment was dark except for a light in the bathroom. Even though he was high above the street, he avoided becoming a silhouette in a lit window. Intense KGB training over twenty years ago had never left him.

He straightened his red-and-gold tie and buttoned the ill-fitting jacket over it. A colonel's pay never had been enough to afford a good suit. His was still Russian. If you wanted anything with style, it had to be imported. Generals wore them, high-ranking government officials wore them; maybe after today he would too. Maybe by next week he would *be* a general. All it involved was continuing to break a few rules.

An hour ago telecommunications at Dzerzhinsky Square had called him. A coded message had been received from Andreas Dukoff in San Francisco, saying that a man had contacted them, claiming to have the film that had been stolen in New York. The man was going to deliver it to them at eight P.M. San Francisco time, about eighteen hours from now. He immediately issued orders for the drop to be secured. Agents were to be brought up from Los Angeles if needed. Direct lines to Moscow were to be kept open on the prime communications satellite until the drop was made. They would risk Washington monitoring it.

As soon as he hung up, he had called Karpolov. Even at three A.M. he had been sharp and alert.

"Karpolov here." The words were always distinct and enunciated. Perfect diction twenty-four hours a day. He remembered other days when they were roommates over twenty-five years ago at the Voltaya Academy outside Leningrad. Viktor had come to the school from a small town in Moldavia and spoke in a Ukrainian regional dialect. "Farmer boy. He's a farmer boy with potatoes in his mouth," the upper classmen had said. They taunted him unmercifully day after day. But it didn't last for long. Viktor managed to borrow one of the two tape recorders in the school and stood before it for hours, ridding himself of the dialect. Karpolov had used him as a sounding board, sometimes as late as three or four in the morning. Within three months all traces of the dialect were gone. Viktor hadn't stopped using him since. And now he was doing it again, this time with the possibility of dire consequences.

He told Karpolov about the message received from San Francisco and what orders he had issued. Viktor was at first elated. If the film supported that the weapon didn't exist, the timing was perfect. He could use it as further evidence of U.S. military deficiency and send the ships off to Cuba with complete confidence. But then there was silence on the other end of the line. He knew what Karpolov was thinking. Maybe the film would prove otherwise. If that happened, the timing would be disastrous.

Karpolov's orders came quickly, one on top of the other. He was giving Zarov complete charge of the San Francisco operation, directing it all through Dukoff. At its conclusion the film was to be transmitted to him directly for evaluation. In the meantime the operation would remain in Code 3 status and not come under POL-1 review.

Zarov refused. There would have to be POL-1 Politburo approval before he would take any more responsibility.

Karpolov had shot back with the fact that he was already responsible for two other directives previously carried out: the ordering of New York agents to find the film, and the murder of James McFarland. Both had been failures—his failures. He would deny any participation or knowledge of them.

Zarov had gotten irate and yelled at Karpolov over the phone. Yes, he had carried out his despicable order to have McFarland tortured, and it hadn't gotten them anything. The man had died defending the fact that the weapon was real. So what. It didn't prove anything except that it was one other fact that had to be hidden from the Politburo. He had gone far enough. He wouldn't hide anything more.

Karpolov's final words had been soft and completely in control. Even though he was totally discarding over twenty-five years of friendship, they were emotionless, cold—and, to Zarov, devastating.

"I will wait two hours and then I will send a coded message to Dukoff in San Francisco," he had said. "If the operation is not in motion by then, I will order your arrest for withholding military information from both me and the Politburo. Within twenty-four hours you'll be in prison, awaiting a trial that won't take place until the ships are in Cuba."

And then, in a more conciliatory tone, he had added, "Be reasonable. You don't know what's on the film. It may very well support my position and will go to the Politburo, anyway. Next week you could be a general."

"No," was the reply.

"You leave me no choice," he had said.

"Very well," Zarov had answered, and hung up. Then he had disconnected a cord from the receiver that led to a small cassette tape recorder.

Now he held it in his hand as he saw his car pull up under the streetlight. Even though he despised Karpolov for what he had said, the fact remained that no one knew what was on the film yet. He was in too deep now. He had to go along for now until he knew more. Maybe the real answers would come that night. Maybe the film was a phony. Alerting the Politburo would then be entirely stupid.

He walked over to the hall closet, put on his topcoat, and placed the tape in the inside pocket. He would bring it to the office and lock it up for safekeeping. It wasn't needed now, but it might be in the near future.

9.

CHERYL RUSHED DOWN the stairs of the safe house carrying a small overnight bag. Jankowski was right behind her with two other suitcases. He was moving so quickly, he practically pushed her down the stairs. LaSala was waiting at the bottom.

"C'mon, let's move it! We gotta get out of here!" he was shouting. "The car's been waiting five minutes already. Let's go!"

"Jesus, it's four in the morning. What d'ya expect? I don't even know if I packed everything," she answered, zipping up the top pocket of her handbag.

"It doesn't matter," he said, holding the screen door open for her. "Just get in the car."

She hurried outside into the darkness. Three cars were already lined up with their lights on. Jankowski helped her into the lead one, threw her luggage in the trunk, and got in beside her. LaSala squeezed in on the other side, slammed the door, and told Jesse Moscowicz, the driver, to move.

The car spun around the circular driveway and sped toward the main gate, gravel flying behind it. It made a left turn and, with a screech of tires, headed down a narrow residential street toward Van Nuys.

Cheryl sat pressed between the two agents as the car swerved
left and right, making its way through a maze of back streets.
Finally they turned on to Lankershim Boulevard and began a
straight run through intersections with blinking caution lights. She
shifted in the seat to get more room and then turned to LaSala,
who was opening his battered briefcase.

"Are you going to tell me what this is all about or what?" she
asked. "Steve, here, comes banging on my door and tells me to
pack up and get downstairs. Just like that. No warning, no
nothing. What the hell is going on?"

"Barry is what's going on," LaSala said, calmly taking a small
cassette player from the briefcase. "He made contact with the
KGB earlier this evening."

"You found him?" she asked. There was a mixture of surprise
and satisfaction in her voice. "Where is he?"

"In San Francisco. He called the Soviet Diplomatic Agency
there, and we intercepted it on a phone tap. The call almost
slipped by the first agent who heard it, but his relief got bored
around midnight and replayed an earlier tape. Thank God he was
alert and found it."

"Is that where we're going now, San Francisco?"

"As fast as we can get there," LaSala answered, taking a quick
look at his watch. "There's a plane waiting at the Van Nuys airport
that'll get us there in about forty minutes, but right now I want you
to listen to this tape. We need to be absolutely sure it's Barry."

He turned on the tape and then added, "The quality's pretty
bad. It was taken over the phone from one tape to another, but I
think it's good enough for you to hear."

Barry's voice came crackling over the small speaker. Even with
the poor quality she could sense his nervousness.

". . . but a friend of mine in New York, Armando Lucci, said
you'd be able to recommend something really good for my
client."

"Ah, Mr. Lucci. Just one moment," a Russian voice replied.
"I'm going to switch you over to someone who may be able to
help you."

The tape was silent now. Cheryl stared at it and felt the anger
of yesterday all over again. Just the sound of Barry's voice
brought back all the hatred she felt for him. It brought back his
lies, his deceit, his hands and body all over her.

"It's him," she said softly. "There's no question about it. The son of a bitch is as clever as ever. Using Lucci's name as an introduction was pretty goddamn smart."

LaSala cursed the FBI agent who had missed the call completely. The KGB operator had been a lot more alert.

Cheryl listened as the second agent came on the line. This one spoke perfect English and was thoroughly prepared to deal with the caller.

"Good evening, sir," he said in a confident tone. "My name is Andreas Dukoff. I understand you know Mr. Lucci in New York."

"Yes," Barry answered. "He suggested you might be able to recommend a good Russian restaurant here. My client is arriving—"

"Ah, yes, your client, I know," Dukoff interrupted. "I would suggest Mr., uh . . ."

"Hines."

"Yes, Mr. Hines. Your client might enjoy the Volga Boatman on Janes Street. The food is excellent and the atmosphere is very Russian. On weeknights three cossack dancers put on a performance that's quite unique. They'll be there tomorrow night. I suggest you call and make a reservation about an hour and a half from now. They won't be very busy then."

"I see," Barry said a little tentatively. Apparently Dukoff was writing the information down. "Would you say that eight o'clock would be a good time for dinner?"

"Yes, but do call them tonight in about an hour and a half."

"I will, and thank you. You've been very helpful."

"Please send my regards to Mr. Lucci in New York," the agent said, with emphasis on the words *Mr. Lucci.*

There was the sound of a dial tone and then the tape stopped. LaSala switched off the recorder and turned to Cheryl.

"So now you know why we got you out of bed at four in the morning. Our friend Barry is going to meet with the Russians in about fifteen hours, and between now and then we have to work out a way to stop him."

"Well, at least you know where they're going to meet," Cheryl said hopefully.

"Maybe," Jankowski answered, rubbing his eyes, which were tired from only two hours' sleep. "Don't forget we didn't hear the second call Barry made an hour and a half later. The meeting place could have been switched to another location if they were afraid of a tap."

"What do you do then?"

"Nothing," LaSala said, clicking his briefcase closed. "All we can do is try to stop him from making the eight-o'clock drop at the restaurant. That's going to be tough enough. You can bet the KGB is going to have that place covered from top to bottom." He leaned forward in the seat to speak to Moscowicz, who was trying to pass a truck taking up two lanes.

"How close are we to the airport, Jess?"

"About five minutes, if we can get around this guy," he answered as he leaned on the horn.

"Good. When we get there, call San Francisco and tell them it's a positive identification on Rossiter. Also that the command post has to be as close as possible to the Volga Boatman Restaurant. We don't want communications running five or six blocks. Make sure they know that."

"Got it," Moscowicz answered as he swerved around the truck and sped through a red light.

"What about San Francisco P.D.? Who's contacting them?" he asked Jankowski.

"Kovacs spoke to them about twenty minutes ago. They'll cooperate, but they want an official request from the FBI office there. This is where all the political shit starts to happen."

"Well, we don't have time for it," LaSala said, banging his hand down on the briefcase. "If we have to go through all this bureaucratic crap, the whole deal is going to slip through our fingers."

"What about Shupe? Can he help?"

"Yeah," LaSala replied in a calmer voice. "He's already spoken to Craig, the FBI chief there, but I'll get him to light a fire under the locals too—"

"I thought you had to keep this all secret from the local police," Cheryl interrupted. "You said that if the KGB found out you were involved, it would blow the whole thing."

"That was last night. It's gone way beyond that now. If we're going to stop Barry from getting to that restaurant, we're going to need help, and that will mean taking some risks. There just isn't any other way to do it."

The car swerved to the left as they entered the small airport. It was totally dark except for a few buildings across the field. Red and green lights flickered in the distance, outlining the one runway in operation. Moscowicz drove by a row of large hangars and headed for one off to the left, where there were lights on inside.

"You're going to kill Barry, aren't you," she said without looking at either of them.

LaSala was staring at the hangar up ahead. He was silhouetted against the lights, and for the first time she saw that the normally friendly face had the lines of a killer. The eyes had narrowed and the jaw was set and determined. His shoulders were squared and his body alert, as if it were ready to pounce at the first sign of its prey.

"We're going to try not to," he said hesitantly, "but if we have to . . . we will."

She looked at the darkened face and a shudder of fear ran through her body. What about her? She knew the truth about the weapon, just as Barry did. Would they do the same thing to her? Would they kill her if they had to? LaSala turned and their eyes met. He said nothing.

As they pulled up to the hangar a small business jet parked on the tarmac started its engines. The fuselage door opened and a dark figure waved them over to the boarding ramp. As each of the three cars pulled up behind them LaSala yelled to the men to forget the vehicles and just get on the plane. Within minutes they were inside, their equipment stored in the belly, and the plane roared down the runway.

Washington, D.C.

In a small dining room down the hall from the Oval Office, President Hayden was having a breakfast meeting with the governors of New York, Connecticut, and New Jersey. A new transit bill had just reached the floor of the House, and they were lobbying for his support. He sat across the table from them sipping coffee and nibbling on a Danish. It was as if he were watching a silent movie. Their lips were moving but he didn't hear a word they were saying. His mind was three thousand miles away, thinking about what was happening in a safe house in California.

Another report from intelligence in Tallinn through Prague had arrived earlier. All six vessels were fully loaded with SRV-60 missiles, their crews aboard and ready. No one was allowed on or off the ships except the highest authorities. October 22 was only five days from now.

There had been no response from the Kremlin regarding orders for the 181st Airborne. The information had been released to the media twenty-four hours ago, but surprisingly, Moscow had remained silent.

Sentinel IV, the Air Force's newest reconnaissance satellite, had been reorbited to pass over Tallinn. Photographs of the docks with resolution sharp to ten meters would be available in the morning.

Alan Benton, the governor of Connecticut, was speaking. Hayden heard a word here and there, enough to get the sense of what he was saying. If government funds weren't imminent, service on his commuter railroad would have to be cut seventeen percent, which would affect over fifty thousand passengers along the shoreline.

"I realize that, Governor," Hayden replied. "I'll take it under consideration." It was a stock answer, but enough to get him off his back.

Transit money, the environment, road construction. All these issues seemed minuscule compared to the crisis Hayden now faced. If these men knew how desperate the situation was, they wouldn't even be having this meeting. The only reason they were was because the president had to maintain a schedule, as if nothing were happening. That would continue until the media found out about the Russian missiles. Then all hell would break loose.

Benton started on another tack, talking about how little government had given him for road construction, which was forcing people to use mass transit. Hayden nodded his head in response and then heard a knock on the door. His aide, Ted Miklos, asked permission to come into the room and Hayden motioned him in. Miklos handed him a folded piece of paper with perforations on the edges, which meant it was fresh out of a Telex machine. He hadn't even bothered to tear them off.

"Excuse me, gentlemen," he said politely as he quickly read the three lines of capitalized type.

ROSSITER LOCATED AND IDENTIFIED.

HE WILL TRY TO MAKE CONTACT WITH THE SOVIETS THIS EVENING.

CALL ME FOR DETAILS.
      SHUPE

He nodded to Miklos and put the paper in his pocket. Within ten minutes he had forced the meeting to a close and told his secretary to get Shupe on the phone. Maybe they still had a chance of stopping Rossiter before it was too late.

San Francisco

Cheryl stood in front of a picture window twelve stories above the city and watched the sun coming up over Sausalito. The lights of the Bay Area slowly disappeared as the reds and oranges of the sun grew brighter. The Bay Bridge turned from a rust-colored brown to a glistening gold dotted with specks of white from the headlights of early-morning traffic. Dawn, the start of a new day, one that was destined to be one of the worst of her life.

She looked down at the street below. It was empty except for a moving van that was pulling up in front of the building. Farther down the block, filled with shops and boutiques, she could see the sign above the Volga Boatman Restaurant. Yellow neon formed the shape of a gondola that flashed on and off over ornate lettering.

Two men got out of the moving van and started to unload some large boxes. The S.F.P.D. was on the ball. This was the equipment LaSala needed. Cheryl turned around and looked at the large, empty room behind her. Three days ago it had been a bustling accounting firm. In a few hours it would be a command post.

The group had spread out into rows of empty modular cubicles to use phones that were lying on the floor. Most of them sat cross-legged against the walls with their briefcases open beside them. LaSala was in a corner office that still had an old desk in it. He was taping a map of the city to a metal cabinet. Cheryl walked over to the office, stepping over some aluminum partition frames and workmen's tools that had been left behind.

"The trucks are here," she said, standing in the doorway.

"Good, they're right on time," LaSala answered, drawing a

circle around the area they were in. It was the Russian Hill section, just west of Chinatown. "Is Sweeney out there?"

"Yes," she answered. "He just came back with some coffee and pastry."

"Would you have him show the moving guys where to put the equipment?"

"Sure."

He continued to work on the map without looking back at her. Since they had left L.A., she had sort of integrated into the group. The way LaSala ran it, there wasn't much choice. Everyone had their job, and it all worked smoothly as a team effort. After a while she found herself caught up in it and was responding instinctively. In a way it was good, because it kept her mind active and she didn't have time to feel the danger around her. But at the same time she realized that tonight these men would kill to destroy evidence. After that there was only one person left who knew as much as Barry did.

Her.

She went over to Sweeney's cubicle, but he was already out in the hallway, meeting the movers at the elevator. They were bringing three large boxes in on a dolly, and Sweeney had them put in a small interior office that must have been a file room. While the movers went back for another load he and Moscowicz began unpacking them. They took four small television monitors from one and a large radio with all sorts of dials on it from the other. There were cables, microphones, and headsets inside another box, which they spread out over a folding table. Then they began hooking it all up.

There were still three cups of coffee left on Sweeney's desk, along with some pastries. She took a coffee and a Danish and went into one of the cubicles. It was empty except for a moving carton and a disconnected telephone. Using the carton as a table, she sat down on the floor next to it. This was breakfast. It wasn't elegant but it was breakfast.

"This must be the company dining room. Mind if I join you?"

She looked up. Jankowski was standing in the doorway with a coffee cup in his hand.

"Not at all," she said, pointing to the space beside her. "Pull up a seat."

He smiled and sat down on the other side of the carton.

"How are you holding up?" he asked, stirring his coffee with a plastic stirrer.

"Okay, I guess . . . considering."

She looked at him. He was still intent on stirring the coffee. It was obvious he had come in to be friendly but didn't know where to start the conversation.

"Actually I'm scared out of my mind if you want an honest answer," she said.

He looked at her and smiled. Even though he wasn't particularly handsome, there was something about him that was appealing. Still, she couldn't really trust any of them. They were friendly now because they needed her. That could all change in a few days.

"I didn't get the feeling there were too many things that frightened you," he replied.

"I show a tough exterior, but when it comes to fingering someone I've lived with for five years, I turn to mush," she said sarcastically.

"We've got to get him and the film," he answered, watching the steam curl over the rim of his cup. He seemed to be carefully forming a new thought in his mind but was unsure whether to verbalize it or not. "We're going to attempt to capture Barry tonight," he said, avoiding her eyes, "but there's a possibility that we won't be able to take him alive."

"You mean, you might kill him?" The words came out in a gasp and she barely understood them herself.

"We don't know," he said softly. "The plan is simply to snatch him off the street, but if the Russians get too close and we're in danger of losing the film . . . yes, we'll have to kill him."

She had thought about the possibility and it had sickened her. Identifying him was one thing, but killing him . . . just the thought of it made her tremble.

"I didn't think the CIA just went around killing Americans."

"This time we may have to."

Cheryl was surprised at her own feelings. Here she was, afraid for Barry's life, when hours ago she would have sooner seen him dead. But that was only a figure of speech. This was real. Tonight they might have to kill him and she was going to help them do it. How would she justify it in her own mind? As revenge for his having taken her body and then leaving her? Was it to keep the Russians from learning that a weapon didn't exist and saving the country from a military disaster, or was it something more basic? Was it simply to help stop him so she wouldn't also be killed? Survival. Yes, that was it, the basic instinct to survive.

"And if you kill him, what about the other people who know? What about me?" she asked. "Am I in danger of being killed so I won't tell them what I know, either? Can you point a gun at me and pull the trigger so I won't tell them anything?"

He took a sip of his coffee. She interpreted it as buying time to consider his answer.

"No," he said finally. "I couldn't do that, and I don't think anyone else could, either. Not after you've helped us find Barry and returned the film to the Russians. On the other hand, I don't think you're going to walk away from this scot-free, but you're not in any danger from us."

"So I'll go to jail."

"I don't know. You may be just kept under house arrest. They do that in a lot of cases like this. But it's up to Frank and the CIA director, Donald Shupe."

She thought about what he had said. House arrest was a better deal than she would have gotten for passing cocaine. They would have put her in jail for that and thrown away the key. Now what they'd probably do was keep her under guard somewhere until it didn't matter whether the Russians knew they had the weapon or not. Maybe it would only be a year or two. Not bad, considering.

"Well, let's hope it's a nice house," she said, finishing her coffee.

They sat quietly for a moment without saying anything. He seemed to be considering his next question.

"I've wondered," he said hesitantly, "what made you get into passing what you thought was cocaine? You're good-looking, intelligent, talented, and nice. What made you get mixed up in something like that?"

"Everything you just mentioned."

"I don't understand," he said, crossing his legs so he was sitting Indian style.

"You think I'm good-looking? There are thousands of girls in New York who are better-looking. They got the acting jobs I was looking for because they had great bodies. And in some cases they were willing to use them when I wasn't. Intelligent? Not really. Maybe street-smart but not intelligent enough to hold my own with really sophisticated New Yorkers. And talented? Ha . . . that's what really surprised me, not being talented at all."

"What do you mean? You told me you were in a Broadway show for over a year."

"Yeah, in a bit part. Two lines. Not what you would call your big starring role."

She drew her knees up close to her body and rested her chin on them. "You see, I wanted all the good things in life that come with success and talent. Since I couldn't get them on my own, I simply decided to take them. There I was, working in Armando's in order to have a few luxuries, and coke was passing right through my fingers; hundreds of thousands of dollars four or five times a year. I'm no coke dealer. Nor am I a user. And I resented the fact that Armando, that sleaze, was forcing me to get involved in his dealings. Many times I thought of quitting my job, but then I got a brainstorm. Armando was a cold-blooded crook. And stealing from a crook couldn't be that big a crime. So I stole the cocaine to get all the things that my lack of looks and talent would never get me."

She shrugged and looked around the empty room.

"But I never thought Armando would be passing military secrets mixed in with his drugs."

"Yeah," Jankowski said sympathetically. "But if it was really the money you wanted, why didn't you go along with Barry when he first wanted to sell the film to the Russians?"

"Listen," she said, raising her voice. "He was asking me to do something a lot bigger than passing drugs. It scared me to death even to think about it. Passing drugs is one thing, but selling military secrets to the Russians is another. I couldn't walk around with that on my conscience."

She leaned her head back against the wall and let out a deep sigh.

"But then I thought, once I called you, that would be it. Instead this horror is just continuing. Tonight I'll have to identify Barry so you can capture him or even kill him. I really don't know if I can do it."

"You'll have to do it," he said, crumpling the paper cup in his hand, "and so will I."

"What do you mean?" she asked.

He looked at her, and she noticed something different about his eyes. There was a sadness in them but there was also something else. Yes. It was fear. When he answered, his voice was so soft, she barely heard the words.

"If he can't be captured and has to be killed . . . I'm the one who has to do it."

By noon the room was a flurry of activity. Technicians from S.F.P.D.'s surveillance team were working with LaSala's communications men to set up video and audio relays. Bud Kovacs's agents were dressing as workmen and delivery people. Cables were being run for a transmitter on the roof. LaSala and Jankowski were finishing a meeting with a police battalion commander to coordinate their men's assignments. There were about thirty people in all.

LaSala looked out the glass windows of his office onto the assembled group. So far everything was going well. Careful planning during the night over the telephone had paid off. Little things, such as having the men arrive individually or in small groups, hadn't disturbed the normal routine of the neighborhood of small businesses. Most were told to wear business suits, as if they were going to work in either the law or the accounting firm in the building. Equipment, along with any change of clothes, had been carried in a briefcase or a gym bag. The KGB was watching the street. That he could be sure of.

He was playing a very delicate game. Not only did he have to stay out of sight of the KGB, he couldn't tell S.F.P.D. or even some of the federal agents what was really happening. All they knew was that a man was about to make a drop that contained top secret information at the restaurant. They were to assist his men in subduing him.

LaSala walked into the main room. Off in a corner there were some empty cartons on which he put his map. It was now filled with a maze of red circles and intersecting lines. As he turned around to the men the room quieted down. Activity came to a halt.

"All right, everyone, after five o'clock we're on alert until the target shows up. It's supposed to be at eight, but it could be later."

He put his hands in his pockets and took a few steps out toward the group. He noticed that Cheryl had come into the room and was sitting off in a corner, next to Jankowski.

"Now, you all know that the target is carrying film to be delivered to the Volga Boatman. It's a KGB drop, and they'll be all around the place like flies. Their advantage? They know exactly when he's coming. Our advantage? We have a young lady here who can identify him. They don't know what he looks like."

He turned to the darkened room behind him, where the glow from four TV screens could be seen.

"Our video communications room is set up now. It'll receive transmissions from three cameras trained on the target's most likely approaches into the area. The fourth camera is in a California Electric van that will track him once he's been located."

Using a small wooden ruler as a pointer, he referred to the map.

"We're covering a four-block-square area from Washington Street on the north to California on the south, Kearney on the west to Battery on the east. Only one cable car comes directly into the area—the California Street one. The most likely approach from there would be through Washington Street, so we've positioned a camera in a blind on the roof at the corner of Washington and Montgomery. The other main intersections are California and Kearney, and here, the corner of Clay and Kearney. There's one camera in a parked van at California and Kearney; the one at Clay is in a vacant apartment."

He paused for a moment and looked across the group.

"Any questions about the camera locations?" There were none.

"Okay, audio communications. At five o'clock we're putting four men on the street with buttonhole microphones. We're going to select men who're familiar with KGB agents working in California, in order to try to identify them. If they spot someone, they'll radio in the location, and at six, the mobile camera will make a sweep to photograph them. We'll continue to monitor their positions until the target enters the area."

"What if we're spotted by a KGB agent? They're going to be playing the same game with us," one of Kovacs's agents asked.

"We just can't let that happen," LaSala answered emphatically. "S.F.P.D's undercover squad has provided us with everything from beards to motorcycle jackets. Use them."

"What about frequencies and code identification?" another agent asked.

"That'll all be gone over later, when you receive your individual assignments."

He reached into a manila folder and took out a small photograph. "The target, as you know, is attempting to deliver top secret information to the KGB. He'll probably be carrying a package containing two videocassettes, so look for something that size. His name is Barry Rossiter, he's thirty-two years old, five-foot-ten, about one seventy, medium build, brown hair, brown eyes. I have a picture taken from his apartment, that appears to be about two years old. I'll pass it around."

LaSala handed the picture to the man closest to him and then turned back to the map to explain the options should the target take a particular route. Cheryl watched as the picture was passed around the room. Each man took a quick look and then directed his attention back to LaSala. Finally it made its way around to her. It was the picture that had been on Barry's bedroom dresser. He was standing next to his sailboat, which now looked to be about thirty feet long. The sun was shining and she could see that flags on some of the other boats in the marina were blowing in a brisk wind. He looked happy standing there in a bright yellow tank top and cutoff jeans. Now she noticed there was a pink boat bag lying on the deck. A woman's floppy hat was on top of it along with a flowery print shirt. That day Barry had had everything—the boat, the wind, and whoever had taken the picture. She passed it on to Jankowski.

Her attention returned to LaSala, who had turned away from the map and was now addressing the men directly. "Now, one last word about what this guy is carrying," he began. His voice was softer now, and some of the men in the back strained to hear him. "Obviously it's important or we wouldn't have scrambled like we did to put this whole thing together. Also, it's obvious that an operation like this should have been planned days in advance, not hours. But hours are all we've got, so we have to make the best of it."

He took off his bifocals and put them in his shirt pocket. Then, holding the ruler, he paced back and forth in front of the group.

"Rossiter has film that can put this country militarily behind the Russians into the next century. The plan is to capture him and recover the film. We'll succeed in doing that if everything goes perfectly with a complex plan that involves perfect timing. Steve

Jankowski and Bud Kovacs will go over it in detail. However, I've got to tell you that as carefully as we've planned it, there's still room for error."

He looked over at Cheryl for a moment and then said, "If something goes wrong, we're prepared to take alternate steps. Our goal is to capture this man, but if we're forced to, we may have to kill him.

"You've all got to remember," he continued, "that the KGB knows about this film and are as desperate as we are to get it. You can bet there's a bunch of them assembled within a few miles of here, figuring out how they can stop us from getting it first. And like us, they're planning everything they can in advance to assure they get it. But let me tell you, no matter how much planning goes into this, the difference will be in which side acts the quickest in the heat of the moment: who responds the quickest when the unexpected happens; who reacts to take advantage of a situation that suddenly appears out of the blue.

"By eight o'clock the streets out there will be filled with Saturday night traffic. It's going to be crowded. There are three restaurants on the block, a bunch of shops, and a movie theater. We've got vehicles ready to move through here on a split-second schedule, but it's probably not going to work that way. So stay alert. When something isn't happening, look for another way in which it can. The KGB isn't good at that. They never were, and they won't be tonight."

He looked at the ruler in his hand and put it down on one of the cardboard boxes. He'd have to remember to use something like that the next time he spoke to a group. It kept his overly expressive Italian hands in check.

"That's all I have," he said, looking at his watch. He had gone on too long, as usual. "Bud Kovacs and Steve Jankowski will fill you in on the details and give you your individual assignments. Thank you."

Cheryl watched as Steve got up to replace LaSala in front of the men. LaSala said something to him as they passed each other, then came over and sat down next to her. She noticed that he was perspiring, although she thought the room was a little chilly. He wiped his forehead with a wrinkled handkerchief and then whispered to her, "The real difference tonight is going to be you. If you don't identify him before he gets within two blocks of the restaurant, the whole thing's over with." Without waiting for a reaction from her, he turned his attention to Steve, who was covering the map with colored pins to show individual assignments.

She wondered if she could identify Barry that quickly. If he was wearing glasses or had changed his hair color, it would be difficult, especially in a crowd. And God knows what else he would do to make himself look different. Would she know him just from his walk and physical manner? And even if she did, could she point him out, knowing that she might be sentencing him to death? Could she do that?

Like LaSala had said, ". . . maybe in the heat of the moment." But only then would she know for sure.

By seven-thirty Cheryl had been staring at the four TV screens for over two hours. The small filing room was dark and crowded with two technicians, LaSala, and herself, along with Bud Kovacs, who was constantly in and out. In order to get the sharpest reception on the screens, the door was kept closed whenever possible. It only added to her discomfort, because she was starting to feel a mild case of claustrophobia coming on.

One KGB agent had been identified on the street, and that had only happened during the past twenty minutes, just after the streetlights had come on. He was working with a woman, who went into a number of shops while he waited outside. "Clever," LaSala had remarked. "The typical American couple. He'd rather stand out in the cold than watch her spend his hard-earned money."

Chauvinist, she had thought. How did he know it wasn't her own hard-earned money? He didn't.

She looked at Camera 2 at the corner of Clay and Kearney and saw the disguised mobile unit turning into the block. It would make another pass by the KGB agent, focusing in on another close-up of him and the crowd in general. As he came into the picture she noticed there were little puffs of vapor coming out of his mouth. It looked like he was talking to himself.

"He's got a buttonhole," LaSala said into the microphone on his headset. "Either there's another agent on the street or he's talking directly to a command post. Turn the camera around to the other side."

As the truck moved along the street, the camera panned across the pedestrians on the opposite side. A beggar wrapped in a plastic bag for warmth was reaching down into a trash basket. He was wearing earmuffs, and pulled the collar of his coat up to cover his mouth. The restaurant was no more than a block away.

"The guy wrapped in plastic," LaSala said excitedly, "he's the relay. Plastic Man's got a headset on under those muffs. Maybe you ought to stay out of there now, until we pick up the target. Move to the corner of California and Sansone, just in case Rossiter comes in through the back door. This guy's not going to move, so we've only got the other one to be concerned with."

LaSala turned to her and lifted the headset slightly off his ears.

"We must be getting close now. They wouldn't put their men out any sooner than they had to. Barry must be keeping the eight-o'clock date we heard on the tape, so stay alert."

She rubbed her eyes and leaned toward the monitors with her hands under her chin. Her mouth was getting dry and she could feel her heart beating inside her chest.

"You all right?" LaSala asked.

"Yes, why?"

"You look like your mind is somewhere else. This isn't the time for that."

"I'm doing the best I can. This isn't easy for me, you know."

"What's not easy, picking him out in the crowd or pointing him out to me?"

"Both."

"The first I·can help you with, but the second I don't have time for," he said coldly. "I thought you agreed to help us."

"I know, but now I actually have to do it." She paused for a moment to avoid having her voice break. "And once I do, there's no turning back."

"That's right, there isn't."

He looked back at the screens, scanning them quickly. Then he continued. "There isn't any turning back for Barry once he approaches that restaurant, either. He's made his choice, and he's made it over you. His choice is to make a few million dollars selling out his country to the Russians without caring what happens to Cheryl Branigan. What would he do if he were sitting where you are now? Would he point you out? Have you thought about that?"

"No," she answered softly.

"Think about it," he answered, pulling the earphones back down over his ears, "but don't take your eyes off those screens."

She looked across the four cameras scanning the sea of faces. Maybe Barry wouldn't show up. Maybe he would chicken out. Maybe she wouldn't recognize him at all—that would be the best of all possible worlds. But then the film would get to the Russians. Yes, but it wouldn't be her fault. Or would it?

Camera 3 showed the approaching lights of the California Street cable car. For what seemed to be the hundredth time, she watched it pull up to the corner of Kearney Street to discharge its passengers. About ten people got off. Two went directly into the all-night Rexall drugstore. The others turned toward the camera, waiting for the traffic light to change.

Camera 1 showed a group of people walking down Washington Street toward the Embarcadero Plaza, but she couldn't see anybody close enough to identify them. A close-up on Camera 2 caught her attention. Some well-dressed men had come out of the Holiday Inn and were walking across Portsmouth Square toward the camera. One man was lagging behind and didn't seem part of the group. He was dressed in a full-length leather coat like she had seen in Barry's closet, but he wasn't close enough to see his face yet.

The traffic light had turned green, and the group of men started across the street. Camera 3 pulled back to follow them. They were close enough for her to see two women, probably a grandmother and her daughter with a small child between them. Trailing behind was a man who had not yet reached the old-style gaslight lamp and was still in shadow. He also was wearing a hat with a long coat, but it was an ordinary trench coat. As the camera continued to pull back, a sign for a disco appeared in the foreground. It was flashing red and yellow, two dancers moving back and forth with each flash. The sign reminded her of the disco where she'd first met Barry almost ten years ago.

"Hi, my name's Barry. What's a pretty girl like you doing here all alone?"

The man passed under the sign and it threw a yellow flash of light across his face for just a split second. It reflected off his glasses, revealing thin wire frames.

"Here's to the fork in the road where we choose our separate ways."

The man's face was back in shadow again as he moved away from the sign. But he was coming closer. The older women in front of him stopped to say something to the child, and he passed them. She could see him more clearly now, and the slight bounce he took on the balls of his feet with each step.

"Want to see what's going to make us millionaires?"

She turned to LaSala, who was saying something into his headset.

"Can you move the camera on the third monitor in closer?" she asked anxiously.

"Sure, what is it?" he asked.

"That man in the trench coat," she said, pointing to the screen.

LaSala barked orders into the headset, and immediately the man's upper body filled the entire screen. Then he passed under another streetlight. His hat cast a shadow over his eyes, but his mouth was in the light. He was smiling.

"This whole thing has brought us both together. We'll never be apart again."

"Is that him?" LaSala was covering the microphone with one hand and pointing to the screen with the other. She barely heard him. The man was practically looking right at the camera now. *"Would you like some more wine? It's very good wine."* The smile was still on his face. He was laughing at her. The son of a bitch was laughing at her.

She was surprised by her lack of emotion, because there was only one: anger. Her whole body shook as her hand came slowly up and pointed to the screen.

"That's him," she heard herself say. The words came out easily. She had always wondered how difficult it was to pull the trigger of a gun. It was this easy because that's what she might be doing now. And then came the verbal coup de grâce. "I'm sure," she said.

LaSala leaned forward to study the screen. Barry's face was in full light now, and he saw him clearly. Even wearing glasses he looked much younger than LaSala had expected and seemed to be calm under the circumstances. In fact, Rossiter looked very confident with what he was about to do. As he came under the next streetlight he stopped and checked his watch. The two women and the girl moved away from him, and he stood under the streetlight like an actor onstage under a spotlight. LaSala looked for a package. There wasn't any.

He turned to Cheryl. Her eyes had not left the screen, and both her hands were clenched in fists.

"You're *sure* it's him?" he said one more time. "There's no turning back from here."

"Yes, goddammit, yes. Do you want me to run out in the street and capture him for you too?"

LaSala turned a switch on the radio in front of him that opened up all channels.

"All stations, this is Command 1. We've located the target, and Camera 3 is tracking him. He's at California between Kearney and Montgomery. Mobile 1, get there quick, Camera 1's going to lose him any second now. Station 4, come in."

"Station 4 here."

"Get the cab rolling."

"Roger, we're on our way."

"Station 5?"

"Station 5 here."

"Start your countdown . . . now. Sweeney and the vehicle are four minutes behind the cab."

"Ready and counting."

"Station 6, where're the two covers on the street?"

The reply was muffled, mixed with static from the agent's buttonhole microphone. "Plastic Man is still in the doorway, but the couple shopping are heading down Montgomery, away from the restaurant."

"Shit. They're on a collision course with the target," LaSala shouted.

He turned to the technician next to him. "Where's the cab now?"

"Coming into Camera 2's range," he answered. "You'll see him any second."

Cheryl hadn't taken her eyes off the camera tracking Barry. He was a lot smaller in the picture now as he started to move out of its range. He was turning onto Montgomery Street. The restaurant was just three blocks away, and Montgomery was crowded with people. Within seconds he had disappeared into the mass of moving shapes.

LaSala continued to bark orders into his headset. Cheryl's heart was pounding. She had pointed out the victim and now he was about to be captured or even killed. Why was she still watching? Was it some sadistic need to see her revenge satisfied? She didn't know, but something was keeping her there. Maybe it was because the whole thing was happening on the screen. Maybe it was just a TV movie that wasn't real at all. Maybe she would still wake up and find herself back in her New York apartment.

"Do you see him, Steve?" LaSala was shouting into the headset. "He's the guy with the tan trench coat in back of the young couple with the punk haircuts. . . . Yeah, glasses and a wide-brimmed hat. . . . Right . . . that's him."

The mobile camera had picked up Barry. Now Cheryl saw the cab coming into the picture. It was a blue Dodge, moving slowly with two cars in front of it. It stopped about fifty feet from Barry. Cheryl saw Steve and Gene Zeller get out. They rushed through the crowd toward Barry. The cab was moving alongside, keeping pace with them.

Barry turned and saw the two men. His pace quickened and he pushed his way around the people ahead of him. Then, suddenly, he darted across the street. The cab tried to follow, but a car coming the opposite way blocked it. LaSala saw the KGB husband and wife come into the picture. They had spotted Barry, who was now moving toward them. The woman waved her arms to signal Plastic Man, who was hurrying up the street.

"Command 6!" LaSala shouted. "They've spotted him."

"I know" came the reply, "but I've lost them in the crowd."

"Jesus Christ," LaSala screamed. He was on his feet with the microphone in his hand, shouting at the TV screen. The woman was less than a hundred feet away, hurrying toward Barry. The cab was still trying to get to the other side of the street against the traffic. It couldn't.

"Steve," LaSala shouted, forgetting about code and radio procedure. "They're going to get him. You don't have any choice. Kill him." He repeated the words again so there would be no doubt. "Kill him!"

Cheryl saw Steve pull his .38 out from under his jacket.

"No," she heard herself say, "no, you can't do it!" Her hands were waving at the screen as Steve brought the weapon up with two hands and aimed it. But he didn't have a clear field of fire.

The crowd was between him and Barry. But suddenly Barry's glasses flew off his face, his arms flung outward, and he slumped forward. As he fell, she saw Zeller behind him, his gun drawn.

Barry fell to the pavement, clutching his chest. He was on his knees, looking directly up at the camera. Cheryl heard herself try to speak but nothing came out. She heard the words forming inside her brain, but they couldn't be spoken. "I'm sorry, Barry. I'm sorry."

The crowd was screaming. Some had run to the opposite side of the street; others fell to the sidewalk in anticipation of more shooting. Steve was holding up his identification while Zeller moved people away from Barry. The three KGB agents had ducked into a doorway during the shooting but were now in back of the crowd, trying to force their way through. Suddenly a policeman who had come from the opposite direction was standing over Barry. It was Moscowicz. He took one quick look and radioed for an ambulance.

LaSala was watching the sweep hand on his Timex.

"Open the door!" he shouted at the technician behind him. "I want to be able to hear that ambulance!"

The door to the room was opened and he continued to stare at the watch. Finally a siren could be heard several blocks away, but it didn't seem to be getting any closer.

"Command 1, this is Station 6."

"Yeah, go ahead," LaSala barked.

"Plastic Man's on his buttonhole. We'll have more KGB here any minute."

"Goddammit, where's the fuckin' ambulance? Station 5, where the hell are you?"

"Just around the corner, but we can't get through the traffic."

"Well, take the gurney and go on foot!"

Cheryl could see the female KGB agent trying to break through the crowd with Plastic Man, who had shed his wrapping. His hand was inside his jacket. Zeller and Moscowicz were doing their best to keep the crowd back, but the woman was succeeding in moving closer to Barry.

The ambulance attendants came running around the corner and the crowd nearest them opened up. They pushed the gurney through and lowered it to the pavement alongside Barry. Without any examination he was lifted onto it, and the attendants snapped it back to an upright position. LaSala saw that two of his agents were now on either side of Plastic Man and the woman who was pressing against them to get a better look. Moscowicz and Sweeney continued to push the crowd back as the attendants quickly moved the gurney back around the corner. The female KGB agent suddenly broke free and tried to circle around the crowd to get to the ambulance. Moscowicz intercepted her and pushed her back with his nightstick. She was yelling something, but he kept pushing her. LaSala heard the ambulance siren from around the corner. It was under way. Cheryl heard him exhale all the air in his lungs as he got up from the chair. It was a sigh of relief. Part one was over.

He threw off his headset and put on his jacket, which was hanging over the chair. For the first time Cheryl noticed the snub-nosed .38 holstered over his hip.

"I'm outa here," he said to the technician. "Stay in contact with the ambulance. I'll get on the car radio as soon as we're under way." He turned to Cheryl. "We all would have preferred it had gone another way . . . but we did what we had to do."

"Yeah," she said, looking away from him, "sure."

He looked at her for a moment and she felt he wanted to say something more consoling, but instead there were more orders.

"Be ready to move with your bags," he replied, moving toward the door. "It may be as soon as an hour. We're going to have to clear this place in a hurry." Without waiting for a reply he was gone, heading for a car waiting at the back of the building.

Cheryl watched as the crowd in the street began to disperse. Some milled around and seemed to discuss what had happened, while others went on their way. Plastic Man and the woman, however, were rushing off in the direction of the Volga Boatman. Moscowicz was filling out a mock report with two apparent witnesses, Agents Zander and Sloan.

Suddenly all five sets went dark and the technician switched on the one overhead light in the room. She stayed in her seat as he quickly began to dismantle the equipment. After a few minutes she saw she was in the way and moved outside to the larger room. It was dark, except for one desk lamp that was lying on the floor at one end of the room.

She walked over to the window and stared down into the street. People were waiting in line at the movie theater while others were going in and out of the shops and restaurants. It was a normal Saturday night for everyone down there.

She listened for the sound of the siren, which had been fading off in the distance. It had stopped.

LaSala's car pulled into the underground garage of a vacant building about a mile from the California Medical Center. Its tires screeched as it wound around the narrow turns down to the second parking level. The car passed a large numeral two painted on a column and then slowly came across the empty floor of the garage. Another vehicle was parked off in the far corner, its interior lights on. It was the ambulance.

LaSala got out of the car and the driver drove it back upstairs to watch the entrance. The ambulance door opened, sending a bright light across the far wall. A man was silhouetted in the doorway. He was holding a gun.

"That you, Frank?"

"Yeah," he answered, stepping farther into the light.

Bud Kovacs holstered his weapon and motioned him forward.

"Get in," he said, extending his hand to help him into the ambulance.

LaSala climbed inside and sat on the bench against the wall. There were three other men crowded in the back: the two attendants, both from S.F.P.D., and Dr. Jack Bloom, medical consultant to the CIA in California. Barry's body was on a stretcher, covered with a white sheet. He wasn't surprised by his lack of emotion at seeing the body. This was only one of many over the years, but probably the most important.

"Did he die right away?" he asked, lifting the sheet from over the ashen face. Rossiter's eyes were shut and his glasses had been removed. He looked very young.

Bloom referred to a sheet of paper on the clipboard he was holding.

"At 8:04 P.M. About two minutes after we got him into the ambulance. There wasn't anything we could have done. The bullet penetrated the aorta and exited through the sixth vertebra. His lungs were filled with blood almost immediately."

LaSala nodded and replaced the sheet over the body. He turned to Kovacs.

"Was he carrying the film?"

"No," he answered, reaching for a manila envelope on the shelf behind him.

A tremor ran through LaSala's body. If they didn't have the film, all they had succeeded in doing was stopping any further passing of verbal information. That wasn't enough. They had to have that film. Did Barry make other arrangements to deliver it on the second call—the call they didn't hear? If he had, there was no way they would ever be able to recover it.

Kovacs removed a hotel key from the envelope. He handed it to LaSala.

"He was carrying this."

LaSala took the key from him and examined it. It hung from a brass holder with a room number, 218, inscribed in the center. On the back was the name of the hotel, the Shelbourne.

"That's all he had?" he asked.

Kovacs emptied the rest of the contents onto the bench. There was a handkerchief, some small change, a digital watch, and a wallet. LaSala picked it up and started to examine it.

"Nothing unusual," Kovacs said. "Some small bills, credit cards, and a driver's license. The hotel key is all we've got. It better lead us to the film."

"Yeah," LaSala replied, turning the key over and over in his hand. "We may have silenced Mr. Rossiter, but those tapes can still speak for him. The race between us and the KGB is still on, I'm afraid. We've got to get the film before they do."

"But they probably don't know where he was staying," Kovacs said hopefully.

"We don't know that, Bud," he answered, looking toward the door. "There's no chance you were followed, is there?"

"I doubt it. We came out through a crowd of people. There weren't any cars behind us then, unless someone picked us up later."

"Well, I've got to get to the Shelbourne, and I've got to get there fast." He turned to one of the S.F.P.D. officers. "Can you radio the driver upstairs?"

"Sure," he answered.

"Tell him to pick me up at the corner of Sixth and Irving Way, just in case they did follow you and are watching the garage. I'll go out the back entrance. Also call Command 1. Jankowski should be back there now. Have him meet me at the Shelbourne, Room

218." He turned to Kovacs. "When do you plan to move the body?"

Kovacs looked at his watch.

"Right now. We radioed the hospital that we'd be on the way as soon as we heard your car. They know it's a DOA, so we're going right to the morgue. The medical examiner will examine the body in a few hours. Don't worry about this end, we're all set."

"Okay, I better get going," he said, putting the hotel key in his pocket. "You all did a good job, thank you." He shook hands with each of them and left. He thought of a football analogy. His men had scrambled and gotten the first down.

But had they lost the ball?

Moscow

Viktor Karpolov sat in the living room of his Moscow town house playing chess with General Parkovsky. The elegant room was always slightly rearranged for the games. Viktor set the chessboard up on a folding, hand-carved antique table Ivana had bought for his birthday five years ago. A soft, high-backed chair was then moved from the far side of the room for the general to sit in. The chair and the table were the only two period pieces in the otherwise modern decor of the house.

He and Ivana had had the nine rooms redone three summers ago. They had visited Paris on a combined business and pleasure trip. It was her first time there and she was greatly impressed by modern French furniture and interior design. The simplicity of line, the contemporary use of metal, and bright red and orange fabrics opened up a new dimension in decorating for her. It represented a new concept of what a room could be. There wasn't any reason to live in the dull, drab surroundings that many of their friends lived in. This was different and exciting for Ivana. But it was all too much of a departure for Karpolov.

Ivana argued that the town house should reflect more of their thinking and life-style. He was attempting to bring new, aggressive concepts into government. She was involved in moving the Bolshoi from just doing the classics to introducing modern ballets. If their friends chose to live with the mundane, so be it; they were in a position to take a leadership role.

But tonight, events were taking place in San Francisco that threatened to affect Karpolov's career drastically. Events that were completely out of his control. But once again, he had taken the necessary steps to protect himself. He had disassociated himself from the laser-weapon film. By keeping it from POL-1 review, he personally was the end of the line as far as knowledge of the operation was concerned. He had made Colonel Zarov the man responsible. Zarov had continually hidden his failures from him, while at the same time ordering further operations to obtain the lost film. Tonight was just another one of those same attempts. If the results failed to support his plan, it would remain secret. On the other hand, if it proved the weapon was a phony, as he still truly believed, he would use it tomorrow morning at his meeting with the premier. Tomorrow was the twenty-second of October. Tomorrow the ships would sail.

There was no turning back now, unless there was undeniable evidence that the weapon existed. The answer would come shortly. He looked at his watch. It was after eleven. Zarov should be in touch with him momentarily.

The general was becoming impatient. He sat across from him, wearing a white turtleneck sweater under a navy-blue blazer. His dress was always somewhat formal when they played. "Chess is more than merely a game," he had always said. "It's an intellectual battle of wits, and one should not come dressed as if he were going to play checkers." This forced Viktor to dress more formally than usual while relaxing in his own home, but then again, chess with the general was never relaxing. Right now the general was winning. Viktor was in check, with only three possible options for a move.

"Viktor, are you solving the problems of the world, or are we playing chess?" the general asked impatiently as he waited for him to make a move.

"I'm sorry," he replied. "It's a big day tomorrow and I guess my mind was wandering."

"It is a big day, for you and all of Russia. He makes us all proud, doesn't he, Ivana?"

His daughter was curled up on the sofa reading *Elle*, a fashion magazine from Paris.

"Yes," she said, smiling at Viktor. "He always makes us proud."

"Well, I can't wait," Parkovsky said, finishing the last of the cognac in his glass. "It's going to be a moment I've been waiting for for a long time." He leaned back in the chair and his body relaxed as his mind shifted from the game to the excitement that tomorrow promised to bring. "Those ships are going all the way to Cuba this time. And once they get there, the United States will have to think twice before they push us to the brink of war." His eyes narrowed and he repeated his words again. "This time we won't turn back."

Viktor met the general's stare, which was looking for the slightest hesitancy on his part as he replied, "I'm not supposed to say anything, but I'll tell you both a little secret. We're going to hold a major press conference in Cuba when the ships arrive. It will be to celebrate their arrival and to announce to the world that we're prepared to defend Cuba and the rest of the world against U.S. aggression. I would like you to attend, General." He turned to Ivana. "And how would you like to be in sunny Havana in about five days?"

"Oh, that would be wonderful," she said excitedly. "I would love to see the ships arrive. And the weather. It will be gloriously sunny. Oh, Viktor, I can't wait."

"I'll make arrangements for you both tomorrow," he said, and then for the general's benefit added, "And yes, it would be exciting to be at the completion of a mission that began thirty-two years ago."

"It will be a great day for Russia," Parkovsky said, extending his hands outward. "And for you, Viktor. After all, it was your efforts that made it all possible."

"That's kind of you, General, but there were others. . . ."

"No," he insisted, "it was your idea to take advantage of our submarine-launched missiles under the Arctic. My friends in the Politburo told me how effective you were at your initial presentation over six months ago. Until then, no one had thought of what a great moral and military victory could be achieved by doing what you proposed. No, you're responsible, Viktor, and don't you forget it."

"That's why I think going to Cuba is exciting," Ivana said enthusiastically. "Everyone will know it was your plan that completed what Premier Khrushchev started years ago."

He smiled at her and said, "I'm looking forward to it also, dear, but first we have to get through tomorrow."

The general looked at Ivana and nodded in agreement. Viktor took the opportunity to glance at his watch. It was after eight-thirty now in San Francisco. Did Dukoff have the film yet? What was on it? Would it support what he was about to do tomorrow or would he have to continue hiding the information? He looked up, and the general had turned his attention back to the game.

"It's getting late," the general said, referring to Viktor's watch. "Perhaps we should postpone my beating you until some other time. You have a big day tomorrow."

"I don't have to meet with the premier until after ten. If we can play a little longer, I'll be able to execute my master plan to bring you down to defeat."

"Very well," the general replied, "but only if you promise not to take ten minutes between moves. That would automatically defeat me, because I would fall asleep. Ivana, watch him if I doze off, so he doesn't replace one of my knights with a pawn."

"Oh, Father, Viktor would never do that," she said, laughing, and then added, "He would replace the queen."

Viktor smiled at her and then put his hand on a pawn, preparing to make a move. He was glad the general had agreed to continue the game because it served to keep his mind occupied while he waited for Zarov's call. He moved the pawn to a position where the next move by the general would result in his queen no longer being protected by his knight.

It was a move the general hadn't anticipated. But at the same time he realized that it was a logical progression of a plan of which Viktor's last three moves were a part. The general still had an option that Viktor didn't seem to notice. He acted quickly, before Viktor saw the one possible route of attack still open to him. With one quick motion he moved his rook one square forward.

The move took Viktor by surprise. It seemed to be a defensive move by the general, the first of the game. Viktor continued with his plan of attack. Three more moves and he would have checkmate.

The general saw the plan clearly now. Timing suddenly became important. He would take his time deciding the next move, although he already knew what it was. His play had to continue to appear defensive, but his rook was now the key to his winning on the fourth move.

"May I have another cognac, Ivana?" the general said, holding out his empty glass. "I seem to be in a difficult situation here."

Ivana got up from the sofa and came over to the table. As she took the general's glass she smiled at Viktor. If he won, it would be only the second or third time since he had started playing with her father.

"Do we have an upset in the making?" she asked, reaching for the decanter of cognac. "Maybe we'll witness a historical event tonight, as well as tomorrow."

"I would almost trade tomorrow for a victory over your father," Viktor said pleasantly. "Sometimes I think he's a far greater adversary than the United States."

"Well, you two finish your little game," she said, handing her father the cognac and kissing him on the forehead, "but I can't keep my eyes open anymore." She kissed Viktor lightly on the lips before going up to bed.

Viktor continued to see the rook in a defensive position rather than as a threat to his plan. He moved his bishop in for the kill. As he put the piece down the general took a sip of his cognac. He looked over the glass at his son-in-law. Without taking his eyes off his opponent, the general moved a pawn next to Viktor's black knight. It took a moment for the move to register, but then his eyes dropped.

"Check," the general said quietly.

Viktor studied the board, looking for a possible escape route that he might have missed, but there wasn't any. He had one move left and then it was checkmate. Again he studied his position, hoping to find a way out that he might have missed, but there wasn't any. The general had covered all contingencies. He was beaten. Without wasting any time, he went through the motions of making his last two moves and the game was over.

"Well played, General," he said, pushing his chair away from the board. "Again I must bow to your superior skill and complete mastery of the game."

"No," the older man said in a surprisingly stern voice. "I'm afraid you've bowed to some presumptive and inflexible thinking: two flaws that are often fatal in chess."

"Well, it was probably presumptive of me to think I could beat you in the first place," Viktor answered, trying to lighten the tone of the general's admonishment. "As far as the inflexibility goes, I guess I don't understand quite what you mean."

"I mean you could have won the game. You had a plan of attack. You were on the offensive, but you presumed that my rook was a defensive move in response to your attack. You didn't think that it could be a counterattack. If you did, you would have made the proper adjustments and gone on to win. There were several options open to you at that point, but you didn't take advantage of them. It cost you the game."

Viktor thought about what the general was saying, and suddenly realized that it paralleled what would happen tomorrow. He was putting the country on the offensive by sending missiles to Cuba. Like the game, his opponent had made a move to try to stop him. He had presumed that it was strictly defensive, in this case a weapon that didn't exist, and pressed on with his plan. But was the enemy operating from a defensive position or was he going on the offensive with a weapon that really did exist? Would he, Viktor Karpolov, again lose the game?

He looked back at the general. The old man wasn't revealing any of his inner thoughts. He simply began to remove the pieces from the board, putting them into their velvet-lined box.

This was the first time the general had openly criticized his play. And that criticism seemed to be laced with anger.

"Thank goodness it's merely a game," Viktor said, trying to lighten the moment.

"Chess is not just a game," Parkovsky stated. "The way a man plays it is a measure of how his thought processes work."

Viktor decided to confront him directly, now that Ivana had left the room.

"So you're concerned that my thought processes may be presumptive and inflexible."

"I didn't say that."

"You implied it."

"Maybe so, but you can be excused for tonight's play. You have a lot on your mind, I'm sure. Tomorrow will be an important day in your career."

"You're still concerned about tomorrow, aren't you? I've noticed it all evening." He wouldn't let it go now. "Even though it will avenge one of the darkest moments in our history, you're concerned that sending the ships may be a mistake."

"Yes, I am."

"Why, General?" The question was not posed with anger or frustration, but rather as a need to understand his concern.

"An old friend from Serpukhov visited me yesterday. He came to my apartment and we had a little cognac together. His name is Alexei Boroshnov. Do you know him?"

"No, I'm afraid I haven't had the pleasure."

The general started to raise his glass to his lips but then decided he had had enough cognac. He moved it just out of arm's length and then continued. "He's a scientist at the Institute of High Energy Physics. A specialist in what he calls the "subatomic area." He went on to explain that, but it became far too difficult for me to understand. One thing he did say, though, was that he was involved with laser technology."

Viktor was prepared for what he had just heard. The general was watching him closely, but years of training had taught him not to reveal anything through facial movement. His eyes remained fixed, unflinching and emotionless.

"Really," he said in an even tone of voice. "And what did he tell you?"

"He said that he was involved in writing the report you requested about a week and a half ago. That was just about the time we had our little lunch, wasn't it?"

"Yes, I believe so."

"Anyway, he went on to say essentially what you had told me at the luncheon—that the Americans had been testing something called RFQ . . ."

"Radio frequency quadrupole."

"Yes, that's it. And he agreed that he didn't think the technique was feasible as far as developing a destructive laser weapon was concerned. But then he said something that alarmed me. He said that his laboratory had received stolen plans from the United States during the past year for evaluation. The plans indicated that the Americans were making progress. What do you know about this?"

"I know all about it, General. The plans he's telling you about were sent to him by my people. We've been monitoring them for over a year now."

He watched the general's reaction to what he had said. The old man was surprised, and he also seemed somewhat relieved.

"The plans were being passed to us by an informer, and we have been carefully evaluating them. At present the consensus by the scientists at the Institute and at Sary Shagan is that the Americans' progress is minimal; they're still two years away from testing the weapon. This is further supported by satellite reconnaissance that shows no testing of a laser weapon during the last six months. Scientists at Sary Shagan also say that without proper testing, conclusions made in the plan remain unproven and highly speculative. My report to the Politburo contained all this information, and it was reviewed very carefully."

"So the Politburo is aware of this?"

"Yes," he answered. There was a very positive tone to his voice. However, he had neglected to say that the review had occurred over six months ago, just prior to the presentation of his Cuban missile plan. Once the plan was approved, he hadn't sent any additional reports. As long as there wasn't conclusive evidence that the weapon existed, he had decided then and there not to put the plan in jeopardy.

The general seemed to be more relaxed now. The muscles in his lined face loosened as his mood changed from anxiety to a feeling of reassurance. Karpolov sensed this and saw it as an opportunity to further that reassurance.

"I have something else for you to consider. Let's just say for a moment that the weapon *is* in development. Let's also give the Americans a year, instead of two, in which to have it tested and operational. By then our SRVs in the Arctic and in Cuba will be surrounding the United States, and we'll already have taken West Germany and moved across Europe. With a two-minute delivery time to major targets, we'll still have an advantage over a laser weapon. Our SRVs will be as fast, but much more powerful. At best, a laser can deliver a twenty-megaton payload. We deliver almost four times more than that.

"If we don't move into Cuba *now*, it'll be much more difficult to do. By the time the Americans have an operational laser, we'll have lost our advantage, probably forever. Our time is now; it's tomorrow."

When the general spoke again, his voice was much softer. "You support your plan admirably, Viktor."

"I firmly believe in it, General."

"You must realize that my friend and I come from a different generation. In our lifetime Russia has always been on the defensive. During World II we fought desperately to protect our land and homes from Nazi Germany. Our generation is defensive by nature. It's very difficult for us to understand the concept of moving aggressively thousands of miles away to protect our homeland. I know it's not rational. Today missiles travel tremendous distances in a matter of minutes. Men no longer confront each other face-to-face but from opposite ends of the earth. Nevertheless it's a difficult concept for us to understand."

"I can sympathize with that," he replied. "However, it's necessary to seize the moment while it is there."

"Agreed," he answered, getting up slowly from the chair. "I've been an annoyance to you on the eve of your great achievement, and I'm sorry for that," he said, extending his hand. "But your candid and knowledgeable answers have reassured me, so I'll be able to sleep tonight. I hope you do too. It's going to be a big day tomorrow."

He extended his hand and Viktor took it.

"You haven't been an annoyance, General. I'm glad I was able to support the plan to your satisfaction. In fact, it gave me an opportunity to organize my thoughts verbally, and that will be useful tomorrow. It was a good rehearsal. Also, I think we so-called 'modern, aggressive mavericks' need people like yourself to keep us in check. We need a sounding board to keep us from jumping into a pool that may be empty. Our little talk was very helpful."

"Well, if nothing else, you still need me to play chess with," the general said, releasing Viktor's hand.

Viktor was relieved to have convinced the general. Parkovsky had close friends on the Politburo. It was important that he supported him.

By the time Zarov finally phoned, Karpolov was at his wit's end. He answered the phone before the first ring was even completed.

"Dimitri?"

"Yes, Viktor."

"Tell me in one word, success or failure?"

"Failure. I must speak with you immediately."

"Hold on one moment, I'm going to transfer you over to another line." Karpolov pressed a series of buttons and the call was automatically transferred to another line, one that was cleared for taps every two weeks.

"Are you there?" he asked, the new line having been connected.

"Yes," Zarov replied. "I don't want to talk on the phone. I have to meet with you . . . now."

"Where are you?"

"In my apartment." He paused for a moment and then asked, "Can you be here in thirty minutes?"

Karpolov was surprised at Zarov's tone of voice. It was stern and commanding. There was a determination in it that was totally unexpected.

"I will be there in thirty minutes," he said sharply, and hung up.

Within ten minutes Karpolov's car pulled up in front of the house. Mikhail, his chauffeur, opened the door for him and he settled into the backseat. The car pulled away from the curb and Mikhail looked at him through the rearview mirror.

"Where to, sir?" he asked impassively.

"To 186–79 Sadovaya Boulevard, just past Mayakovsky Square. Actually, one block from that address. Leave me out at the entrance to the square. I'll walk the rest of the way." He didn't want to take the chance of anyone seeing him arrive in a limousine. It would stick out like a sore thumb at this time of night. He had also taken the precaution of wearing an unobtrusive woolen waist jacket over his turtleneck, along with a peaked cap. Hopefully he would look like someone just getting back to his apartment after a long night.

"After you leave me off," he continued, "park on a side street a few blocks away with the motor running. I'll be meeting Colonel Zarov in his apartment. I'll call you when I'm ready to leave. Meet me on the same corner."

"Yes, sir."

He looked out the window at the falling snow. The streets were empty except for a few trucks making late-night deliveries. Moscow had become more deserted at night than usual during the past three weeks. The weather was so cold, people didn't want to come out of their apartments after dinner. He pulled the jacket up around his neck. The heaters in these damned Russian-made Zhigulis took forever to warm up. Then he wondered if it was the cold, or his body responding to the fear inside him. The timing of events during the past two weeks had been incredible. Just as his plan was being put into effect, what had been a routine operation in New York had suddenly become a crisis. Now that he was only hours away from achieving his goal, everything was going against him. But this was the kind of situation he thrived on. Where other men would panic, he methodically planned for the unexpected and was ready to react with other options, if needed.

They were coming into Kolkhoznaya Square. The pentagon-shaped Soviet Army Theater was dark except for one floodlight in front, which illuminated its tall columns and ornately sculptured arches. Across the square was the Memorial Museum; the park next to it was the scene of many summer concerts. Now its trees were frozen into icy fingers that clenched to hold the snow within them.

They continued down the Sadovaya, the Grand Boulevard of Moscow. It was one of the streets in the city where the builders had the foresight to see the need for a wide boulevard. Many of the other main streets were narrow and congested with traffic during the rush hour. At this time of night, however, they were the only car on the road. Karpolov looked over Mikhail's shoulder. The lights from the Hotel Peking and Mayakovsky Square were up ahead.

Mikhail pulled into a side street one block from the apartment. He continued about halfway down the street before stopping under a streetlight. There would be enough light for his passenger to get out of the car safely.

Before Karpolov got out of the car, he repeated his order one more time. "Wait for my call. Don't come for me before then."

He stepped into the snow and started down the sidewalk toward the corner. The wind blew in his face and he wished he had taken a scarf. Around the corner, walking became a little easier. The Sadovaya was brightly illuminated and the wind wasn't as gusty. In a few minutes he was in front of Zarov's apartment.

He climbed the steps and went through a revolving door into a dimly lit lobby. He looked for Zarov's name on the rows of neat tabs next to the call buttons. Finding it, he pressed the button. Zarov answered.

"Yes?"

"It's me," he said quietly. There was a buzz and a loud click as the bolt in the door released. He went inside and rang for the elevator. Hopefully it would come quickly. He didn't want to stand out in the lobby any longer than necessary. Within a minute the doors opened, and he was relieved to see there was no one inside.

He rode up to the fourth floor and stepped out into a narrow, carpeted hallway. It smelled musty and he noticed that the carpet was worn and frayed at the edges. The building wasn't the height of elegance, but there were few in Moscow that were. He found number 431, rang the mechanical bell over the doorknob, and waited.

Colonel Zarov opened the door, holding the stub of a cigarette in his hand. He was wearing a soiled white shirt, his tie open. His trousers were unpressed and the tips of his shoes were wet. He hadn't been in the apartment much longer than the time it took Karpolov to get there.

"Come in," Zarov said, looking down the hall over his shoulder.

Karpolov stepped inside and closed the door, locking it with the bolt. Zarov walked to the opposite side of the small living room and stood with his back to Karpolov, facing a drawn window shade.

"What happened in San Francisco this evening?" Karpolov asked quietly.

"Nothing happened," he answered sharply. "We didn't get to our man, and we didn't get the film."

"What do you mean?" He could feel the fear and anger building inside him.

Zarov turned suddenly and faced him. "The man who was supposed to deliver the film was killed before he could get to the restaurant."

"He *what*?"

"He was shot by two men in the street less than two blocks away. There were police, an ambulance, and a crowd gathered. Before our people in the street realized he was our man, he was taken away by the ambulance. The whole thing happened in four or five minutes."

"Goddammit." Karpolov took off his hat and threw it on the

floor. "Those idiots! The man calls them up and makes an appointment and they can't manage to get to him." He unzipped his jacket down to the waist.

Zarov took one last puff of the cigarette and smothered it in an ashtray on top of the TV.

"Dukoff is certain that the CIA killed him. He was shot right in the street. The men who did it identified themselves as policemen, but then other police showed up within seconds. An ambulance was no more than two blocks away." He pointed a finger for emphasis. "It was all very neat, too neat."

"The CIA," Karpolov repeated. He wanted to hear the words himself.

The colonel continued. "We can't hide this any longer, Viktor. I said that last night, but now it's gotten even worse. With the CIA involved, we can't . . . I can't . . . go on without it being reported."

"You're reporting it to me, Dimitri."

"What the hell does that mean?"

"It means that as a member of the Politburo, you've done your duty by reporting it to me."

"You're responsible for total policy in the Soviet Union now?"

"For this operation, yes. I still believe the Americans don't have this weapon."

"But do the premier and the rest of the Politburo?"

"That's not your concern. Your responsibility lies with reporting accurately to me what occurred tonight in San Francisco, and that's what I want you to do right now." His words were cold, devoid of any relationship that existed between them. Zarov turned away and sat down in the soft chair next to the window. Karpolov remained standing.

"All right, what do you want to know?" There was no attempt to hide the vindictiveness in his voice.

"Everything," he replied. "You said it was the CIA that made the hit?"

"Yes."

"Did the man die immediately?"

"He was dying."

"What about the film? Did he have it?"

"No, there was no sign of any film."

"You're sure."

"From what our people could see, he wasn't carrying any film."

Karpolov turned away and walked over to a large oval mirror that hung above an old, worn sofa. He stared at his reflection and saw a tired man under immense pressure. But now was the time to think clearly, to put the pieces together. This was what he was good at, assembling the pieces of the puzzle to find the clear picture.

Events of the past two weeks slowly began to come together in his head. The real piece of information was that the CIA was definitely involved. Dukoff was right. No one else would have been able to pull off a hit in the street simultaneously with the immediate arrival of the police and an ambulance. CIA involvement was key.

Karpolov wondered if this tied in with Berkhin's report from Sakhalin that discovery of the receiver devices planted there had been too easy. Perhaps the American who had arranged for their burial was working for the CIA, and wanted them to be found.

Also, Karpolov had always had doubts about the information being passed in New York through Lucci's restaurant. For two years McFarland had given them data indicating that the Americans had a laser weapon ready to be tested. Yet Russian scientists insisted that it was years away from being developed. Did the Americans have it or not? Would this film have proven anything one way or the other? He doubted it.

And what about McFarland? Was he working for the CIA? McFarland had denied it right up until his death and insisted that the weapon was real. Karpolov didn't believe him. He believed his scientists. The weapon couldn't possibly exist.

What concerned Karpolov now was how close his KGB was—or the CIA, for that matter—to finding the film. Time was what he needed.

He still felt confident in tomorrow's decision to send the ships to Cuba. Right now no one had the film. The weapon was still nothing more than hearsay. His detailed report to the Politburo had supported his scientists. He would stand by that report and send the ships off in good conscience. His biggest problem was Zarov.

Zarov was sitting in the chair, awaiting the next question, his hands folded in his lap. Karpolov decided on a gentler approach in dealing with him. Aggressiveness would only result in furthering the colonel's insistence on going to the Politburo. That could be dangerous.

"We didn't fail completely tonight in San Francisco, Dimitri," he said. "In fact, I'm certain now more than ever that the Americans don't have the weapon. Our scientists say it's impossible, and there's still no concrete evidence to dispel that."

"Agreed," Zarov said, taking a cigarette from his breast pocket. "But this film might have told us whether the Americans have it or not. Instead it was snatched right out from under us, and the man who delivered it killed. I call that failure, complete failure."

"No, Dimitri, it isn't. What was on that film? No one knows. Would it have proven that the weapon existed or not? No one knows. The film is moot, Dimitri. It proves nothing, because we don't have it, and neither does the CIA.

"In the meantime I have committed ships to Cuba that will sail tomorrow. On the basis of what I've heard you say, there's not enough evidence to prevent them from sailing. If this film was in our hands, and if it could prove beyond all doubt that the Americans had the weapon, I wouldn't send them. But it isn't. No one knows where it is, and probably won't for some time.

"By then our missiles will be aimed at the United States, surrounding it from all sides. And most important of all, the Politburo will have achieved what it set out to do over thirty years ago. Do you think you have enough evidence to deny them that? I don't think so."

Zarov got up from the chair. It was as if he wanted to be on an equal level with Karpolov, rather than surrendering to all of his points sitting down.

"I still feel this should be reported," he said weakly. "There are still many unanswered questions that the Politburo should know about."

"What are you going to tell them?" he asked, raising his hands over his head. "That the Americans have a weapon our scientists say is two years away from development? That a girl stole some secret film that might have proven otherwise, but nobody has seen the film or knows what's on it? Come on, Dimitri! They would laugh you right out of their offices. You don't have the film, the girl, or the guy. You have nothing."

"It just doesn't feel right," he answered, raising his voice in frustration. He had run out of facts. He only had his gut feeling left, which was worthless.

"Listen, we both would like to have absolute proof there isn't any risk in sending the ships off. We don't have it. However, there's more reason to believe they should go than not. And there certainly isn't enough evidence to go in front of the entire Politburo without making a fool of yourself."

He waited. Zarov needed time to retreat from his position without damaging his ego. Without saying anything, he walked across the small room to the window and back. His head was bowed and his hands were in his pockets. Finally he looked up.

"What are my orders?" he asked. There was complete resignation in his voice.

"I want you to get some sleep. It's been a long night for both of us. Tomorrow will be time enough to pick up in San Francisco where we left off. I would follow up on all the leads and identify the man who tried to deliver the film. Finding out who he was may lead you to the girl. Above all, I would try to pick up the CIA's trail. They're frantic to get that film and could eventually lead you to it."

"What about the transmissions?" Zarov asked.

"Continue to keep them off POL. There is no reason to change that. The ships will sail tomorrow, and in five days we'll be in Cuba, with missiles aimed right down the Americans' throats. My plan will be completed and you'll be a general. I'll see that the papers go in right after the press conference in Havana."

They stood awkwardly facing each other. Neither spoke.

"I need to use your phone to call my driver," Karpolov said finally. Zarov gestured toward the hallway where it hung on the wall.

Karpolov walked over to the telephone and called Mikhail. When he finished, he came back across the room to pick up his hat from the floor. Before he could get there, Zarov quickly bent down and got it for him.

"Thank you," he said. "You'll start checking everything in the morning." It was a statement, not a question. "Call me at my office if you need anything at all."

"Yes," Zarov answered, opening the door. "Good night."
Karpolov nodded.

"Good night," he replied, and went out the door.

Zarov listened as the sound of his footsteps receded down the hall. Then he knelt down where Karpolov had thrown his hat, and reached under the sofa. He pulled out a tape recorder and pressed the off switch. Tonight's conversation, together with what he had recorded earlier, was enough to incriminate Karpolov of withholding information from the Politburo. Should the need arise, he was protected. For years his so-called "friend" had used and outsmarted him to his own advantage.

Now it was his turn.

San Francisco

LaSala jumped out of the car as soon as it pulled up in front of the Shelbourne Hotel. He came through the revolving doors into the lobby, which was one of the most elegant in San Francisco. He had stayed at the hotel on numerous occasions and had liked everything about it—except the price. One hundred and eighty dollars a night was outrageous, even if it was on the government.

Quickly he scanned the line of people at the front desk and saw Jankowski talking to a white-haired man at the far end. He hurried across the lobby through the maze of bellhops, people checking in, and piles of luggage. Steve saw him coming and waited at the counter. The man had gone into a small office.

"What have you got?" LaSala asked, knowing that his young assistant had already acted on the information he had received.

"Nothing yet." He gestured toward the office. "That's the night manager, a Mr. John Phelan. He knows who we are and is checking Room 218 now." Steve went into the very efficient-looking office. LaSala followed him in and shut the door.

"Room 218 has a Mr. Steve Hines in it. Arrived at 1:35 P.M. yesterday, and is checked in through tomorrow," Phelan said without looking up from the computer.

"How's he paying?" LaSala asked, standing over the desk in front of him. Phelan turned to Jankowski, who quickly introduced him to his partner.

"Does he have anything checked in your vault?" LaSala asked quickly

"We don't have one, Mr. LaSala," Phelan answered. "Instead

we provide individual safe-deposit boxes in the room to which our guests have the key."

LaSala took the room key from an envelope in his breast pocket. "Would this smaller one be it?" he asked.

"Yes."

"Then let's get up to Room 218. We need to check that box."

They went back across the lobby to the elevators and rode up to the second floor. Room 218 was just to the right of the elevator. Phelan put the key in the lock and opened the door. They came into the room, and LaSala saw that the bed had already been turned down. There was an overnight bag sticking out from under the bed. The television set was on the opposite side of the room, a VCR and a cabinet above it. Phelan went over and opened the cabinet. Inside was a metal box. LaSala let out a deep breath. It was large enough to hold two cassettes.

"Shall I open it?" Phelan asked.

LaSala just nodded his head.

He inserted the key into the lock at the top of the box. The cover snapped open. There was a black videotape container inside, with a red KNBC logo in the corner. "Excuse me," LaSala said as he removed the cassette from the box, revealing a second one underneath. He took it out and placed both of them on top of the television set. This was it. These two little black boxes could have proven to the Russians that the country was defenseless against their SRV missiles. Now at least they still had a chance to convince them otherwise. He looked at Steve. He was wiping his brow with a handkerchief.

"This is what we were looking for," he said, hiding his emotions from the hotel manager. "You've been very helpful."

Phelan edged back toward the doorway, not knowing whether he was excused or not.

"There are a few other details we'd like your help with," Steve said, looking toward his partner.

"Yes," LaSala said, drumming his fingers on the cassette box. "We'd like you to keep the room under Mr. Hines's name even though he won't be returning."

"I see," Phelan answered, obviously not wanting to pursue the statement any further.

"In addition, we'd like you to include Mrs. Hines on the register as having checked in with her husband. We'll move her into this room later tonight. Also, we'll require two more rooms in the hotel, one about halfway down the hall on this floor and a suite three or four floors up."

"I'll take care of it immediately."

"There's one more thing." He moved closer to Phelan, putting his hands on his hips so the shoulder holster under his jacket was visible. "It's absolutely essential that you don't tell anyone that we're in the hotel. I mean nobody—your employees, your wife . . . nobody. Do you understand?"

"I understand perfectly. I'll be on duty until two A.M. If you can have . . . Mrs. Hines . . . in by then, everything will be taken care of before the other manager arrives."

"She'll be here."

"Well, then, I'll be off to see to your other rooms."

"Thank you."

Jankowski opened the door for him and he left. LaSala immediately put the tape with the KNBC logo on it into the VCR. The control room came on the screen; the countdown was beginning. He pressed the fast forward and ran through the entire demonstration. At the end he rewound the tape and took it out of the machine. Quickly he inserted the second tape, pressing the fast forward to get by the station's cue numbers. Then the damaging title appeared on the screen: WASHINGTON REPORT, SECRETARY OF DEFENSE WALTER COMMACK, MARCH 6, 1994. Commack began to speak, and LaSala ejected the tape.

"That's it," he said, putting the tapes back in the boxes. "There's the proof that Commack couldn't have been at the weapon test. Barry had enough here to blow the whole plot wide open. I gotta tell you, it was close, too close. And the hell of it is that it's not over yet." He held up the original film. "We've got to get this to them, and do it convincingly."

"Well, that's where our star actress comes in," Steve said, sitting down in a leather recliner near the set. "Only she doesn't know it yet."

"I know. She's going to have to deliver this film to them personally. If one of us tries to do it and they spot us, the film's credibility goes right out the window. Hopefully it can be a simple drop; she can just be seen with it and leave. But if they take her, she's going to have to be prepared for an interrogation. And what she tells them will be crucial.

"It's going to take a lot of preparation."

"I know. We can give her the script, but she's got to be in enough control to give a performance. Then it'll be her ball game. I get very uncomfortable when things are out of my control, and this might be one of them. I don't like it."

"I don't know," Steve said, loosening his tie. "She's a pretty gutsy lady. I think she'd do all right."

" 'All right' won't be good enough. This won't be an audience of playgoing suburbanites, it'll be the KGB; and you can bet they'll send their best. They'll be looking beyond what she says. They'll be watching every move. One false blink of the eye and they'll catch it."

He looked at his watch. It was eleven o'clock. The sun would be coming up over Moscow, bringing on the dawn of October 22. He reached for the TV remote control and turned on the set. NBC's senior news anchorman, Adrian Kostigan, was reporting from Washington. A late report had just come from the Pentagon that the 182nd Airborne was being ordered to Germany to participate in maneuvers. There had been an immediate outcry of opposition by members of the Senate, but President Hayden had defended the move as being necessary, due to a Soviet buildup of troops in Czechoslovakia.

"So with just a little more than a week until the thirty-second anniversary of the Cuban missile crisis," Kostigan said, a picture of the Pentagon behind him, "the Soviet Union is again threatening the borders of a friendly nation. And there's little comfort in knowing that those borders are thousands of miles away."

LaSala lowered the volume. "The borders are a hell of a lot closer than that," he said, reaching for the phone. He handed it to Steve and sank into the chair next to him.

"Call Command 1 and get Cheryl," he said. "It's showtime."

Cheryl leaned against the bathroom wall in the command center and tried to catch her breath. The mirror on the wall verified what she had thought; all the color had drained out of her face. Her skin was a chalky white and there were tears under her eyes. She had just vomited up everything she had in her stomach. It seemed like three days' worth.

From the moment she had seen Barry fall to the street, her stomach had formed a knot that grew tighter and tighter. She had tried to control it by taking deep breaths and staying in a sitting position. But her stomach was connected to her brain and her brain said she had just killed a man. Forget about whether she loved him or not, whether it was justified or not; a man lay dead because she had pointed a finger at a television screen. The finger might as well have been the barrel of a gun, because it had killed him.

Her stomach tightened again and she leaned back over the bowl. Nothing came up. Even though it was empty, she had not spilled the guilt. She wondered if she ever could.

"Are you in there?"

The voice came from outside the bathroom door. It was Jim Sweeney.

"Yeah," she answered loudly. "Be out in a minute. Give a girl some privacy."

"Hurry it up," Sweeney answered. "They want you checked into a hotel within an hour. Steve just called."

"All right, already."

She came out into the hallway and found both Sweeney and Zeller waiting for her. Zeller handed her her coat.

"Where are my bags?" she asked.

"In the trunk of the car. We've got everything. Let's go."

"To where?"

"We're taking you to the Shelbourne. It's only five minutes away."

"The Shelbourne Regency?"

"Yeah, your boyfriend had good taste," Sweeney answered.

She stopped and looked at him. Her fingers clenched into a fist at her side and the muscles in her neck tightened. She threw her coat on the floor.

"He wasn't my boyfriend, understand! He wasn't!" she screamed at the top of her voice. "I killed him, so how the fuck could he have been my boyfriend? Don't ever call him that again. Don't ever!"

"Okay, okay," Sweeney replied, holding his hands out in front of him. He didn't want to upset her. Nobody did. She was too important to them. He picked her coat up from the floor and handed it to her. "I'm sorry," he said quietly. "Let's go."

Cheryl didn't say anything in the car on the way to the hotel. It was a cold October evening for San Francisco, and there weren't many people on the street. She sat in the backseat behind the two agents and felt the car tilt backward as it started up a hill, then forward again as it came over the crest. It reminded her of her first roller-coaster ride. Barry had taken her on it at an amusement park in Santa Monica. The Zigzag Twister. She would never forget the thrill of that ride. As they came over the crest of the first rise, she screamed so loud, she thought her throat would burst. The roller coaster plummeted down and went into an ess curve and into a tunnel. It was dark, and she buried her face against Barry's chest to block out the fear. She wished she had someone now to bury her face against. Maybe when she opened her eyes again, the fear would be all gone.

The car pulled up in front of the hotel and Sweeney got out. As he headed for the lobby Zeller pulled the car out of the valet parking lane and drove to a spot around the back of the building. He took Cheryl's two bags from the trunk and led her down a ramp to a heavy metal door. They waited a few moments and then a light went on inside. Sweeney opened the door and they stepped into a waiting elevator. When they reached the sixth floor, Sweeney got out first and checked the corridor. Then Cheryl and Zeller followed him to Room 625. The door opened immediately. LaSala and Jankowski were waiting inside the three-room suite.

"Any trouble getting here?" Steve asked Zeller.

"None. We went one block out of the way, but the streets were pretty empty."

"Good." He motioned for them to sit down. Sweeney took Cheryl's bags and put them against the wall. LaSala walked over to her and took her arm.

"How are you holding up?" he asked, leading her over to the sofa.

"Okay, I guess," she said, avoiding his eyes.

There was a tray of sandwiches and salads on the coffee table. He pushed it closer to her. "Help yourself," he said. "You'll feel better." Then, turning to the other agents, he added, "You never ate anything so expensive."

Cheryl moved away from the food. LaSala took note of it as he reached over for a sandwich. He put a napkin under it, then walked over to the TV set, putting the sandwich on top of it. Finally Cheryl sat down.

"I told the guys in the ambulance, and now I'm telling you.

Everybody did their jobs well tonight. We pulled off a beauty right under the Russkies' noses. We—"

"You saw Barry in the ambulance?" Her words were barely audible.

"Yes," he answered, putting down his soda. He thought she would add to the question. When she didn't, he continued.

"The doctor we had inside the ambulance said Barry died almost instantly. He probably didn't feel much pain."

"I saw him double up in pain on the TV."

"Yes, but within seconds he lost consciousness. By the time he got to the ambulance, he was dead."

LaSala watched Cheryl closely. Her eyes were staring into space, and she was absentmindedly picking polish off her nails. He could see that what had happened earlier was just starting to affect her. She would need time to recover. The question was, how much time? By tomorrow they needed a strong, aggressive Cheryl Branigan to go up against the KGB's best agents. And they would be suspicious. Tonight's operation would be obvious to them as more than a man shot in the street by the police. They would throw trick questions at her, try to intimidate her and threaten her. She would have to respond assertively and with authority. Right now she was a long way from that.

LaSala had to draw her out of her shell. Something had to be done to get rid of her guilt for Barry's death. Revenge for what he had done to her had to resurface again. LaSala had to make her angry.

"This is what the Russians almost got from Barry," LaSala said, holding up the cassettes. "Why? Greed. Plain and simple. Did Barry care about his country? No. About you? No. He only cared about himself and his own greed!" He put the cassettes down. Then, leaning back against the wall with his hands in his pockets, he continued. "He says I can get millions for these tapes. Why should I share it with Cheryl? She wants to return them to the CIA, anyway, so I'll pretend to go along with her. I'll tell her she's right, they should be returned, and we'll do it in the morning. To make sure she gets a good night's sleep, I'll slip a little Valium into the dinner wine. Pretty neat guy, this Barry."

LaSala stopped and waited for a response from her. There wasn't any. She just stared at the cassettes. She closed her eyes and saw a montage of images. Barry was holding up the film and laughing at her. Barry was kissing her neck and breasts. Barry was under the streetlight, looking straight into her eyes. Barry was grabbing his chest and falling to the ground. Barry was dead. She wished she were too.

There wasn't any room left for her to be angry at him anymore. The impact of his death had overshadowed that. Now she felt like she was walking around in a void. There was this giant, stark, gray, empty room, and she was in it. It was devoid of anything sensual. There wasn't any happiness or sadness, light or darkness, passion or delight. It was a living limbo. She really didn't care what happened to her. She would just exist. Nothing more.

The whole thing had finally overwhelmed her. When she first discovered that she had microfilm, there had been fear and panic. Barry had come and offered protection. Fear had returned when she saw what was on the film, but then she felt peace, even love, for Barry when they'd decided to turn it in. Suddenly he had left and there was hatred for what he had done, relief at turning herself in, and finally sorrow—mixed with revenge—in identifying him so he could be murdered. Now she felt guilt for what she had done and wondered if she could ever forgive herself, no matter what happened now. The whole roller coaster of emotions had finally caught up with her and broken her spirit. The ups and downs were just too much to take. She would settle on one solid level of nothingness and exist there. Then she could force it all to end. If it couldn't end in reality, then she would force it to end in her mind.

So let them do what they wanted with her. She really didn't give a shit anymore. Maybe that would be her inner strength—not caring if she lived or died. She opened her eyes and looked around the room.

"Am I sleeping here?" she said finally.

LaSala was surprised at the question, which was totally irrelevant to what he had said. Although it caught him off-guard, he realized quickly that his little attempt at provoking her into gaining revenge had failed. She was staring at him with a blank look that said her mind was in another place altogether. If this continued, it would be fatal. He would have to force himself to act with patience, even though time was running out. Tomorrow the Russian ships would leave for Cuba and the American people would know they had another crisis on their hands. They had missed the first deadline to get the film to the Russians; now they only had six days left before the ships reached Havana. Once they got there, it would be nearly impossible to get the missiles back out. Even if they proved to the Russians that the weapon existed, it would be too great an embarrassment for them to accept.

He couldn't risk sending Cheryl in front of the KGB before she was ready. But on the other hand, he had to prepare her for the fact that she might come face-to-face with them. The film had to be returned with credibility. The question was: When would she be ready?

He returned to her question and answered it in a low, calm voice. "You'll be sleeping down the hall in the room Barry checked into. We've changed the hotel register to show you checked in with him yesterday afternoon. Your name is Hines, Joan Hines. Got that?"

"Yes," she answered. "Cheryl Branigan, Carolyn Mulcahey, Joan Hines . . . what's the difference?"

"I know. You've been through a lot," he said sympathetically. "A lot has hit you all at once, and I want you to know we're all grateful for what you've done so far. But there's something more you must do."

She looked at the men sitting in the room. Most of them avoided her eyes while they picked at their food. She looked at LaSala. There had been an emphasis on the words *must do* that made them unequivocal and final.

"I called you, told you where the film was, helped you *kill* Barry," she answered. Her voice was heavy and she spoke slowly. "What more, Mr. LaSala, what more?"

"We need you to make contact with the Russians to return the original film. It has to be done as soon as possible. We're running out of time."

"And you want me to bring it to them." She pointed to herself, as if LaSala were asking something totally ridiculous.

"Yes," he answered quickly. "That's the only way the film will be credible. You stole it, they know you contacted Barry, were with him, and probably still have it. If anyone else returned it, it just wouldn't have credibility. They've got to believe it was the same film that was stolen in New York."

She looked down at her hands, which were folded in her lap, but said nothing.

"We need you to call them and arrange for a drop that you'll make in person. But you have to be prepared to make that call. They may ask you a lot of questions, and if they do, you'll have to answer accurately and convincingly."

"How do you expect me to do that?" she asked without looking up.

"We'll brief you on everything you have to say. You'll know the answer to every possible question they could ask. It'll be like learning a new part."

"The only parts I've ever had were one or two lines. You need an actress, not a bit player."

"We have an actress."

She looked up at him and he thought he saw tears in her eyes. But suddenly she stood up and picked up her purse.

"I want to go to my room now," she said, looking toward the door. "I'm tired."

LaSala decided she couldn't stay in her room alone. The door couldn't be locked from the outside and a guard in the hallway was out of the question.

"Steve will stay in the room with you tonight. There's a nice comfortable recliner in there he can sleep on." He turned to Jankowski, who nodded in agreement. Cheryl stood silent, her eyes fixed on the door.

Steve gathered up his things and brought Cheryl's bags over to her. To his surprise she picked them up and walked to the door. She waited there while LaSala talked to Steve.

"Go easy with her, " he said quietly. "Reassure her that everything will be all right. I'm going to talk to Shupe and see what kind of incentives we can work out for her to do this. Don't let her answer the phone, no matter what. Above all, be sympathetic to what's happened to her. She trusts you, so use that to your advantage. If you need any help, call. I don't care what time it is."

"I think I know how to handle her," Steve answered.

"Good. And one other thing," he said. "She's got to be convinced she's capable of pulling this off. She's got to do it. You're closer to her than any of us, Steve. That's why I'm leaving this to you."

"I'll do my best."

"That's all we can ask."

Steve walked over to Cheryl and opened the door. Sweeney checked the corridor. Then Steve and Cheryl left.

LaSala sank into the nearest chair. Fatigue was beginning to catch up with him. During the past three days he hadn't gotten any more than three hours' sleep a night. Usually in these situations his adrenaline pumped so much that he didn't even realize he was tired. But age had slowed the adrenaline and it became harder to keep mentally alert for long periods of time. Physically, forget about it. He was overweight, ate poorly, and got very little exercise. Thank God there were younger agents to do the physical stuff.

Sweeney and Zeller were watching him. That was the other hard part of the job, providing leadership. He didn't like to think about it, but he knew the men looked to him for a positive attitude. On an assignment like this he set the pace and tone for the group. He had to stay aggressive.

Zeller reached over for a container of mayonnaise and spread it over the top piece of bread on his sandwich. LaSala had watched him while he was talking to Cheryl. At thirty-one, he was already considered an expert on KGB operating techniques and procedures. Washington took pains to keep a small group of men like him familiar with the latest KGB thinking. Defectors were sent to him for interrogation and he was supplied with the latest manuals. The man knew their systems better than anybody. He would play a big part in preparing Cheryl.

"What do you think, Gene?" LaSala asked. "Do you think we can get her ready?"

"In the amount of time we've got left to do it? No."

"Why?"

"She's too emotionally unstable. I don't think she can stand up to Dukoff. He's very tough."

LaSala knew of Dukoff. Although listed as the information officer at the San Francisco Diplomatic Agency, he was really a senior-ranking agent in the KGB. His last assignment was in France, where he had been involved in the assassination of two of the Shah of Iran's top aides, who were organizing support against Khomeini. The job had been done cleanly. Neither the French police nor Interpol had any clue as to who the killers were.

"What can she expect from him?" LaSala asked.

"She can expect the manual from him," Zeller said, cutting his sandwich into equal halves. "If Dukoff sees a crack in her armor, he'll cut her to ribbons." He considered his sandwich for a moment and then looked up. "I just don't think she'll be up to it emotionally."

"She's got to be. Besides, she's an actress. She can learn the part."

"That's the trouble, it's not just a part. It's her own life they'll be talking about. Her emotions will be harder to control. They'll be hers, not something a writer built into her lines. She'll be more vulnerable to any attack because those emotions are very real—they're hers, she's lived them."

"So what do you suggest?"

Zeller took a bite of his sandwich and considered his answer.

"One thing I wouldn't do is what you attempted a few minutes ago. I think trying to stir up revenge for what Barry did to her is dangerous. It can lead either to anger or to deep depression, and from what I can see, it's the latter. What she needs now is reassurance. She's got to know that if she pulls this off, she'll be taken care of."

"I'm going to work on getting some financial incentives for her." LaSala replied.

"It'll help," Zeller said, "but I still think it'll be close to a week before she'd be able to go up against somebody like Dukoff."

"We don't have the time. The ships sail tomorrow. She's got to be in touch with the KGB no later than that. If Moscow doesn't get that film before the ships reach Cuba, it'll be too late."

"I think it's leading a lamb to slaughter."

"Do we have a choice?" LaSala asked, stabbing his fork into a pickle.

"No, I guess we don't," Zeller answered. "But I don't like it." He looked at the tape cassette, which was lying on top of the television set. "What about that duplicate film the lab was working on? Isn't there any way we could get that back into KGB hands and avoid this?"

"With McFarland gone, it's impossible. The guys at the lab are working around the clock, but they say they're at least a week away from completing it. I'm afraid she's our only chance." LaSala heard the finality of his own statement. He liked things neat, in control, well planned, precise. This was none of those. This whole thing had suddenly come down to two people, one a seasoned KGB interrogator, the other a frightened, jilted actress. In the balance was the establishment of military superiority by either the U.S. or the Russians. The actress would have to sell something that was make-believe to the professional. And that still wouldn't be the end of it. There was yet another man who had to buy Cheryl's story.

Viktor Karpolov had to be convinced enough to humiliate his country and destroy his career in the process.

Twenty minutes later Shupe called from Washington. The call had been forwarded from the command center, still manned by three agents. As soon as LaSala heard his superior's voice, he suspected bad news.

He wasn't disappointed.

A message had been received from COTSAR, Coded Transmission Satellite Receiving, moments ago. The transmission was from Prague and had been sent directly to his office. He had read it and immediately passed it on to the president. It was as they had suspected. A convoy of six ships led by the *Poltava* would leave the port of Tallinn on the next day. The Russians were celebrating the thirty-second anniversary of the Cuban missile crisis right to the day. They were going to Cuba. The trip would take no more than five days. The clock was running.

He told Shupe that Cheryl wasn't ready to contact Dukoff. They needed more time to prepare her. The normally placid CIA director had flown off on a tirade.

"Then, goddammit, get her ready! This is no time to be cautious, dotting the *i*'s and crossing the *t*'s. Worrying about every fucking detail may be right under normal conditions, but now the barn's on fire and the horses are running out. Get that film to the KGB, and do it quick!"

LaSala calmly tried to make his point that sending an ill-prepared Cheryl to them would be dangerous. A compromise was reached. Two days. No longer.

Reluctantly LaSala asked what incentives could be offered to Cheryl in return for her cooperation. Shupe's response was as he had expected. They would protect her, but she would have to remain under lock and key. LaSala suggested a safe house and Shupe thought that was a good idea; he would have to think about LaSala's thought on a financial offering.

"Tomorrow is going to be quite a day," Shupe had said sarcastically. "We're sending a reconnaissance satellite over Tallinn by 0100. If we see that convoy out in the Baltic, the president will be on the phone with Chebrikov by evening. Then we'll start playing poker with them. The only trouble is that they're holding all the cards. We've only got a few. And you're holding one of our aces." With that, Shupe hung up.

LaSala went into the bedroom and sat on the bed. He took off his shoes and lay back on the bedspread. There wasn't any sense in getting under the covers. He wasn't going to sleep tonight, anyway.

Tallinn, USSR

Admiral Nikolai Yurchenko stood at the wheel of the fifteen-thousand-ton freighter *Poltava* and guided it down the narrow channel leading to the Baltic Sea. It was six A.M., and the sun was low on the horizon off his stern, casting brilliant slashes of golden light in the sky above. Ahead, a red buoy flashed on and off, marking the port side of the channel, while a striped black one bobbed lazily a hundred meters away on the starboard side. Two deck officers and the helmsman stood behind him while he spun the wheel left and then right, to negotiate the last turn in the three-kilometer channel.

The older deck officer nodded to the young helmsman beside him. It was a silent communication urging the seaman to observe Yurchenko's technique. It wasn't often one got to watch an admiral behind the wheel of a ship, much less one who had the skill to steer it.

At fifty-one, Yurchenko was lean and fit, but the sea had left its marks. His face was a mass of lines resembling a photograph that had been crumpled up and then stretched out again. Dark brown eyes squinted through lids that were merely slits from long hours in the sun. A narrow mouth was framed by a high jawline, giving him a look of determination and purpose. The look was appropriate. He had not had anything handed to him in life. It had all been gotten the hard way: by scratching and clawing his way up through the ranks.

Thirty-two years ago he had been a young helmsman, standing

behind the same wheel, heading down the same channel. The
morning had been much like this—clear with calm water and a
chilling October north wind blowing off the starboard beam. He
had felt proud, as he did now, being at the wheel of the flagship
heading for Cuba. But five days later, off the coast of North
Carolina, they had been ordered to turn around. President
Kennedy had sent destroyers to intercept them. Kennedy and
Khrushchev literally had been on a collision course from which
they would have to steer clear. Because Kennedy had the upper
hand in military might, he won the game.

Even now he could hear the orders crackling over the small
speaker above the radar screen. They were terse words, spoken by
the radioman with anger and disgust. He practically spat the words
out. "Reverse course to three zero degrees northeast immediately
and proceed to Checkpoint 14." Checkpoint 14 was three hundred
and thirty nautical miles from Bermuda, heading them back on a
course that would return them to the coast of Sweden. He
remembered turning the ship hard to starboard and back into the
wake that had been trailing behind them. No one spoke, no one
moved. They had suffered a defeat worse than if the ship had been
sunk and sent to the bottom.

But this time would be different. This time, as commander of
the convoy, he had been given personal assurances from Chebrikov, himself, that the ships would not be stopped. The United
States no longer had the upper hand militarily. Their SRVs gave
the Soviet Union the advantage, and the placement of them in
Cuba would seal that fact. Nothing could stop them. In five days
they would sail into Havana Harbor to a tumultuous welcome.
They would avenge the defeat of 1962, and establish their country
as a military power in South America, thereby surrounding the
U.S. with missiles.

The freighter headed out into the open sea, leaving the
flickering lights of Tallinn behind. Yurchenko checked the line of
ships behind the *Poltava* and saw that all had cleared the final
marker. The pilot boat fell away off the port side and signaled
three short blasts. Yurchenko returned them and the convoy closed
up to set the formation.

He turned to the officer beside him and asked for a communications headset. The lieutenant handed it to him and he slipped it
over his head.

"Main engine room," he said sharply.

"Main engine room" came the quick reply.

"Sergei?"

"Yes, Admiral."

Sergei Veronikhin had also been on the *Poltava* thirty-two years ago, serving as an apprentice seaman in the engine room. Like himself, he had been devastated by the orders to turn back. Nevertheless he had gone on to serve in the navy and had put in a total of thirty-five years. During that time he and Yurchenko had remained close friends. Last year Sergei had finally retired with the rank of chief petty officer and settled down with his wife to collect his retirement. But a month later Yurchenko had called him to be his chief engine-room officer. Sergei had accepted immediately. Two weeks later he came aboard.

"Your engines are purring like kittens," Yurchenko said with a rare smile.

"But are ready to run like tigers" came the reply.

"Then full ahead."

"Full ahead it is, sir. Let me know when we get to Cuba, because I'm not touching a thing until then. That includes a bottle of champagne I'm keeping down here just for the occasion."

"I hope you're saving some for me."

"Wouldn't think of touching it without you," Sergei answered happily.

"Good, my friend. I can taste it now."

Yurchenko motioned to the helmsman to take the wheel, and pointed to the compass in front of him.

"Bring her to two-ten degrees."

The ship turned to starboard and the sun streamed through the port-side windows.

"Two-ten degrees, sir."

"Good," the admiral replied. "Lock it there until we reach Havana Harbor."

10.

PRESIDENT HAYDEN SAT facing a large television screen in the newly constructed communications room of the White House. After years of audio communication by way of a "hot line" to the Soviet premier, both sides had agreed to a video linkup so they could see each other face-to-face. If the commercial networks could talk on camera to people around the world, why shouldn't they?

As a result, a room in the East Wing had been turned into a small studio. It was totally white with fixed overhead lights that automatically adjusted to whoever was seated at a white Formica table. Slightly angled padded walls kept out noise from the outside.

Hayden straightened the small microphone clipped to his tie and glanced over at General Cabot, who was going over some handwritten notes. Senator Park, Chairman of the National Security Committee, was getting final adjustments to a small earpiece from a technician. The clock on the pristine white wall in front of the three men read 3:58 P.M. In two minutes they would make contact by satellite with Premier Chebrikov, Defense Minister Borskeyev, and Politburo member Karpolov.

Hayden thought back over the ten hours that had led to this call. Early that morning Secretary of Defense Commack had called. He had spoken to Borskeyev the previous night and gotten nothing from him. Although he hadn't broached the subject of Tallinn, he had tried to get a sense of the marshal's mood. It was the same as usual: friendly, warm, and cordial. However, he had brought up the subject of military maneuvers in Germany that had just been reported to him. "Why not in the summer?" Borskeyev had asked Commack. "Germany is dreadful this time of year."

At noon Sentinel II had flown one orbit over the Soviet Union, aiming its cameras at the port of Tallinn. By two o'clock Cabot had shown him pictures of the convoy, which was now twenty nautical miles out in the Baltic. Close-up photographs with ten-meter resolution from an altitude of twenty-six thousand kilometers showed cargo on the decks, covered with tarpaulins. When the photographs were examined closely by experts, it was determined they were probably not missiles. More likely they were turbines or some other type of machinery. That, however, contradicted intelligence reports from Prague. But when Prague tried to contact the informer at Tallinn, he could not be reached. They hadn't been able to reach him for over twenty hours.

Hayden then met with the Senate party leaders and the Speaker of the House, all of whom had been standing by. Decisions were then made as to how Premier Chebrikov would be approached. It was decided that Hayden would take a tough approach, realizing at the same time that the Soviet Union did hold the upper hand militarily. However, once missiles got into Cuba, the situation would be disastrous. A balancing act was required of him.

He looked up and saw the red light over the television camera go on. It was operated by remote from a small control room where a technician and a translator were located. The technician pointed up to the clock and he saw the sweep hand come up to four o'clock. Suddenly the large screen lit up and was filled with an image of Chebrikov, Borskeyev, and Karpolov seated at a conference table. Chebrikov sat in the middle, Karpolov to his right.

"Good evening, gentlemen," Hayden began. "I know it's late in Moscow, but I felt it most urgent that we speak this evening. Thank you for your cooperation."

He waited for the one-second satellite delay and the translation to be completed. Chebrikov shrugged his shoulders and leaned forward slightly. Although he was seated, it was apparent that he was a big man. At six foot four, his two hundred and ten pounds were evenly distributed over a large frame, dressed impeccably in a dark gray suit. His thinning hair was snow white and neatly parted at the side. A red handkerchief was tucked in the lapel pocket of his jacket, which fit snugly against his barrel chest. He spoke in Russian with a quick, animated style, although both his hands remained on the table.

"You're most welcome, Mr. President. Now, what's on your mind that is so urgent?"

"I'll get right to the point," Hayden replied. "It's about a convoy of ships that left Tallinn this morning. Reliable intelligence reports have identified their cargo as SRV missiles bound for Cuba."

Chebrikov turned and said something to Borskeyev that wasn't translated.

"The only shipment we know of to Cuba is a shipment of gas-powered turbines that was requested by the Castro government. That's not unusual. We have a trade agreement with the Castro government."

"We think it's more than turbines," General Cabot replied. "We think you're sending SRVs to Cuba."

"And why do you think that, General?"

"They left on October twenty-second from Tallinn with the freighter *Poltava* as the lead ship. What would you think if you were us?"

"I wouldn't think much of anything if I didn't have proof," Karpolov said. "You are making wild accusations on the basis of unverified intelligence reports. We, too, gather intelligence information, but we are a little more prudent before we accuse anybody."

Hayden watched Chebrikov as Karpolov spoke. His head nodded almost imperceptibly.

"We also have information that was very readily available in your newspapers during the past few days," Karpolov continued. "It says that you are involved in military maneuvers in West Germany. Our intelligence is studying this most unusual move, but we won't be making any accusations until their report is complete."

"That 'move', as you call it, was not only in response to what's happened at Tallinn but to intelligence that says you're building large troop reserves near the East German border," Senator Park answered. The translation was delayed for a moment as the translator struggled with his Southern accent. "And I must tell you that the Congress will support the president's decision to send more troops if you continue to build reserves there."

"Come, come now, gentlemen," Chebrikov said, raising both hands so they framed his round face. "Let's not get into a global discussion when the president's concern is specifically directed at ships that have left Tallinn."

"Ships carrying SRV missiles that have left Tallinn," Hayden replied, emphasizing the word *missiles*.

"And we have told you that the shipment is nothing more than turbines," Borskeyev answered, raising his voice. He was about to continue on but Karpolov stopped him with a subtle gesture of his hand. "Your system of justice has always interested me," Karpolov said in a calm voice. "It says that a man is innocent until proven guilty. How are we guilty of sending missiles to Cuba when you have no proof? What do you have, Mr. President? All we're hearing are assumptions. You assume that because we're leaving Tallinn on the twenty-second, we're carrying missiles. But that is merely an assumption."

"We now have a reliable intelligence report," Hayden replied, staring directly into the camera lens in front of him, "and if your ships continue on to Cuba, we will get the proof we need."

"And how will you do that?"

"We'll board and search them off Cape Hatteras."

"In international waters?"

"Yes. We will not allow you to proceed past that point."

Hayden watched their reactions on the large screen. Borskeyev shifted his body to a more upright position. Karpolov looked up from the notes in front of him. Chebrikov smiled.

"And if our ships resist?" he asked.

"Then we'll stop them forcibly."

"I must say, Mr. President, your words sound much like one of your predecessors', President Kennedy, except you don't have his accent." He paused for a moment and then added, "Nor do you have the military strength to back you that he had in 1962. You know it and we know it. So why do you threaten us when you're in a position of weakness?"

"Now it is you who assumes," Hayden replied. "And you couldn't be more wrong."

"You're bluffing, Mr. President, and we know it." The smile was gone now. Chebrikov shifted his body so that he was leaning toward the camera. He pointed his index finger directly at the lens.

"Try us," the president responded quickly. "I'm telling you we won't allow you to place missiles into Cuba that threaten the United States. And we will not allow you to continue to threaten our allies in Europe. It is going to stop, and it's going to stop at Cape Hatteras." He was pointing with his finger now. "Don't go beyond it!"

"We *will* go beyond it." Chebrikov answered. He was standing now, and the camera tilted upward abruptly to keep him on the screen. "You will not stop us like you did thirty-two years ago. Those ships will go to Cuba."

"I have nothing more to say," Hayden said, leaning back in his chair, "except that if you persist in this endeavor, it may result in consequences we may all regret."

"We'll see," Chebrikov responded.

"Hatteras," Hayden said quietly. "No farther."

"You won't stop us," Chebrikov replied. "You're bluffing."

Hayden looked straight into the lens.

"Don't count on it," he said slowly. He waited for a reply but the Russians sat impassively in their seats. He turned back to Cabot and Park but they, too, had nothing more to say. Finally he signaled the technician to turn off the camera. A close-up of Chebrikov remained on the screen for a moment until he realized the transmission had ended. Then the screen went black.

Hayden got up and looked at the blank image. The call had gone worse than expected. He had hoped to get a sense that the Russians were more convinced they had a weapon to retaliate with. But the opposite had been true.

Also, the tone of the call surprised him. There was nothing left of a feeling of détente that had existed up until six months ago. Chebrikov had seemed much friendlier then and seemed to be holding on to whatever was left of *perestroïka*. Hayden now had the feeling that others were influencing him toward a more aggressive stance concerning the United States, Karpolov among them.

Karpolov's emergence as a political power within the Kremlin had fostered a new direction toward aggression. He had depicted the United States as two-faced. On the one hand, the U.S. had pursued friendly relations while at the same time developing a system of potential destruction called Star Wars. Now that Star Wars had failed and the U.S. was left weak militarily, Karpolov was seizing the opportunity for military aggression.

There was no way he and the powers that supported him in the Kremlin could be stopped unless they were convinced the U.S. could retaliate. An old political science professor had once told Hayden that the only thing the Russians understood, and would ever understand, was strength. "When it came right down to it, you had to fight the bear," he had said. "And unless you can break the bear hug, he will destroy you."

He turned to Cabot and Park, both of whom were now standing beside him. "They're not going to stop those ships," he said, "unless we convince them we've got something to stop them with. And all we have right now is a bluff."

"We don't even have that," Cabot replied.

"Well, in five days we'd better have," he answered, still staring at the screen, "or we'll be looking at the possibility of World War III. And if it happens, gentlemen, we're going to lose."

14th Tactical Missile Group
Cheyenne, Wyoming

Specialist Second Class Wayne Morrison climbed into the cab of a four-and-a-half-ton tractor trailer and settled into the soft cushioned seat. The door opened on the passenger side and Colonel Lionel Travis got in beside him. He slipped a clipboard down between the seat and the gearbox and took a quick look at his watch.

"It's 1110 hours, Wayne. We're late. Crank it up and let's get outa here."

Morrison checked the sideview mirrors and saw that the forklift was clear, having loaded the last of the sixty- by fifteen- by twenty-foot panels. With a layer of Styrofoam between each panel, the load filled the entire mirror. He saw the loadmaster check the tightness of the bonding straps and then give him the high sign. He turned the ignition key and the two-hundred-horsepower diesel sprang to life.

A large hydraulically operated warehouse door slowly opened, revealing a clear night sky filled with stars twinkling over the city lights of Cheyenne, ten miles away. He switched on the parking lights and the truck moved out of the warehouse down a dirt road toward a barbed-wire fence. At the fence it made a right turn and the lights played across a sign marked MX 1570 DANGER ZONE.

"This load's the last of it, Wayne," Travis said, lighting up a cigarette. "We've got about five hours to lay these down and then you can sack out. But it's going to be a long night."

"Yes, sir," he answered, shifting the engine through the lower gears. "But none of the guys really want to sleep until we see what this jigsaw puzzle looks like when it's done."

"That'll be at about 0500 hours. I'm scheduled to go up just after dawn and photograph it from five hundred feet. It better look convincing," Travis answered.

"Well, some of the panels look like a hole deep enough to jump into, sir. When it's all put together, it should look pretty real."

"We'll see," Travis said, picking up the clipboard to check the location of the panels. The truck was coming up a rise now and he could see the work lights off to the right, where the first fifty panels were being put down.

With a penlight he went over the grid on the clipboard. With the last fifty panels in place, Missile Silo 16 would look like it had been blown to pieces. And every piece would be in the exact place that it appeared on a film that hopefully would get to the Russians. An overhead photograph of the model used in the film had been digitized by a computer and then enlarged a thousand times on to one hundred and fifty panels. The fifteen- by twenty-foot panels would cover an area the size of a football field over the real missile silo, which lay below them. When viewed from above at a distance of just ten meters, the sophisticated cameras of the Russian reconnaissance satellite *Kirov II* would see a silo devastated by a laser weapon more powerful than anything ever seen before.

Travis thought to himself about the ingeniousness of the plan. The idea had precedent, though. During World War II the Boeing plant in Seattle had been painted to resemble a housing development when viewed from above. It had been crude by comparison. The Boeing roof only had to be convincing from an altitude of several thousand feet. The peering eyes of *Kirov II*, however, would be scrutinizing this deception much more closely. Its sophisticated cameras were capable of photographing with absolute clarity an object just one meter in length. It would be difficult to fool.

"Bring 'er around to where that blue light's flashing," Travis said. "That's where the next sequence of panels starts."

Wayne shifted down into third gear and the diesel engine strained to hold back the truck as it started down the back side of the hill. As they got closer, he could see that the last of the holding pins were being driven into the ground by a small pile driver the size of a pickup truck. It drove a six-inch-long pin into the baked clay of the desert floor, and then a flange at the top opened that held the panel in position. Over five hundred were now in place.

Wayne swung the truck around in front of the blue light and an airman guided him back. He watched his swinging light through the rearview mirror until it stopped. He hit the air brakes and a hiss of compressed air shot out from under the truck.

The airman turned off the light and came around to the driver's side. Wayne rolled down the window and saw it was a buddy of his from the same barracks.

"Hey, Wayne," the airman called up to him, "this the last of it?"

"Yeah, Bobby. How's it look so far?"

"Pretty good," he replied. "I climbed up on top of a payloader to look at it, and those fuckin' Russians are gonna be surprised when they see it."

"Yeah, why?"

"It's a picture of a naked broad and she's givin' them the finger."

Wayne opened the door to get out and the airman saw the colonel for the first time. He got off a quick salute, which Travis returned. Then Travis turned to Wayne and said, "He's right, you know. That's exactly what we're doing to the Russians. We're givin' them the finger."

San Francisco

LaSala was worried.

He had lost a day waiting for Cheryl to be prepared. The convoy was on its way to Cuba, and Washington wasn't letting him forget it. They had been calling constantly since the previous morning. Shupe had informed him of the president's call to the Russians. Hayden had called Shupe afterwards and stressed the urgency of getting the film to the Russians in a convincing manner. "*Convincing* was the key word," he had told Shupe. But Cheryl wasn't ready.

She had stayed in the room with Steve all the day before. Finally, at four o'clock, Steve called and told him they wanted a tape of an old 1944 movie called *To Have and Have Not*. He had just assumed they had wanted something to watch for the evening and had asked what else he could get if that one wasn't available. Steve said it had to be that one. If they got the movie, Cheryl could be ready to call the KGB tomorrow. He thought about pressing him further but decided against it. By five-thirty Sweeney delivered the tape to the room. Steve simply opened the door and took it from him. He said he would call before eight-thirty that morning. Well, where the hell was he?

He and Zeller had both spent a restless night in the three-room suite and had been awake before dawn when Washington started calling again. If it wasn't for the hotel's strong coffee, they wouldn't be able to keep their eyes open. Zeller was reading the morning papers and was about to turn on the television when the phone rang. It was probably another call from Washington. Zeller picked it up.

"Hello . . . yeah . . . Frank? . . . He's right here. . . . Now? Okay, I'll tell him."

He hung up the phone and turned to Frank.

"Was that Steve?" LaSala asked.

"No," Zeller answered. "It was Cheryl."

"She called herself?"

"Yes. She said she was ready to be briefed."

Cheryl was seated in a small sofa when Steve opened the door to let LaSala and Zeller into the room. She was wearing a blue turtleneck over dark gray slacks with a simple gold chain around her neck. Her hair was parted in the middle and hung straight, close to her cheekbones. Light blue mascara accented her eyes and her lips were sharply defined by a ruby-red lipstick. Her legs were crossed and her arm rested on the wooden end of the sofa. With a very deliberate motion she reached for a pack of cigarettes beside her and lit up a filtered Marlboro. LaSala stared at her. It was the first time he had ever seen her smoke.

"How are you doing this morning?" he asked cautiously. Steve had gone over to the window and was looking down at the street.

"I'm fine," she answered. Her voice was lower and had a somewhat gravelly tone to it. "But you're not here to make small talk, are you? You're here to ask if I'm ready to call the KGB." She paused for a moment to blow some smoke into the air. "Well, I am. So let's get on with it."

LaSala turned to Zeller, who took it as a cue to open a folder and spread it out on the coffee table. There were several yellow pages with handwritten notes on them, one of which he picked up. He glanced at LaSala, who gestured for him to go on.

"Cheryl, the first thing we have to concern ourselves with is the phone call you have to make to set up a meeting. That call will be to the Soviet Diplomatic Agency on Market Street, the same place that Barry contacted. It's important that the call be as brief as possible and that you take command of the conversation quickly. We'll tell you everything to say, but the way you say it is what's crucial."

"Who will I be speaking to?"

"Probably an operator initially, but once you've identified yourself as Cheryl Branigan, you'll be speaking to the top man. Andreas Dukoff."

"Is he the man I might be forced to meet with?"

"Yes."

"Is he good-looking?" She took a long drag on her cigarette. The question had taken Zeller by surprise, and she knew it.

"I don't know," Zeller replied, "but he's a tough professional with an excellent reputation as an interrogator. You won't have to worry, though, we'll give you all your lines. You just have to remember them."

"And who's written this Pulitzer Prize winner?"

"Frank and I."

"Terrific. I can't wait to hear it."

Zeller began reading each line to her, along with alternates should the expected line of questioning change. LaSala walked into the other room and Steve followed him. They stood next to a window that looked down on the street.

"How did you do it?" LaSala asked in a low voice. "She's like another woman."

"I didn't do much of anything," Steve answered. "When I finally got her to talk, it turned out we had to find a way for her to get over the fear."

"But how did you do it?" LaSala asked, glancing back at Cheryl in the other room.

"She came up with the idea," Steve replied, "that the only way for her to pull it off was for her to become someone else. To really develop a character so she could step outside herself, lose her own fears and emotions. She'd play a character. It's what every good actress does." Looking toward Cheryl, Steve pointed out, "She's playing her now."

"Who is she?" LaSala asked, watching a blue Pontiac pass by on the street below. It was one of their men patrolling a two-block area around the hotel.

"Lauren Bacall," Steve answered. "She's playing a character called Slim that Bacall played in the movie *To Have and Have Not*."

"She's what?"

"Slim . . . the girl who said to Humphrey Bogart, 'You know how to whistle, don't you, Steve? You just put your lips together and blow.' That's who she's playing . . . Slim."

"Why?" LaSala asked.

"Because she's what Cheryl wants to become. Slim's tough, in control. She's sultry and, most important of all, won't be intimidated. After watching the movie three times she's become her already."

"It's a little strange, my friend," LaSala replied, "but listen, it seems to be working. When I walked in here, I expected a slightly improved basket case, but she really has become someone else."

"I think so too," Steve said enthusiastically. "She may find she's a better actress than she thought."

"I hope so," LaSala said, pulling the window shade down.

At nine-thirty Cheryl was ready to make the call. By then,

Moscowicz had worked on the hotel phone lines. He connected them to an electronic device that would measure any deviation in current, indicating a trace in progress. It would alert them, but tracing the call would be impossible. He had made arrangements with the phone company to scramble any search coming into their exchange. A tape recorder was also hooked up to one of the phones. Everything was set to go.

Cheryl sat at the desk phone with two pages of typewritten instructions in front of her. They were notes, not word-for-word dialogue. They didn't want to give the impression that she was reading from a script. The information would be LaSala's, the words hers.

In just two hours she had learned the essence of what she had to say. The answers to more than fifty hypothetical questions were on the tip of her tongue. There would be no hint of hesitation or indication that she needed time to make up an answer. She was ready to respond . . . instantly.

LaSala nodded to her and picked up his extension. She dialed the number and heard the phone ringing.

"Soviet Diplomatic Agency, good morning." It was a woman's voice and was surprisingly bright and cheery.

"Good morning," Cheryl replied in a short, clipped tone. "My name is Cheryl Branigan and I'd like to speak to the person in charge."

"What is it in reference to, Miss—"

"Branigan, Cheryl Branigan."

Suddenly the operator's tone changed. She spoke more rapidly. "One moment, please. I'll connect you right away . . . to Mr. Dukoff. Hold on, please. He'll be right with you."

Fifteen seconds passed and a man came on the line. His voice was slightly accented and he spoke in a very slow, calculated manner.

"Miss Branigan?"

"Yes."

"My name is Andreas Dukoff, and I'm the information officer. What can I do for you?"

"I have something that was supposed to have been delivered to you at a restaurant on Market Street two nights ago."

Dukoff hesitated for a moment.

"I don't know what delivery you're talking about," he said carefully.

"I think you do," she answered quickly. "My friend was supposed to deliver a package to you, but apparently somebody found out about it."

"Do you have that package now?"

"Yes, but I want to be sure that the line we're talking on is safe. I don't want what happened to my friend to happen to me."

"I see. Well, you can be sure the line we're speaking on is absolutely clean. There's no way we can be overheard."

"I hope so, because whoever stopped my friend from getting to you must have been listening."

"We know that now, Miss Branigan, and the problem has been corrected. Where is the package now that was supposed to have been delivered to us?"

"I have it. My friend didn't have it last night because he came only to negotiate a price. I can tell you now that the price is three million dollars."

"That's an awful lot of money, young lady, for something I'm not sure you even have."

She ignored the comment and referred to the scripted notes in front of her.

"The money is to be deposited into the Bahamian National Bank, account number N-2939440, three o'clock this afternoon. They're waiting for the deposit to be made." She checked her notes again to make sure the information was correct. Dukoff was hesitating.

"And you're asking me to give it to you before I have the film. How do I know you even have it?"

"I have it," she answered without hesitating. "But I'm going to make sure I have the money before I give it to you."

"Even if I was foolish enough to do that, my superiors wouldn't be. They would have to authorize that amount, and I can assure you they wouldn't do it without seeing the film first."

"I understand." She was changing the tone of her voice now. She sounded more frightened and her words came quickly, one after the other. "I'm afraid, Mr. Dukoff . . . whoever . . . whoever killed my friend is still looking for the film. I have to get rid of it before they find me."

Her voice started to break and she appeared to be fighting off crying. There was an audible click on the line and she turned to Moscowicz. He nodded for her to continue.

"My friend told me to arrange an account with the bank, so I did it yesterday. I'm frightened. I want the money put in the account before I give you the film."

"I see," Dukoff replied. He paused for a moment, apparently trying to collect his thoughts. "I would have to consult my superiors before I could pay the kind of money you're asking for. That may take some time. I—"

"I don't have a lot of time. I . . . I want the money deposited right away . . . this afternoon."

"That's impossible."

"No, it's not," she answered. She was sobbing now, and her voice broke down into a series of short gasps. "Please, if you want the film, call the bank by three o'clock this afternoon. Do you have the account number?"

"Yes, I have it."

"Call them and deposit the money. I'll . . . I'll call you back later."

"I'll see what I can do." Again there was a click on the line. "I'll call you."

"Yes, do that if you want the film."

She hung up the phone.

LaSala waited until she had taken her hands away from the receiver, then put his own down. Steve, Moscowicz, and Zeller had been sitting on the bed during the conversation. It was Steve to whom Cheryl looked first.

"I thought you did terrific," he said enthusiastically. "You sounded frightened, yet you knew what you wanted in return for the film. It was very convincing. For a minute there I closed my eyes and really believed you were crying. You found another side to that Slim character. That wasn't even in the movie."

"Yes, it was," she said, brushing back a loose strand of her hair. "Slim was vulnerable even though she hid her emotions. I just let them out for her."

"I also think you did great," Zeller volunteered. "You said you only played bit parts, but you gave one hell of a performance."

"She did very well," LaSala said finally. "But Dukoff's no fool. He was trying to trace the call during the conversation to locate her. Also, I'm sure he suspects we're involved. We've got a way to go before he's going to buy this act, so let's not sit on our laurels. The main event is yet to come."

Cheryl lit up a cigarette and turned away from the desk, crossing her legs in the chair. LaSala noticed how her body movements had changed. Every move was slower now, more deliberate. It made her look sultry, more confident . . . like Slim in *To Have and Have Not*. She was continuing to play the part, even when she wasn't onstage.

"So I don't get rave reviews from our fearless leader?" she asked, blowing smoke into the air.

"I think you did very well," LaSala replied. "I'm just saying we shouldn't let down; the real performance is yet to come."

"Spoken like a true director," she replied. "Don't give the talent too much praise during rehearsal; save it until the show is over."

"Something like that," he said. He realized the danger in responding directly to the Slim character. She was playing a tough part, but underneath was the frightened woman she had played on the phone. It was crucial that he remember that. He moved on to the next call, which hopefully would come from the bank during the afternoon. "When Bahamian National calls," he said, "you'll be speaking to the bank's executive vice president, a Mr. Alan Clark. I want you to sound very efficient and businesslike. The conversation should last only three or four minutes."

They wrote down several notes for her to refer to while speaking to Clark and then started rehearsing for Act II, her next conversation with Dukoff.

Cheryl watched LaSala, Jankowski, and Zeller as they wrote down questions and answers for her to rehearse. They were professionals doing their jobs, but she was a frightened woman caught up in something that was terrifying. She had never been exposed to danger like this before. Tapped phone calls, death on the street, coded messages, CIA, KGB, men trying to kill her—it was like a nightmare. She had to continue the role she was playing. It was her only hope of making it through without her fear getting out of control. And so far it was working.

LaSala handed her two pages of notes filled with questions and answers. After she had studied the answers thoroughly, they began firing questions at her.

"Who was the man with the film? How did he get it? What was

your relationship? How did you meet? What was the address where you lived together? Where did he work? For how long?

"Did you love him? How did you find out about his death? How do you feel about the CIA now? Are you selling the film for revenge? How has his death affected you?"

They went over each question until she responded automatically. Then she added feeling and emotion to the words. She interpreted the answers to the way Slim would feel about them. They were Slim's answers.

At three-thirty she called the bank. A very dignified voice with a British accent assured her that yes, three million U.S. dollars had been deposited into N-2939440. The money had been deposited by the Ursus Research Foundation in Modesto, California. LaSala was pleased. Not only were they getting three million dollars from the KGB, they had forced them to reveal one of their cover corporations from whose account the money had been withdrawn.

Having completed the call, Cheryl turned to LaSala. "Well?" she asked.

"You did fine," he replied.

"Yeah," she answered, ignoring the compliment. "And the CIA is three million richer."

"Two million," he said quickly. "If everything goes according to plan, you'll be withdrawing a million from the account in a few days."

She tried to retain her composure but found it difficult. Before she could ask the obvious questions, LaSala provided her with the answers.

"I spoke to Shupe this morning, and he's agreed to pay you one million dollars from what the Russians deposit. Let's call it incentive to give a good performance. There is, however, one stipulation: You'll have to remain in safe-house custody for two years. I don't know where the house is yet, but it'll be very comfortable. It might even be in the Bahamas."

"What happens after the two years?" she asked. LaSala was watching her carefully. He had chosen this time to tell her about the money, to see how much control she would lose. The answer was very little. She continued to stay in character. However, the hand holding the cigarette trembled ever so slightly.

"You'll walk off into the sunset with a million dollars to do whatever you want," he added.

"No strings attached?"

"One. You'll have to tell us where you are every three months."

"That's reasonable."

"I think so."

Inside she breathed a long sigh of relief. Her worst fear had been that they wouldn't allow her to live because she knew too much. But instead they were going to hold her captive until her knowledge about the nonexistent weapon became obsolete. It was ironic. She had turned herself in and ended up with the money. Barry had tried to get money from the Russians and had ended up dead. *"Here's to the fork in the road where we choose our separate ways. Maybe not because we want to, but because it has to be."*

Twenty minutes later the second call was made to the Soviet Diplomatic Agency. Again the female operator answered, and Cheryl was put right through to Dukoff. This time he seemed friendlier and allowed her to take the lead in the conversation.

"I assume you called the bank and verified our deposit," he began.

"Yes," she replied quickly. "And I want to get the film to you tonight."

"Tonight. I don't know if that's possible," he said hesitantly. "I would have to arrange a meeting where we can be assured the film can be safely transferred."

"It has to be tonight," she said. "I can't hold on to the film any longer. They'll find me. I know they will. I can't wait."

LaSala heard the click on the line again. They were still trying to trace the call. If Dukoff had his way, they'd come crashing into the hotel right now. He held the notes in front of Cheryl and pointed to the instructions for the drop. Dukoff would agree to tonight. As a professional, he was trying to secure a safe drop, but Moscow wanted that film in a hurry. The three million wouldn't have been deposited that quickly if they didn't.

"You'll have to give me time to draw up a plan," Dukoff continued.

"I *have* a plan," Cheryl said. She was injecting excitement into her voice now, which heightened her fear even further. "My friend and I had it worked out before they killed him. It has to be tonight."

"Go on," Dukoff said cautiously.

"Tonight there's a football game between the Forty-Niners and the Rams at Candlestick Park. Are you familiar with the stadium?"

"Yes, I am."

"The film will be left in a black Toyota Cressida in the south parking lot of the stadium, once the game has begun. It will be in the trunk, which will be left ajar.

"How will we recognize the car? There will be hundreds of Toyotas in the lot."

"It will be the only one with a motorized antenna left up, because the engine will be running."

"I see." Dukoff paused for a moment while he considered the viability of the plan. "It will take us a while to locate the car," he said finally.

"Exactly," she answered, "but you will find it."

"Was this your friend's plan?"

"Yes. He thought it would be a safe way to deliver the film if you had agreed to the price at the restaurant."

"Well, Miss Branigan, you hold all the cards right now. You've already got your money deposited and you still have the film. You could just run with it, you know, or simply dispose of it anywhere—a trash can, even."

"No," she answered. Her voice was trembling again. "I want this all to be over with for good. If I didn't leave the film, I know you'd come looking for me and wouldn't stop until you found me. I can't run anymore."

"You're right. We would come looking for you. Remember that tonight."

There was another click.

"There are a couple of questions I'd like to ask you before you hang up."

She turned to LaSala, who nodded in the affirmative.

"Yes, but I have to go. Someone may be listening, and I'm frightened."

"The line is clean," Dukoff answered reassuringly. "Are you calling from a public phone?"

LaSala nodded.

"Yes," she said.

"Have you seen the film?"

"Yes."

"What is on it?"

"A demonstration of a weapon and some plans for it."

"How were you able to see it?"

"My friend was able to put it on videotape and we played it in his apartment."

"What kind off weapon do you think it is?"

"My friend thought it was some kind of laser weapon. Look, I just want to get rid of it. I have to go now."

"Very well," Dukoff replied. "Candlestick Park . . . tonight. We'll be looking for that car. Don't disappoint us."

"I won't."

She hung up the phone.

Again she had done well. LaSala reached over and patted her on the shoulder.

"This time the director is telling you that you did a good job. You came off as a frightened young lady who just wants to be done with this."

"You hit it right on the head," she said, pushing the phone away. "That's me."

He watched her get up and walk over to the window. Steve and Zeller followed her and repeated LaSala's comment of a job well done. If they had convinced Dukoff that she was operating on her own, it had been a big step forward.

Now only one thing was bothering LaSala. Karpolov. Why was he still interested in the film now that his ships were leaving for Cuba? If the film proved they did in fact have a weapon, he might still be forced to turn them back. The humiliation of that would ruin his career, but for some reason the Russians still wanted it. Why? Finding out they had a weapon now could only destroy Karpolov. Why did they still want it?

Andreas Dukoff hung up the phone and wrote a five-line message on a piece of notepaper. He then went to a small communications room located in the basement of the Soviet Diplomatic Agency. There he handed it to a man seated in front of a computer connected to a shortwave transmitter.

"Send this immediately by satellite, encoded," he said, handing the man the note, "to Colonel Zarov."

Atlantic Command Headquarters
Norfolk, Virginia

Admiral Sam Hutchinson hurried out of the backseat of a staff car as his driver opened the door. He was late for his meeting. The goddamn traffic into the city from Newport News had been bumper to bumper, even though it was ten o'clock in the morning.

He ran up the steps and through the door of the newly built 6th Fleet Naval Headquarters. The open elevator was straight ahead. He shoved his leather briefcase into the closing doors, winced as they pressed against the soft leather, then stepped inside as they opened again. Two minutes and six floors later he was standing in front of a Navy lieutenant, sitting at a desk outside the Atlantic fleet commander's office. She pointed to the door on her left.

A heavy wooden door opened into the conference room. He had expected a large group of officers to be assembled for the meeting, but there were only three men. Admiral Alvin Hampel, Fleet Commander, held out his hand for him and he shook it.

"I know . . . traffic was heavy. Sam, I think you've met General Cabot. Say hello to Senator Park here, Chairman of the National Security Committee."

"General, Senator Park, pleased to meet you." He shook hands with both men. There were a few pleasantries and he took a seat offered him by the admiral. The others sat down and looked to Hampel, waiting for him to speak first. There was a large white folder on the center of the table.

"As you know, Sam, we wouldn't have sent you down through all that traffic unless we had something important. And this one's *really* important. Your carrier is going out about six hundred miles, with two frigates and a destroyer. Tomorrow. Hopefully by 2100 hours."

"It'll take some doing to get ready by tomorrow night," he replied.

"Get ready. You're going to come face-to-face with the Russians," Hampel said, emphasizing his point by tapping his pencil on the table. "They're replaying 1962 all over again. They've got a convoy of six ships carrying SRVs to Cuba."

Hutchinson looked at Cabot and Senator Park. Neither said anything but were looking straight at him.

"You're sure they're carrying missiles? We've seen a lot of machinery going down the coast to Cuba."

"The president spoke to Chebrikov yesterday afternoon. He says the ships are carrying turbines, but we've got reliable intelligence that says they're missiles. SRVs. The convoy left yesterday. From Tallinn."

Hutchinson opened his briefcase and started to take a leather-bound notebook from it. He thought about the irony of the carrier *John F. Kennedy* being called upon but said nothing.

"You won't need any notes, Sam," Hampel continued. "All the details are in that packet on the table. Your orders are to track the convoy on radar, set a collision course, and meet them no farther north than Cape Hatteras."

"Why Hatteras?" he asked. "We can probably get up to latitude forty-one in time to meet them."

"No," Hampel replied quickly. "We need the time for other efforts, which the senator and General Cabot will explain. "We'll let them go as far as Hatteras."

The admiral's eyes met his for a moment and Sam thought he was about to say something more. But he hesitated and turned to General Cabot. "General, I think you'd better fill Sam in on what's led up to all of this," he said evasively.

Cabot nodded and then in slow, deliberate words explained the elaborate deception that had been created over two years to bluff the Soviet Union into thinking we had a laser weapon. Hutchinson listened, shocked with disbelief. As a military officer he had always believed the United States was in a position to challenge the Russians militarily, but now he was being told that we no longer had that capability. One of the key components of the military arsenal of the U.S. was merely a bluff.

"The Russians suspect we're bluffing," Cabot said, "but the president has threatened to stop the convoy and search it off Hatteras. In five days it'll be there. In the meantime we're taking steps throughout the world to convince them we have the weapon. If those efforts fail, it will affect your orders at Cape Hatteras."

"How?" he asked, "and what do you mean by 'threatening' to

stop the convoy?" These were questions they all had avoided so far. It was Senator Park who gave him the answers.

"What happens at Hatteras depends on whether or not we can convince Chebrikov that we have the weapon. As the general just said, those efforts are going on right now. But if we aren't successful within the next three or four days, Chebrikov will know we have nothing to counterattack his SRVs with and have no defense against them. He'll realize that he now has unchallenged military superiority."

"And how will that affect my orders?"

Senator Park looked to Admiral Hampel.

"The president, along with key members of Congress who know of the deception, came to a decision last night. You will allow their ships to pass through to Cuba."

Hutchinson looked at the three men. All of them were avoiding his eyes. Admiral Hampel was absentmindedly drawing long diagonal lines down the margin of a yellow-lined pad. They were ordering him to go out and meet the Russians and point his guns at them. But when they came face-to-face, Washington would tell him whether or not his guns were loaded. If they weren't, he was to retreat. The word *retreat* disgusted him. He never had retreated from anything in his life, and neither had his country.

But now, for the first time . . . they might have to.

San Francisco

At four-thirty final preparations were made for Cheryl's departure to Candlestick Park. The three-room suite was busy with activity.

Moscowicz had been working all morning on the Toyota Cheryl would drive to the stadium. The Cressida's motorized antenna had been fitted with a timer which she would activate once the car was parked. The Russians would be looking for a Cressida with its antenna up, but the timer would delay the antenna motor for three minutes. It would give her ample time to get away from the vehicle before the KGB could identify it. By the time they found it, Cheryl would be seated inside the crowded stadium, being watched by Steve and other agents, scattered around in nearby seats. At the end of the game they would leave with the crowd and the car would remain in the lot. Avis would pick it up the next day.

Clothing had been bought for her during the afternoon: a knit Forty Niners hat, a blue down jacket, a white turtleneck over gray wool slacks, and black flat shoes. Her wallet contained her real identification, fifty dollars, her ticket, and her hotel key. She looked like a typical fan out to enjoy the ball game.

LaSala made one last phone call to Jim Sweeney at Candlestick Park, to check if everything was ready. Five agents had been assigned seats within view of Cheryl. Two others would patrol the outer gates. Sweeney would be in a car, pulled off at the side on Gilman Avenue with a flat tire. Gilman was the main street leading to the parking lots. Steve and Kovacs were already at the stadium, and would pick her up once she came out of the lot. Everything was ready.

A final check was made on the Toyota, then Moscowicz and Zeller also left for the stadium. Cheryl was alone now with LaSala. He walked over to the sofa and took her coat and Forty Niner hat from it.

"Ready?" he asked, holding the coat open for her.

"As ready as I'll ever be," she said, turning her back to him and holding out her arms. He slipped the coat on and pulled the collar up around her neck. How many times had she done that for people at Armando's Restaurant in New York? It felt good to be on the receiving end. LaSala held his hand on her shoulders for a moment. She felt them through the coat. They were holding her tightly.

"Be careful," he said softly. "Run everything through your mind on the way to the park. When you get there, head for the main parking lot, park the car, release the trunk latch, activate the timer on the antenna, leave the motor running, get out of the car, and lock it. Head for Gate B and pick up Steve and Kovacs. They'll be behind you all the way to your seat. Then you'll be safe. You'll just be one of fifty thousand people watching a ball game. Now, have you got all that?"

"Yes," she answered. They had been over it a hundred times. She turned around and LaSala was standing there like the father she had never had. Although he was doing his best to hide it, she could see the concern for her in his face. She had never seen that with her own father. He had left her without a strong shoulder to cry on, something her mother never had been able to provide.

LaSala reached for the tape, which was rolled inside a heavy plaid blanket. He held it out to her. "Put it in the trunk when you get in the car. Keep it wrapped until then. It's very valuable cargo."

She took the blanket from him and felt the bulk of the cassette inside it.

"I just want you to know," he said, staring down at the blanket, "that I think you're a very brave woman. I wish we didn't have to put you through all this, but it's the only way we can safely get the tape back to them. If we were delivering it ourselves, it would destroy the credibility of the tape. And they'll be watching, believe me. Dukoff will have men inside the parking lot. Hopefully the antenna device will enable you to get out of there and into the stadium without having to make contact with them. Get into that stadium as fast as you can. Mix in with the crowd. The more people around you, the better. Once you're inside among thousands of people, you'll be safe."

"I know," she said, putting the blanket under her arm. "Don't worry, I'll be all right."

"Good luck," he said, handing her the keys to the car. "Remember, it's in space 3B. We'll see you later, at the stadium."

She nodded and left the room, hoping she would live to see it again.

Traffic was fairly light as she brought the Toyota onto the James Lick Freeway heading south. She had over forty-five minutes to travel the eight miles to the stadium. Plenty of time.

The plan had been for her to arrive at six-fifteen. By then the fifteen-thousand-car lot would be about half full, with tailgate picnics in full swing. There would still be enough vacant spaces for her to park, and enough of a crowd into which she could blend. Also, three different lots would still be open, so the crowds would enter the stadium from many different directions.

She felt her heart beating. Her hands gripped the wheel so tightly, her knuckles were turning white. Hopefully, in another hour, this whole thing would be over with. She took a deep breath and turned on the radio. Some country music came on.

She stayed in the slow lane behind a recreational vehicle with a sticker on its bumper that read, WE'RE SPENDING OUR CHILDREN'S INHERITANCE. Yeah, she thought, she should live so long.

It was beginning to get dark and she switched on the lights. The news came on. She half listened to it. Something up ahead had caught her attention. The red taillights of the cars were getting closer together. The traffic had stopped.

Suddenly she realized that the radio station was giving the traffic report. A female voice rattled off a bunch of names and acronyms, half of which she didn't understand.

"A tractor trailer carrying propane gas has overturned at the intersection of the Lick and Southern Freeways. Two lanes have been closed by the S.F.P.D. and traffic is backed up to Army Street. Police and emergency rescue are on the scene, but only one lane is open at this time. Alternate routes are across Oakdale to the tanks and onto Third, however those routes already have twenty-minute delays."

She looked at the clock. 5:55. She had only twenty minutes. The game didn't start until seven but the spaces would be filling. Every minute past six-fifteen meant more of a chance she would be spotted. What the hell was she going to do?

The car in front of her slowed to ten miles an hour. Finally the brake lights went on and it stopped.

Agent Sweeney stood next to his "disabled vehicle," looking down the long line of cars backed up along Gilman Avenue. It was almost six-forty-five and still there was no sign of Cheryl. She was now over thirty minutes late and he estimated that the fifteen-thousand-car lot was now over three-quarters full. Steve had been on the radio three times, asking the same question. "Where the hell is she?"

He looked across the road at the cars turning into the four lanes leading to the ticket booths. So far he had counted fifty black Cressidas among the thousands of cars that had already gone through. Some had been in the lot for as long as ninety minutes now. Long enough for the KGB to have located and checked them, if they were looking.

To his left he saw a police car approaching, its red lights flashing. It pulled in behind him and a city policeman got out. He walked over to him, his flashlight playing over the flat tire and jack lying next to it.

"Anything I can do to help you?" he asked, looking Sweeney over.

"No thank you, Officer," he replied. "I'm afraid my spare is flat, but I've already called someone. With all this traffic, though, it's going to be a while."

"Yeah, I'm afraid so," the cop replied, looking down the line of lights. "The stadium traffic's normally bad enough, but there's an accident on the Lick, and they're backed up for over four miles."

"How long has it been backed up?"

"Over a half hour. Probably another half hour before they get it cleared. I'm staying away from there if I can. Sure you don't want me to radio anybody else?"

"No. Thanks. They'll get here sooner or later."

The cop nodded and went back to his car. As he pulled away, Sweeney got in his car and radioed Steve inside the stadium. Then he called LaSala.

At 6:55 Cheryl passed Sweeney and drove up to the ticket gate. By now she was nearly hysterical. For nearly an hour and a half she had sat in traffic watching the digital clock on the dashboard click off the minutes. Each one was a precious moment of time that would have given her better odds of not running into the KGB.

She saw that all the cars were being sent down one lane to the few spaces that remained. Up ahead, a man was waving a red flashlight that he used to direct her off to the right. As she turned, her lights reflected off a second man's yellow striped vest. She drove toward it, avoiding people with Forty Niner banners and beer in their hands, rushing for the stadium. Finally she made it to the end of the row and was directed into a space.

She turned off the lights, but kept the motor running. Her hands trembled as she felt for the timer switch that would delay the antenna motor. Her fingers searched under a maze of wires and found it. She clicked it on and then released the trunk latch.

Quickly she pressed the electric door lock, got out of the car and shut the door. As she passed the rear of the car she felt under the trunk to make sure the latch had released. The trunk was ajar. There was less than an inch of space under the cover. She hurried away from the car, glancing back to see that the antenna was still down. Good. The timer was allowing her to get away before it raised the antenna back up.

The crowd rushed by her toward the stadium. She fell in among them. A man behind her tossed a football to a friend who was running between the cars. Two men sitting on the tailgate of a pickup whistled at her. Another man, who was carrying a small boy on his shoulders, bumped into her. A woman turned to talk to a friend and almost hit her in the eye with a Forty Niner flag. To her right Cheryl saw two parking attendants moving a barrier in place that closed the lot. It was full.

Up ahead were the tailgaters. There was a line of recreational vehicles parked close to the stadium entrance. She thought she saw a woman sitting outside one of them wave to someone behind her. The entrance gate was no more than a few hundred feet ahead now. She was almost there. Soon she would see Steve and Kovacs. Just a few more minutes. She heard a roar from inside the stadium. The game was starting.

The crowd pressed tightly against her as they headed for the narrow entrance that led to the gate. The woman at the RV waved again, and suddenly Cheryl felt someone behind her grab her arm tightly. For a moment she thought it might be the man with the boy on his shoulders, but then she turned around. It was Plastic Man.

He pushed her forward toward the woman, who now had been joined by another man. "Cheryl," the woman yelled, "we didn't know you were coming to the game! Frank," she said to Plastic Man, "what a surprise!"

Cheryl started to scream, but the woman pressed against her in an embrace that muffled it. The crowd moved around them, rushing for the gate, while Plastic Man pushed her toward the RV. Again Cheryl tried to scream, but the woman held her tightly, trying to kiss her. As the crowd headed for the gate she kept up a running dialogue that was close to hysteria. "We haven't seen you in such a long time! Cheryl and Frank, of all people! You've got to have a drink with us. There's still time. Herb, do you believe it? It's Cheryl and Frank!"

Suddenly Cheryl was being pushed into the RV. She struggled to fight her way back out, but Plastic Man and the other two Soviet agents were blocking the door. It closed behind her and she saw a man seated at a small dining table. The venetian blinds next to him were drawn, but the stadium lights shined through, casting long horizontal shafts of white light across his face. He got up and took a few steps toward her. As he came closer, Cheryl saw his features more clearly.

He was short, slightly overweight, but extremely handsome.

His white, wavy hair was cut stylishly close, and it framed a face that looked like it had been chiseled by a classic Greek sculptor. His features didn't have the usual Russian look—thick eyebrows, narrow eyes, and heavy chin. Instead his face was delicately shaped, the nose straight and narrow, the eyes big and very blue. She thought he might be in his late fifties but looked younger. He smiled at her and extended his hand.

"Hello, Cheryl," he said pleasantly. "I'm Andreas Dukoff."

She stood looking at him. Her whole body was shaking and she struggled to get control of herself. The whole elaborate plan that had been put together by LaSala had failed. A goddamn overturned tractor trailer had made her an hour late, and now she was on her own. Her mind raced to call upon the character that was her strength. Slim. She quickly had to become Slim. She had to have her strength and her composure.

"I'm sorry to have forced this meeting on you," he said, smiling, "but it's necessary that I not only see the film but also that I talk to you. Do you have the film?"

"It's in the trunk of the car, like I said it would be."

"Where is the car? What area?"

She tried to think. The space hadn't been important. Then she remembered.

"There's a large 21 on the pole in front of it. It's somewhere in Section 21." Her voice was shaky.

"Get the film," Dukoff said to Plastic Man, who immediately went out the door with the other agents.

She took a quick look at her watch. Only a few minutes had passed since she'd left the car. Would the antenna be up? What if it went up just as Plastic Man was approaching the car? Oh, God.

Dukoff turned to her. "May I take your coat?" he asked, extending his hands. His smile revealed a small dimple in his chin. She took off her coat and handed it to him. He folded it neatly and laid it on the driver's seat. She watched him and again tried desperately to control her fear by summoning the Slim character. Already she could see that Dukoff was trying to put her at ease, catch her off-guard, and gain an advantage. He was trying his best not to be KGB. They were both going to playact, one against the other.

"Please have a seat," he said, gesturing to the empty chair on the other side of the table. "May I get you some coffee while we're waiting?"

She shook her head. "No . . . thank you."

He poured himself a cup, then sat down at the table with his hands folded in front of him. She didn't dare look at her watch.

"We thought you had stood us up," Dukoff said, stirring the coffee. "You were over an hour late."

"I got stuck in traffic," she said quickly. "There was an accident."

"We heard it on the radio. Did you come directly from a hotel?"

"Yes," she replied.

"Downtown?"

"Yes."

"I see," he said. He was studying her carefully. His blue eyes darted from side to side, watching her every movement.

"You said you had a cassette copy of the film that your friend made. How was he able to make it?"

"He made it where he works. He's a film editor."

"And then he came back to the apartment with it and you looked at it. Is that right?"

"Yes. We saw it would be valuable to . . . to your people . . . and then we left for San Francisco as soon as we could."

"Why didn't you contact us from L.A.?"

"We wanted to get out of the city. We were afraid that Lucci's people or the CIA would be following us."

Dukoff was about to ask another question when the door opened. Plastic Man came into the RV carrying the blanket with the film inside. Her heart started to race again. He placed the blanket on the table and opened it. The cassette and two boxes of microfilm were inside.

Her eyes closed and she let out a sigh of relief. Dukoff got up and put the cassette into a VCR that was built into a cabinet.

Cheryl took the opportunity to get a pack of cigarettes from her jacket pocket. Slim would need to smoke in this situation. She lit the cigarette. It was easy. Her hands were steady. She was in control.

Dukoff clicked the recorder on, and an image came up on the screen. He stood with his hands behind his back during the entire four minutes without moving. She was surprised. He showed no emotion or reaction to what was a very impressive demonstration. When the control-room sequence ended, he was about to turn off the VCR but then realized there was more. The schematic drawings appeared, and he used the pause button to study each of them carefully. At the last drawing he rewound the whole tape and then started over. Again the control room came on the screen and he froze the image.

"So what did you and the film editor think this was?" he asked, leaning against the set on one elbow.

"I told you on the phone, some kind of weapon demonstration," she answered, remembering her prepared lines. She would give short answers until she knew what direction he was headed in.

"Do you know what kind of weapon?"

"The drawings made us think it was probably a laser."

"Ah, I see," he said, smiling again, "something out of science fiction. Star Wars, right?"

"No," she said. He was attempting to oversimplify. To follow this tack would make her seem naïve. "My friend said the drawings showed a laser weapon, or something that reflects a laser off a satellite down to a ground receiver."

"Very perceptive," he said, looking at her with a slight tilt to his head. Every word she spoke was being evaluated carefully. He turned back to the machine, ran the tape to the second scene, and paused again. This time he leaned forward and studied the image for what seemed to be close to a minute.

"Do you know who these men are who are watching the demonstration?"

"One of them is Walter Commack, the Secretary of Defense."

"And the others?"

"Obviously high-ranking military men."

"Very high-ranking," he answered. "From left to right, General Dwight Cabot, chairman of the Joint Chiefs of Staff, General Arnold Fogel, Air Force adjutant, General John McMahon, NATO commander, and General Milton Lowe, Congressional liaison officer for the Pentagon. Quite an impressive group."

He ran the tape forward again and stopped where the laser exploded into the missile silo.

"You're absolutely correct," he said without taking his eyes off the screen. "This is a laser, a very powerful one, probably in the seventy-five to eighty thousand ton range. It easily destroyed a silo in Wyoming that we've been monitoring for several years now."

She didn't answer. He started the tape again and watched the celebration in the control room. Then he fast-forwarded to the schematics again, pausing only once. The tape ended and he placed it back on top of the set. His smile was gone.

"You know, Miss Branigan, stealing this tape in New York was a pretty daring thing to do for a young lady like you. Why did you do it?"

"I thought I was stealing cocaine, not microfilm."

"So you stole what you thought was cocaine and ran to Los Angeles. When you got there, you checked into the Belmont Hotel?"

"Yes."

"And then you called Barry Rossiter."

Cheryl hesitated. She hadn't told him Barry's name. How did they know who he was? "Yes," she answered, recovering quickly. "He came to the hotel and I showed him the microfilm."

"Then what?"

"We went to his apartment. I told you, the next day he brought the film to where he worked."

"KNBC."

"Yes," she replied. Again he had information beyond what she had told him. This time she decided to press him. "How do you know?" she asked.

"We've done some checking," he said, brushing the question aside. "Your friend Barry then transferred the film and you saw what was on it for the first time. Is that right?"

"Yes," she said, blowing smoke up into the air.

"And what did you think?"

"At first I was frightened. I knew that Lucci was involved in more than cocaine and that the man passing the film was probably selling it. He would be looking for it. And Lucci would be looking for me."

"How did Barry react?"

"He wanted to turn it in to the CIA, but I thought it would be worth a lot of money to the KGB."

"What made you think that?"

"Because the guy who had come into the restaurant must have been getting a pretty penny for what he was passing, so this would be worth plenty." She hesitated for a moment while she inhaled her cigarette and then added, "I was right."

"So how did you convince Barry to go along with you and sell the film to us?"

She hesitated and then answered. "I slept with him."

She noticed him look down at her hand that was holding the cigarette. It was steady. Slim was playing the role for her, right down to the proper body movements. She leaned back in the chair a little, letting the turtleneck tighten against her breasts.

"So," he said, "you sort of rekindled the old flame, I suppose. You had lived with him for a period of time over five years ago, isn't that correct?"

This was something else they knew that surprised her.

"Yes," she answered in a slightly irritated tone. "We lived together for a while, but then I left him."

"Why?"

"Because he was into coke and we didn't get along."

Dukoff nodded in response to her answer, then sat down on the opposite side of the table.

"I'd like to know more about you and Barry," he said, finishing his coffee, "because what happened to him two nights ago seems very suspicious to me. It was the CIA that killed him. You realize that."

"Yes, but your phone was tapped. Otherwise they wouldn't have known he was coming to meet you."

"Maybe so, but the question remains, why did they have to kill him? Was it simply because they didn't want the weapon to fall into our hands, or was it for other reasons?"

"What other reasons?"

"I'm not sure yet."

She flicked the ash off her cigarette and moved the ashtray nearer to her. Dukoff was watching her closely now, for a flaw in her story.

"Where were you last night when Barry tried to get us the film?"

"In the hotel," she answered. This was a line of questioning LaSala had thoroughly rehearsed.

"Why weren't you with him?"

"He thought it was too dangerous and wanted me to stay there."

Then, remembering her lines, she said, "Besides, I thought it was foolish for him to go, anyway."

"Why?"

"Because arrangements should have been made for the money to be paid beforehand. He wanted to negotiate in person to see how much he could get. If it wasn't for me, he would've been carrying the film too."

"But you stopped him."

"Yes."

"Your plan was then to open an account in a Bahamian bank and have the money deposited first. How were you able to do that so quickly?"

"It was easy," she answered. "I wired ten thousand of my own money with the stipulation that a deposit of over three million would follow within forty-eight hours. When they heard that, it wasn't very difficult."

Dukoff looked down at his empty coffee cup and ran his finger around the rim. The lines in his face seemed to have grown sharper, and his handsome features took on a different look. A roar came up from the stadium. The Forty Niners must have scored. He glanced at the window for a moment, then turned back to her. Now the smile was there again. He, too, had stepped back into his character role.

"Did you love Barry?" His hand was around the bottom of his chin, which emphasized his dimple.

"Yes, a long time ago."

"But when you came back to L.A., terrified with what you had found, he helped you." He paused and waited for her to answer.

"I needed to find out what was on the microfilm. He's an editor, a logical choice, so I used him." She heard her own words and realized that Slim was giving her more confidence now, and she was becoming more aggressive. She decided to make the transition. A more aggressive role would be needed to get her out of this.

"Barry was a fool," she continued. "He likes nice things— boats, cars, a nice apartment—but he never made any real money. So when I finally convinced him it was worth the risk to sell the film, he went along."

She paused for a moment, making sure her story was straight.

It was all lies now. She had to make them up quickly and they had to be convincing.

"I used him six years ago to get started acting here in L.A. and so I just used him again."

Dukoff looked at the cigarette lying in the ashtray, then moved to another line of questioning.

"How did you find out that Barry had died?"

"On the eleven-o'clock news," she answered, going back to the script in her head.

"The news reports said he was killed on the street by the police. They said he was wanted for murder. That report was obviously set up by the CIA."

"Of course," she said. "The CIA killed him to prevent this film from reaching you. And they'd kill me, too, to get it. That's why I want to get this over with quickly. I'm leaving the country."

"Maybe what you say is true, but there are a number of things that trouble me." He got up from his chair and moved around the table until he was standing next to her. Suddenly he appeared much taller, and his smile had gone again. "I have a lot of respect for the CIA, Miss Branigan. I think they're very intelligent men and women, truly formidable opponents. However, during the past few days they have reached new heights. They suddenly have been able to appear out of nowhere and kill a man just as he was about to deliver film to us. They were able to identify him, knew exactly when he was to meet us, and then killed him right under our noses. Now, that's a tall order even for the CIA. I think they had some outside help. I also think you had help in coming here tonight. You say that the plan for this drop was Barry's, but I don't think he was that smart. But the CIA is. I think you're working with them, Miss Branigan. Maybe not because you want to, but because you have to."

She wanted to respond, but this had gone farther than anything on which LaSala had briefed her. Her rehearsals had been like the football teams out on the field. All the plays were supposed to work. The other team was supposed to fall down like dominoes. It wasn't happening.

Dukoff continued. "The big question was why they had to kill him. Was it simply to keep him from getting to us with the film, or was it something else? I think you know the answer to that question, and probably to many more."

"How the hell should I know why they did anything?" she said, trying to hold on to Slim. "They must have wanted to stop the film from getting in your hands. You let your own goddamn phone be tapped."

"That's true," he countered quickly, "but I'm afraid you're going to have to come with me, Miss Branigan. We're going to have to get some more answers out of you before I'm convinced you're not lying."

"Where are you going to take me?" she asked. Her hands were beginning to tremble and she was losing her character.

"To our offices on Market Street. We'll want to examine this film more closely and continue to question you."

"No," she said as she got up and moved toward the door. Maybe she could run outside into the parking lot. There still would be people around. Maybe she could get help. Suddenly the door opened. Plastic Man stood over her.

"You will stay because you have no alternative," she heard Dukoff say behind her. "Even if you are involved with the CIA, they can't help you because that would simply prove my theory. So we're going to sit here and watch the game on television. As soon as the lot starts to empty, we'll leave. In the meantime, please don't try anything foolish. You're such a pretty young lady and it would be such a shame to end your life now that you're a millionaire."

"You're crazy," she said in one last desperate attempt to hold her fear in check. "I'm not involved with the CIA. I'm selling you information that can be valuable, and you're subjecting me to meaningless questioning. It's crazy."

"We'll see. Maybe we'll know if you're involved with the CIA before we leave the stadium. They've killed before, to stop us from getting the film. Maybe they're waiting out there to do it again. They're probably trying to find you right now."

Cheryl sank back into her seat. Dukoff was right. They couldn't reveal their involvement with her as long as there was a chance she could convince them the film was real. Well, so far she hadn't convinced anybody.

She was on her own, with only her instincts and abilities to help her. And goddammit, she would use them. If convincing the Russians was all going to fall on her shoulders, then she would give a performance. She would draw on whatever toughness she had and combine it with Slim's strength. Then, fuck it. If that failed, she had done the best she could.

LaSala stood in the upper deck of the stadium, looking out at the parking lot through his binoculars. It was nearly midnight and the stadium lights were dimmed while the ground crew finished covering the dirt sections of the field. He focused the glasses on the fifty or so cars left in the lot. Under one of the overhead lights he saw the Toyota Cheryl had driven. The antenna was up and smoke was coming from the exhaust as it hit the cool night air.

He scanned the rest of the lot, moving carefully from car to car, but there was nothing suspicious. They had taken her out of the lot in one of the thousands of vehicles that had left over an hour ago. The last report on her had come at six fifty-five, when Sweeney radioed in to Steve that her car was entering the parking lot. That had been three hours ago. She had never made it from the car to the gate where Steve had been waiting.

By the time he had arrived, the first quarter had ended. The Lick Expressway had cleared and he had made good time to the park. But Cheryl hadn't. The forty-five minutes she had lost had meant failure in terms of her avoiding contact with the KGB. Now she was in their hands. His worst fears had become reality.

Dukoff had correctly calculated that he could take Cheryl from the stadium. There was nothing the CIA could do to stop him without revealing themselves. He had known this but had hoped Cheryl could make the drop and get away from the car before Dukoff could get to her. The accident on the Lick had prevented that.

He thought about the options left open to him. There weren't any. All he could do now was wait. They had prevented Barry from reaching Dukoff with evidence that the film was phony. Now they were back to square one with what should have happened a week ago in New York: getting the original film into Russian hands. But they had lost precious time. The convoy was already at sea, and there were just five days left to turn them around. Now Hayden would be forced to play poker with the Russians, not knowing whether he had the film to back him up or not.

The validity of that film now rested in the hands of a twenty-nine-year-old actress who would have to stand up to KGB interrogation. He thought about what they had done to McFarland

and what Cheryl had told him days ago: "I may have the strength to be a heroine, but not a martyr."

Moscow

A small Zhiguli sedan pulled up in front of a two-story building in the exclusive district of Novopeschannaya. It was 5:56 A.M., and the night sky was giving way to dark clouds that rolled overhead, driven by the winds of a heavy snowstorm. About twelve inches of snow had accumulated during the night, and the trees along the narrow street glistened as the streetlights reflected off them.

The car door opened and a man wearing a heavy, dark coat and fur hat got out. He pulled his collar up to shield him from a gust of wind and then turned to the building marked with the number 78. A single light shone through a window on the second floor. He waved to the driver and the car pulled away, disappearing at the end of the street behind a curtain of falling snow. Then he carefully climbed up the unshoveled steps, his boots leaving deep tracks behind him.

There was a row of call buttons along the side of the door. He pressed the third one down and waited. Turning back to the street, he saw that it was quiet except for a bus that passed by slowly, stopping at the corner to pick up three people huddled under a shelter. A light went on behind the draped door and he heard a dead bolt click. The door opened and Colonel Dimitri Zarov stepped inside. General Ivan Parkovsky stood in front of him wearing a heavy blue robe, pajamas, and slippers.

"I'm sorry to have awakened you, General, but it was urgent that I see you immediately," Zarov said quietly.

"So you said on the phone," Parkovsky answered, looking down at Zarov's battered briefcase. "I hope what's in there is important enough to have awakened me from the soundest sleep I've had all week." He turned to the stairs and slowly went up them one step at a time, holding the railing tightly. "You said it was something involving Viktor," he said without turning around.

The mention of Karpolov's name caused a change in Zarov's voice. It suddenly became higher and he had to clear his throat. "Yes, it's something I have to talk to you about privately," he replied.

"At six in the morning?" Parkovsky said, opening his apartment door, which had been left ajar.

Zarov brushed his overshoes off on the mat outside the door and went into the small apartment. The general's retirement had provided him with a neat, comfortable four rooms, which were furnished with an odd mixture of traditional and modern.

"Would you like some coffee?" the general asked, going straight into the kitchen. "I made a pot as soon as you called."

"Yes, thank you," Zarov said from the living room, draping his coat over a chair. He sat down on a small sofa and put his briefcase on the coffee table. Opening it, he took out a folder containing ten pages of computer printout, which he put alongside it. A quick glance at his watch showed it was after six. He was already an hour late in reporting to Karpolov. Karpolov would be calling his apartment now after trying to locate him at the communications center in Dzerzhinsky Square.

The general set a silver tray down in front of him and poured two coffees. Then he settled back into an antique high-backed chair, holding the coffee in his lap.

"Now, what is so urgent?" he asked calmly.

"This," Zarov answered, holding up the stack of printouts. "And this," he added, taking a cassette from the briefcase. "It's the result of a transmission received just an hour ago from San Francisco. It shows that the Americans have a powerful new laser weapon that's already been tested and is ready to become operational."

The general sat upright in the chair. Zarov was surprised at the immediacy with which the general reacted to what he had said.

"Does Viktor know about this?" he asked quickly.

"About the operation? Yes. The results—no."

"So why don't you go to him with them?"

"Because he'll do what he's done with the reports of two other operations within the past three weeks. They will be kept secret from the Politburo."

"What other operations are you talking about?"

"These," he said, separating two paper-clipped sets of computer printouts from each other. He read from the top sheet of each set. "Sixteen October, New York . . . Information being passed through an informer to our agents was intercepted by a hatcheck girl at the drop. It was to contain film concerning a new laser weapon being developed by the Americans . . . report kept from POL review. Thirteen October . . . The girl ran off with the film and later showed up in Los Angeles. Again report kept from POL review. Sixteen October, San Francisco . . . A friend of the girl contacted our diplomatic agency there and tried to deliver the film to us but was stopped, probably by the CIA. Again it was kept from POL review. Eighteen October, last night . . . The girl called and succeeded in delivering the film. The report of that meeting is here, along with a copy of the film transmitted to us by satellite from San Francisco during the night."

"Have you seen it?"

"Yes, it shows a full demonstration of the weapon in front of high-ranking American officials, including Secretary of Defense Walter Commack."

"Who was in charge of running these operations for us?"

"I was."

Parkovsky took a sip of his coffee and looked at Zarov over the rim of the cup. He was obviously frightened, and was reporting this at great risk to his career and to his relationship with Viktor. But Viktor had deceived him, too, and he was furious. On two occasions he had questioned Viktor about the laser weapon and had been assured there was no need for concern. There *was* a great need for concern, and Viktor had known it for some time. Withholding information from him was bad enough, but lying infuriated him.

Zarov fidgeted with the reports, then continued, expanding on his role in running the operations.

"As soon as I received the reports, I forwarded them to Viktor. I told him the Politburo must be informed about what was happening. The whole Cuban missile plan was based on the assumption that the Americans couldn't retaliate with a superior weapon, and he was keeping the leadership of the country in the dark about information that could have proved otherwise. He said he would be the decider of that. In his opinion the Americans were bluffing. When I suggested that he let the Politburo decide that, he threatened me with insubordination and possible imprisonment. General, he's possessed with protecting his missile plan, even if it's at the expense of the country."

At the expense of the country. The words echoed inside

Parkovsky's brain. The cost to the country would be there no matter what happened now. If the ships were turned back, the cost would be in morale. For a second time the people would suffer the humiliation of bowing to the United States. On the other hand, if he said nothing, an eventual confrontation would cost lives. And there was one other consideration: His daughter, Ivana, would suffer the disgrace that would be cast on her husband. The dishonor would be a terrible blow from which she might not be able to recover.

"May I see those reports?" he asked, holding out his hand to Zarov.

The colonel got up and placed them in the general's lap. He leafed through them, stopping occasionally to read a paragraph or two. When he got to the last page, he closed the folder and placed it on the coffee table.

"You say Viktor doesn't believe there's sufficient proof the Americans have the weapon. What do you believe, Dimitri?"

Zarov was looking at his watch. This was all taking too long. Karpolov would be looking for him. Every minute now was precious.

"I believe there's sufficient evidence that the Americans have the weapon. They have film showing a demonstration of it, for God's sake. But that's neither here nor there. The premier and the Politburo have the right to see it along with all the other information and make the decision, not one man, not Viktor Karpolov. I think—"

The phone rang.

Zarov paused in mid-sentence while the general slowly got up to answer the phone in the kitchen. It rang with a strange persistence that caused a chill to run through Zarov. Viktor knew he was there. Viktor always knew everything. Parkovsky picked up the receiver. Some words were spoken on the other end, and then the general turned toward Zarov.

"Colonel Zarov? No, Viktor, I haven't seen the colonel for nearly three weeks now. . . . No, you didn't wake me. . . . I was just about to make some breakfast. . . . Where are you? . . . I see. . . . Yes, I'll let you know if he calls, but I don't expect he will this early. . . . Yes, I will. You too." He held the receiver in his hand for a moment, then placed it in the holder on the wall.

Zarov was visibly shaken when the general came back into the room. He was gathering his reports together and cramming them into the briefcase. There wasn't any time left to waste. Viktor was desperate to find him—and he would. His tracks were in the snow outside. Even they were enough to give him away.

The general was standing behind his high-backed chair, leaning on it for support. "Where are you going?" he asked. There was concern on his face.

"I must get back to my office," Zarov replied nervously. "I can't stall Viktor any longer."

"I agree," Parkovsky replied, "and here's what I want you to do. I want you to give him the report immediately after you've copied it, along with the tape."

"I've already copied that."

"Good. Then tell Viktor again that it's absolutely necessary that the Politburo be informed about the operations immediately. Be adamant. Do everything you can to convince him. If he refuses, I want you to call me. I'll be waiting here all day."

"Thank you, General," Zarov said, putting on his overcoat. "I'll call you, one way or the other, before noon." He hurried out of the apartment and down the stairs.

Parkovsky stood at his living-room window and watched as Zarov got into his staff car, which had been waiting at the corner. As it drove off, he turned away from the window and picked up a picture of Ivana from an end table. It had been a gift from her just before her mother had died. He picked it up and held it toward the light. Ivana had been just twenty-two, and was dressed in a ballerina costume. How young and graceful she looked. He remembered her first recital. Like a swan, she had moved across the stage, her every movement pure delight. From then on he had become a ballet aficionado. The Bolshoi became his second home as he followed her career from a young student, to prima ballerina, to director of the Bolshoi School.

Ballet had taught her to appreciate the finer things in life, and her marriage to Viktor provided the means to enjoy them. Her position in Moscow society had flourished to where it had become a large part of her life. But now all of that was in jeopardy. Now he had to make a choice that would either protect it all, at the risk of endangering the country, or he would have to expose Viktor, sending Ivana's world crashing down. Morally and rationally he knew what he should do, but could he bring himself to do it?

He took the picture into the kitchen and placed it on the table. Then he sat down in front of it and waited for Zarov's call.

Latitude forty-five degrees, aboard the *Poltava*

Admiral Nikolai Yurchenko was sitting in the small mess room of the *Poltava* having coffee with Boris Stavronov, the *zampolit*, or political officer, assigned to the convoy. Stavronov was not comfortable at sea. The only reason he was on the *Poltava* was that he hadn't any choice. This mission was of absolute importance to the Soviet Union, and he had been ordered by the chief of Naval Operations himself.

The only positive thing that could come from this was that he might lose some weight. His two-hundred-fifty-pound body ballooned out at the waist, causing difficulty when he moved through the hatches. Almost all of the crew, including Yurchenko, were lean and strong. He was constantly in the way as they moved around the ship. At least today the seas were calm and the weather warmer as they came closer to the coast of Nova Scotia. The previous day had been horrible. The ten-foot waves off Newfoundland had combined with a southeasterly wind that sent the ship pitching and yawing until Stavronov's stomach felt like a soccer ball bouncing around inside his body. At least today, at breakfast, he had managed to hold down some toast.

"What is our position this morning, Admiral?" he asked, maintaining the formality of addressing Yurchenko by his rank.

"An hour ago it was two hundred miles east of Sable Island, Nova Scotia. We're approaching latitude forty-five. Our present course will take us off Cape Hatteras, past the Florida coast, into the Gulf of Mexico and on to Havana within three days."

"Good. I can't say it'll be a bit too early."

Yurchenko looked at him with disgust. He never had had any respect for these *zampolits*, who were put on ships supposedly to assure that the wishes of the Party were carried out. Although he was in command of the convoy, the *zampolit* could overrule him if a situation involved a political decision. In Yurchenko's twenty-five years at sea, it had never come to that. But there had been many petty squabbles and he thought all *zampolits* were nothing more than excess baggage. He disliked Stavronov in particular. Apart from his disgusting obesity, the man had done nothing but exercise his rank in front of the crew, diminishing his own authority. What really infuriated him, though, was that Stavronov had actually studied to be a submarine commander at the Frunze Academy near Moscow but had failed miserably. From there he joined the Party and rose through the ranks quickly, with his only other experience at sea coming on a carrier two years ago. The man belonged on land, like a beached whale.

The metal door on the bulkhead opened and a seaman stepped inside. "The lieutenant commander requests the admiral on the bridge." he said hurriedly. There was an unusual urgency in his voice.

Yurchenko took one last sip of his coffee and followed the seaman out the door. As Stavronov struggled to get out from behind the table, Yurchenko followed the seaman up two flights of stairs to the bridge. There, he found Lieutenant Commander Tulchin, huddled with the radar man, a computer printout in his hand. Seeing the other men in the room manning their stations, Yurchenko knew that something was wrong.

"Admiral, we have activity on radar," Tulchin said excitedly, looking up from the screen. "Three AV-B Harrier attack fighters, bearing 0010, range twenty-two kilometers . . . closing quickly."

"How long have you been monitoring them?"

"Seventeen minutes. We weren't sure what they were until now."

"Order the convoy into a dispersed formation. I want two kilometers between ships. Reduce speed to fifteen knots. Hold present course."

"Yes, sir."

He heard the message broadcast and immediately saw the *Kerenov*, behind them, begin to fall back.

"How close are the Harriers now?" he asked.

"Range six thousand meters, still bearing 0010, sir," the radar man said without looking up. Yurchenko picked up a pair of high-powered binoculars from the console in front of him and looked out the forward window. He saw two tiny specks just off the horizon. The Harriers were coming fast, and they were coming low.

"Shall we contract REDNAVCOM?" the commander asked. The specks were visible to the naked eye now.

"Not yet," Yurchenko replied, his binoculars again fixed on the approaching fighters. "Let's see what these three are up to first."

The fighters lost altitude at two thousand meters and came directly over the ship, their jets screaming with a thunderous roar as they passed over the command bridge. The helmsman and the navigator ducked instinctively as they passed overhead.

Yurchenko spun around and went to the opposite side of the bridge. He saw the Harriers split formation and then begin a circular route over the convoy. They buzzed each freighter, then made one more pass over the *Poltava*. As they came back over, they suddenly turned and rose sharply, heading directly into the sun.

He watched as they disappeared into the blinding light, leaving just a vapor trail behind them. Then the door opened behind him and he heard Stavronov's voice.

"Those are American planes," he shouted, pointing to the Harriers which, again, were specks in the distance. "What's going on?"

"A warning, Comrade Commissar," Yurchenko replied calmly. "The Americans are finally showing their displeasure at our bringing missiles to Mr. Castro."

Stavronov was perspiring heavily, both from climbing the three flights of stairs and from what he had just witnessed. He wiped his brow with a wrinkled handkerchief and turned to the radioman. "Have we received any communication from REDNAVCOM 1?"

"No, sir," Tulchin replied.

"Then contact them," he shouted at Yurchenko.

"We will," Yurchenko replied. "In the meantime, we proceed on course."

Tulchin looked up from the radar screen.

"Admiral, the aircraft are proceeding south now at 0182 degrees. Range 20.9 kilometers."

Yurchenko went over to the table and looked at the large chart spread out over the entire surface. He took the course plotter and laid it over the compass rosette. Carefully he drew a line from their present position along the 0182 degree course. It went down the American coast and didn't cross land until Haiti. The planes weren't land-based. They were carrier-based.

The carrier was somewhere along the 0182 course, probably headed for them. At present it was still over four hundred kilometers away, or he would have picked it up on radar. But it was out there, and the planes had been a warning. They had fired the proverbial shot over the bow in anticipation of a confrontation that was yet to come.

Stavronov was looking over his shoulder and had seen the Harriers' course on the chart.

His voice rose to a higher pitch as he realized what was happening. "What are we going to do?"

"As I said, proceed on course," Yurchenko replied calmly.

"But they've got a carrier out there!"

"Then we'll just have to go through it," Yurchenko answered, turning to the helmsman. "Maintain course 0021," he said calmly. "Increase speed to thirteen knots."

The *Poltava* leapt forward, its engines pushing her bow through the water on a collision course with the *John F. Kennedy*, five hundred kilometers away.

San Francisco

Cheryl sat in a soft leather chair staring at a picture of Lenin on the fireplace mantel in front of her. The stern face with arched eyebrows and pointed goatee seemed to be defying her to hold on to her story and the role she was playing. Her performance had been going on for nearly fourteen hours now, and the ornate clock on the wall behind Dukoff's empty chair read eleven A.M.

It seemed like an eternity since she had arrived at the elegant Soviet Diplomatic Agency. The three-story building was filled with eighteenth-century antiques, Oriental carpeting, and delicate crystal—a setting quite different from the bare interrogation room she had expected. Sitting behind a hand-carved walnut desk, Dukoff had surprised her by resuming the role of the gentleman he had played at the stadium. He had calmly questioned her for three or four hours, then left the room for an hour. She had slept in the chair while he was gone. When he returned, the interrogation had continued at a faster pace, his staccato voice firing questions right and left as he tried to find inconsistencies in her answers. Then suddenly he had left again. This had happened three times since the questioning began. The only time she had been out of the room in fourteen hours was to go to the bathroom.

The process had worn away at Slim's character, even though she had fought desperately to hold on to it. However, Slim's impertinence had caused Dukoff to become impatient, and his last questions had come in rapid-fire succession. She barely had time to think. He had asked things that weren't in her prepared script and she had made up answers that she now realized were flawed.

"What time did you check into the Shelbourne Hotel?" he had asked.

"At about ten o'clock two nights ago." The answer had been rehearsed with LaSala, and she had responded without hesitation. He had made note of it on a yellow-lined legal pad.

"How did you get there from L.A.?"

That wasn't in the script and she had made up an answer. "We rented a car."

"Where?"

"In Los Angeles."

"At what time?"

"I don't know. Sometime around noon the day before."

"From what company?"

"Avis." The word was no sooner out of her mouth than she realized the answer could be checked. Dukoff had also noted that on his pad, smiled, and gone on with his next question.

"Where is Barry's body now?"

"I don't know," she had answered, and then added, "I don't care."

"I think you *do* care, Miss Branigan." Plastic Man had come into the room and whispered a few words to Dukoff.

"I have to leave for a few minutes," he had said to Cheryl. "Why don't you use the time to reconsider your answers, because we're going to check on them." He had smiled politely and followed Plastic Man out the door. That had been over an hour ago.

Cheryl took a small compact from her purse and looked at herself in the oval mirror. Not only was Slim fading in her mind, but she was losing it physically as well. Her hair was scraggly, and the mascara under her eyes was smeared. She was exhausted and hungry. Quickly she freshened up her makeup and put on new lipstick. Then she combed her hair, getting it to hug the side of her face.

The door opened behind her. Through the mirror she saw that it wasn't Dukoff; it was Plastic Man.

"Get up," he said in a voice that was now harsher than before. "We're moving to another room."

As Cheryl started up from the chair Plastic Man grabbed both her hands, pulled them behind her back, and tied her wrists with twine.

"What are you doing?" she shouted. "Where is Dukoff?"

"He's waiting for you downstairs," he answered, knotting the twine tightly so that it cut into her skin. Before she could say anything more, he spun her around and pushed her toward the door. Grabbing her arm, he guided her down a long carpeted hallway. At the end was a stairway that led to the basement. There was a light at the bottom, and she could see the woman who had left the stadium with them waiting there. Her face was expressionless, except for a slight curl to her mouth that said she would take pleasure in what was about to happen.

"Get in there," she said, pointing to the right as Cheryl stumbled off the last two steps. Plastic Man gave her one final shove and she found herself in a cluttered storage room. There were metal racks on both walls, filled with stationery supplies, audio equipment, and some cameras. A wooden table was in the center of the room with a folding chair on one side and a comfortable high-backed one on the other. Behind the far chair was a photographer's strobe light, mounted on a tripod. A control switch rested on the table alongside a tape recorder.

Plastic Man pushed her down into the folding chair and then took a seat against the wall. The woman loaded a tape into the recorder and looked up at her. The smile was still there. She was going to enjoy this.

Cheryl looked at her but said nothing. Fear was mounting inside her. She had to get Slim's character firmly fixed in her mind again or she wouldn't be able to go on. Taking a deep breath, she straightened herself in the chair and looked hard at the woman. When she spoke, her voice was calm and in control.

"I want my hands untied and I want to see Dukoff," she said

confidently. Her tone suggested that he was late. How dare he not be there right now!

"Oh, you'll see him soon enough," the woman answered. Her sarcasm was apparent.

As if on cue, Dukoff came into the room. He nodded to the woman to turn on the recorder and then sat down across from Cheryl. After placing his pad, now filled with notes, in front of him, he looked up at Cheryl for the first time. Where there had been a slight gentleness to his character, now there was a look that was threatening and intimidating. She looked him straight in the eye, determined to become Slim again, determined to hold her own.

"What is the meaning of this?" she asked. "I've answered all your questions. What more do you want from me?"

"The truth," he said flatly.

"I've told you the truth," she countered without hesitation. "And I'll continue to if you untie my hands."

"I'm afraid not," he said, looking toward Plastic Man and the woman. "You see, we need to make you a little uncomfortable, because my timetable for getting straight answers has suddenly been collapsed."

He looked down at his notes and then continued, "I've just received a message from Moscow, and they need to know immediately whether the laser weapon on the film is real or not. You're going to tell me the answer to that question right now."

"Listen," she replied quickly. "I'm just a girl who thought she was running off with a couple hundred thousand dollars worth of coke and ended up with your film instead. How should I know if it's real? Why wouldn't it be?"

"Because we believe you're involved with the CIA, that's why," he answered, raising his voice. "We're not going to play any more games, Miss Branigan. We've got a convoy of ships headed for Cuba with nuclear missiles that can destroy the United States. We think the CIA is trying to prevent them from getting there by threatening us with a weapon they don't really have."

"What do you mean 'don't have'? It's on the film right in front of your eyes."

"We don't think so. We think it's a demonstration created on film by the CIA."

"You're crazy. That's impossible."

"Not really," Dukoff answered, glancing down at his notes. "It could have been created with sophisticated film techniques so that nobody could tell the difference. Not even experts. That's what Barry saw, wasn't it?"

"I don't know what you're talking about," she said in an attempt to divert this line of questioning, but he persisted and his next questions came quickly, one after the other.

"Did Barry notice anything unusual about the film?"

"No."

"Did he use special equipment at the station to blow it up?"

"I don't know. He didn't say."

"Yet he knew it would be valuable to us. Why?"

"Because it was a laser weapon. We both could see that."

"Then why did he try to come to the restaurant alone?"

"I already told you," she said defiantly, "I was at the hotel. I was holding the film while he went to negotiate a price. He didn't want—"

"Liar!" Dukoff shouted, throwing the notepad down on the table.

He flicked the switch in front of him and the photographic strobe light began pulsing directly at her. The brightness was blinding, and instinctively she closed her eyes, but it was too intense to shut out completely.

"Open your eyes!" he shouted.

"No," she replied. "I'm telling you the truth. You can check the hotel."

She felt fingers around the twine that held her hands. Then suddenly her arms were jerked upward and she felt a searing pain tear through her shoulders. She expected that it was Plastic Man, but when she opened her eyes, he was seated off to the side. It was the woman.

"Look straight ahead," she ordered, "or I'll jerk your arms out of their sockets."

Cheryl looked at Dukoff. He was a blurred shape now, in front of a pulsing sun that seared through the pupils of her eyes.

"We checked the hotel, but that register could have been altered," he replied angrily. "Other information proves much more interesting. Avis had no record of a car driven from L.A. to San Francisco during the time you say you rented one. And what's even more interesting, a check of area hospitals showed that the man the police shot was brought into San Francisco General almost forty minutes after the shooting. Why? Where did that ambulance go after Barry was picked up? Where did it go?"

"I don't know," she answered feebly.

"But the CIA knows, don't they? Don't they! Answer me!"

He was losing control, and she realized now how desperate he was to find out the truth. Those ships must be getting close to a head-on collision with the U.S. Navy, and he was under orders to find out, at all costs, whether the film was real or not.

The pain in her shoulders had spread to the back of her neck, and her eyes were burning from the strobe light. Each pulse seemed to bore into her head, causing it to pound. She tried to look away, but the woman jerked her arms higher, until the pain became unbearable.

The past two days had been spent rehearsing for an interrogation, not physical torture. She had never been able to withstand pain and didn't have confidence to hold out against it. Also, Slim's character was becoming useless. This was Cheryl Branigan's body that had to bear the pain, not someone in her imagination.

She didn't know if she could do it.

Aboard the carrier *John F. Kennedy*

Admiral Sam Hutchinson puffed on his cigar and turned to his executive officer, who was watching a radar screen with the Russian convoy superimposed over four hundred square miles of ocean. The red safety lights of the carrier command center made them look like tiny points of light against a red sea. "What's his range now, Ted?" he asked, blowing the smoke from his cigar toward the ceiling.

"Just under two hundred miles. He's got us on his radar now, but he's increased speed and is coming right at us."

"Son of a bitch," Hutchinson answered. He ground the cigar into a plastic ashtray and pushed it aside. Get COMFLEET on the horn again. If this guy's going to go right through us in twelve hours, they'd better know about it every step of the way. Give 'em our position and request confirmation of our orders."

The exec turned to the radioman beside him and gave the order.

Hutchinson moved closer to the superimposed chart. Inside the large concentric circles he saw the *Poltava*'s position in relation to his own. A long diagonal line was being drawn by a seaman wearing earphones, confirming that the 181-degree course was on a direct line to Cuba. His ships would meet them at approximately 0600 hours at daybreak the next day.

He thought about the orders he had received at ATCOM. If the Russian convoy didn't reverse course, he was to confront them at 0600 the following day. If they still didn't turn around, he was instructed to allow them to pass through without any interference.

He had lost control at the ATCOM briefing. "Why the hell are we letting them sail through after just token resistance?" he had asked. "If they don't turn around after some shots over their bow, we'll start shooting for real. They'll turn around."

"There's to be no direct action taken against them," Admiral Hampel had replied. "If they don't change course, you're to let them through. Do you understand?"

"No," he had persisted. "I don't understand why we can't stop them. We did it in 1962, we can do it now. We can—"

"There are a lot of things you don't understand, and one of them is following orders," General Cabot had thundered from across the table. His face had gotten red with anger and he had pointed to the orders that Hutchinson held in his hand. "This isn't 1962. Up until a few months ago we were in a tight race with the Russians, and now we've lost it. We're in no position to confront them head to head. Also, you don't start shooting at someone until all your diplomatic bargaining has been exhausted. If the president is successful in convincing Chebrikov that we can defend ourselves, the ships will turn away."

"And if he's not?"

Cabot had glared at him for a moment and then answered with one simple sentence. "Then you will follow your orders, Admiral."

He stared at the glass chart and his face reflected over the outline of the eastern seaboard where he would meet the Russians. The white lines that formed the contour overlapped his features like a chalk drawing on a blackboard. Hundreds of times he had charted courses to targets that he was to attack. But this time he

was charting a course that could lead to surrender. It went against
every fiber in his body. To lose a battle because it had been fought
and lost was one thing, but to surrender without a fight was
unthinkable.

11.

VIKTOR KARPOLOV SAT across from Premier Chebrikov while twenty-five men, who sat on both sides of a long conference table, bombarded him with questions. Chebrikov no longer wore a friendly smile. A phone call at eight A.M. had taken that away forever.

The call resulted in Chebrikov immediately assembling this group of scientists, film experts, and members of the Politburo for a two-o'clock emergency meeting. It had already gone on for three hours, with a showing of the film and an evaluation of it by the experts. The consensus was that the film was authentic, but more time would be needed to study it carefully. The scientists had always been somewhat divided, but now they had a majority that said the weapon could have been far enough in development to be tested. Those who disagreed, however, conceded that more time would be needed to disprove the theory. But time was what they had run out of.

Zarov had betrayed him. At seven A.M. Zarov had finally told him that the Branigan girl had delivered the film and was being questioned by Dukoff in San Francisco. He showed him the film and demanded that the premier be informed. When he refused,

Zarov had remained surprisingly calm and quietly had left the office. However, within an hour, the premier had called him to his office. When he got there, he found that Chebrikov was irate. Chebrikov accused him of withholding information from both himself and the Politburo. He immediately tried to put the blame on Zarov by saying he was running the entire operation without keeping him informed. But Chebrikov played a taped conversation Karpolov had had with Zarov, which disproved that. Now he sat with his back to the wall, trying to defend whatever dignity he had left, and to convince them of what he truly believed: that the Americans were bluffing with a weapon that didn't exist.

"Why did you continually withhold the reports from us?" Chebrikov asked, banging his fist on the polished walnut conference table. "You knew the information was critical in deciding whether your plan was viable or not."

"Because I didn't think they were conclusive enough to jeopardize implementation of the plan. I still don't think they are." He scanned the table quickly and saw one or two of the scientists nod in agreement.

"Isn't this film enough?" Chebrikov shouted, pointing to the frozen image of the explosion on the screen behind him. "Isn't a demonstration of a weapon more powerful than we've ever seen convincing when there are receivers for it scattered all over our air bases? Maybe the Americans have already put some in Cuba and are waiting to destroy our SRVs as soon as we get them there. Maybe then you'll believe it!"

"I don't think that's likely," Karpolov replied, addressing the entire group as well as the premier. "Again, those boxes were meant to deceive us into thinking they have the weapon. If you study Berkhin's report, you will see they were planted by amateurs. They were meant to be found. Believe me, if the CIA wanted to bury them secretly, they wouldn't have selected bungling idiots to do it."

"However, those boxes are capable of handling a 100,000-ton laser," one of the scientists from the Institute of High Energy Physics said, interrupting. "That in itself is new technology. Also, how do we know there aren't more that haven't been found?"

"I would seriously doubt it," he replied quickly. "Once the first one was found, we increased security around all our bases. Every inch of ground was gone over with metal detectors, and we found nothing more."

The room grew silent. There were no more questions to be asked, and the group consensus remained the same: They were not convinced. He continued on, attacking the film's validity.

"I don't believe the film is real," he said, sitting with his hands folded in front of him. "I think it was created to dupe us into thinking they have a laser weapon. I'll admit there's some disagreement within our own scientific community, but the majority of scientists support me in my contention that a vibration laser weapon is still two years away from being tested. I ordered a full investigation, which resulted in this report." He held up the five-hundred-page document so that all could see it. "It states categorically that a vibration laser cannot be effective at an altitude of more than eighteen thousand kilometers. Higher than that, it loses its destructive power. At a lower altitude we would be able to shoot it out of space with missiles that even now are obsolete. I tell you, the Americans are bluffing."

"They may not be," Yuri Kosmanovich, the scientific director at Sary Shagan, said sharply. "It's true, most of us believe the weapon isn't feasible at high altitudes, but nevertheless, the receivers found at Sakhalin have not been thoroughly studied yet. They may enable the satellite to be at a much higher altitude and still have the power to destroy."

"Then why didn't the Americans do a better job of hiding them? They were found too easily at Sakhalin. I believe the CIA wanted to make sure they *were* found."

"Speculation, mere speculation," Chebrikov replied. "You don't have any proof of that. And I'm telling you, we aren't going to find ourselves in Cuba with the Americans ready to use a weapon on us against which we have no defense. In 1962, world opinion wasn't with us. The same is true today, if not more so. Today NATO is stronger and we're pressured in the U.N. to withdraw from countries under our control. We're attacked politically on many fronts. It was only because we thought we had overwhelming military superiority that we made this move." He slammed the reports down on the table, then picked up the empty cassette box. "At this moment there's no evidence that says this film isn't real. We have no alternative other than to withdraw the ships. Right now the American Navy is less than a day away from confronting them.

Several of the men at the table started to interrupt him, but he brushed them aside with a wave of his hand.

"I know what the arguments are. I know what it will do to the morale of our people, and what world opinion will be. But at the same time, we can't put ourselves in what will later be an untenable position by not facing up to our mistake now." He put the cassette back down and pointed to Karpolov. "This man's mistake," he said loudly.

Karpolov knew there was nothing more he could say that would convince them they were wrong. The Americans had done an extraordinary job of bluffing. He wondered who was responsible for the CIA's impeccable execution of a very difficult assignment. As a peer, that man had earned his respect; as an enemy, his hatred.

There were still two more things he could do to prove the film a fake. Some quick phone calls would have to be made: one to Dukoff, the other to General Anatoly Dubrinen, chief of Air Defense.

Karpolov pushed his chair back from the table and stood up. With both hands on the brushed metal edge, he leaned forward in the direction of Chebrikov. In a calm but forceful voice he made a plea for one more chance to prove that the Americans were bluffing.

Fifteen minutes later, Karpolov emerged from the conference room. He was perspiring heavily and had to stop in the waiting room to loosen his tie and pull out his handkerchief. He was trembling so, the handkerchief dropped from his grasp. As he bent down to pick it up, someone approached him. Karpolov's humiliation was such that he hesitated to stand upright and face whoever it was standing inches away. After a few moments, which seemed like an eternity, Karpolov stood up. He was face-to-face with General Parkovsky.

The general's eyes were fixed on him like an automatic gun-sight tracking a target. Karpolov held out his hand in what he knew was a feeble gesture of reconciliation. The old man ignored it. When he spoke, his voice was louder than Karpolov had ever heard it. It echoed off the marble walls in a booming sound that sent a shudder through Karpolov.

"You have disgraced me, but that is unimportant. I'm an old man," he said. "You have disgraced my daughter, whom I love more than life itself, and for that I can never forgive you. But most of all, you've disgraced yourself with an insipid ego that had to be satisfied even if it meant destroying the morale of your countrymen. I regret that I ever loved you as the son I never had, but most of all, I regret aiding you in your rise to power. For that I, too, have betrayed my country. My only consolation is that I was able to expose you for what you are."

STARSAT tracking station, Palo Alto, California

High on a hill outside Palo Alto, a large satellite dish swept the night sky, the light from a full moon reflecting off its silver covering. It made a low, growling sound as the gears beneath it meshed to rotate it a full three hundred and sixty degrees every ninety seconds.

Inside a low concrete building to the right of the antenna, Airman First Class Bill D'Ambrosio sat at a screen watching a tiny blip move through a series of concentric circles superimposed over North America. Looking over his shoulder was the commander of the facility, Colonel Pat Neary, who nervously drummed his fingers against the side of a phone linked directly to the Pentagon. A third officer, Captain Roger Cranston, monitored the blip's course.

The Russian reconnaissance satellite *Kirov II* was passing over Newfoundland, beginning a routine orbit that would take it over Washington, D.C., northern Texas, southern California, and out over the Pacific. Radio reports from another tracking station in Scotland had already noted the usual automatic course correction over the Soviet Union, positioning it for orbit. If the last series of corrections were repeated again, *Kirov II* wouldn't pass over Cheyenne, Wyoming, until fifteen more orbits were completed, sometime the following day.

It was Neary who noticed the first deviation in its course. Suddenly the digital numbers monitoring it started to flash.

197.69 degrees, 197.63, .62, .59. *Kirov II* was slowly moving to the west. Neary turned to Cranston.

"Rog, she's changing course almost a half a degree a second. Run a projection down to the target and see what the heading is to it."

Cranston typed the data into a DEC mainframe computer. Instantly a series of numbers came up in front of him while projected course lines were automatically displayed on D'Ambrosio's screen.

"If she comes to 194.72 degrees, she's on her way to Cheyenne," Cranston answered. "Is she still deviating?"

"Yeah," Neary replied without taking his eyes off D'Ambrosio's screen.

The airman had now visually displayed the satellite's present course and the one needed to fly over the covered missile site. The two courses read on the screen as a solid yellow elongated triangle. As Neary watched the digital numbers continue to change, the triangle got narrower and narrower. Within two minutes it was one solid line, a line heading directly to Cheyenne, Wyoming.

"Give me the projected ETA for the target," Neary ordered as he reached for the phone.

"Nine minutes, fourteen seconds," Cranston answered, scanning the numbers on his screen.

Neary stabbed at the digital buttons on the phone, activating the direct Pentagon line. An anxious voice answered on the other end and within twenty minutes President Hayden was given the information. The Russians were coming to take a very close look at missile silo MX-27.

Although it would pass over the site at an altitude of fourteen miles, it would view the destruction from the equivalent altitude of two thousand feet. At that distance it could read the license plate on a car. Its cameras would transmit what it saw to a Soviet receiving station outside Moscow and relay it to Karpolov at the Kremlin. Experts would compare the destruction, piece by piece, to what was on the film. Hopefully they would believe what they saw.

The defense of the United States depended on it.

San Francisco

"Open your eyes! Open them, I said!"

Dukoff was shouting and Cheryl felt her arms being lifted higher, until she thought they would break at the shoulders. The pain ripped across her back like a whip cutting into her skin. She couldn't remember the last question he had asked her. The pain must have caused her to black out momentarily.

Slowly she opened her eyes to face the blinding light. Dukoff was barely visible, having moved farther away from the flashing strobe. Off to the side, she could see Plastic Man moving toward her with something in his hand.

"I'll ask you again," Dukoff said in a lower voice. The words were carefully enunciated so there would be no misunderstanding. "What did Barry find on that film that caused the CIA to kill him?"

"Nothing," she answered, surprised at her own words. "He found nothing."

She knew the response would result in another violent wrenching of her arms but somehow she had said it, anyway. What had happened to the pact she'd made with herself? "She could be a heroine, but not a martyr" was what she had said. Yet she was defying Dukoff, knowing it would bring on a jolt of excruciating pain.

It came swiftly. This time the shoulder was wrenched so far, she thought she would pass out again. For the first time she screamed. It was an involuntary shrill that her body had forced her to make. Even though she still had the mental will to resist, her body had been stretched to the limit.

"Why don't you listen to reason?" Dukoff said through the screeching in her ears. "Who are you trying to help by lying?"

She didn't answer. Her head slumped down to her chest and she waited for the woman to pull her shoulders back even farther. But nothing happened. Instead the woman came out from behind her and walked to the side of the room. She stood against the wall with her arms folded. Her job was finished and she was pleased with herself.

Cheryl tried to focus her eyes, but they were filled with the tears she was holding back.

Dukoff looked at his watch. Then he said something to Plastic Man, who took a few steps toward her.

"Do you know who James McFarland was, Cheryl?" Dukoff asked. He emphasized the word *was*.

Before she could control her reaction, her eyes widened and her breathing quickened.

"I see you do," he said, watching her closely. "He worked for the CIA, didn't he, Cheryl? And do you know what happened to him?"

She shook her head.

"I think you do but maybe Mikhail should show you, anyway."

Plastic Man plugged something into a wall socket, then turned to her. The strobe light was momentarily blinding. Then he moved in front of her. Suddenly she saw what was in his hand. It glowed fire red and the end was so hot, it shimmered. Her body recoiled instantly in an attempt to move away, but he held it inches from her face. LaSala's words echoed in her ears. "McFarland had been interrogated very heavily." Tortured was what he had meant. With a fire starter.

She started to shake uncontrollably. Every nerve ending was in motion and her breath came in short gasps. *Oh, God, don't let him burn me. Don't let him do this to me.*

In her mind Dukoff's voice seemed amplified a thousand times as he asked the same question again. "What did Barry find on that film? Tell us, goddammit! Tell us now!"

Plastic Man turned the starter so it was vertical. It looked like the burning frame of a hand mirror, moving within an inch of her skin. Just a slight movement would put the fiery metal against her entire face.

She had to tell them everything. The weapon wasn't real. Barry had seen Commack on the film and knew he couldn't have been there. Yes, the film was created with models because a real demonstration had never happened. Yes, Barry was coming to them with a film from a Commack interview taped the same day, at nearly the same hour. Yes, she was working for the CIA and they had killed Barry. *Yes, yes, yes, only please don't burn me. Please.*

Could she get the words out? Her breathing was a series of

quick gasps and she struggled to speak. Plastic Man moved the starter closer so that her nose actually protruded through the open frame.

Dukoff shouted something at her, but she couldn't hear the words. There was just the sound of her heart pounding. It felt like it was coming up through her chest into her throat. She tried to speak, but the words wouldn't come out. "Yes, I'll tell you everything, everything," she wanted to say, but just couldn't.

Plastic Man was framed in the fiery oval of the starter. A slight movement of his lips told her he was going to touch the burning metal to her forehead. She closed her eyes, pressing the lids together. The words . . . they had to come now. She struggled desperately to get them out, but her pounding heart forced her to breathe faster and faster. There wasn't room for words . . . just a scream.

It was a deafening shriek. Her eyes opened and the blinding light silhouetted Plastic Man's face. A weakness surged through her and suddenly the light went out. Everything was black. Plastic Man's face receded into darkness along with the glow of the starter, and she was falling through space.

Cape Hatteras
Aboard the *John F. Kennedy*

Admiral Sam Hutchinson stood on the bridge of the *Kennedy*, scanning the horizon with his binoculars. The Russian convoy was now in sight. They were a cluster of black dots sitting atop a gray horizon with a pink, early-morning sky at their backs.

Off his bow, a mile ahead, was the frigate *Austin*, plowing through the calm three-foot seas toward the convoy. She would be the first barrier the Russians would come up against. Running at fourteen knots, she would sail a collision course at the lead ship, the *Poltava*, and was instructed not to turn short of a thousand yards. Off the starboard quarter was the destroyer *Macmillan*, and to port admidships was the *Conway*. If the Russians passed the *Austin*, all three vessels would be lying perpendicular to them, directly in their paths. However, the gap between them would be over five hundred yards, enough for the convoy to pass through.

And if the orders came from Washington, they would be allowed to do so.

Hutchinson turned to his exec, who was looking over the shoulder of the radar operator. "What's her range, Dave?" he asked.

"Sixteen miles, closing at six . . . no, five knots."

"She's slowing down, then."

"Yeah, they may be waiting for orders too."

"What do we pick up on them?"

The exec spoke into his headset to communications in the red room below and then waited. "Nothing," he replied. "No communication as of the last hour."

"What about among themselves?"

"They're translating the latest one now. It's . . . wait a minute . . . yeah, okay . . . they're closing up tighter . . . a thousand meters between ships."

"To sail through us," Hutchinson answered, raising his glasses again to the horizon ahead. "What's their heading?"

"One-eight-zero degrees and steady."

"He hasn't changed that heading for thirty-six hours. It's pointed right at Cuba."

"Reducing speed further, sir. Three knots. They're practically dead in the water."

"Reduce speed to four knots," Hutchinson ordered. "Radio the *Austin* to do the same. If this is going to be a Mexican standoff, we need to do what they do. Get ATCOM on the horn."

"Coded?" asked the exec.

"You better believe it," Hutchinson replied. "If we're going to turn, we goddamn well don't want them to know it until the last minute."

**The White House
Washington, D.C.**

President Hayden sat alone in the white communications room staring at the blank screen in front of him. In just two minutes Chebrikov would appear on it and he would play out the final moments of a bluff that had begun over two years ago. Although they were now potential enemies, both had agreed on one thing: to face each other alone. If one had to back down, it would be in private, even though he was sure his conversation was being recorded, as was the premier's.

Events of the last twenty-four hours went through his mind as he tried to organize his thoughts. The American people were now up in arms. The network newscasts the previous day had ignited them. Once the nation was told that Russian ships, possibly carrying missiles, were headed for Cuba, the White House phones had started to ring and hadn't stopped. All three networks had shown Kennedy's speech, which, point by point, called upon Khrushchev to pull his missiles out of Cuba. In words that were both stirring and forceful, Kennedy had called upon Khrushchev to "abandon this clandestine, reckless and provocative threat to world peace and to stable relations between our two nations." He then went on to show Khrushchev stating his own case for the defense of Cuba but finally breaking down and returning the missiles to the Soviet Union.

The newscast had fired the emotions of the nation.

The right-wingers had come out screaming for an immediate attack on Cuba. An American occupation of the island would prevent a military threat forever. Oddly enough, there was considerable support for the plan, and several senators came on the news in favor of it.

Although the vast majority of Americans were more reasonable, they still expected Hayden to act decisively. Chebrikov had to be dealt with in the same way Khrushchev had: with tough language and tough actions. By evening, the people had spoken out clearly in demonstrations around the country. Signs held up for TV cameras read, DON'T LOSE WHAT KENNEDY WON! MISSILES IN CUBA ARE SECONDS AWAY FROM WASHINGTON and KEEP THE RUSSIANS AWAY FOR J.F.K. An overnight poll taken by *The New York Times* showed that a majority favored a total blockade of Cuba by five to one. The people wanted him to face the Russians and force them to back down, just as Kennedy had done before him.

A meeting with key Congressional leaders that morning had produced the same outrage. There was support from both parties to double the force that was already in West Germany. NATO members were contacted throughout the morning, to gain support for multinational resistance against the Soviets. The Pentagon was told to prepare for an order that would put forces throughout the world on alert.

As the *Kennedy* drew closer to Cape Hatteras, Hayden had conferred with members of the Cabinet in preparation for his call to Chebrikov. It was decided he would have to take a hard stand against the Soviet leader. The people would not stand for anything less than the convoy turning around immediately.

The clock over the large screen now read 1:28 P.M. The last report still had the *Kennedy* and the Russian convoy fifteen miles away from each other at Hatteras. They were both holding their positions now . . . waiting. The next hour literally would make all the difference in the world.

He looked down at a yellow-lined pad, where he had written key words that would provide background for his talk with Chebrikov. They were the unknowns on which the entire bluff centered. There were four of them.

McFarland was the first word. Did he tell the Russians about his connection with the CIA and that the weapon didn't really exist? No one knew. If he had, this call had failed before it had begun.

Cheryl Branigan. Up until an hour ago she was still in Russian hands. She knew the truth about the weapon. Was the KGB subjecting her to the same things they had done to McFarland? If so, she could have told them everything by now.

Cheyenne, Wyoming. Had the photographs from the Soviet reconnaissance satellite *Kirov II* convinced Chebrikov and the Politburo? Did they believe a laser weapon had destroyed a missile silo with more power than a conventional missile could ever deliver?

The film. Had it convinced scientific experts that it showed a real laser-weapon demonstration?

If any of these had failed, the entire bluff would fail. He was coming up against Chebrikov not knowing what cards actually were in his hand. It was one hell of a way to play poker.

Moscow

Premier Chebrikov sat in the Kremlin communications room looking at photographs taken by *Kirov II* over Cheyenne, Wyoming. Twenty black-and-white shots clearly showed massive destruction to a missile silo that had been classified as impenetrable unless it received a direct hit. Even at that, experts had still been doubtful that an SRV could destroy it to the extent the photographs showed. Clearly the weapon was more powerful than anything military experts had seen to date.

A quick comparison of the destruction had been made to the film sent from San Francisco. A computer-generated image that translated ground-level destruction to an overhead view proved they were identical. The picture confirmed conclusively that what the film showed was exactly what *Kirov II* had photographed from an altitude of 120,000 kilometers.

He slipped the photographs into a folder beside him and thought back to the meeting that had just ended moments ago.

Karpolov had still maintained to the Politburo that the film was phony and that the devastation in Wyoming had been achieved through other means. He still believed the Branigan girl would break under Dukoff's questioning and reveal that she had been involved with the CIA to put the film created by them into KGB hands. None of the facts supported this.

However, scientific experts again expressed their belief that the weapon was not yet feasible and could not have destroyed the silo. They also pointed out that an explosion of this magnitude, in the 150,000 to 175,000 ton range, would have registered on Richter scale instruments throughout the world. But then again, this may not have been a conventional explosion. A vibration laser simply could have shattered the silo's molecules, causing them to crumble.

The conservative Politburo still was in favor of withdrawing the convoy at Hatteras. If the United States had the weapon, they would confront their ships and search them. Once they found the missiles, world opinion would be on their side.

Karpolov still insisted they were throwing away military superiority that had taken five years to build. The U.S. was bluffing. They had tried with Star Wars and failed.

He had made one last effort to stir the Politburo's emotions. He said that media in the Soviet Union and around the world had shown the Russian convoy sailing toward Cuba, as they had thirty-two years ago. The whole world knew they were carrying missiles, and once they were in Cuba, U.S. aggression would be stopped forever.

A press conference had already been scheduled in Havana to coincide with the convoy's arrival. Press from around the world would be in attendance. They had to proceed and call the Americans' bluff.

The Politburo listened to Karpolov's words and realized the tremendous demoralizing effect it would have if the convoy was turned back. To suffer the humiliation of being defeated by the Americans a second time would be devastating. After they recovered emotionally, they would look to their leaders to blame. Karpolov would be the first, but Chebrikov, as premier, would suffer politically as well.

Chebrikov thought for several moments before making his final recommendation to the Politburo. "Although there seems to be enough evidence to support our retreat from the American task force," he had said, "there also is some doubt as to their weapon's credibility. I don't think we'll ever settle it among ourselves. My suggestion is to play out the Americans' bluff, if it is one, all the way. None of us wants to suffer the humiliation of turning the convoy around, and we shouldn't until we're absolutely sure Hayden isn't bluffing. The only way we can be certain is to take him right to the brink of confrontation. I will confront him one-on-one and play out the final hand. Let's see what's in his eyes. It may be more important than what he says. Let's see if he still is willing to stop our ships and board them now that they're standing face-to-face. Let's see if he still has the will to do that."

A technician signaled from behind the glass window to Chebrikov's left, and suddenly Hayden was in front of him on the television screen.

For a moment neither man spoke. Hayden looked calm, with both hands resting on the table in front of him. A yellow-lined pad was off to his right. He looked straight into the camera, both eyes fixed on the lens that was sending his image over five thousand miles in less than a second. Chebrikov looked for signs of nervousness, lack of confidence, uneasiness. There weren't any.

"I think we had better get right down to business," Hayden said through an unseen translator. "Our ships are just miles apart, awaiting the outcome of our conversation."

"Very well," he replied. "However, I think there is little to discuss. Your ships are blocking our path to Cuba. We have every right to international waters in order to support our allies, and you are preventing us from doing that."

"We will not allow you to support them with missiles that are a threat to our security."

"They are missiles for an ally to defend themselves against aggression from South America and from the United States. They've been requested by the Castro government."

"So you admit they're missiles."

"Yes. SRVs." He had suddenly decided to make the admission.

Hayden shifted slightly in his chair. This had come as a surprise to him. His hands turned upward and he moved them slightly apart.

"The request by Castro to put missiles in Cuba is very familiar. It was used in 1962, and was rejected by President Kennedy. His reasons hold true . . ."

"Come, come now," Chebrikov answered, brushing off the translation with a wave of his hand. "This isn't 1962. Right now, as we speak, there are SRVs in the Arctic aimed at over two hundred targets inside the United States, concentrated around twelve major cities. They can destroy those targets in less than three minutes. You have nothing to defend against them. Frankly, Mr. President, you're in no position to argue with us."

"That's absolutely correct, Mr. Chebrikov," Hayden replied. "We have nothing in our arsenal to defend against them. I'm sure your intelligence has verified that. However, we have the means to retaliate swiftly, at the first indication that your missiles have been launched."

"With what? A laser weapon that is still two years away from development?"

"No, with a laser that has been tested and is fully operational, ready to strike against the Soviet Union if we're forced to use it."

"A myth, wishful thinking. You don't have the technology or the weapon. You're bluffing!"

"Then what was it that destroyed a missile silo in Wyoming that your reconnaissance satellite went out of its way to photograph?"

"These?" he asked, holding up the pictures. "A deception to demonstrate the power of a weapon you don't really have."

"The silo isn't wishful thinking," Hayden answered coldly.

"It's a force greater than anything ever used in a weapon before, one hundred times more powerful than the bomb dropped on Hiroshima."

"A force that didn't even register on the Richter scale."

"Because it simply crumbled concrete over four feet thick that your SRVs wouldn't have been able to destroy. The same way it'll crumble targets inside your country. We have over two hundred receivers inside the Soviet Union that will draw the laser down to reduce military targets to ashes. We won't use it unless we're provoked, but if we are, we're prepared."

Chebrikov listened to his words closely. There was conviction behind them. If he was bluffing, he had rehearsed himself well. The time had come for him to call the bluff with one of his own. He put the photographs aside and ran Karpolov's unproven logic through his mind.

"I think we're wasting each other's time, Mr. President," he answered. "We know the weapon doesn't exist and we're going to proceed on to Cuba. You're aware of the Branigan girl, are you not?"

"No, I'm not."

"I think you are, but nevertheless she's in the custody of our agents in San Francisco, where she's been interrogated for several days now. She approached us there with film of this weapon being demonstrated before some of your high-ranking government officials, Walter Commack among them."

"The weapon was demonstrated several weeks ago, yes, but I don't know of any such woman who has film of it."

"Come now, Mr. President, she's working for your CIA."

Hayden felt the premier's eyes on him even though he was five thousand miles away. He was watching every movement now. Subtleties. A quivering of the lips, a sideward glance, an involuntary move of the hand; any of them could reveal the fear he suddenly felt inside.

"I don't know what you're talking about."

"The woman, this Cheryl Branigan, has told us that the weapon doesn't really exist. That film we have of the demonstration was created by the CIA to make us believe it was real. She admitted everything."

"I know of no such woman," Hayden replied calmly.

"You're lying," Chebrikov answered, raising his voice.

Hayden went on. "I would suggest you remove your troops from the Czechoslovakian border and turn your convoy around. Neither serves any purpose other than to provoke a military confrontation that can result in the destruction of this planet. And I suggest you do so immediately."

"I think you're bluffing, Mr. President. You're bluffing but don't have the guts to back it up. Because you have nothing to back it up with."

"Don't try me," Hayden replied. His voice remained calm and steady.

"Oh, but we intend to," Chebrikov answered. "And we will. Our ships will not be prevented from delivering missiles that Premier Castro has requested for his defense. You will not stop us."

"I hope you realize what that decision will mean, because we will not allow you past Hatteras."

"We'll see about that, Mr. President. Because we're going to call your bluff."

Chebrikov motioned to the technician behind the glass window and the screen went blank. For the next few minutes he thought about the conversation that had just ended. If Hayden was bluffing, he had calmly said all the right words. But could the bluff stand up to action? Would he stop them if he really didn't have the weapon? He decided that his recommendation to the Politburo would remain: to bring Hayden to the brink of confrontation.

Then they would find out for sure.

12.

Cape Hatteras
Aboard the *John F. Kennedy*

"THEY'RE MOVING, SIR."

The radar man looked up from his scope and turned to the exec. "The lead freighter is back on one-eight-zero degrees, coming right at us."

Hutchinson grabbed his glasses. The goddamn sun was beating through the windows of the bridge and he could barely make out the *Poltava*. But yes, she was on the move, with the rest of the convoy following.

"Get ATCOM on the horn again," he said to the exec, who was already putting on his headset. But before he could relay the message, the teleprinter next to him suddenly came to life, its matrix head printing out characters at two hundred words a minute. The communications officer handed him the perforated sheet of paper and he read the message.

TOP SECRET
10046Z******45895

ATCOM HDQT

KNDY ANV 336

ORDERS FROM ATCOM BRIEFING 30 OCT. REMAIN IN EFFECT
XX CONTACT DEFINED 1000YDS XX REDNAV VESSELS AL-
LOWED TO PROCEED BEYOND. XX CONTACT ATCOM 100.75
MGHZ AT CROSSPOINT.

ATCOM SENDS

1022Z

He handed the message to the exec. "If they get closer than a
thousand yards, we're to open the door for them," he said, trying
to keep himself from raising his voice. "Relay it to the others. See
if they're as disgusted as I am."

He turned back toward the bow and watched the *Poltava* as it
headed directly at him.

"Turn, you son of a bitch, turn," he heard himself say under his
breath. But he knew that nothing he could say or do would make
a difference.

The decisions had already been made.

Aboard the *Poltava*

Admiral Yurchenko had personally given the order from the
bridge to Chief Engineer Sergei Veronikhin for one-third ahead.
He had used the intercom rather than the mechanical signaling
device to do it. He wanted Sergei to hear his voice. At last, after
four hours of waiting, he had finally received orders from
REDNAV. The bureaucrats in Moscow were having second
thoughts. He was only to proceed at one-third power toward the
Kennedy. At two thousand meters he was to contact REDNAV
again. Orders would follow immediately. They were going to play
cat and mouse with the Americans.

Already he could sense the Kremlin bureaucracy's cowardice.
What had happened to Chebrikov's determination to succeed
where Khrushchev had failed? Chebrikov had personally assured
him that this time they would get the missiles to Cuba. What had
happened to that conviction?

Yurchenko turned and saw Stavronov peering over the radar
man's shoulder, watching the distance close between the blips on
the screen. Beads of perspiration were forming on Stavronov's

forehead, either from nervousness or his body's inability to cope
with nearly three hundred pounds of weight. The man continued
to disgust him. It was under these situations where men of
substance and courage came to the fore. Stavronov was losing
control.

"Range?" Yurchenko asked as he trained his binoculars back on
the Americans.

"Twenty-two hundred meters" came the reply from Commander Tulchin.

"We should be contacting REDNAV!" Stavronov was shouting
from behind him. "We'll be at two thousand meters in less than
three minutes."

Yurchenko continued to look through the binoculars. The
markings on the American frigate were clearly visible now:
0163 AUSTIN. She was lying directly in his path, three hundred
meters in front of the *Kennedy*, whose superstructure towered
over her. Through the glasses he saw activity on the carrier's
deck and bridge. Three aircraft were being moved into launch
position, and two others were being readied. A helicopter was
taking off from the stern. The frigate and the destroyer were
lying in a straight line. There was barely enough room for the
convoy to pass through unless the carrier moved to one side or the
other.

"Range?" he barked without lowering the glasses.

"Twenty-one hundred fifty meters," Tulchin replied.

"Radio the convoy. Close to two hundred meters behind
flagship in a straight line . . . one hundred meters apart. Do it
quickly!"

"Yes, sir."

"What are you doing?" Stavronov shouted, rushing up behind
him.

"Obviously, putting the convoy in a tighter line so we can pass
between the American ships," he said, lowering the glasses.

"We need orders to do that! And we need them now!"

"We will get them," Yurchenko answered, turning to Tulchin.

"Radio REDNAV," he said calmly. "Give them our position.
Slow to three knots."

Tulchin quickly gave the order over his headset as he looked at
the huge carrier looming ahead. Figures were clearly visible now,

and many of the *Kennedy*'s crew had lined up along the starboard side, watching their approach.

A minute passed. The helmsman remained frozen at the wheel, the compass in front of him locked at 0180. Yurchenko still had not deviated from the course.

Two minutes.

The *Austin* was only eighteen hundred meters away now, lying in their path. With the *Poltava* traveling at three knots, she would have to move within minutes to avoid a collision.

Three minutes.

The telecommunications printer next to Tulchin started to clatter, its printing head racing back and forth across the carriage. It printed for just five seconds and then stopped. Tulchin ripped the paper out across the perforations, quickly scanned the message, and handed it to Yurchenko. He took it and read the five lines. Then he read them again. It had to be a mistake. This could not be happening to him twice in his lifetime.

"No!" he shouted, crumpling the paper into a tight ball and throwing it across the room. "Never! We stay on course!" His face was white with rage as he stormed over to the helmsman to check the heading on the gimboled compass.

Stavronov picked up the paper that was lying at his feet. He stretched it out, quickly reading the words crowded between a maze of crumpled lines.

REDNAVCOM

15444300Z . . . . 48265 SATCOM 4160A

1655 HRS.
POLTAVA 446244ARN

ARV CONVOY ORDERED TO ALTER COURSE XX NEW HEADING XX 00342 NORTHEAST XX PROCEED TO RNDVOUS LAT 38.44.67N XX LON 70.67.59W.

MAKE CONTACT WITH SSR 451 AT PT. 5479, 1800 HRS. 29 OCT. XX ORDER VERIFIED XX POL-1 XX REDNAVCOM XX TALLINN.

EXECUTE IMMEDIATELY.
END BULLETIN.

105992 K

Stavronov rushed over and thrust the message in front of Yurchenko. His pudgy index finger jabbed at it as he shouted words that were almost incoherent.

"What are you doing? You've been ordered to turn around! Don't you see? The order is from the naval group at Tallinn. POL-1. The premier himself has ordered it. It's verified."

Yurchenko said nothing and stood behind the helmsman.

Stavronov pointed out the window at the *Austin*, lying directly in their path.

"The orders were to execute immediately. Don't you see how close they are? Do it!" His teeth were clenched together but his voice was loud and shrill. "Do it! Do it immediately!"

"I will do nothing," Yurchenko shouted back. "I will not be dishonored again, and neither will the Russian people. The premier gave me his word, personally, that there would be no turning back. I stand by that assurance."

"But now he's ordering you to turn around!"

"Full ahead," Yurchenko said sharply. The seaman next to him repeated the words into his headset to direct the engine room, then turned back to Yurchenko.

"Full ahead, sir," he repeated. The *Poltava*'s engines increased power and it plowed through the water toward the *Kennedy* at fourteen knots.

Aboard the *John F. Kennedy*

Hutchinson watched through his glasses as the *Poltava* bore down on the *Austin*. The frigate was rapidly changing course to avoid a head-on collision. Even so, it would be close. The two ships would come within fifty yards of each other as the *Poltava* steamed by.

The door had opened for the Russian convoy. Now all that was between them and Cuba was his carrier, less then fifteen hundred yards away. This goddamn Russian was staying locked on his course. They were the ones that were being forced to move. Son of a bitch, it galled him.

"Three minutes to collision contact," the navigator called out behind him. Three minutes to go and he would go down in history as the one who had allowed the Russians to sail to Cuba. Hayden and the rest of them were gutless. That's what they were . . . gutless. How could they allow this to happen when it had been prevented over thirty years ago? The country would be disgraced before the world, and he along with it. He heard Hampel's voice in his ears: "*One thing you're not good at is following orders.*" He wished he wasn't good at it. Maybe then he wouldn't be carrying out one that he despised.

Hutchinson turned to the exec, who was looking alternately at the digital clock overhead and the *Poltava,* which was now less than a thousand yards away. His index finger was poised over the intercom button of his chest set. Hutchinson knew he wouldn't give the order. It had to come from him, and it had to be now. This little game of chicken was over with. The Russian was racing down the center stripe and they had to pull away.

"Radio the *Conway,*" Hutchinson ordered. "Prepare to make a starboard turn in two minutes to avoid collision."

He heard the order repeated, then looked back at the *Poltava.* She was flying the hammer and sickle from her bow, and it blew triumphantly toward the stern. The *John F. Kennedy* was going to stand still while a path opened up for the Russians to bring missiles to Cuba. Everything Kennedy had fought for was being sacrificed at this moment. Hutchinson's stomach tightened and his hands began to shake, making it difficult to stay focused on the ship. He pulled the glasses away. They had been given to him by his father the day he took command of the *Kennedy.* He threw them to the floor and the lenses exploded into a thousand pieces.

Washington, D.C.
The White House

Ten men sat with the president in the Oval Office, staring at the white phone on his desk. It was the same group that had originated the deception two years ago: General Cabot, Donald Shupe, Senator Park, Walter Commack, the vice president, and three members of the Cabinet. No one had said anything for the past few minutes for fear of interrupting a call that would come momentarily. It was as if the phone were part of the group and was waiting for an opening in the conversation to speak.

They had all watched the tape of his conversation with Chebrikov. Everyone agreed that the premier was going to go all the way to a final moment of confrontation. In his mind the question of whether or not the United States had military superiority would be tested at sea. He was going to force the U.S. to stretch their credibility to the limit. Both sides were going to race down the centerline of the highway toward each other. It was just a question of who was going to turn away first.

Hayden looked at the group seated in front of him. Every man sat silently, alone with his thoughts. The clicking of the eighteenth-century clock on his desk became a series of loud staccato sounds that echoed throughout the room. What was the *Poltava* doing, and why didn't the phone ring?

Aboard the *Poltava*

Chief Engineer Sergei Veronikhin listened as the order to reduce engine speed came down from the bridge. Something was wrong. Yurchenko had just ordered full ahead minutes ago, and now they were cutting power. They were in the open sea. There was no need for such maneuvering unless—the thought sent a shudder through him—they were about to turn.

Suddenly he felt the angle of the oily floor beneath him shift slightly. An empty can of hydraulic fluid rolled off to one side. They were turning. It was a wide turn. A one-hundred-eighty-degree turn.

He took off his communications headset and threw it on the hook in front of him. Then he ran past his second mate, knocking him against the turbine control board. The hatchway was open to the deck above, and he ran up the metal stairs. At the top he stopped to look off the port side. There was a carrier ahead of them and a destroyer turning to starboard. He ran up the last flight of stairs to the bridge. Putting his shoulder against the heavy metal door, he pushed against it and nearly fell into the room.

Stavronov was struggling to get the wheel away from Yurchenko, who had pushed the helmsman out of the way. "Our orders are to turn!" he shouted hysterically. "You are disobeying orders from the premier himself. Turn away! Now!"

"Never!" Yurchenko replied, gripping the wheel tighter. His eyes were fixed on the carrier ahead of him.

Veronikhin looked to his right. The carrier was almost on top of them, but the destroyer was moving away.

"We will not disobey our orders!" he heard Stavronov scream behind him, and then two shots rang out. He turned and saw Yurchenko fall away from the wheel, his admiral's tunic turning red beneath rows of military decorations. Yurchenko tried desperately to utter some words to the crew behind him, but they were no more than a gurgle coming from his blood-filled throat. Finally his legs collapsed under him and his body crumpled to the floor at Stavronov's feet.

Veronikhin raced forward, his face white with rage. "What have you done?" he screamed at the *zampolit*. "Why are you turning the ship?" He moved around him toward the helmsman, but Stavronov turned the gun on him.

"Don't touch the wheel, I warn you," he said. His immense body was shaking and the gun wavered in his hand. "Our orders are to turn immediately and we will do as we've been ordered." He screamed at the helmsman, who had taken the wheel. "Complete the turn to a 0359 degree heading."

Veronikhin ignored him. He looked down at Yurchenko and then turned to the pilothouse crew. "What's the matter with you all?" he asked, snarling out the words. "Where is your honor? Are you going to listen to him instead of to your captain? Thirty-two years ago Captain Yurchenko and I were on this same ship, and we had to show our tails to the American destroyers. Are we going to do it again?"

Lieutenant Commander Tulchin stepped forward and handed him the crumpled orders they had received.

"This is what we have to obey," he said quietly. "It just came over the computer and it's verified from Tallinn. We're not going to disobey an order from Chebrikov himself." He looked back at the *Kennedy*, which was now almost astern, and added, "An order that if disobeyed might start World War III."

Veronikhin read the orders, then handed them back. Slowly he knelt down beside his friend. He leaned forward and kissed him on the forehead, then shut the eyes that were staring up at him. The bureaucrats, the politicians, the men who sat behind large desks had won again. Thirty-two years ago they had made a decision that, in hindsight, was a mistake. Many believed if they had defied Kennedy and gone on to Cuba, they would have called his bluff. Maybe these bureaucrats were making the same mistake all over again.

If they were, his friend had died in vain.

Washington, D.C.
The White House

Hayden couldn't bear staring at the phone any longer. He got up from his chair and started toward the other end of the office. Just as he got there, the phone rang. It went off like an alarm, the shrill pitch sounding like an ambulance rushing to a stricken victim. Maybe that's what was happening.

He approached the phone slowly, as if picking up the receiver might cause it to explode. On the other end would be Admiral Alvin Hampel, commander of ATCOM, who was now at the Pentagon. The message would be brief. Either Hutchinson had allowed the convoy to pass or the Russians had turned around. Hayden picked up the receiver.

Shupe watched the president closely as he spoke to Hampel. Hayden's eyes were squinted under eyebrows pointed downward. The pressure he was feeling inside was translated into lines along both sides of his mouth where the lips were drawn tight. Later Shupe wouldn't remember what he had said, just his expression. Suddenly Hayden took a deep breath and his shoulders and chest relaxed, as if a tremendous weight had been lifted from them. He dropped the receiver back into its cradle and stuffed his hands into his pockets.

"They bought it," he said jubilantly. "The sons of bitches bought it. The *Poltava* reversed course right at the last minute. I tell you, it was close. Hutchinson almost let them through, but now they're already five nautical miles down the reverse course. I'm going to call the *Kennedy* just as soon as we make the announcements. We pulled it off, guys, we really pulled it off!"

Senator Park stood up and let out a rebel yell. The others joined in with applause and Shupe hurried around the desk to be the first to shake hands with the president. General Cabot remained in his seat and reached for his briefcase.

"I didn't want to appear overly optimistic," he said in his booming bass voice, "but I did come prepared for this." He took several sheets of paper from his briefcase. "I don't know what you fellas are going to say to the press, but I'm all set."

"That's fine, General, but before we call them in, I think a celebration is in order," Hayden said.

He went over to a cabinet and took out some glasses and a bottle of champagne. "I'm prepared too," he said, smiling. He poured for each of them and they raised their glasses. Hayden turned to a portrait of Kennedy over the fireplace mantel. "To Jack Kennedy," he said in a solemn voice. "He would be proud to stand with us today."

"Here, here," they answered.

"As for you guys," he said, turning back to the group, "I've never met a better bunch of poker players."

They all joked and laughed for a few minutes, then Hayden turned to the one task remaining.

"We've got one final bit of playacting to do, and that's to announce to the press that we've got the weapon and were about to use it on the Russians. We'll release the film to them, but once we do, they'll ask a lot of technical questions. I'll need you, General, to field most of them. They'll also ask why the weapon was kept secret so long. The answer is that it had to be in order for the receivers to be put in place. We'll qualify that by saying that within six months the receivers won't be needed. That's in line with what McDonnell Douglas is saying, anyway. Senator Park, I'll need you to assure them you'll be doing everything you can in Congress, on both sides of the aisle, to express your enthusiasm for the weapon and to raise financial support for it."

"You can count on me," Park quipped. "I was enthusiastic about it when it didn't even exist."

"Well, as of right now it exists," Hayden said, laughing. "Hell, even the Russians believe it."

San Francisco

A man sat at the window of a vacant twelfth-floor apartment overlooking the Soviet Diplomatic Agency on Market Street. His binoculars swept along the entrance of the ornate building and then across the dome-shaped windows with drawn shades. The lights inside occasionally silhouetted people moving from room to room, but at ten P.M. there wasn't any unusual activity. He reached for the last cup of coffee from a thermos bottle on the windowsill. There were two more hours to go before he would be relieved. Two more hours without coffee.

He took a moving carton, folded it, and laid it against the wall behind him. Maybe it would ease the pressure on his back, which was starting to stiffen. Ten minutes ago he had taken a few minutes to walk around, but the rest of the time had been spent at the window.

Again he focused the binoculars on the window nearest the door. There were three figures clustered together now, and they were moving toward what was probably the foyer. Suddenly the lights went on in the entrance hall and a figure appeared behind the leaded glass door. It opened and a woman stepped out into the street. It was Cheryl Branigan.

The man picked up a two-way radio that was lying on the floor and flicked the on switch. There was a hiss of static until he pressed the talk button.

"Yellow One, this is Sentinel. She's out of the building and on the street . . . alone. Go." He waited for a response and it came immediately. "We're on the way."

Cheryl stumbled out onto the street, barely able to stand. It was dark and the night was bitter cold. A brisk wind was coming off the bay and it whistled down the empty street. Her whole body was shaking and she was terrified. After twenty straight hours of questioning, every ounce of physical and mental strength had been exhausted. She was totally drained, but inside there was a feeling of satisfaction. She had survived. Whether or not they had bought her act, she didn't know, but she was still alive and free. That, alone, was success.

The thought of the flaming-hot fire starter just inches from her face sent a tremor through her again. She reached up and touched her forehead, where the skin was still tender even though the burning metal had never actually touched her. Somehow she had been spared just as Plastic Man was about to burn her. She had passed out and then later awakened to find herself slumped on the floor of the storage room. The woman had untied her and brought her to Dukoff, who simply said she was free to go. "We have no further use for you," he had said. The woman had then given Cheryl her things and shoved her out the door.

"No further use." Did that mean they had run out of time? Had she held out long enough that they thought the film was real, or had she told them things before she passed out? Maybe they had won, after all. Maybe the Russians now knew the film was a phony and their ships were already in Cuba.

The question now was, where would she go? She felt for the wallet in her jacket pocket. The fifty dollars LaSala had given her was still in it. It would be enough for a meal and a night in a hotel, anyway. She needed sleep and something to eat desperately.

Suddenly she was aware that the entire block was empty. She had to move—anywhere, it didn't matter. The main thing was to get away from this building. A taxi turned onto Market Street with its for-hire light on. She waved for it to stop even though it was more than a block away. But as it got closer, she saw that it was a blue Dodge. Her heart started to pound and she began to move away from it. It was the taxi that had pulled up behind Barry three nights ago. Jankowski and Zeller had jumped out of it and killed him. Now they were coming for her. Her job was finished and she was expendable. Why should they pay her a million dollars and allow a witness to their deception to live? There wasn't any reason. They had come to kill her.

Her legs were stiff, but she ran to the corner and turned it, heading down a quiet, residential street. There were lights on in the houses and television sets visible in the windows. Looking back over her shoulder, she saw that the taxi was right behind her. Maybe if she ran into one of the houses, someone would help her. She picked one out and started to run for it, but the cab was right alongside her now. It stopped.

Jankowski jumped out and ran toward her. "No!" she shouted. "Please, leave me alone!" She turned quickly and ran for the next house.

"Wait!" she heard him yell behind her, but she was running desperately to get to the entrance gate. There were lights on in the house. His footsteps were hard on the pavement behind her, coming closer and closer. She tried to open the gate. It was locked. Frantically she pulled at it, and then she felt Jankowski's arms around her. She would feel his gun against her back now, and the pain of the bullet entering her body. Then she would go limp, as Barry had done, and fall to the pavement.

"Stop," he said, pulling her away from the gate. "I'm not going to hurt you. I've come to take you back to the safe house."

"You're going to kill me," she said, sobbing. All her defenses were crashing down around her now. She had used up all of them during the past twenty-four hours.

"No," he said, turning her around to face him. "You gave a great performance. They bought your act and turned the ships around about four hours ago. They're taking their missiles back to Russia. Everybody's back at the safe house. Let's go."

She looked up and studied his face. That boyish smile said everything was all right. "C'mon," he said softly, "they're all waiting for you back there."

It was over. She felt her body go weak and fell into Steve's arms. He held her, gently stroking the back of her head. They stood for a moment without saying anything, and gradually she began to accept the fact that maybe she was safe at last. She wouldn't have believed it from anyone else but Steve. He had been the one who was the most caring right from the start. He had comforted her and helped her to become Slim. Without him she wouldn't have made it. She reached up and took his hand, holding it tightly.

"You've pulled it off, kid, you really did," he said excitedly. "Frank always said you needed to give the performance of your life, and you did."

At the safe house, Cheryl was met with cheers, congratulations, and thanks from the men. LaSala filled her in on the American triumph at sea, a triumph made possible by her tremendous courage. Suddenly it all seemed worthwhile to Cheryl; the enormity of what she had accomplished became clear.

Half jokingly, Steve asked Cheryl if she was ready to be recruited by the CIA permanently. Cheryl winked, and then slipped back into her Slim character, which by now had become second nature to her.

"If you need me, just whistle. You know how to whistle, don't you, Steve?"

Everyone in the room burst into laughter as Steve joined Cheryl in answering.

"You just put your lips together and blow!"

Epilogue

Ivana Karpolov turned the key in the lock of her town-house door. She had just returned from the drugstore with a prescription Viktor had asked for, to calm his stomach. He hadn't felt well after a meeting with the premier and members of the Politburo. Ivana had been sure Viktor's ailment was caused by nerves. Their trip to Cuba had been canceled, along with the press conference. Everything he had worked so hard for had suddenly turned against him. She would try to cheer him up as best she could this evening, with some hot tea and brandy. It would settle his stomach better than the medicine.

She struggled with the lock. It always turned hard in the cold weather. Finally it clicked, and she hurried inside.

"Viktor, I'm home," she said as she hung her coat in the hall closet. There wasn't any answer. He must have gone to the upstairs bedroom to rest.

"Viktor?"

She took the medicine and started up the stairs. At the landing there was a trap door that led to the attic. It was open, allowing light to stream into the darkness of the attic above it. She saw a dark shape hanging from a crossbeam, slowly swaying back and forth. At first she thought it was clothing she had hung there months ago, but then she moved closer to see the shape more clearly.

Suddenly she screamed.

It was her husband.

Washington, D.C.

Three days later Frank LaSala came down the steps of the Pentagon. It was a beautiful afternoon and it felt good to get out into the sunlight after an austere but moving ceremony he had attended earlier that morning. President Hayden, CIA Director Shupe, and Secretary of Defense Walter Commack had gathered there secretly to present the Presidential Medal to Mrs. James McFarland, in honor of her husband, who had given his life for the security of his country. Mrs. McFarland never knew what her husband had been involved in, but the president assured her that his sacrifice had been extremely important to the security of the nation.

LaSala walked down the street, passing through the lunch-hour crowd. At the corner was a newsstand where a deliveryman was just dropping off the early-afternoon editions. As he passed by, the headline on a stack of papers screamed out at him: KGB HEAD VIKTOR KARPOLOV FOUND DEAD.

LaSala bought a paper, shoving the money into the hand of the newsstand owner. He walked around the side of the stand to get out of the way of the crowd, and read the front-page article.

"The Soviet news agency, Tass, reported hours ago that Viktor L. Karpolov, chief of the KGB and newly elected member of the Politburo, died two days ago at his apartment in Moscow. Death was attributed to a massive coronary, which struck him unexpectedly. He will be buried tomorrow in a small, private ceremony. Karpolov was architect of the plan which sent missile-carrying ships to Cuba five days ago in an attempt to place newly developed SRVs there. The ships were turned back when intercepted by the carrier *John F. Kennedy* off the coast of North Carolina.

"Intelligence sources inside Moscow report, however, that Karpolov's death may have been a suicide, in response to the failure of his plan. The accusation was totally refuted by high Soviet officials, but American intelligence has reason to believe it true." The article went on to detail Karpolov's rise to power, as well as details of his failed plans.

LaSala put the paper under his arm and took out his wallet. Carefully he slipped the picture of Mark Ellis and himself from inside the plastic insert. Then he removed a paper clip that held the picture of Karpolov to it. He looked one more time at the fiery eyes that had haunted him for too many years and then slowly he tore it into tiny pieces. He never thought he would get the chance to avenge Mark's death, and he never really would, but at least those fiery eyes were closed . . . forever.

Eighteen months later the United States had fully developed the high-vibration laser weapon and launched it into space. The Russians were forced to remove their now vulnerable, missile-carrying submarines from beneath the polar ice caps. For the moment the United States had, once again, achieved military superiority.

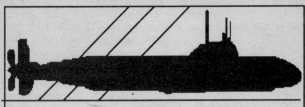